"I WANT YOU

Hugh stared at he_____ I refused the king's requ___ __ ___ you, my beauty?"

"You would've had a hole in your life, as I would've had in mine." Passion had given her power.

"What say you? Think us to be a match?"

She nodded, tracing his mouth with her finger. "Having come from a country of upheaval, I'm not fool enough to think that all could go smoothly with any alliance, Milord—"

"Hugh," he murmured, brushing his mouth over hers. "Hugh," he whispered again, taking her mouth in a strong kiss that went on and on, fire licking through him . . .

Books by Helen Mittermeyer

The Pledge
The Veil

Published by
Warner Books

THE
PLEDGE

Helen
Mittermeyer

WARNER BOOKS

A Time Warner Company

WARNER BOOKS EDITION

Copyright © 1997 by Helen Mittermeyer
All rights reserved.

Cover design by Elaine Groh and Diane Luger
Cover illustration by Michael Racz

Warner Books, Inc.
1271 Avenue of the Americas
New York, NY 10020

W A Time Warner Company

Visit our Web site at
http://pathfinder.com/twep

Printed in the United States of America

First Printing: February, 1997

10 9 8 7 6 5 4 3 2 1

To Cristine, my youngest child. Your courage and generosity are a constant inspiration. You remind me of this heroine.

HM

Dear Readers,

I hadn't started out to be a historical novelist, but found that once I entered those hallowed halls, there's a fascination that won't release me.

I've always been interested in Scotland, the land of my forebears. My maiden name of Monteith is one of the oldest there.

As I researched my family background, I found it had been peppered with an assortment of entrancing rogues. My heroes are an amalgam of hero, warrior, rogue, and good fellow.

The heroines are even more intriguing to me. My research taught me that many women were as intrepid as the men. Many were battlers, protectors, defenders. Scores were as courageous as a good share of our women in modern times. To the credit of all females, many, today and yesterday, were of the heroic stamp of the ancient warrior Queen Boudicca; of Flora MacGregor, who went to the new world and whose antecedents fought for the South; and of course, Elizabeth I.

I value the brave, of both past and present. So it is with great pride I give you their stories. If you're looking for simpering misses, you won't find them here.

Good readers, you've been with me from my first book, fifty some volumes ago. I will try not to fail you or myself as we embark on this journey entitled *The Pledge*. Bonne chance!

Helen Mittermeyer

PROLOGUE

Duchy of Trevelyan, Wales—1327

Was all of Wales caught in the miasma that swirled around Castle Trevelyan? The fog caught and exaggerated every sound that ebbed through the dry branches smacking against the stone walls.

At fifteen Morrigan Llywelyn was untutored in the ways of the world, all but cloistered, some would say. Wales was a dangerous land. Protecting women was a necessity and always had been in the Duchys of Llywelyn and Trevelyan.

As a princess of Wales, Morrigan had been lettered by the monks and good sisters. She could converse in Latin, Greek, Anglo, and her own Welsh, the purest Celtic. She'd been taught to be cautious and reserved because in some quarters of the world female opinion wasn't to be considered. But Morrigan knew her value, taught by a father who revered her.

For the most part she wasn't quick to express her thoughts, her feelings. Though her brothers seemed to value her, they were often busy handling the huge holding of Llywelyn. So, many of her yearnings she kept to herself, though nothing could tame her wild heart. Her wise father had sensed this, and had allowed his only daughter to be tutored in war games, as well as her beloved scholastics. Often she challenged her brothers, Califb and Drcq, and her cousins, Goll and Cumhal.

She also knew death. At the request of the duchess, she was staying at the Duchy of Trevelyan, alone but for her old nurse Nell. The Duchess Gwynneth, her cousin once removed on her mother's side, was dying.

"Is there nothing can be done, Diodura?"

"Nothing."

Morrigan gulped, thanked the witch, and watched her leave. Old Nell had balked at calling the witch. Morrigan had been desperate, and overriding her nurse's protests, she'd sent for Diodura.

Nell approached Morrigan. "I'm sorry that witch couldn't help her."

Morrigan nodded, choking back her grief. "I don't want to lose dearest Gwynneth."

"I know."

Morrigan went back up the stairs to the suite, to sit near the bed watching Gwynneth, whose visage was pasty white. She wouldn't last the night, said Nell and Diodura. The babe had torn her insides something fierce. Morrigan was sure they could have saved her had they called Diodura or her sister in time.

Morrigan blamed herself for listening to Old Nell.

She should've called the witch at once, at the very beginning of birth pains.

It had taken too long to bring forth the baby boy who was heir to the deceased duke's fortune, name, vast estate, and wealth. The tiny creature was the Duke of Trevelyan, by writ and God's grace. He would be beset and besieged on every side by those greedy for the great consequence and gold the title could bring.

The duchess, too weak to hold her newborn, let her hands touch his brow.

"Don't forsake me, Morrigan. We're Welsh Llywelyns, descended from Dafydd ap Llywelyn, unafraid of the dread English and Scots who killed my beloved Ruric. We are sworn to uphold our name and honor. You must give my son the name of Llywelyn, and not that of Trevelyan. If you don't they'll find my babe and slay him. Swear to me."

"I swear by Saint David and Llywelyn, he shall be mine and none other."

Her dear cousin smiled and tried to lift her hand.

When Gwynneth closed her eyes, Morrigan thought her cousin slept, until she saw that no breath lifted that fragile chest.

"She's gone, so she is, milady. Come, we'll ready her for burial."

Morrigan stared, stunned, at Old Nell, the only mother she'd ever known and her own nurse since birth. What was to become of them? They were alone, far from their home of Cardiff, with the enemies of

Trevelyan ready to snap at the estate, to carve and slice into its richness. She'd have to leave Trevelyan, go to the isolated holding bequeathed to her. It was her only choice. She was not so young that she didn't realize how she'd be castigated when it became known that the child was hers.

Frightened, and more alone than she'd ever been, she scooped up the babe and hugged it to her. "You shall be Rhys Llywelyn and mine alone."

"Milady, come. You're wanted."

"Tell them I'm in mourning—"

" 'Tis Lord Tarquin of Cardiff, milady."

Morrigan glanced at Old Nell's flat expression, then away. The funeral had been private. Word had been sent forth a sennight after so there'd be no question. Rhys was upstairs with his nurse. Her brothers had been far removed from the private holding deeded to her by her father. None knew the secret but Diodura and Old Nell, who hadn't looked up from her tatting.

Now a childhood friend had arrived. For years Morrigan had been sure she would marry Tarquin one day. That wouldn't have been disagreeable to her. They'd known each other since babyhood. She could be comfortable with him. A verbal agreement of betrothal had been made with Tarquin's family and her brothers. Now it could never be. "Send him in, Alea."

The handmaiden bobbed a curtsy and left on the run.

"Will you not tell this one who be betrothed to you?"

Morrigan inhaled a shaky breath, then shook her head. "There's word among my family that war is brewing on the borders. I cannot speak vows now, nor can I break my covenant to Gwynneth."

Old Nell nodded, passing the newcomer on her way out. He gave her not one glance.

"Beloved!" Tarquin approached, hands outstretched. "You should've sent runners when you were so beset. I long to take on all your troubles as my own."

She smiled when he enfolded her in his arms, thinking of the babe in the upper suite, and how her life had changed because of him. She closed her eyes when she pondered how Tarquin would look upon her when she announced the boy was hers. Adulteress! It would hurt, but she wouldn't shirk her duty to the babe and to Gwynneth.

She was happy with Tarquin, not at all adverse to being courted by him, mayhap exchanging vows with him. But now, it could not be. The babe must be her priority.

Though not a word had been set to script, she would break off the verbal compact between them. She would spare Tarquin the shame of being thought cuckolded by his betrothed.

ONE

Courage, daughter! May the Lord of heaven turn
your grief to Joy!

Edna

Scotland—1332

Morrigan was unable to protest or stop time. Her wedding day was ticking away on the water clock as the giggling women dressed her.

It had been a whirlwind of treaties, diets, compacts, then compromises at the last with herself as pawn. That she should become the key to end the hostilities of Wales and bring peace to the borders still mystified her. She'd not thought that the triangle of land deeded to her, a portion of the Llywelyn holding, would become a rallying point for both sides uniting them at last.

Her brothers had told her that they wouldn't contest the holding, that she could remain there, even designate her son as heir to it. Why would they contest her right to the holding? The lonely piece with one isolated castle on a craggy outcropping, battered by the sea on one side and Bude Bay on the other, had never seemed a treasure to them. Its very remoteness had been her protection.

"Rhys can succeed to the holding, and thereby not be a penniless lord when he comes to maturity," her brother Califb, Earl of Llywelyn, had told her.

"Thank you." Not even to her kind brother could she disclose Rhys's identity. If even a word was whispered about, it could imperil the boy.

Now, she was in Scotland because of the strategic placement of her property. Of more importance was her relationship to the most powerful lords in Wales. With her union to the Scottish lord, English Edward could be neutralized. They would marry to bind the borders and bring peace.

Never had Morrigan looked on her holding as prime until it had become a bone of contention in hammering out a treaty among the triumvirate of Wales, Scotland, and England. It would be an uneasy peace. That the lords at Cardiff would take such measures, that she would become the linchpin of Edward Baliol's shaky claim, had not been a triumph to her. Nay! It could become her death warrant. Too many secrets tangled through this union. She had little choice but to keep them.

Edward Baliol, monarch to Scotland, had taken up a startling cause. His drumbeat was peace and a united peoples consisting of Anglos who called themselves English, the great Welsh, and the unconscionable Scots who were little more than brutish bears wearing their outlandish costumes. Was Morrigan the only person to call the king's declarations foolhardy?

But once her brothers had become convinced that a peoples united through her marriage was the only way to peace, no word of hers could change their minds.

It had all come too fast to her remote corner of Wales. If her own family hadn't prevailed upon her to make the sacrifice to prevent bloodshed, she'd have never agreed to align herself with a Scot. If Califb and Drcq had demurred she might've had a chance of getting out of the unholy alliance. They thought they were protecting her and her issue by such a marriage.

She'd had little choice once the lords began to come to agreement. The veiled threat of turning her out of her castle, of donating her home and land to the Church, had been mentioned by the earls of Wales. Though her brothers had protested, their protests had been the impetus to her agreement. She couldn't cause a conflict that could endanger her brothers' holdings, even their lives, if they had to fight in her defense.

The cavalcade north into wildest Scotland, bordering an even wilder ocean, was as arduous as the seers had predicted. She was to marry one of the mightiest lairds in Scotia to seal the king's bargain, not a border lord as she'd supposed, but a warrior descended from the mighty Vikings. The most barbarous of Scots! Aodh MacKay wouldn't have agreed to the marriage had he not so much to gain. The promise of reclaiming his own lands, lost when he'd battled against Scottish Edward's fight for the throne, had been the powerful inducement.

Now she was here with the godless Scots in a land as wild as they were, with a host of ladies surrounding her as she was readied for the vow taking. She felt more like a lamb led to the slaughter than a bride prepared for her groom.

Perhaps her primitive betrothed might be able to speak Anglo. She could. She'd not admit to understanding the discordant Gaelic that tripped off their lying tongues but she knew it well, having had a housemaid from Hibernia who could speak the language. She needn't tell her husband of her understanding. Just a small deception on the list of larger ones. The handmaidens who spoke freely in front of her did not realize she comprehended.

"If you'd but smile, milady . . ."

At Morrigan's cold look the handmaiden's broken Anglo faltered then subsided.

Morrigan glanced over at Rhys, who jumped and fidgeted no matter which lady tried to entertain him. She forced a smile. He would feel her tension just as he always sensed her moods. At five years of age he was a brawny, healthy lad. Rhys was a pure Celt and she was proud of him. Recalcitrant at times, bullheaded too often, he was a true son of Wales. That he called her Mother, and knew no other, was his safety net.

"Be good, Rhys," she commanded quietly. It wouldn't do to show fear, though if truth be told she'd been frightened on and off, since Rhys's birth. Even protected by the Llywelyn name she'd been the subject of scorn. More than one illicit liaison had been offered to her. Some had all but threatened. Somehow she'd prevailed, even in the absence of her brothers.

Her husband could put her to death if he discovered her secret. She would do anything and everything to protect the knowledge buried in her heart. Keeping silent about Rhys's true birth was the only protection for both of them. Old Nell was gone. Though Diodura, the only other person who knew the truth of Rhys's birth, was still alive, she'd say nothing. No doubt her sister, Lature, would also know. She would be silent, as well. They were the only ones, outside of Morrigan, who knew Rhys was heir to the vast holding of Trevelyan. One day when Rhys reached his majority, when he could manage an army, his true identity would be revealed.

That didn't hold sway in her mind at the moment. Getting free of the Scottish entanglement, and how to manage it without war, had filled her head for weeks. So far she'd not come up with any workable plan to liberate herself and Rhys from the terrible alliance that faced her. Choices dribbled away as fast as time on the water clock. It was getting late.

Rhys roared his disapproval when one of the ladies tried to wipe the chocolate from his chin.

"Rhys! Remember your place," Morrigan chided.

He scowled at her, opening his mouth.

Before he could speak the gong sounded throughout the castle and the merriment increased. Shouts and laughter bounced off the walls. Perhaps it was this that made the tapestries sway, and not the sudden bitter wind that'd swept down from the northern isles.

It had been pointed out to her that the castle was on the coastline of the Pentland Sea. Beyond the mists were the dreaded Orkneys wherein the Vikings, loyal to the MacKays, dwelt. Not only were they aligned with MacKays, they were kin. What could be worse? A combination of savages. Could the mighty traders be any more dangerous than those on this forbidden land called MacKay?

"The king is here, milady! Edward Baliol, himself, will give you to the great laird of the Norlands. The wondrous Highlands will be blessed by the presence of MacKay. His mother came from the Orkneys, you know. A rare beauty she was. 'Tis said she spoke naught but the Icelandic tongue so common there. What a twist of families there is this day, wouldn't you say?"

"I . . . I know not your meaning," Morrigan said.

"Is it not strange that your name, Morrigan, is the same as the clan you'll marry into, milady?"

Morrigan whirled around, upsetting the seamstresses who were putting the last stitches in her raiment. "I thought the name was MacKay."

"Not Mak-kay, milady. 'Tis Mac-key, or as the laird, Aodh, calls it, Ma-ky', milady, with the heavy accent on the last syllable."

"I see. Then why not call it Clan Morgan?"

"To be sure, milady, such was it called, eons past. 'Twas such a wild and woolly group of roisterers they didn't much care what they were called. And so it was Morgan."

"And as mine is Welsh and pronounced Morgan, I see a faint similarity, but not enough to be important," Morrigan replied. Perhaps she sounded stuffy. Nervousness had always made her poker up, rather than cry, which would've been more acceptable, mayhap. Nay! She'd not satisfy any of their black prayers. If they expected her to beg for mercy, plead to return to Wales, they'd wait till their bones rotted. She was Llywelyn. Her chin lifted.

The giggles increased to hoots as word of what she said flew among them.

"I think she just insulted her future rib," one of the ladies called to another.

" 'Tis not a thing she'll do often if all that's said of Aodh MacKay is true."

"Aye, 'tis true he's ruthless, that he'd skewer one for frowning at him."

Morrigan steeled herself not to shiver. She was happy no one could see her knees. They quaked like dry branches in the wind.

" 'Tis a shame the laird is so closedmouth about his liaisons. 'Twould be a grand tale to know it all."

"My, I think not. Yon one would faint," said one, her head jerking toward Morrigan.

The hilarity increased.

Morrigan rubbed her wet palms on a piece of precious material that'd been trimmed from her garb. She couldn't close her ears to the ribaldry that was so much a part of the Scots, though she wished she could. Hearing about the outlander who'd be her spouse put a bad taste in her mouth.

These Scots were an unseemly people with little good sense. She'd never experienced such in Wales. The men might talk in a lascivious way to one another. She'd overheard such when she'd been hidden away in a cupboard. No such talk of coupling was stated openly by Welshwomen as was done with Scotswomen. Had they no shame? If truth were told she knew a goodly amount of what went on between animals. She'd been raised among the hills and dales where sheep and goats played and rutted. Weren't the actions of men and women the same? She knew enough, and didn't care to hear her future privacy with her spouse discussed. Nor did she wish to ponder how their coupling would progress.

". . . and they say he's hung as a destrier is. What a ride she'll have . . . 'struth he's bedded enough wenches to people a village . . . nay, they were glad to be plowed by such a stud."

When they grinned at her, Morrigan nodded as though she had not understood such words, though she struggled to control the blood flowing to her cheeks.

The women thought her illiterate, as some were in Wales and their own land. How could they know she'd been tutored as her brothers had been, in Greek, Latin, with a background in Euclid and the Egyptian healing ways? She'd been instructed, too, by the witches in the keeping and preserving of herbs.

To be sure they were no different from most who thought her an adulteress, a woman who'd bedded a man not her spouse, and had only been protected by the Llywelyn name. So, now she was mother to one thought to be a Llywelyn by bastardy, not a Trevelyan by birth, who was heir to a large, imposing holding. It was not in Rhys's best interest that anyone know he was not a natal Llywelyn. One day—

"Milady, do not thread your hands so," one of the seamstresses urged. "Each motion pulls the fabric out of the stitching line."

"Sorry," Morrigan whispered. Her life could be over that day when it was discovered she'd not known the touch of a man. Would she be entombed in her bride's clothes? She had to force herself to remain still and standing. How ironic that she could and might be castigated for being a possible conspirator against the Scots because of her virginity, if only because they believed her to be a mother.

The solution to her dilemma had eluded her these many days since her betrothal was first trumpeted throughout Wales. Many of the Welsh thought her little more than a human sacrifice. They understood the need, but pitied her, and she could expect little more, being a fallen woman. None of them knew her problems were greater than they perceived.

As the ceremony grew closer, her desperation grew. She had to find a way to protect herself. If her husband decided to kill her who would take care of Rhys?

Taking a deep breath, she stared at the water clock. It took all her mettle not to grab Rhys and run. Foolhardy! She wouldn't get far.

That very night she'd be joined with a man she didn't know. She'd seen the joinings of animals and such. It didn't assuage her trepidation. If anything such ponderings magnified her fears. She didn't know, beyond that, nor did she care to, about the detailed intimacies a man and woman shared, since she was a virgin. Most in Scotia and Wales thought her well past bedding and breeding because she was beyond two decades by three changes of the moon, and had a child by another man. Proving them wrong didn't set well. It could mean a very painful death if her new husband questioned her, demanded an explanation. If she could save Rhys by confessing his parenthood, she would. Mayhap the wild MacKay would listen to reason and spare Rhys. Lord knew he was as much at risk as she.

She glanced out an open lancet and tried not to shiver. Scotland with its gaunt and endless mountains seemed not a country at all, but a place of darkness and goblins.

One of the ladies patted her. "I'm Lilybet, milady. Not a chatterin' gomeril like some is," the retainer said, jerking her head at the giggling ladies. "Time to go, 'tis.

Dinna fret what 'awn say. 'Tis naught but the wind, ye ken. Aodh MacKay is a man of great wealth. Were he not to wed and bed you his lands would be forfeit since he fought against the earls who put Edward upon the throne. Since the king knows 'tisn't wise to battle the Norland lairds, that the Highlands are peopled with stalwarts he cannot afford to gainsay, he's opted for compromise, ye ken. 'Tis proud you are to be the key to such."

The words fired Morrigan's inner strength. Proud, is it? she fumed. To be a pawn makes no Welsh woman proud. Am I not Boudicca's spawn who fought the Romans to their knees before their duplicity caused the great queen's death? More fool Aodh MacKay if he thinks I will bend, that I will be grateful for his name. I am a princess of Wales. He's naught but a barbarian from the north. Instead of voicing her fury, Morrigan smiled and nodded.

"Were you not to procure an heir for MacKay, yon lad could lose his Welsh monies and holdings that come from you. Not so?"

"Why do you say so?" She struggled to stay calm. Had Lilybet the power of vision? How could she know about Rhys?

"Fret not. Yon boy will not do ill with MacKay. You'll see. The we'en will not need your own monies. He'll benefit from MacKay, and rightly so."

Not so! His wealth is Trevelyan! He will inherit! Her mind screamed it. Her mouth muttered ayes as she passed the canny Lilybet, and preceded her ladies-in-waiting from the tower room.

"Aodh! Ready yourself, the king comes."

"I'm ready, Toric." He turned to look at his men gathered around him in the keep below the west turret. Looking upward, he scanned the battlements. It would not be impossible to storm the castle at the first sign of treachery. Though Edward had given his gauntlet, the sign of his honor, Scots were not fooled by such. Had not Wallace lost his life because of English infamy?

"Toric, you, and the others"—he let his eyes rove his large complement of soldiers—"know what you must do. Protect our guidon, our tartan, our name." A smile touched his mouth. "I'll unbend a bit more and use my Anglo name. No more will I be called Aodh. The Gaelic gives way to the English Hugh." He nodded once when some groaned a complaint. "Flinch not at small cost. The name, honor, and our wealth are in balance. Even if this comes off with the dreaded Welsh woman, naught changes for us. We are Scots and MacKays." The expected roar to such a battle cry was greeted with the silence of wisdom. Not one word of their counterplan would be known to the royal. Nay, his very existence as monarch would hang in the balance until the moment when they would have their rightful heritage returned.

Only to spare his people further death and pain had Hugh MacKay agreed to having a Welsh spouse. If Edward Baliol thought him cowed by the pact he didn't know his Scot.

If the Welsh wanton sold herself to gain power among her people and his, she didn't know MacKay. He'd bed her until she brought forth another son. The one she had now would inherit some of the MacKay holding, but no Welshman could ever command the land, name, and people. If she brought no heir, then he . . .

His thoughts were jarred by the second striking of the gong. He sucked in a breath and looked at his men.

Bratach Bhan Chlann Aoidh!

The murmur grew until it was on all their lips.

The White Banner of MacKay!

Shields were brought forth with the bulrush painted on the white banner. Shoulder clips were touched with the same insignia. Man looked to man, standing straighter. Clenched fists slammed into chests, the Viking signal meaning death before dishonor that had come to them from the Icelandics who'd married into the clan. The warlike MacKays would never suffer perfidy. If Edward Baliol sought to betray them with the Welsh tart, he'd swallow revenge before the sun set.

One more time the gong sounded. Hugh smiled at his cousin Toric and his men, patting his sword.

They smiled back and followed him, many breaking away from the serpentine procession to the glen. Some melted into the throng, others disappeared through passageways. More than a few climbed to the battlements, while a complement went to the bailey and beyond.

There'd be MacKay warriors to man the walls, though the king's forces might not notice them. These were almost a match in number to those who already dotted the woods, and surrounding areas. A full contingent would mix with the wedding crowd. They'd be prepared for anything. The MacKay Clan hadn't survived so many generations by being careless.

TWO

**A little thing indeed is a sweetly
smelling sacrifice.**
Judith

The dankness, dimness, and rank scent of the old rush-
ings in the ancient castle mirrored Morrigan's soul. She
looked down into the vaulted entry, spying the royal at
once.

Edward Baliol was certainly not the romantic ideal of
a king. His bandy-legged, narrow-chested form was
cloaked with riches that didn't hide the scanty frame nature had provided. His razor-sharp mind had kept him at
the forefront of rule. His greed for power was far more
imposing than his ill-shaped body.

Morrigan took a breath and whispered the vow she'd
made to Gwynneth. Then she rubbed the gold claddagh
pinned to her bodice and fashioned for her by her ma-
ternal Hibernian grandsire. She descended the stairway
carved from the turret wall so that ascending warriors
would find it harder to wield a sword than those coming

down at them. At that moment she'd have felt more at home battling foes than descending to take the arm of the royal who'd escort her to her spouse.

Keeping her chin elevated took grit when all she wanted to do was watch her footing on the treacherous stairway. The stone, the hue of blacksmith's iron, had gone slippery from wear, and since she'd not wanted any of the ladies at her side, she had to pray for balance as she descended.

With a waxy smile upon her face, she reached the bottom and crossed the hall. She bowed to Edward Baliol. Some said he should never have ruled Scotland. It was his ancestor who'd aided in the betrayal of Wallace as did many of the other greedy earls, including the king's henchman, Monteith. "Your grace, I am—"

"I know who you are, Lady Morrigan Llywelyn. Am I not your guardian and as such sworn to protect your person and all you possess?" His smile washed over her.

She looked up at him, inclining her head. You bloated usurper! You'll not get Trevelyan. "'Tis true I am a princess of Wales—"

"Descendant of Dafydd ap Llywelyn, as is your bastard son, Rhys Llywelyn."

She fought the run of blood that washed from her heart at his words. For five changes of the sun she'd heard men's scathing pronouncements against her. If the Llywelyn family hadn't been so cohesive, so strong, so mightily resistant to all who'd dare to insult them, she might've been stoned for what they believed. She was protected by the bastion of her name and wealth. Power and gold! How they turned the world. She could not be ungrateful for the power that protected her. It was a vitriol in her innards that no man would be castigated for fathering a child out of wedlock. There was little justice.

A hand reached for hers, drawing her up. "I ask your pardon for my usage."

" 'Tis nothing I've not heard before, your grace." How she hated the quick condemnation of herself, and a child.

"Milady, I admire your sangfroid at my clumsiness. Do not think I'm unaware of your plight. Men cast their leavings at every turn. They're not condemned. You choose to bear and rear your child, and you are a sinner. I see the inequity, as I know you do."

Stunned, she fought to keep her mouth from falling open at such a declaration. Had she underestimated the monarch? She stared into those bright hazel eyes, alight with warmth, and almost faltered. She swallowed, lifted her chin, laid her hand upon his arm, and turned. "I thank you for your kind words, your grace."

"And I would say you'd not heard much of that outside the world of your kinsmen."

" 'Tis true." She took deep breaths. She would remain calm. It was not in her best interests or Rhys's to lose control.

"We have a walk before us, milady. This castle"—he jerked his head at the walls—"though the closest to the borders and the many families who have need to attend your nuptials, is not large enough to hold all who'd insist on witnessing the nuptials. The clans who clamor to see the deed nailed to the monastery door are numerous indeed, so we have no choice but to have the service out of doors. For once the sun smiles on Scotland."

Morrigan nodded, understanding the feudal powers that would only accept what they could touch or see. Many of those not seeing the vow taking would question its validity. Even some of those who did might protest. Better to let any who wished witness it. Facing straight ahead, not looking at any of the murmuring crowd that lined both sides of their way, she inclined her head to answer. "It behooves you to return Mac-Kay . . ." She stumbled over his name.

Edward chuckled. "How smooth your mouth is when it speaks your Celtic tongue. Worry not about your coming name. Say it this way. Maw-Ky. Come down hard at the last."

"Maw-Ky," Morrigan repeated, eliciting a smile from the monarch, sighs and whispers from the populace. "Once this nuptial commences, such lands revert to MacKay—"

He laughed. "Indeed. Vast properties and wealth untold, milady." When she looked at him he smiled, steering her around a retinue of guards who were clustered along the way. Across the inner and outer courtyards and out the main gate they slow marched as was custom. Then the crowd multiplied until it took many soldiers to hold back the throng who pressed to see, and to greet both bride and monarch.

Morrigan faltered at the first roars of the assemblage. The cheers and huzzahs were honeycombed with boos, though they were not as cacophonous as the happy sounds. The thunderous greetings grew and had her pausing.

"Head high, milady. Aye, that's the way of it. Be proud. You bring your own treasures to this match . . . not to mention the link with Trevelyan."

Morrigan swallowed, bowing left and right, pretending she hadn't heard the last. Had the royal guessed about Rhys? Or was he shooting in the dark as some did when wanting to probe and pry? He'd not gain her confidence.

The king waved his arm in greeting to those about them, as they wended their way to a copse of trees. In the center was the platform where she would promise to love, honor, and obey. Atop the large dais, which looked small from the gate, the vows would be shouted to those great numbers of persons dotting the heather-thatched hills. The far-off ghostly gray and snowcapped mountains half circling the area, the other half open to the wild and noisy sea, would be the sentinels, the silent witnesses to the vows.

When a raven and seabird flew above her, Morrigan wondered what the soothsayers would say. Ravens brought death; seabirds brought messages. The meaning was too obscure.

"For a sadly short or blessedly long time hence, milady, your name and person, both Scottish and Welsh may have the power to stem an invasion."

Morrigan swallowed. "Then to protect the peoples I embrace the decision to unite Llywelyn and MacKay."

"Well said."

"Surely peace hangs upon a stronger cord," she remarked.

"Does it? I wonder."

"You must know any ties we fashion will need to be knotted into peace and prosperity."

"That's what we do this day," said the king.

"You're very sure, it seems."

"I am sure of might, milady."

"And this would be MacKay?"

The king nodded. " 'Twould seem my English cousin would pause in his conquests if he stared into the sights of MacKay and Trevelyan might be aimed his way." The king's smile was sour. " 'Twould be better if I knew the enemies closer to me than my cousin."

Morrigan slanted him a glance. "I can assure you they are not among mine."

"I can agree with you, milady. I'm honored to have the might of MacKay and Trevelyan."

Morrigan smiled at the political sally, though her mind turmoiled with worry. Why had he not said Llywelyn? Three times he'd mentioned Trevelyan. Was it a sign? Would he guess who Rhys was? Had others? Certainly Aodh MacKay would ask questions once he found her to be virginal. He might not put her aside, for to do so would allow disclosure and questions about his right to keep his holdings. There were other ways to handle it. MacKay could consign her to a remote tower until she wasted away to death. To be parted from Rhys would be the greatest punishment.

If MacKay were as private a man as he was touted to be by the gabbing women, he'd not want his marriage business aired. Yet, if his anger was fierce enough he might not weigh the consequences. Dispatch her with a sword? Of course, he could put her aside by the simple expedient of ignoring her. In Wales women would protest. In Icelandia women would have an advocate to speak for them. No doubt in Scotland they merely burned them alive. Lord! She'd not dwell upon it.

At least there'd be no lords and ladies inspecting her wedding couch to see if she was in truth virginal. As a woman who, according to gossip, had had an unnamed lover and bore his son, she'd not be expected to be chaste. Nay, the rumor among those other than Llywe-lyns was she was wanton. How angry MacKay must be to take her to the marriage bed. Then again, he claimed his estate with her hand. Perhaps the justice of Hammurabi wouldn't prevail. She shuddered when she pictured the myriad punishments that could occur. Dismemberment. Stoning. Lashings.

Closing her eyes for a touch of time, she prayed to St. Dafydd that MacKay would not linger in her bed, nor would he visit it more than one time.

The cool breeze coming down the glen had her lifting

her face to it. Scotland had become too warm. Most said
it never did. Some had told her the sun had never shone
on the godforsaken land. Today it gave lie to the gossip.

Then she saw him. Good St. Dafydd, he was a giant
with naught upon his person but a white shirt, with a
multicolored swag over his shoulder and a kilt of the
same fabric. His knees were bare! Glory be! He was in
truth a barbarian in a sea of such. She blinked at the gi-
gantic men surrounding him, some with the same colors
on their shoulders, some with checks and plaids of totally different hues. A veritable spectrum! And all had
bare knees!

Many tales she'd heard of the mighty giants of the
north, how they looked when they fought. Some garbed
in myriad colors. Some naked and painted blue! Holy
Mother she was in a hell of colors! She'd had some idea
of what she would face after listening to the bitter pros-
ings of her family. To see it for herself was more than
strange. Did not the enemy use the many-hued garments
as targets? The earthen-hued raiment of the Welsh was
much more sensible. Oh to be in Wales . . .

"You pause, milady? Is something amiss?"

My whole life! she wanted to shout. "Not at all, your
grace. I'm just most anxious to see everything on this
auspicious day." She saw the glint of humor on his face
though he bowed as if he accepted what she said.

"A new life begins this day for you, milady."

"So it does, your grace." She forced a smile. What
would he say if it became her execution day?

She was to espouse herself to the largest of the giant Scots, forever, until she was called by her Maker. How unfair life was to the Welsh. She knew one thing. She'd never bend to him. She was a royal from Wales. What was he? An outlaw who'd been pardoned. The condition of his freedom and return of lands and name had been to align himself with the Welsh in marriage so that the King of Scotland could command fealty from its people. So be it. She would not let him forget that she was the mortar that buttressed every stone on his battlements.

If Ruric, Gwynneth's husband who by Welsh mandate could be called her cousin-in-law, had lived, no such infamy would've occurred. She might have been married to Tarquin of Cardiff and Lothb, if all had not been changed by false Fate. What would Tarquin say when he heard of her marriage? She'd not seen him in many turns of the sun. He'd told her he wouldn't have the heart to visit after she'd told him they couldn't marry. She'd read censure in his eyes, but she didn't, couldn't, explain about Rhys.

Had the saints deserted Llywelyns? She'd have to pray harder. Or if things became desperate, she would take up sword and cudgel as she'd been taught and fight her way back to Wales with Rhys on her back. She'd not be defeated. The Scots would soon discover she could wage war as well as any of them.

The king nudged her forward. "Come, milady, meet

your destiny with truth and grace. Are you not a royal Llywelyn of Wales sworn to protect all you hold dear?"

She heard the amusement in his voice as though he doubted she could. She didn't move. Rather she faced the king. "I will go through with this, as is my compact with my family and the House of MacKay. But first, as is my right, as a princess of Wales, I seek a boon from Scotland's king."

The royal's brows snapped together.

She could almost read his thoughts. Such was not the way of things that any woman being used as political tool would deem to seek favor. No matter how the demand was couched, it was still that. Where had female humility gone?

When he stared at her, Morrigan knew he waited for her to beg pardon, to confess that she had erred. Then they would resume their march to the altar without tomfoolery. The silence stretched. Morrigan held his glance. Too much was at stake to back down now.

Edward sighed. "And what would that be?"

"I seek to be named princess regent to a holding."

Edward's throat bobbed with myriad emotions. "By being princess regent, you would become regent, in effect."

"True. I wish to be named regent of the lands known as Trevelyan." When the king bared his teeth, she almost faltered. Then she thought of Rhys and persevered. " 'Tis my right, I believe, your grace. Since my lands run with theirs, my people can protect the holding. Since

I was kin to the last ruler, I can truthfully claim the right of family. This I can do since 'twould seem there's no Welshman of blood to claim the estate. I do not seek to manacle it to my lands. Instead I would ask that my regency run for two decades. 'Tis not unreasonable. After that time it could revert to the royals, or mayhap by that time an inheritor would be found." The blood running up those hard features told her she'd struck a vulnerable point. No doubt the king had meant to sweep the Trevelyan riches into his own keep. Edward Baliol would be a fool if he didn't negotiate some of the riches into his own depleted coffers.

"And why would you want to hold such in trust, milady? You are not a blood tie as you have admitted. Am I correct?" The silky tone held menace.

"You speak truth, your grace. 'Tis my loyalty to my people that makes me want to protect Welsh for Welsh. Would not a Scot do the same?"

The smile was reluctant. "I fear 'twould be so."

"Well, then?"

"Your argument is thin."

They'd stopped and faced each other, neither cognizant of the rising murmurs around them.

Since Morrigan didn't feel she could be any more threatened than she already was by being betrothed and soon to be married to a Scot, she persevered. "I, a true Llywelyn, and as such bound in ancient times to Trevelyan, can be held responsible for this, as my brothers can't. Welsh law allows a woman to be regent for a specified time. I am the only one left who has the blood and connection to hold such riches in trust, honorably, until such an inheritor can be found—"

" 'Twould seem you know your Welsh history and customs."

" 'Tis true." She'd also learned how to wager and gamble at her father's knee.

"And you do not consider this royal person equal to the task of protecting such lands and monies?" the king thrust at her, his face mottling.

She'd risked his anger and it would seem she'd fired it. Morrigan swallowed and wondered if she'd even make it to the marriage dais alive.

The murmurs rose higher through the sudden silence. Morrigan was sure that the onlookers, including her intended, could read the royal's ire as well as she. She looked at none but the king. "I, and all who know your reputation, respect your royal acumen," Morrigan stated.

The royal unbent enough to glance around him.

Morrigan looked to the assemblage on the raised platform. She saw lips move and was sure they were discussing the delay.

"Can you discern their meaning, Hugh?"

"No. They are rigid enough to have argued." He didn't turn to look at Toric. His gaze was fixed to the woman.

"She's not just a princess, but a beauty as well, eh Hugh? 'Tis a surprise, I'll be bound."

"Yes," Hugh said in terse tones.

"Perhaps 'tis a fluke of the sun. Her tresses cannot be midnight black shot with fire? Her brows are like black-bird wings. Even those arches seemed to be touched by that auburn fire. Though her rich raiment covers her from head to toe, I would say that she's as well formed as my mare. What say you, cousin?"

Hugh cursed. "What keeps the monarch and princess from the dais?"

"I sense you're more angered by my words, than by their hesitation."

"Hold your tongue, Toric."

His cousin laughed. "I swear you wouldn't have cared a fig on waking if she had been covered as well as a nun with only the tips of her fingers and face showing. Now you do."

"Must you go on with this?"

"I must," Toric responded, hiding his mirth. "Is she not like the wonderful enamels fashioned in Mercia? And her skin shines like sunny moonlight. Ah, if only we could see her eyes."

"How poetic you've become, cousin."

"I'll ignore the vinegar in your voice, and tell you to remember the covenant that will enrich MacKays with these nuptials."

"I forget nothing."

Ignoring his cousin's restraining arm, he leapt down from the dais and strode toward the duo.

Hugh perused her as he moved, noting the rich elkskin of her boots. The narrow, womanly foot was well shod. The intricate lace of her underdress spelled wealth.

" 'Twould seem the vows are to be put off by discussion?"

Morrigan had to call on all her reserves not to fall back. She knew without looking that the harsh tones barely coated by civility belonged to her future spouse. When had he come upon them? When last she'd looked he'd been among the throng on the platform. She didn't turn her head.

"All proceeds as it should," she said in her haughtiest tone. She was rewarded by the king's elevated brow, and a fractional lifting of one corner of his mouth.

"Your blood beats hot, MacKay. Even from a distance I noted your charge to reach us. No doubt 'twould be my needs that would call you, and not the loveliness of your intended."

"My heat would be for my intended, as you say," Hugh interjected, his smile almost hiding his annoyance. "Perhaps the lady had bewitched both of us, highness."

"To be sure she must be. And more than that the lady has a mind for opportunity, MacKay. Your espoused wife would have me sign over Trevelyan to her regency, MacKay. What think you?"

"I think her perspicacity in enlarging my estates is admirable. What think you, most lovely intended?"

Silence gouged through the gothic curves of the

stately trees dotting the glen. His words had been beyond courteous, though spoken in lazy fashion. Some murmured they had loverlike tones. How could that be? MacKay didn't know the princess, had never met her.

"I think . . ." Morrigan said in measured tones, knowing her enunciated words would carry. ". . . that I cannot receive what is not to be given. My riddle is simple to solve when one is bound in the truth that I alone, by blood, can carry the Trevelyan estates in my regency."

The bald, bold statement brought gasps, sighs, mutters, and groans. Then a light chuckle that began with her intended and brought a reluctant response from the king allowed the onlookers to breathe again.

Morrigan shook inside like a pudding, but she pressed her lips and knees together and prayed for strength. Her gaze touched the man who was soon to be her spouse.

Taller than any man there. His hair seemed dark until it hit the sun, then it was auburn flame as were his brows. His cheekbones were wide. Such breadth of shoulder she'd not seen in all her family. His mouth was as firm as his jaw, and some would call him handsome. The colorful tartan became him. The claymore proclaiming his title of laird looked like a giant's weapon, yet he wore it with ease. His eyes were black, then blue, or both. His skin had a smooth, ruddy tautness that covered his strong bones. Though big, he looked so smoothly muscled one couldn't call him brawny. This man was formidable—and more comely than any warrior she'd beheld.

There was a movement to the right. A woman richly dressed, though in the black of mourning, her gem-encrusted gown and headdress winking in the sun, stepped to the side of MacKay. "Has my godson need of me?"

MacKay turned, noting the agitated frown. "No need to fret, milady. I believe you know our royal."

The woman sank in deep curtsy, bringing a smile to Edward's face.

"And this is my intended, the most beautiful woman in Wales."

There were titters and murmurs. The lady's brow elevated just a trifle.

Hugh touched his godmother's arm. "Lady Maud MacKenzie, my godmother. Lady Morrigan Llywelyn, soon to be MacKay."

Morrigan was impressed by the woman's lustrous skin, the blue-black hair that peeped from the side of her headdress. She was struck at how beautifully the mourning colors became her, how they enhanced that white skin and her bejeweled garb. "'Tis an honor to meet you, milady."

"The honor is mine, dear one, since you are soon to be espoused to my godson." She waved her hand in a languid, graceful way. "'Tis my son who will support the cardinal at your vows."

Morrigan turned to look. "He's a priest, then?"

MacKay chuckled. "Not quite. Kieran MacKenzie

hasn't taken all his vows as yet, though he soon shall. He's too caught up in his Latin and Greek studies."

His mother sighed. " 'Tis true."

The king coughed and Lady MacKenzie bowed, then faded back to the throng. " 'Tis past time for the vows." He glanced at Morrigan. "Shall we, milady?"

Morrigan pressed her lips together. "I would have an answer to my query for regency, if it please your grace." She could tell that the monarch wished she had forgotten it and not mentioned it again.

MacKay stepped nearer. "What say you of my intended, good royal? We stand before you and God to say our vows. This day truth will be spoken."

The king nodded once. "I've been outflanked by the Celt," he murmured for her ears alone, though the widening of MacKay's smile said he'd picked up the words. "Let us proceed." He waved his hand and all the frozen retainers unbent, surreptitious gripping of weapons relaxed.

Morrigan hadn't received a verbal promise, but she felt encouraged that she hadn't had a negative response. She'd persevere.

Instead of returning to his place as custom demanded, MacKay offered his other arm.

She looked up at him, reeling at the heat she saw there, the interest. This was unexpected. That she could be drawn to a Scot had not entered her thoughts. At best she'd thought to tolerate him. Now her innards quivered like treacle because he eyed her.

For the first time her carefully built resistance wavered and Morrigan could feel a trembling at the back of her knees. Her neck was so stiff it'd cramped between her shoulders. Her soon-to-be-spouse was even larger than he'd looked at a distance. His shoulders were like doors, though there was a smoothness to him, a quickness she sensed. Danger surrounded him like the lunar aureole.

His face had been chiseled to rock hardness, his eyes the brown of a Welsh hill with golden slashes around the outside. He'd made such a quick complete impression on her, she could recall the slight scar at the corner of his mouth, a similar one to the side of one eye. She felt the beat of his blood under his hand. Not as fast as hers. She'd not expected to like his features, to find him winsome in a manly way. She must be sickening with something to find a Scot appealing.

Her hesitation was enough to make MacKay aware she was more of a reluctant bride than he'd been led to believe. Annoyance had him moving closer to her so that her right hand slid down over his, his thumb locking her there. The flowers she carried drooped between them.

Morrigan was out of breath and off balance. She didn't know why MacKay had such an effect, but she knew it was he who'd caused it. All at once her modish raiment felt mussy, uncomfortable, lumpy. Each and every step had to be handled with care for her limbs had become like softened wax.

It was more than awkward to try to traverse the glen,
manage the train of her gown and the heaviness of the
bliaut, with her arms lifted to the limbs of two haughty
men. To make it more cumbersome, the chin guard of
her headdress began slipping up and covering her
mouth. She took a deep breath and wished for the long
trek to the altar to be over, when just short minutes past
she'd wanted it to go on forever. What a paradox. She
needed an ending that she sorely didn't want.

Her two escorts paused at the foot of the platform. As
quickly and quietly as she could she pushed and pulled
at her raiment, trying to keep it in order.

The king preceded the bride and the laird upward. He
held up his hands to the crowd, accepting their huzzahs,
ignoring their boos.

Morrigan looked up the short steps to the platform
and sighed. Too steep. Were they rickety as well? Surely
she'd fall from them and break her neck. That might
solve the problem. She lifted one foot.

MacKay bent toward her, eyes alight. "Let me assist
you, milady." He scooped her up to thunderous ap-
plause.

"Fool! Would you have them scorn us?" Morrigan
felt dizzy, disoriented. She clutched at him. Never had
she felt anything but a need to handle her own destiny.
In one quick swoop MacKay had rendered her helpless.
It was not a wholly unsatisfying sensation, though unseemly. She was surely going mad! Not minding being
held by a Scot! Ridiculous.

"They dare not," he answered her shocked query.

Why did he look at her so? He seemed taken aback. Did she repulse him?

"Surely your flashing emerald eyes would tell them they are in the presence of a queen."

"Surely not, since I'm a princess," she shot back, more shaken by his touch than she'd ever been. No other living person had wielded such potency over her. Black magic, that's what it was. MacKay was in league with Satan himself. Consigning him to the devil had a leavening effect on her nerves, though her being continued to tingle from his touch.

The papal representative, Cardinal Campbell, was a long-suffering, sour man who'd taken martyrdom as his cloak when only a young priest. He wore it like a second skin and it had served him well. His glowering glance would've stayed upon the Welsh woman, had not the hard glance of MacKay intercepted it. He schooled his features into what he was sure was a pious look.

Morrigan looked up, off balance, relieved to find the altar in front of her. When the cherubic face next to the prelate grinned in encouragement, she had to smile back. Who was this monk, tonsured as required, but not as obsequious as the others who attended the lofty churchman? When she saw a slight bow to the left of the monk, she noted the younger, almost pretty, young man standing not quite behind the cardinal. When he smiled, she smiled back. That must be Kieran MacKenzie.

The cardinal lifted his hands and there was a semblance of quiet. He turned to the altar and began.

Morrigan took her place and bowed her head, startled when she felt the warm body of MacKay touch hers.

The mass and ritual droned on until most fidgeted, some yawning and wiping their faces, some sneaking away for various reasons. Finally, the vows were to be repeated.

"Whosoever would come forth and find against this woman, let him speak now?" the cardinal intoned, his words ricocheting from the mouths of the many callers.

It was on Morrigan's tongue to tell him that she was as good as any man there, and a good deal better than the man next to her, if all of the foibles described by the ladies and laid at his door were true. Let them come forth who would find against the man, not her. She said nothing. The world she would be living in henceforth would not be much different from the one she left. In the Llywelyn world, and among some of the other families in Wales, there was a difference. Women had to make decisions, lead families if that was their duty. The old Celtic laws and customs had come down from Boudicca, whose very fierceness and courage colored all Welsh declarations. None among the Llywelyns thought them strange.

"Wise," her intended whispered, bending down under the guise of pushing back her veil.

"What is that?" she whispered back, trying to recall what was said.

"If I read your thoughts, you see the prelate as I do. And though I applaud your desire to call him for the jackass he is, better not to do it. He's a pompous idiot, more than willing, milady, to bring our peoples to war over the merest slight—"

" 'Twouldn't be mere," she muttered back, mirth pushing at her throat. He'd make her laugh at this solemn occasion? He was unruly. She put a shaking hand to her mouth. "Stop," she pleaded behind her fingers.

He chuckled, his fingers going over her headdress and lingering. ". . . that's why I sent for Monteith to aid the cardinal during the mass. He has a way of moving things along, and he's much less puffed up."

"You . . . must . . . not . . . say . . . so," she muttered, hard-bent not to double over. Unaccustomed to hilarity as she'd been the last five years, she almost didn't recognize it. Morrigan had to press her hand tight to her lips to hold back the laughter. She tried to glare up at her husband, but the monk called her attention to repeat the binding words. That sobered her. She'd not looked forward to saying them. The words stuck in her craw.

"Ah, I will, under God and Wales . . . er, ah Scotland . . . ah, er . . . and England, keep the vows pronounced by me, Morrigan Dafydda Nemed Agnomon Llywelyn, nor will this bond ravel or be broken by me on this day and forever. I swear this as a royal princess of Wales."

MacKay pronounced his the same way without stumbling over the countries as she'd done.

It startled her when her husband leaned down and kissed the corner of her mouth. Monstrous! Then to compound the infamy he turned her to the assemblage.

Since she'd been too flustered after making her request for the regency to look about her when walking with the king and her intended, she'd not noticed how huge the throng had become. For most of the day she'd sensed good feeling among the people, though a time or two she'd felt that there were malicious gazes on her. Now, she was too taken aback to do anything but stare at their numbers.

When her husband raised her hand with his, a roar went up thundering through the trees, surely bending the bracken to the ground and making her jump. If that was their battle cry, no wonder good men blanched.

Her mouth fell open when a woolen was thrown over her shoulder in the same pattern her husband wore. The thunderous cacophony was accompanied by a dreadful occurrence. The warriors with the same plaid as her husband howled another dreadful battle cry, then heaved their mighty claymores high in the air. Morrigan was appalled. "They're slaughtering the people!" she gasped.

"Nay, milady. They honor you. None shall be hurt, I promise. Would I mar the day of our espousal?"

It was already scarred beyond redemption by the mouthing of the vows. She didn't say it out loud. It surprised her when her husband moved closer to her. The dreaded Scot was a comfort who made her blood bubble. Surely she was coming down with an ailment.

Everyone laughed when people clustered under the quickly drawn shields that caught the brunt of the weapons when they tumbled downward.

"A tradition, milady. What think you of your clan?"

"Their mirth escapes in strange ways," she murmured.

He laughed. "You are quick, milady."

"Not quick enough," she muttered.

He leaned over her. "I heard that. Had you hoped to escape me?"

"Fortune disallowed it," she blurted, seeing the flash of what she assumed was ire in his eyes. "I beg pardon. I do not mean to wound you." He was prodigious handsome. No wonder the handmaidens and ladies-in-waiting discussed him.

"Thank you. I'll stanch the blood flow."

A smile pulled at her mouth. She liked his tart humor. "You could be hurt only by one of your mammoth swords, milord Maw-Ky."

He laughed. "So someone has tutored you in my name."

She nodded. " 'Twas necessary." She pointed to her mouth. "I couldn't get my lips about it." She blinked when he stared, his eye pinpointing what her finger touched. "Have I offended?"

"Only if you are, in truth, a Circe?"

Taken aback she stared at him. "Have you been imbibing that infamous brew called uiskah made by the monks?"

His laughter increased. "I would not let the churchmen fashion a drink for me. My people make it."

"I hear 'tis passing cruel to sample."

He put his arm around her waist, still laughing. "Then I'll only drink a tot when you do, wife."

"That'll be never." Had he no shame? Clutching her like she was a doxy! He deserved a good set down. If she could think of one she'd have dished it to him. "I should join Rhys. He'll be wondering what has—"

"He'll not be worried. He knows you're with your spouse."

Had she read his thoughts aright? He did not seem eager to dispose of her. "What are you pondering?"

"How intriguing Welshwomen are, in truth."

Flustered, she struck rather than simpered as was her way. "How monstrous wrongheaded you are not to have known. Our comely women are sung of, far and wide."

"I'll have to punish my people," he murmured, leaning over her.

"Rubbish! You'll do no such thing."

He laughed. "Why has no one described your beauty? Surely that calls for torture."

"Nonsense." She could scarce get a breath.

"Would you believe I would give half my holding to see your tresses at this moment?"

She coughed. "We . . . we were talking of Rhys."

He chuckled. "I told you he'd be fine."

"Don't be too sure about him. He's more than passing unpredictable," she muttered.

Hugh caught the words. "Worry not. Your son will come to accept."

She caught his look. His grin didn't mask the curiosity that lurked in those eyes.

Had he guessed that Rhys had decided to despise him? Would he care about the feelings of a five-year-old? She did, but even explaining to him that she must marry to protect Wales had not penetrated the ire of Rhys's factoring. Someone was taking his mother from Wales, and he had to leave with her. Not good. She agreed it was wrong to align with a Scot! Safety demanded she put her feelings on hold for the good of the Trevelyan heir. Convincing Rhys was a different story since he must be kept from the truth. She'd spent much of the journey north on the task of disabusing him of hating all MacKays.

She was on her way away from her new spouse when the gong sounded and he pulled her back, anchoring her to his side. "Will you not gainsay this?" She hissed at him, bringing his laughter to the fore once more.

" 'Tis only my deep passion responding to your charms, good wife."

Morrigan gasped. "Such barbaric words. Have you no shame?" She said this between her teeth, knowing her overheard words would send the scandalous Scots into hilarity.

"I have. Shame that I had to make bargains to regain

what was mine. Shame that I have to bow my head to
yon monarch whose blood is too thin of good Scot lin-
eage to be the powerful liege lord he must be to stand
against our enemies." He grimaced. "I have shame."

His hurt was a hurled spear that had her choking on
her own ire. That he should be shamed by an alliance
with her, no matter the reason, shouldn't have pained.
But it did. Her anger flared. She pulled free, gazing up
at him.

He seemed puzzled when he looked down at her,
opening his mouth as though he'd query her glower.

She felt heated, trapped in that look. It whetted her
fury even more.

"The king!" The attendant blasted on a horn after the
gong sounded again.

Morrigan had the sensation that time had stopped,
that she and her new spouse had created a world
wherein they dwelt alone. All because they'd looked
into each other's eyes and couldn't look away. She
couldn't remember what last they'd said, or how long
they'd been still and staring. She swallowed. "The
king—"

"I heard," Hugh said, his face tight. He took her hand
and put it on his arm and they turned together to face
Edward Baliol, who now stood behind a trencher board
on a podium, his crest raised by an attendant.

Most inclined their heads in respectful silence. A few
glared or sneered, though they were quiet. Some

glanced at MacKay as though he dictated their stance. MacKay stayed close to his wife, looking at the royal.

"I, Edward Baliol, your king, do pronounce that the Trevelyan holdings in Wales shall be ceded to the regency of Milady Morrigan of MacKay, royal of Wales, heir to the Llywelyn holdings and spouse to Hugh, Earl of MacKay, laird to Clan MacKay."

The roar of assent far outreached the nays in sound and fury. Some shouted protest at the anglicizing of MacKay's Gaelic name.

"You've won power, wife."

"Not for myself," she murmured.

Hugh frowned, not sure he'd heard her right.

Morrigan rocked with the enormity of it. She'd triumphed, and by royal writ that would be shouted throughout the hills and dales of Scotland, England, and Wales. Gwynneth's son would rule as God and Wales had ordained. She swayed in teary joy, not even pulling back when her husband embraced her, though a sense of decorum had her whispering a protest.

"What, milady?"

"Scots have little in the way of courtesy, milord, if you think this acceptable."

"I do."

She looked up at him, not sure what to say. She didn't mind his touch. She'd begun to like it. Surely she'd become addled by being aligned to a mad Scot.

"Come, lady wife. 'Tis time for you to greet your people, then we shall sup together as man and wife."

She hesitated, drawing in air. Perhaps the greatest battle was still ahead. The wedding night! Trying to put it out of her mind, she moved to the steps that would take her off the dais.

Hugh was there, lifting her again.

"We can't keep doing this," Morrigan protested.

"We can and will," he riposted as he settled her on her feet.

The words of recrimination failed her. She placed her hand on Hugh's arm and walked along at her husband's side.

"Milady!" Men and women bowed toward her, some kissing her hand.

It didn't surprise Morrigan to see enmity on more than one face. She was Welsh, a sworn enemy to Scots and Anglos alike.

One group of people parted, and Morrigan saw the reason. There were two young children walking with the aid of sticks. To many of those who kept the old ways, the children would be marked as witches or their spawn. Such thinking had never been to her liking. Morrigan paused, gesturing that the children come to her.

There were gasps, protests. Some hid their eyes.

"You would bring the cry of witch upon yourself, milady," one of the coterie of churchmen muttered.

Father Monteith pushed his way to her side. "Forget the foolish talk, milady. These children depend upon the generosity of too few to help them. They have no kin."

Morrigan nodded, understanding the fear. She'd seen the same in some areas of Wales. It would seem the same among the Norland people in Scotland. The common explanation was if they couldn't walk straight, surely their souls were twisted. That such conclusions could be false was not accepted by many. She put her hands on their shoulders. "Your names, if you please?"

"Conal is mine, milady. And this be my sister Avis."

"I give you greeting." Keeping her hands upon them, she looked up at her husband. "I would ask a boon on this nuptial day."

"You may."

"I want them to live where we do, and eat as we do, don the same garb, touch hands as the sun rises and sets."

There were shouts of surprise and protest, as her words of adoption were repeated and eddied out among the crowd.

MacKay lifted one hand. Silence fell like a mantle over the throng. He made a complete circle, seeming to stare at each of the thousands who looked at him. "My wife will have her boon."

Except for the shuffling of feet and some downcast eyes, there was little response. MacKay had made a dictum, as was his right. That no Scot had to agree or disagree was accepted. That none gainsay him was also irrefutable.

MacKay's narrowed gaze found hers. "As you say, it will be, wife."

"Then I, Morrigan, Lady MacKay, do ordain it this day."

Shock that she'd taken it upon herself to bequeath family on orphans, instead of going along with her husband's dictum, caused a silence. Then a river of sound grew, louder by the second, as approval outshouted disapproval. It sailed on the winds, rustling the trees, sending out a message of goodwill. Not all the responses had the same feeling.

A woman came forward. "I will take them in hand, milady, and I thank you."

"And who are you?" Morrigan inquired, not releasing the children.

As though she sensed the new Lady MacKay's reluctance, the woman smiled. "I'm Dilla MacDougal MacKay, milady. I've known these two since their birthing and would not harm them, milady."

Morrigan stared at Dilla for long moments, then looked down at the two. "Go with her. This day you will belong to the Clan MacKay. Fear not."

The boy sucked in a breath. "We've been under their care, and have feared."

A hand reached past Morrigan and touched the lad. "No longer, lad. You're in our care," MacKay said, his voice carrying.

Morrigan smiled at the boy's courage to voice the truth. She understood what lay behind the words. They'd been shunned, or worse, by some. "You will be as our own. So are the words of the laird and my own."

The words waved over the guests like the wind, the meaning of protection and high placement for the less than stalwart youngsters understood by all.

Neither said a word, nor moved when she walked on, greeting others.

"Come, young ones, a bath and nuncheon for you. This day Fortune has smiled. You must pray it will continue." Dilla put a hand on each shoulder, letting her own gaze rove the crowd. "You've heard the words, take heed," she said to those who stared at her.

The crowd parted as she led them away. She smiled when she felt the company of warriors at her back. So the laird had backed his lady, fully. This was a day of surprises. What would Lady MacKay do next?

A sharpened gaze followed the children, then went back to studying the bridal pair. Anger and frustration had hands clenching behind the flowing robe. Though it was not necessary to hide the features from most of the horde of guests, it was necessary not to show fury. It'd become difficult to hide the animosity since discovering that a pact had been made and mortared by Wales and Scotland. One day justice would be served. Those who had usurped and thwarted would be eliminated.

THREE

**There was also an extraordinary goddess
named Morrigan . . .
from the Celtic Myths and Legends**

Huge trenchers were set up throughout the glen. Custom dictated the bridal couple dine within the castle walls where it was safer and more comfortable. After dining and drinking, which could take hours, they were then expected to move among the throng, greeting those who'd attended their nuptials, taking part in the dancing and revelry. Since most would not be served until well after the vow takers, there was ample time to sup and rest at table, and prepare for the rigorous celebration of music, singing, dancing, and games.

When Hugh stopped she looked up at him. "If we follow mores we dine in the great room. Since the weather is so unusually fine I think we can set our own rules. We may eat out here, or inside. Today you choose, not only for me, but for the monarch."

"Today only, I'll be bound," Morrigan murmured.

Hugh caught the words though he was sure she didn't think so. She'd made more than one enigmatic remark that day. It would be most interesting to delve her reasons. Despite his wife's seeming fragility, he sensed there was iron behind that beauty. The Welsh were famous for allowing their women much freedom and full learning of languages and the sciences.

In his short acquaintance with his wife he'd come to some conclusions. Morrigan had been taught to be her own person. He knew she'd lived in a remote section of Wales, no doubt shunned by many because she'd had a child at the age of fifteen. To some she'd be a woman below the salt, unacceptable in royal circles. Perhaps without the protection of her powerful brothers and their families she might've been stoned. His informants had told him she'd lived much like a hermit since the boy's birth. No doubt she'd learned to be self-reliant. What choice had she?

She took a deep breath, smiling. "Since the weather is so fine 'twould be a shame to shut ourselves off from it."

Hugh watched her. That the lady had more on her mind than the weather was apparent. "That's true." Hugh gestured to some attendants, pointing to a trencher board.

In minutes places were set, so that they might choose.

Morrigan smiled at those around her, not recognizing any.

Hugh watched her, sensing rather than seeing her agitation. No doubt her mind boiled with thoughts of her new husband. Mayhap she'd not looked forward to their mating and she'd counted on disliking him to bolster her for the night ahead. He smiled, fully intending to win her over. When she glanced at him, he grinned. She looked caught in a maelstrom, not like a blushing bride on her nuptial day.

He watched her move farther and farther away from the castle. Did she think being out of doors kept her farther from the nuptial chamber? He excused himself and moved to her side. "Milady, I would not have our guests think you avoid me."

She stopped as though she'd struck a wall. "They must know I'm entranced to be in your company."

He laughed, then sobered, when he saw the flash of fear in her eyes. "If there is anything troublesome in your heart, milady, please tell me." Her smile wobbled, making him more suspicious.

"Would you not say we all have secrets, Milord MacKay? Sometimes a person dissembled not to hurt but to protect. Would you not agree?"

Wariness filled him. "Have you something to tell me?"

Her smile trembled. "Won't we have many things to tell each other? This is the first day of our meeting, Milord MacKay."

"Has someone hurt you since your arrival, milady?" By her hesitation, he could almost believe it'd been something he'd done.

"You are known to be a charmer, milord."

A jolt of happiness went through him. "Am I?"

She nodded. "So I've heard. 'Twould not be wisdom to reveal all to you . . . lest you sink into ennui."

She was dissembling! Why? "True, there is the enticement of mystery," he said, hoping to provoke more conversation. The sudden relief that crossed her face deepened his suspicion.

"I'm glad you agree. We shall get to know each other in small ways. Our life shall not be throws of the dice. Besides, there are too many watching us. Today we'll just enjoy the proceedings, if we can." She seemed to sink into a reverie.

"Milady?" Hugh bent over her, his mouth quirked in humor, keeping her words in his thoughts. There would be time when he would probe for the truth. For now they could take part in the fete.

"What?"

"We should follow the attendants so that our food is served to us at proper time."

"Oh." She looked around her. "Yes. We must go." She sighed. "There's much to see in the castle and I would study it, but I'll be happy to be in the fresh air."

" 'Twould seem our monarch agrees. He approaches."

The bite of acid in his tone didn't escape her. "He honors us with his presence."

"So he must think," Hugh murmured, inclining his head to the king, then bending his gaze to her again. "So what can I choose for you as libation, milady?"

Morrigan indicated the earthen jugs being passed

around the table. "I would fancy the strawberry juice. And 'twould be grand to have it out here. I would visit with . . . our peoples." She didn't look at him when she spoke, but she heard the sighs around her, Hugh's low chuckle, and the king's answering one.

"I think I should keep your wife with me. Her winning ways would bring me much," Edward Baliol said to his now most powerful earl.

"I thank the most gracious royal," Morrigan said, bending in curtsy.

Hugh watched her. "She has a way with her," he murmured. Not to Edward, not to his nearest and dearest would he confess to being poleaxed by his bride. He wished king, pawn, and all attendants to perdition that he might bed the winsome Morrigan from Wales. She not only excited his sexual appetites, she teased his intellect as well. His wife seemed a most unusual woman. He wanted her.

In his wildest dreams he'd not envisioned a woman such as this. He'd not wanted the marriage, but he'd been ready to marry anyone in order to regain his holdings. He'd not looked for a lovely visage, for sparkling green eyes, for a tall, strong body curved so sweetly. Beauty, wit, courage, canny understanding of the world where she had a special place, had not been how he'd envisioned her. He'd pictured a conniving Welsh woman who'd wormed her way into prominence with family and name. The knowledge that she'd broken the laws of the church by conceiving a child carried far less

weight with him than that she was Welsh and came from
a powerful family that had been inimical to his clan. It'd
rubbed him raw that he'd had no choice but to obey the
command or lose all.

Now he cursed the stupidity that had kept him from
finding out more about his intended. Either she was the
greatest daughter of Janus, the god of acting, or she had
a genuine beguiling sweetness to her. Under that he
sensed a tensile strength.

The threesome took seats and began to sample the
myriad dishes rushed for their inspection.

More than one approached the new Lady MacKay.
Most were shy, wary, uncertain.

It touched a core in Hugh when she seemed to exert
the most effort with those filled with trepidation at meeting her.

"What think you, Hugh? Did the council choose
well?"

Hugh nodded, loath to express his inmost feelings to
anyone, and certainly not Edward Baliol. "She has a
regal way about her."

Edward laughed. "God knows she should. Most
would tell you she's a direct descendant of Boudicca.
That, I'm not sure I credit. She is related to one of the
oldest names in Wales, and she comes by her royalty
honestly."

Hugh smiled. "Whatever her blood, I think Morrigan
would be royal." Hugh was looking at his wife. He didn't

see the surprise that crossed the king's features before they were swiftly schooled to blandness.

"Then I think all the time it took to fashion this treaty was worth it," Edward ventured.

Hugh's head whipped his way, his smile touched with vinegar. "Do you? That I was kept waiting for too many turns of the moon mightn't have bothered you, your grace. It pricked at me mightily."

Edward crooked a brow, then sipped ale from his tankard. "I cannot be displeased at the outcome. Nor can you."

Hugh didn't answer. His bile was rising as he recalled the long days that had brought him to this one.

It'd taken almost a full turn of the sun to mortar the compact to everyone's satisfaction. In those long weeks since the settlement he'd been in constant company of the king. What he'd wanted was to see to his people who'd been sorely pressed and depleted by the many conflicts engaged in by the clan. He'd taken no chance that something could go amiss, that all that belonged to Clan MacKay wouldn't be returned to it. So he'd accompanied Edward everywhere, bartering any way and with anyone to reclaim his title and holdings.

He'd given little thought to the bride, considering her a necessary factor to the negotiations, a pertinent anchor to his life in order to provide for his clan. Well worth the risk of vow taking to ensure the future for himself and fellow MacKays. He'd been a fool not to seek her out.

He watched her magic touch with his people. The built-in suspicion of all MacKays for outsiders, after years of being proscribed, melted in the gentle onslaught of his spouse. Her very natural charm wooed and won all those with whom she conversed. It pleased him to see her unbend with his people.

The king nudged him, gaining his attention. "Will you join us, Hugh? Some of the lords are gathering their lads for the games. Will you not toss the caber to impress your bride?"

Hugh's chuckle was dry. "Let the others test their mettle. I'll be along to watch."

Edward's glance skated between the Earl of MacKay and his lady. "You never cease surprising me, my lord earl."

" 'Tis my fondest hope," Hugh retorted.

Edward hesitated. "You do not ask for her brothers or cousins or about their absence at the nuptials."

"I assumed you would know and inform me. I have not missed them."

Edward's lips lifted. "I was asked to represent the family since all were about on the business of their families."

"I'm sure," Hugh said, irony in his tone.

Edward nodded. "I thought the same, but my informants have told me they were indeed tending to their businesses that take them far and near. The oldest was in Afrique. The cousins were in Cornwall. The other brother was aboard a ship."

"Now I can be at peace," Hugh responded in the same tone.

Edward laughed and rose. "You are a suspicious man, Hugh. Remember the compact was drawn in a most rapid fashion. 'Twas your wish to bring it together quickly."

"So it was." Hugh's brow lifted.

"You're a rogue, MacKay." The king tapped his arm. "Bring your lovely wife with you when next you come to Edinburgh."

"We'll see."

Edward still chortled as he left with the others, but his eyes had narrowed on the powerful MacKay.

Hugh was glad to throw aside the worries that had plagued him for months and just watch his wife gather an ever larger coterie of admirers around her. Though she seemed carefree, Hugh noticed she'd eaten little, that she'd barely touched her ale or wine. She had concerns, this wife of his. He would find out what they were, and he had a lifetime to do it.

He pondered again that foolhardiness that had him ignoring her until their spousal day. Since it was not uncommon not to see a bride before wedding her, he'd just accepted what those around him had said. Welsh bitch had been how most had referred to her. That most of them had never met the woman consigned to an isolated corner of Wales had not weighed with him. What an ass he'd been not to check out what was fast becoming an important segment of his life. His wife. He'd not have been so careless choosing a destrier. Not since boyhood had he let another choose his mount, but he'd been lax about knowing more about his most important "mount."

Morrigan turned to look at him. "Why did you just laugh?"

"You wouldn't like what I was thinking."

"Oh?"

What was she thinking? Would there ever be a time when she would probe his thoughts? Would she wonder what it would have been like to be wooed by such as he, without the trappings of treaties, compacts, debts of honor? Mayhap she thought him a womanizer. If she'd heard the women's gossip she would.

Now that she'd met him would she discount the gossip or put more credence to it? It annoyed him that he had an urge to explain.

"Do tell me. I would be amused."

"What?" She sounded aloof. He sensed temper under the coolness. He applauded restraint, and self-control. It had carried him far. "Are you in bad tid, milady?" He used the Gaelic term for waspishness.

She faced him, head up, eyes flashing. "Do you say that I ponder you with a host of loose women? That such would make my blood cook?"

He bit back a laugh. "Nay, milady, I—"

"Perhaps you think your profligate life would not matter to me until our vows were spoken. Be at peace, milord. I will not have you drawn and quartered."

"Thank you."

"Why do you elevate your brow? Do you not believe me?"

"I do."

"Then contain your mirth and regale me with your tale."

A spitfire! Under all that smoothness and serenity was an unleashed wolf cub! He was delighted.

"Your story, milord." She moved back from the trencher board, rising, turning away from the guests to concentrate on her spouse.

He stood as well. "All right." He leaned down and whispered his thought about choosing a horse and a wife.

When she turned that benign smile on him, wariness seized him. He backed a step just as she brought her knee up in a sharp, meaningful thrust.

Few noticed the move. One who'd not taken eyes off the pair since the vow taking did. Keeping the smile in place to hide the hatred wasn't easy, but observation provided more and more information. Mayhap this day the couple would be sped to Hades. But . . . if they lived there was another way to level the enemy. Divide and conquer, Caesar said. Wife and husband could make interesting adversaries. It could foment troubles for Wales and Scotland. The smile widened. Intrigue was delicious. The dispatching of foes was an even more delightful repast to ponder. Dishing up either wife or husband, or both, to torturers had the greatest appeal.

Who first? Surely the least vulnerable would be the wisest. No sense setting up vigilance in one who battled well. Let the strongest go first. The gaze fixed on Hugh MacKay.

"Very good," Hugh said, leaning over her, his hands fitting around her waist. "Had I not moved you would've taken me to the healers instead of to our nuptial chamber."

"Release me."

"No, wife, I won't." He smiled down at her. "I told you what crossed my thoughts, sweet bride. How unkind to strike at me. I was only being truthful." He grinned again. "How quick you were to retaliate. You'll make an uncommonly good Scot."

"Do not downgrade a Welshwoman, sirrah."

He laughed. There was a melting in him when she joined him. He loved teasing her and for all her words, he knew she liked it. "You do not hate me, wife."

"No. Actually I would like to throw back my head and let levity take me as it does you."

Surprised, happy, he inched her closer. "Tell me you're not insulted, but entertained."

She bit her lip. "I will admit I feel less threatened."

He chuckled. "I'll take that. Worry not that you'll lose your way on MacKay land."

"I must be alert . . . but this day had brought good feelings and I have enjoyed it."

His booming laugh echoed across the glen, bringing

smiles, inquiring looks, some frowns. "I regret not meeting you and courting you as I could've done." Despite the good feeling he'd caught the word "alert." It stayed in his mind.

Stunned, she could only stare. "You are uninhibited, Hugh MacKay."

"I am. I still am sorry we did not have a courting." His laughing eyes probed hers. Tell me what keeps you wary despite your mirth, good wife, he said to himself.

"Why is that?" Foolish question!

His hands tightened at her waist. "Because you're very beautiful. Because you have a great kindness. Because your laugh is like the sweetest honey." He squeezed her waist just a bit. "You joust with me, your wits are quick, and you're unafraid."

"I . . . I am glad you are pleased."

"I am." His words had unsettled her. "You are a woman of many parts." She was struggling for composure. She didn't want to give in to him. He would get through the barrier she'd made.

"I should think so. I'm Welsh."

"You create a heat, milady. I fear that all around us can see your deep beauty."

"You must unhand me, sirrah. 'Tis not circumspect."

" 'Struth, 'tis, for this day you're my bride, my beauty. Have you forgotten so soon?" He lifted her higher, her feet leaving the ground, until he could look into her eyes. He'd never seen such womanliness. Yet there was iron in her, mayhap embedded so deeply she'd not shown it to many. He wanted to see it all, to know all about his intriguing, bewitching bride. "Though you have the courage of a warrior, you have the loveliness of the most beauteous of women. That pleases me." When he saw how her eyes widened in surprise, how they searched his for the lie, he wanted to laugh. Little conceit had his wife. An amalgam of loveliness and goodness. No wonder other men had wooed her, had fought her betrothal to a MacKay. What had been the name? Tarquin of Cardiff. He'd remember it. Had he been the one who'd given her a son? Was he the one who'd known the delight of piercing her maiden's veil? He was furious at the thought. A raging jealousy shook him that was most difficult to bury before reason calmed him. She was his now. No other man would get close to her. He smiled.

"What?"

"I think on your virtues, good wife."

"Virtues?"

He chuckled when suspicion crossed her face. "Shall I list them?"

"You might have to, Hugh MacKay. But first you must put me down for we draw eyes to us."

"No matter. 'Tis our spousal day. Let them look. Shall I tell you?"

"Pardon my interruption."

"I do." He grinned when she looked chagrined. "Let me see. When you should've been preening from the adulation shown you in all your wedding finery, you stopped and assured two children they would always have a home with us, and then claimed them as ours. You have passion and caring, love. I like that."

"How do you know for sure?" she blurted.

Her blush told him she was referring to the night ahead and he laughed again.

He had to be careful of her magnetism. She could make him let down his guard. As keeper of the vast estates belonging to MacKay he had to be wary of any and all. Lusting after her didn't mean she had his full trust. There were few, whether they be Welsh, Anglos, or even Scots outside his clan, who did.

He couldn't deny the wanting. It had grown into a seething sea that he could've drowned in if it weren't for the damnable guests. He pictured her under his tartan, with nothing but her bare skin touching his. His blood cascaded to his lower body, hardening it. He hadn't been so aroused so quickly, so fully, in memory. Aye! It would be a monumental task to keep his spouse in proper perspective. She had the visage of an angel. He shouldn't allow himself to think she was one. She netted him with her look. Though caution told him to glance away, he was loath to break the moment. Rather he would stay buried in her eyes.

Hugh lowered her to the ground. "Shall we wander about and greet our guests?"

" 'Twould be proper."

The hand she placed on his arm trembled. When he covered it with his own, fire burst through him.

There was a flurry upon the knoll leading to the castle.

Both Hugh and Morrigan looked. She noted how he angled her to the back of him, just a hair.

"Maman!" Rhys roared from his place up the glen between two burly MacKays. He ran toward her, legs and arms pumping, falling and getting up again to race faster than the two MacKays at his heels.

MacKay cursed, allowing her to move to the side of him again.

Still dazed she turned to the boy, opening her arms wide. He threw himself into them. "They's said I'm to be them. I aren't, are I? I'm Welsh like you."

Hugh felt a stab of feeling unknown to him. Damn! To watch her cuddle the child, rain kisses on his face, raised his ire, and more. He wanted her touch over him instead of on the boy. "You are MacKay, and Welsh," he told Rhys, lifting him away from his mother, more than irked when she showed reluctance to release the boy.

Lifting him high, Hugh commanded that Rhys look about him. "All that you see belongs to MacKay. A portion is yours one day."

White-faced, Morrigan watched.

Hugh felt her glance. Was it through a veil of deceit? As her husband he'd just offered land to the boy and made him an heir to a portion of MacKay holdings. Did she resent the offer? He knew that her Welsh hectares would go to the boy. Did she think he should have more than he'd bestowed on the lad?

"I do not think you need to worry about estates, Rhys." Morrigan lifted her arms, but his circled Hugh's neck.

"No, maman, I'll stay here." He shoved his thumb in his mouth and grinned around it at Hugh. "I can see everything."

Taken aback, Morrigan could only stare.

Father Monteith came up to her side. "The boy surprised you, milady?"

"Yes. Rhys connects with few people. He's very possessive of me, and short-tempered with most, including his peers, Father." She bit her lip. "Sometimes I've worried that he might be too attached to me after our arrival in Scotland." She shook her head. "He takes me aback, Father. To see him look around him, cuddled up to Hugh's shoulder, feeling at home, seeming content, is a relief."

"Children find their way," the priest whispered.

Morrigan nodded, listening to what Hugh was saying to the boy.

"And why do you speak the patois of the Galls, Rhys Llywelyn?"

Rhys removed his thumb. "Maman says I must."

"Then you must speak Gaelic as well." Hugh laughed when the boy rolled his eyes. "Go with Tor and Andrus. They would show you your horse."

Rhys's eyes widened. "A horse? Truly?"

"A MacKay is never false to his own, by word or deed, nor does he walk when he can ride. You have a horse."

"Oh." Rhys pondered that. "And am I MacKay or a Llywelyn?"

"Both," Hugh told him.

Rhys smiled. "Good. I want to see my horse."

Morrigan put out her hand.

Hugh could see she wanted to protest that the boy had been given more than enough. He didn't need anything else. Hugh shook his head and she paused.

"I wouldn't wipe the joy from his eyes," she murmured. "Be good for Tor and Andrus." She took him from Hugh and hugged him. "Have you eaten?"

"Yes. And I'll be good." He pushed against her, wriggling to get down and run ahead of the two warriors who were after him in an instant.

It crossed Hugh's mind that the boy was as dark of eyes and tress as other Welsh he'd known. Neither did he resemble his mother with his stocky build and skin that would brown in the sun. He would be a big man one day and he, Hugh of MacKay, would call him firstborn.

"I fear Tor would rather fight a boar than monitor your son."

Morrigan chuckled. "He's a handful."

"But you don't mind."

"I love him," she said, looking up at Hugh.

A terrific force hit him in the chest. He'd never needed what some referred to as love. The power to lead his clan and protect it was all he craved. Now another potency had taken the breath from his body, and had his heart hammering against his ribs. Used to seeking, finding, and nailing down his needs and wants by cajolery, battle, or intrigue, it stunned him that he was all but impotent to gain what he desired most. The woman and all the feeling she could have. It would have to be freely given, for in no other way could he savor the passion he knew was there, embedded in those eyes and in his wife's wonderful form. He wanted it all, not from duty, but from the same emotion that spurred her feelings toward the boy.

Hugh was glad when a border laird caught her attention. It allowed him to study her, and steady himself. It wouldn't do to let her know how many times she'd shaken his equanimity. She had power enough.

"Och, milady, you honor all of Scotland wi' your words."

Hugh blinked, concentrating. What had she said to old Gordon?

"Not at all, sirrah. I've been to your border lands and seen your wondrous herds of sheep and stoat. Marvelous they are, to be sure." She swept her hand in a small arc. "The hills so green and purple, the sky so blue. Even your mist has magic." Morrigan felt Hugh's gaze even as she conversed with the bluff borderer. "I've also heard of your family, er, clan, Laird Gordon. Their wondrous deeds are sung far and wide."

Pushing out his chest, he put his ham hand on her arm. "You'll do, missy, you'll do." He gazed at Hugh. " 'Tis blest you are, MacKay. So I've said it. Give her good care or answer to me."

Hugh ground his teeth staring at Gordon. When the borderer glared for a moment, then roared with mirth, Hugh's fists ached to connect with the older man's jaw. Ian Gordon had been like a father to him. Damn his eyes!

"Be on your guard, missy. Your laird is a jealous lump."

"What . . ." She was talking to air. Gordon had wandered off. "What did he—?"

"Nothing. We'll tarry here, and taste the sweets that've come from the kitchen." Hugh took hold of her waist and swung her over the nearby bench, then seated himself at her side. As custom demanded, he tasted the cakes and buns first, then fed them to her. He didn't hear the ribald remarks. His attention was on his bride, who had only bites of the sweets and sips of the wine.

Much of the time she continued to bow, smile, and greet those who dared to approach, despite the glares from the Earl of MacKay. His own clan gave his trencher board a wide berth. Others were not so wise.

FOUR

Now Eros had shaken my thoughts, like a wind
among the highland oaks.

Sappho

Interminable platters of food, crocks of wines and ales
continued long after most had finished and contributed
to a queasiness that shook Morrigan. She declined offer
after offer, understanding the generosity, the labor, the
honor, bestowed by the many workers, but she wasn't
able to swallow anything more. She stared at the
mounds of food left after most were sated.

"What is it, wife?"

His smile, his golden eyes that seemed molten, went
over her, heating her. He was too appealing. She'd not
expected that. Not just a brawny barbarian, but a perceptive man, one who'd showed care to a five-year-old.
Such gestures were not common in the known world.
Since meeting him she'd come to understand that most
women would find him attractive. The shock was that
she'd come to agree with that and hate that other women

would look upon him so. She should seek a priest and confess her vagaries. Ponder something else, anything. "I want what's not eaten given to the indigent."

"None without food or shelter reside upon your land, Princess. MacKays see to their own." He touched the heavy ring on her finger. "So the princess from Wales considers her people. Wife, I didn't need to find more of your virtue. You entice me enough."

Morrigan just stared. He'd shocked her once more. He wanted to see her hair. He'd called her a woman of virtue when all believed her to be whore. When he touched her headdress she trembled and blushed. "Sirrah, I . . ."

"Pardon. You said?"

"What of neighboring—"

"It shall be done. 'Tis your bride's day, so it shall be as you wish."

"Thank you." She couldn't look at him, though she sensed he wished she would. He made her dizzy, as though she suffered from the winter weakening.

The worst of it was ahead of her. It hurt to admit that she'd come to feel a measure of admiration, and a liking for her spouse though they'd only met hours ago. What was there about him that made her blood rise, that caused her innards to squeeze, her heart to jerk instead of pump? Such had never occurred even with Tarquin of Cardiff, who'd told her he would approach the elders in the Llywelyn family and request a betrothal. Not once had she had this uncomfortable beating of blood, the hammering of heart that occurred each time Hugh MacKay was near. MacKay had a strange effect, indeed.

What would he be like in a temper? He could rage and beat her. None would interfere. That could happen that very evening. The knowledge that she came to him a virgin . . . with a son, could be too much to bear. He could scream perfidy, and the thrashings could begin. To some it was the normal way of things. The pain of lashings made her fearful. She'd not ever been struck. Her father had been a gentle man.

Even more it sickened her to think of the contempt that could mar those strong features of Hugh MacKay when he discovered she'd deceived him, that she hadn't birthed a child. He might consider it an even more pernicious act that she'd dared to request and receive the regency of Trevelyan lands, when she'd hidden the heir to the holdings under the guise he was her son. Would he see her as greedy schemer? He might perceive her dealings with Edward Baliol as dire intrigue, as taking control of the estate under false pretenses for her own uses. He could be angered that her actions could jeopardize his own holdings, his fragile, new grasp on his ancestral lands.

To her eyes there was nothing about the night ahead that boded anything but ill for her. If only he'd been an unconscionable boor, an ignoramus, or a gross barbarian. Hugh MacKay was none of those. Nay, he was a man of many parts. She sought distraction from her black thoughts and found none. Woe to the woman who carries a secret to her marriage bed!

"Have all these festivities tired you, Morrigan?"

His whisper went through her like a sweet knife. "No . . . no, I can carry on, milord."

" 'Tis not necessary. I shall—"

A sudden flurry at the gates was a welcome sound until she saw Rhys coming at her again, this time riding a horse! Not a small steed, but a destrier. "Sweet mother of God."

"Shhh. Don't fret."

"Good Lord! He shouldn't have had such a large horse, should he? Is that not a destrier used for war?" She moved around Hugh, fully intent on intercepting the cantering beast and Rhys, who hung on to the mane, his short legs flapping on the animal's back, his mouth wide open.

"Ma-man! Lo-ok a-at me-e!"

Before she could do more than take one step, Hugh moved in front of her. "Wait. Nothing must startle the animal. Trust me." Then he strode toward the horse. "Everyone remain still." He saw the harried MacKays behind the steed, but spared them barely a glance.

"Hugh! There were four of us. He eluded us all. How the hell he mounted Orion, I don't know."

"I have him, Toric. No one move." Hugh put his hands up. The destrier, independent and able to factor predicaments because of his highly intelligent ways, glared at Hugh, his ears back.

Morrigan held her breath, moving step by step toward Rhys.

"No, milady, you mustn't interfere with the laird. Orion is one of his. The steed knows the master. 'Twill be fine. You'll see." Laird Gordon tried to pull her back. She wouldn't budge. "So, you are as headstrong as your spouse. I see chaos in your future, but then again, 'twas what I had." His dry laugh pulled no answering one from her. He held her at his side.

Hugh put his hand on the destrier's snout. "You would defy me, old friend, when I've given so many gracious ladies to your keeping. Consider your mare, Eufeme. Was she not sweet and gracious?" Hugh's soothing tone droned on, even as he took hold of the stallion by the nostrils with one hand, and reached for Rhys with the other.

"No," Rhys said, edging backward, making the destrier quiver. "We're friends. He wants me here. He said so."

Morrigan's hands twisted together. She fought for breath.

"Is that right?" Hugh said, seeming to ponder what Rhys said. "You've made a choice, then?"

"I have."

"Fine. For now, you must come down so that Orion can be fed and pastured. Would you deny your friend his meal? He's a great warrior and has earned good care."

Rhys's face screwed into thought. Then he nodded and moved toward Hugh's hand that scooped him from the back of the huge horse.

The concerted sighs of relief drowned out Morrigan's shaky thanks to God.

Hugh kept the boy on his shoulder and handed the reins to Toric.

"The boy reminds me of you," Laird Gordon said to Hugh, keeping hold of Morrigan as they moved toward her husband. "You were always pigheaded."

Morrigan didn't see the humor. She had eyes for Rhys, catching him in her arms and hugging him.

"Maman! Don't. I have to help Toric with the horse . . ." Before he could finish what he was saying a giant yawn caught his lips and parted them.

Morrigan looked at Hugh as she set Rhys on his feet. "I thank you, milord."

His smile came and went. "You're welcome." He looked at Rhys. "As for you, for disobeying the Mac-Kays who were put in charge of you, you will clean out the stables for one week with Jaxe."

Morrigan opened her mouth.

Rhys was ahead of her. "I will do that."

She looked down at him, shaken that he would so easily accept his penance. His eyes were shining!

"And you'll mount nothing unless Jaxe, Eamon, or Toric is with you."

Rhys's head bobbed up and down, his eyes fixed on Hugh, seeming unaware of the silenced party guests who watched.

Morrigan touched the top of the boy's head, her hand

only shaking a bit. "Come along. This party has gone on long enough for you. We'll find your bed."

"No. Don' wanna'," he told her, his mouth opening on another yawn.

"Yes, you do." Grasping his hand firmly, she turned the boy. She was about to tell Hugh where she was going when she realized he was deep in conversation with Toric and Gordon. She hoped he'd know where she'd gone. Speed was necessary. If Rhys became too tired he'd cause another ruckus. His lung power could be awesome.

Whisking him from the dining and drinking guests took too much time as it was. Many had her pausing to comment on the courage of her son riding a destrier. She had every intention of telling Rhys he'd never ride another horse until he was a man if he ever attempted to mount a destrier again. She tried not to slight anyone, but Rhys was getting crabbier by the minute.

Finally she reached the castle and hurried him through the bailey, then in under the portico and through the wide open doors. She was all but running. She didn't care. Throwing aside dignity was better than having a battle with a five-year-old with a mind of his own.

Passing no one, she all but carried the hefty lad up the stairs that hugged one wall. Getting him into the chamber that connected to her guest chamber took time. He whined for milk, for sweets, for ginger beer, for strawberry ale. His eyes were closing as she undressed him, gave him a quick wash, and put him beneath the covers.

He was mumbling protests as she tucked him in and kissed his cheek.

"Oh! Milady, I didn't think you'd be up here. I'll take care of the boy, if you wish."

"I wish to let him sleep. You are Lilybet. I remember."

At the nod, Morrigan continued. "He's exhausted. Let him sleep. If he awakens before the last feast is served, he may wish to eat something else. Otherwise let him sleep the night away."

Lilybet nodded. "I will."

Morrigan tried to smile, but nothing quite buried the rising panic she felt at the coming night. The sun had gone. Flambeaux lit the glen and castle. Soon there'd be the awful "headache heaviness," as the wedding night had come to be called. Taken from the Celtic and Latin customs by the Scots, they'd brought it to a methodology unheard of by the ancients, she was sure. It had become one of their cherished traditions. Charivari! The dreaded night of copulation when the bride would be sport for all the groom's friends, where rape occurred at regular intervals, where women . . . She swayed, pondering what could occur.

"Milady! You are faint. Here, let me help you. Lie down—"

"No! I . . . I must go."

"Ya canna gang awa' this way," the handmaiden broke into the patois of Gaelic and Anglo. "You're fair sickened, swaying like a reed you were."

Morrigan pushed at the hands that held her, the moist pieces of lint held to her head. "Please, I—"

The door crashed open. MacKay stood there, others of his clan behind him. His eyes found her, the sleeping child, the ministering women all faster than the light that courses the sky when Thor himself rumbles across the heavens. His Viking connections allowed the great gods into his life. Not that he believed in much beyond his own powers. She was sure he didn't. Did the mighty MacKay believe in anything but himself? It scored her feelings to know that whatever small trust he had in her would be flayed alive that very night.

"What ails milady?"

His mild query didn't fool Morrigan. His eyes danced with fury.

"Nothing," she answered, cursing the hoarseness in her voice.

He went around the handmaiden hovering over Morrigan. She faded back as though a large besom had swept around the room. He lifted Morrigan's hand, his fingers pressing on the inner wrist.

Stunned that he should know where to find the pumping of blood, Morrigan could only stare.

"And are you ailing, wife?"

"No."

"Then what of this?" He lifted her hand, his fingers still at the pulse. "Your drumbeat is too fast."

"I was hurrying."

"Why is that?"

"Rhys was tired. When that happens he can become recalcitrant. I didn't want him to mar the celebration," she said truthfully. Did she imagine that his features lightened, that his eyes melted away from their slate hardness of moments past?

He studied her for long moments. Then before she could do more than gasp, he'd lifted her into his arms and strode from the room. "You've nothing to fear," he told her as he marched down the dank corridor.

"So you say," she muttered in Welsh.

"So I do," he answered in the same tongue, chuckling when she stiffened. "I've battled in Wales. One learns to speak the language, milady."

"Of course." Her tone was sharper than she'd wanted and it didn't quite cover the quaking in her frame. "I'll have to remember to pick up the language if I ever venture to foreign lands to conquer," she said in rapid Celtic, trusting he wouldn't pick up all of it.

"I'll keep you at my right hand, then, and you can help me lead. We'll battle together, milady."

Morrigan's mouth dropped open.

MacKay kicked open a door to a much more splendid suite. Setting her on her feet, he slammed the door shut again. When he saw her looking about, he inclined his head. "You were expecting your Celtic assassins, mayhap?"

Stung, she lifted her chin and glared. "No! I was expecting your infamous voyeurs. Is this moment not for their delectation?"

He shook his head. "If you're expecting the charivari, do not. I'd not allow it." He turned and lifted the heavy wooden bar across the door. "There. 'Twould take an army to get through and I'd not countenance it."

Morrigan swallowed, looking at him fully for the first time. Her secret wouldn't become tattle for the word mongers. If her husband put her aside it wouldn't be in front of a contingent of drunken men spitting ribald remarks. If he didn't kill her on the spot, she could live with the infamy of being returned to Wales. She and Rhys would be under the protection of the Llywelyn name until such time as he could attain his inheritance. The law would protect her when her deceit was unmasked since she was regent of the Trevelyan estate.

Hugh frowned at her. "I have to wonder what takes your concentration, why you wander in thought."

"I've . . . I've not been here before, there is much to see."

"Join me in wine, or an ale." He looked around him, smiling when he saw the tray with cups and skins upon it.

She nodded, needing soothing. So did he.

"I went wild when I couldn't find you below stairs, wife."

"Why? Surely you knew I'd see to my son."

Hugh shrugged. "I didn't. I missed you," he said through his teeth.

"And that is why you came through the child's door like one of the bulls of Afrique?"

His smile twisted. " 'Twould seem so." He looked toward the drink table, then back at her. "I was crazed when I couldn't find you."

Morrigan smiled, feeling a glow spread through her. Even as she looked, his eyes seemed to deepen in color, his face hardening, but not in a fearsome way. There was a hotness there, almost a wanting. It shook her that she wouldn't have minded had he pulled her into an embrace. What would it be like to feel his strong mouth on hers?

He went to the wine table. "We'll toast our nuptials, wife."

"I would have fruited water, milord, since I cannot stand spirits when I've had little sustenance since rising from my pallet."

"You should have supped."

She tried to smile. "The day was too exciting." She didn't lie about that.

"I found it so."

His lazy hot gaze went over like silky flame. Her head snapped back. She studied his bland expression, wishing she could read his thoughts. Did he make sport of her?

He glanced around the room again, spying the stone jar that would hold the cold, fruited water. He indicated it. "Then you can drink this, and I will take the wine."

She smiled. He was being kind. God help her, she was beginning to like him more and more. She mustn't let herself like him too much. When he eventually turned his fury on her, rejecting her dissembling, she felt it would be easier to bear if she could remain aloof now.

"Thank you." She took the glass and willed her hands to stop their shaking. They didn't.

He poured wine into a goblet and sipped his brew, eyeing her in puzzlement. "You're frightened. Why? I'll not let the hordes enter here. Is that what sets your skin to jumping?"

She sipped her water. "That's part of it."

He quaffed his drink and poured another. "Then why don't we talk and then we'll see how we feel." He indicated the reclining couch near the fire, then he swiped a hand across his brow.

Morrigan frowned. Sweat had broken out on his visage. Though it was comfortable in the chamber, it was far from hot, yet rivulets ran from hairline to chin. When he blinked a few times and staggered she went to him. "Sirrah! Have you a chill?" When he would've finished his wine, she took the goblet from him, ignoring his slurred protest. His body was boiling, yet there were shivers. She glanced at the goblet. Could it be? Was there an assassin amongst the guests? It couldn't be so. Who would dare try to poison the laird on this day?

Fear was a lance in her soul. No Llywelyn would do this. She closed her eyes, counting to ten, calling on Boudicca and all the old Druidic women who'd aided so many of the Welsh. Think! Think! Not only would she die if she were blamed, but Rhys could be victim as well. She would save Hugh to preserve Rhys's life and her own . . . and because she couldn't bear to lose the great MacKay.

"Mor . . . gannn," Hugh said, swaying, frowning as though the effort to look at her was burdensome, well nigh impossible.

"I'm here. All will be well." It wouldn't be if the laird was found in such a state. She had choices. Leave him to die, or succor him. In her mind there was no choice. She had to help him.

Either way, whether he lived or died, she could be hanged as perpetrator or accomplice. A Greek dilemma. So often they had tragic endings. She shuddered, not wanting to dwell on that.

They looked at each other, he so weak, though beginning to comprehend.

"I would help you, husband."

"Cannnn youuu?"

She nodded. Even if she hadn't begun to like her newly avowed husband, she wouldn't and couldn't let him expire without using her skills to try to bring him back to health.

Her hands flew to tearing strips, getting water on to heat, finding tongs she set into the fires. Every move she made was driven by desperation.

A part of her concentrated on her chores. As she worked another part of thinking went over her life, as though she needed the past as impetus.

Living her life in jeopardy had given her sharpened instincts. In the years since Rhys's birth, she'd been imperiled by the righteous, who might've abducted her at any time. Their reason for hanging or burning her would have been the sundering of the commandment against adultery. That she'd had a child out of wedlock would have been the proof. Now she faced an even greater danger. The MacKays could draw and quarter her for killing their chief. She'd be such a handy criminal, they might search for no other. Another paradox where women lost. She wondered why such thoughts were crowding her mind when she was in crisis, even as she began ripping cloths and pulling back the bedcovers.

At the moment her hard-won ability to smell danger gave her an edge in factoring out deception, deceit, even attempted clan treason, mayhap. An assassin had tried to kill the laird, and she would be the obvious culprit. Or if the alternate plan had taken effect, she would've drunk the tainted wine also and expired with the laird before any could help. Were there any among the wedding guests who would know the ways of healing? No time to think of that. She had to act. No way could she let such infamy occur.

Hugh staggered forward. With a grunt she caught him, nearly unbalanced herself by the breadth and height of MacKay. Oh, if only the witches of Wales had accompanied her. She'd learned from them. If only her brothers and cousins hadn't been busy abroad they would be here. Welshmen were often canny when it came to medicaments. God help her. She was alone.

It was a boon that he'd fallen not far from their marriage bed. Though it took a bit of tugging and pulling, she was able to ease the laird down upon it.

Quick! Quick! Running all the Celtic medicaments she knew around her head, she concluded she had to get an emetic into him before the cramping began, before the poison spread. Had this been meant for her? Had a MacKay targeted her for destruction? Would a disgruntled Welshman do such a deed? There were enough of those who wished no liaison with the hated Scots and their monarch. What would've become of Rhys? Steady. Vigilance. She might save him if she followed the recommended treatment of her Druidic ancestors. Think of nothing else. If she was to conquer she had to hurry and she couldn't make an error.

Racing to the door, his low groans in her ears, she removed the heavy bar, though it took effort and time. A MacKay as big as Hugh and twice as broad was there. She stared at him. "You must trust me."

FIVE

Mankind censure injustice fearing that they may
be the victims of it, and not because they shrink
from committing it.

Plato

Morrigan held her breath, knowing her life could end in
an instant.

A hand as big as a ham slammed across the warrior's
chest. "I serve MacKay and will till I die. I'm Diuran,
milady. None shall pass this door." He studied her, his
eyes narrowing, then fixing above her head. "MacKay?"

She took a deep breath, aware she'd never been more
imperiled. "Your laird is in severe straits. He could suc-
cumb. No! Don't go to him. Go to my quarters. Under
the boy's clothing is a box. Bring it. You must hurry, or
we'll not save him."

Diuran stared at her for a wisp of time, then he was
gone, on the run.

Cold moisture pearled her body as she sagged against
the heavy door for a moment. She closed it behind her

without the bar, and hurried to the fire, stirring it up, sweeping the water pot over it. Then she turned back to the couch. She winced at the sight of her spouse. His parchment-white skin beaded with moisture sent her fear spiraling. "No! Be calm. I will prevail," she muttered to herself.

As though her words commanded MacKay and not her, his eyes opened, somewhat opaque with the beginnings of deep fever. They slid around the room until they found her, barely able to focus.

"And did you kill me, girl?"

Stunned by the words, though she knew they'd come from a soul and spirit beleaguered by evil humors, she could only stare. "I did not."

The door was flung open and Diuran was there with her box, slamming the door behind him.

"Bar it," she ordered.

He did and moved to her side, his eyes on his laird. "What did this?"

"I'm not sure. I think the wine." She jerked her head at the skin on the table.

Drawing in a deep breath, Diuran snarled. "Who?"

She shook her head, not looking up as she laid out her medicines.

"What magic is this, milady?"

Morrigan heard the fear and anger in Diuran's voice. Without looking up, she answered. "We must make all speed, or we will lose the laird. The emetic will empty his innards. The other purgative, though dangerous, will clean out the rest before the evils travel the way of the blood. If we don't stop the flow of poisons, nothing will save him." She looked up. "Will you help me?"

"As long as you know that if he convulses, you'll die with him."

Morrigan sighed. "I cede to your code . . . with qualifications. We cannot discuss them now." The concession was big. In essence she gave up her life to be martyred if her spouse expired. Caravans from the east who traveled the way of the Venetian, Marco Polo, spoke of the strange cultures in the alien lands that marked the path to what was called Cathay. There was much talk of the human sacrifice of spouses. Morrigan had not thought to place herself among them.

Medicating the very large man who'd become her husband wasn't easy. Turning him, lifting him, getting the needed herbs into him would've been awesome tasks.

Without Diuran's help she wouldn't have been able to cleanse his fevered form, bathe him as often as needed after his body rejected the poisons that'd been administered. As it was both Morrigan and the warrior were exhausted by the time they stripped and bathed him for the hundredth time, it seemed, and again put the limp form between clean covers.

"He breathes well," Morrigan said, trying to smile through her fatigue at her helper. "You've done fine work this eve, good Diuran."

"As you have, milady." Diuran slammed his hand across his chest. "While you live I shall serve you."

Morrigan exhaled. "I would have a bath, but I want none in this room, but me." She hesitated. "My boy, Rhys, could be endangered as well because of this." She stiffened. "Whoever plotted this is still about, and very dangerous. We must take every precaution, Diuran."

Diuran shook his head. "No one will bother the lad, nor you, milady. My cousins will attend him. Oengus and Ian MacKay, plus Eamon, his appointed guardian, will ensure the safety of the boy. I shall make sure they know there was an attempt against our laird. They are closemouthed and wise, milady. They will be ever vigilant."

"I thank you, good Diuran. I shall remain with the laird. If I have need of you, I'll rap upon the door. None must enter but you."

Diuran nodded. "There're others I'll call to my side, and we'll hang the assassin who dared assault our laird. 'Twill not be done quietly." He glowered. "For now, you and your son will be safe, milady. Fear not that any craven will pass this door."

"Thank you." It might've been more of a relief to know she and Rhys were totally safe. Suspicions had crowded her soul all the while she ministered to her husband. Who had put the wine in the chamber? Who had such free and easy access to the sleeping area of one of Scotland's most powerful lords?

Something told her that MacKay's enemies were hers

as well. What did it matter who first tasted the wine? Or if they'd drunk it together? 'Twas a mere happenstance that she'd not tasted the brew. Had that been the plan? That they would die together? Who plotted the deed? Were they the enemies of Llywelyns or Trevelyans, as well as MacKays? It didn't take a soothsayer to tell her that despite what had happened she was safer with MacKay than abroad in an unfriendly world, that keeping him alive and well was the best bulwark for both Rhys and herself against known and unknown foes. Even back in Wales, where she had the protection of the Llywelyn name, all was not without peril. Her relatives were flung far and wide throughout the country, not within call. At least MacKay was here. She glanced at the supine figure. For now he was. It looked like he would recover, but she couldn't be sure. Evil humors were known to attack without warning when one was debilitated. She would use every care to aid in his recovery. It was her best hope.

She laid the hot cloths she'd immersed in the fireplace cauldron onto his chest and stomach. She could create a fever to burn a fever. God help her if Diodura's ways were wrong. She sped between bed and fire, her mind tumbling with queries as she worked.

And what of other MacKays? Would they be her allies after finding out what happened to Hugh? Were some among them false to Clan MacKay? Yet, how could she fault the loyalty of Diuran to his laird? He commanded great loyalty. Could it protect her and

Rhys? Her innards crawled with the certainty that there was an element that would see her brought down, along with the Earl of MacKay, but she didn't know who it was. She needed MacKay's long, strong arm of protection.

She could comprehend Diuran's loyalty. It touched her that after their duties to the patient were done he seemed to brook no suspicion about her. That he could believe her innocent of such a heinous crime made her weak with relief. She needed friends among the Mac-Kays.

She yawned, all but cracking her jaw. At the moment she was too fatigued to care about anything but sleep, though she was sure that MacKay would wake her in the night with his wants and needs. The fever could rise again. There would be sweats and chills demanding cloths and warm woolens. She might catch a nap, not much more.

Diuran returned with a retinue of helpers whom he hurried through their assigned tasks. Though there were curious glances, there were no queries.

In short order the steaming copper tub was readied for her, then Diuran waved away the attendants assuring her they were loyal MacKays. "I'll guard the door through the night, milady, and there will be others beside me who will be ever watchful. No one will enter unless you call them."

"Again I give you thanks, good Diuran. I think the laird will win this bout."

"Assuredly he must, milady." He hesitated.

"What?"

"You have a bar for the door, but perhaps 'twould be safer for you unbarred, in case you have need of me."

She nodded. "True."

She waited for the door to shut, then went to the copper bath, stripping her stained wedding raiment from her body.

After laving herself and seeing to Hugh, she sank down on the couch.

The much-needed rest eluded her because she rose many times when Hugh required her assistance. He was so dry he needed water time after time, or a biscuit to settle him. Then he shook as though from ague and she had to embrace him with woolens. More often than not she had to change the sheets every turn of the glass since he soaked them with sweat.

Finally, almost too tired to move, after changing his bedding for the umpteenth time and the last she hoped, she gave him a soothing draft. Tired to the bone, she finished what was in the goblet herself, and climbed into the big bed next to him, rather than go back to the uncomfortable couch.

Deep in sleep she thought herself caught in a storm. She couldn't free herself from the maelstrom. Tossed and turned, she heard a mumbling as though Taranus, god of lightning, had come among them. Though a follower of the Christian ethics, Morrigan was too canny to underwrite the great gods and goddesses of Boudicca and other great Celts. When she had to, she soothed their capricious ways. She opened her eyes to mutter a prayer to the power god and looked into the eyes of her spouse.

"Wha . . . ?"

"Be still, my beauty. You've come to my bed and I give you welcome. This night this warrior has need of the likes of you. 'Twould seem I've sustained a wound, though I know not with what or how." He frowned. "Nor can I recall what day 'tis nor what battle beset me. Must have been a blow to the skull with a cudgel. No matter, I'm strong enough for this and seek it. I have a great flame in my innards I would bestow upon thee, my beauty. Forsooth I'll give you the hottest of loving as you'll give the same back to me."

"Wait! Hugh MacKay—"

He kissed her, his tongue jousting, tickling, teasing, cutting off her sputtering ire and protest. "Resist not, lovely one. I care not that you've given your favor to others, though if truth be told I would prefer that all your talents be mine, alone." He grinned at her struggles.

"Will you listen—?"

"Nay! This night you'll belong to me, as I will be yours, and we will pleasure each other until I must rise from your pallet and battle once more." He leaned over her, kissing her neck, her cheek, returning over and over to her mouth. "I'll fill you with my heat as you will drown me in your charms." He kissed her lips again. Then his mouth slid between her breasts, caressing the skin, taking one nipple into his mouth and sucking there, muttering shocking encouragement that she imitate such on his body.

"Sirrah! I cannot—" Morrigan was spinning. New sensations filled her like rare wine in a goblet. She couldn't describe what was happening. Nay! She'd never known there was such. She was on fire with a need she couldn't name. Her hands clutched Hugh MacKay even as she told herself it couldn't be happening.

"You can, my lovely. Tomorrow, I'll war again, and not know your name. Mayhap I'll not forget you so easily, though. You're a rara avis to be sure. This night you'll be my mate in passion and ecstasy . . ." He kissed her, openmouthed, eager, wanting.

Unused to such endearments, to such a clasping of bodies, to such daring words, Morrigan was rigid with outrage. Yet there was a melting in her, a yearning that ignored his shamelessness. Nay! She would've spurred him on if such was necessary. Hugh MacKay had no need of impetus. He set a fire and fed the flames with an eagerness that left her breathless.

It would seem he was not as sick as she'd believed. That he thought her a common strumpet raised her ire. Then she felt the coldness of sweat brushing her skin and knew that he was indeed in deep fever. Her umbrage melted, her rage seeped away. She wrenched her mouth from his. "Stop, MacKay, you're ailing. Stop!" She felt her garment tear. Good glory! The evil humors had taken his hearing.

"Seek not to tease me, lovely one. Remove this wrap and I will love you as you seek."

"Seek? Me?" Sputtering, Morrigan tried to reason with him. Then she caught sight of his glazed stare. "You know me not!"

"Of course I do, sweet one. You're my whore—"

"What? How dare—"

He kissed her, his mouth filling hers, taking, giving such heat that her fury had no focus. A drumbeat began in her belly, throbbing until she was deafened by it. Her limbs had turned to hot honey and all they wanted was to entwine with MacKay's.

When he lifted his mouth a mere breath from hers, she couldn't get enough air to voice more protest. He didn't seem to share her problem. His eyes held more than fever. The look made her fire anew. His body, though pearled with sweat, seemed to have a seductive, sinuous strength that magnetized her. "Hugh—"

"In the east you're honored as kadim or houri. If you suit me, I'll keep you with me. 'Tis not uncommon to keep such as you in a castle." He lifted her torn garment from her body, seeming not to notice her protests. "I will inform my people that you will be an honored guest."

Gulping breaths, she glared at him. "Oh? Is that the way of it? You'll not keep me—"

"I shall . . . until I battle again."

"Monstrous! You cannot," she argued with him as he

was freeing her from the last of her raiment. "I am not a houri, Hugh MacKay. Hear that plain."

"Sweet one! Do not seek to entice me with false shyness."

"False, is it? I'll take a claymore to you, I will. And one more thing, you ungracious lout, I'm not . . ." All at once she realized she'd been poking her finger into his naked chest. "Good glory! Have you no shame?"

"Nay. Nor should you, my bare beauty."

"Bare? Don't be . . . Eek!" She scrambled to cover herself, slapping at his hands when he continued to ignore her modesty. She was stunned to realize their bodies were entwined. "Stop!"

"I can't," he muttered. "Nor do you wish it."

"I do . . ." Words dribbled away when he put his head upon her breast, pulling her nipple into his mouth.

"Beautiful," he muttered, his lips still surrounding her.

Aghast, she opened her mouth, exhaling and inhaling deep breaths, words of denial caught deep in her throat. "No . . ." she wheezed.

"Shh," he muttered, taking her other nipple and repeating the torrid ritual. "I would wash you with my tongue, sweet lady. Lave you up and down from your woman's place to your eyes, I will."

"Good Lord!"

"Seek me, not the Maker, lovely one."

He was a barbarian! If she'd had the strength, if she weren't so hot, so trembly, she'd smite the bastard Scot for such effrontery. His language was atrocious! He spoke in the most outrageous way. If truth be told he was blasphemous. Ohhh! His mouth upon her middle must be sinful. Surely such wild sweetness could be nothing else.

" 'Tis not often I'm made so hot. You have done this," he told her, growling the words. "This is where your magic is." His hands went down her middle until they touched her female center. Then his mouth followed, darting at her navel, then moving lower, his lips pulling at the curls there, licking, making her body as feverish as his. When she bucked beneath him, he increased the rhythm until she thought she'd go mad.

Stunned by the surge of sensation, building inside her like the mudslides from the cliffs overlooking the Irish Sea, she could only grip his shoulders and wonder if she was living or dying. The heat she'd never known, nor imagined, grew and expanded, filling her. When there seemed there could be no more, there was. It cascaded through her like the sea crashing on the shore.

"Hugh!"

"I'm here, beauty."

"I can't . . . I don't . . ."

"Ah, 'tis the same for me. You've set me aflame."

Her body writhed upon the bedding as though she, not Hugh, were caught in a miasma. Trying to gainsay him, to find the words to stop his wonderful onslaught, seemed impossible. Appalling that she wanted him to continue, yet she couldn't stem that wondrous tide of desire. The thought crossed her mind that he thought her another, that he might not have wanted her as much. Then it evaporated like the mists in the glen. Why could she not find the strength to stop this thunderous wanting? What magic did MacKay have? It was a bittersweet certainty that, even if MacKay didn't know he made love to her, she wanted more and didn't want him to stop.

She'd had the swelling sickness in her throat once and her body had burned into watery rashes. She'd thrashed for days on the edge of oblivion. She had a similar sensation now. If she released her hold on MacKay she could spiral away into nothingness. He was her anchor to life and hot, melting beauty.

The heat in the core of her was beyond any fire she'd ever thought to have. How to define the mushrooming need that had nothing to do with hunger and thirst, but was even stronger? It was not for cool, fruited water her being cried. What then? She couldn't comprehend the great gnawing that filled her, making her form move with his upon the big bed. What unseen rhythm had them in thrall?

"So, my sweet, you call me as Circe has always beckoned with your lovely form."

How outrageous he was! Being with him was more than right, it was a clarion call from spirit to spirit . . . and much more. She ached to be closer though she was skin to skin with him. Letting their bodies abrade, their limbs entwine was a command she couldn't ignore. That heat from within was building to a pyramid of feeling she'd not had an inkling of until that moment. Wanting choked her. Air left her body in great gasps, to be sucked in again in huge gulps.

Her intent to tell him to desist crumpled like the dried sage put into the bedcovering, turning to dust her resolve to make him lie back, rest. Their sweat-slick bodies rubbed each other like flint against stone, turning them into glowing embers. Hands gripped hands, legs tangled and tightened, bodies pulsed against each other.

Morrigan forgot protest, forgot inhibition, lost reluctance. She wanted him, and no other. Needed him, no other, and she didn't know why, or how it happened. And she didn't care. She'd never been so weak, so strong, so rejuvenated. What was happening?

"That's it, my beauty, move against me."

"I . . . I do not—"

His mouth took her words, tasting them. When his tongue found its way between her lips and began a dance with hers, she tried to cry out. Instead her tongue began its own jousting and the intolerable heat built again.

Her arms pressed against him to be freed. When he backed a hair's space away to give her room, some far-off thought was sure she'd smite him. Instead she let her arms encircle his neck.

"Hold me tight, little love, I shall carry you with me to Valhalla."

'Twas blasphemy, an errant voice whispered. Why

would a Scot wish to go to a Viking heaven? True, some said his mother was Icelandic . . . Thought dribbled away. Her body, heeding its own clarion call, began to inch up and down him anew. When he cursed, his voice hoarse with urgency, she stopped, uncertain, hot, eager, but afraid.

"No, sweet thing, I have no anger. You just make me so hard, so needful. I could plunge into you now, but I've a fantasy to make you as wanting as me." He kissed her hard, his one hand holding her, the other stroking up and down her form.

Euphoria and excitement were a wild paradox that held her. When he looked into her eyes, smiling, he took away all resistance. She wanted this coupling, enough to drown the fear deep within her. It was madness to desire a Scot. Surely she'd lost all sense to want him in such a way. No doubt of it. She was depraved.

He turned her body so that the candlelight flashed over it, creating a sunburst of color. "You are a goddess. What deed have I accomplished that brings you to me from your star?"

Morrigan didn't have an answer even if he'd expected one. She knew he didn't when he pressed his face between her breasts, his tongue laving her, his hands massaging her.

Eager for more, she let her hands touch his back, her fingers feeling the strong, smooth skin, crisscrossed with many scars. She caressed him as she'd done to no other. Excitement built anew, even as she was sure there could be no more. It was as though another had taken her life and given her a new one, bubbling with a delight, a desire to mate with MacKay.

He lifted his head, smiling at her, his eyes glittering. "You taste sweet, my beauty." His mouth closed over her breast again, the touch arching her body into him.

He put his arms around her buttocks, lifting her closer. He lifted his head, gazing at her. "I shall make you flame with desire, beauty."

Morrigan swallowed. "Yes."

He smiled, his lazy mouth descending to her skin, scoring down it to her navel, entering and exiting in a wonderful rhythm that seemed right, though she'd not known of it before Hugh MacKay had done this.

She pulled at his hair when she felt his breath on her woman's place. None should go there except to plant the seed of a child. She knew this as did all women. But he'd been there before and she wanted it again. "Ohhh." The cry escaped her as she felt his tongue there, going in and out as it'd done in her navel. She would've protested, but she couldn't find the words.

His tongue plunged again and again into her woman's place. Then she seemed to rip apart in heat.

"MacKay!" she called aloud.

"I'm here, beauty."

She was being torn by MacKay's flame the way that lightning struck a tree. There was no pain, only a building, hot sensation then blackness took her, her body bucking against his mouth.

"I come to you, my beauty."

Sliding up and into her body, he began the rhythm again, taking her beyond anything she'd ever known. There was a sudden surprising pain through all the boiling need, then there was nothing but a surging, pounding desire.

His body worked over hers. She rose to meet every thrust, finding a burgeoning fullness that suddenly carried her beyond any sight or sound she'd ever imagined. She gripped him, thinking that she'd risen beyond the castle, the battlements, the land of miserable Scots.

She shuddered over and over again, feeling a subtle rawness, but it was not unpleasant. She was still locked into MacKay's arms, his mouth in her hair. Then as though a far-off plan was executed, their two bodies strained in an ultimate journey of joy. For long moments after she couldn't move, nor could she see or feel. After a while sensation appeared again. She knew where she was, what she'd done. She tried to free herself. His hold tightened.

"Nay, lass, I already want you more." Though the words were slurred his hold was fast.

Twice more in the night he loved her, each time better than the last, longer, sweeter, until she was wrung out with new feelings she'd thought never to experience.

When he began to sleep she gazed at him in wonder. He was devilishly ill with fever, still he'd made love to her over and over and it'd been wonderful. She was truly wed to a giant of a man. How frightening that, mayhap, she might come to love this man because of the night of love he'd given her. His feelings wouldn't be involved because he thought he'd joined with a courtesan. Would he change his feelings on the morrow and realize he'd made love with his wife?

She rose, easing him away from the coverings, eyeing the blood there. Her husband would never know he took a virgin as bride and she could never tell him. She began changing the bedcoverings. In a rage he could deny Rhys his heritage. He could put her aside and the boy, as well. No, she couldn't confess that Rhys had been born to another mother. Her pledge overrode her need for truth. The pathos, the irony shook her and she felt a tear on her cheek.

SIX

What fools these mortals be.
Seneca

Morrigan watched the children while they had their lessons with Father Monteith. She bit back a smile when Rhys rolled his eyes at Avis, who labored as hard as he over the Greek words.

Her attention went to Conal, who seemed to eat up every word and thirst for more. She caught the eye of the priest, who gave some directions to the children and then moved to her side. " 'Twould seem we have a scholar, Father."

He nodded, smiling. "Conal is eager for any knowledge and is able to digest a good mix. His language skills are excellent, milady, and his curiosity is boundless."

She smiled. "Both he and Avis have responded well to care."

"You have shown them love, milady. They flower because of it." He bowed to her. "And we owe you much for the nurturing you've given the MacKay. As a man who has studied the medicaments, I know how dangerous and varied are the poisons that surround us. You saved his life. Though he chafes at his slow recovery, I've told him many times he should be grateful he can move about at all."

Morrigan frowned. "He insists on riding over his holdings, yet I'm not sure his innards are in as good shape as they should be."

"A most headstrong man is the laird, milady. In another turn of the moon he should be in guid tid as the country people say, if he does not undo all your nursing by being precipitous."

"He's most impatient."

"Yes. Milady, I would ask a boon."

"Of course. What is it?"

"If I have your permission I should like to take the twins to the monastery. Conal wishes to see the great books, and Avis would accompany him." His smile lurked. "Rhys has told me he's seen such things."

Morrigan chuckled. "Rhys is happiest in the stable, I think."

"And with the dogs," Father added. "I thank you for letting me take Avis and Conal."

"Of course. The outing would be good for them. I'll take Rhys for a ride on his new mount, though I'm quite sure he would prefer working in the stable."

The priest chuckled, then went back to his charges.

* * *

"Why do you have to go with me? Eamon will do that."

Morrigan looked at Rhys, wanting to laugh when his chin jutted out, his eyes narrowed. He looked so much like her beloved cousin Gwynneth at that moment. "You have run poor Eamon ragged. I've decided to spell him."

"You're tired. Dilla says you are. She says that you take care of MacKay all the time, and that wearies you. Then she laughs," Rhys told her. "So you should return to rest. I can watch myself."

Morrigan was glad at that moment when he looked away. Her face flamed. Nay! Not just the visage, but all of her felt heat. Some was embarrassment. Most was the heat that MacKay engendered though he wasn't beside her.

He was improving every day, though there was still great weakness that was akin to such poisonings even if one was fortunate enough to survive. Though he required little in the way of nursing, he wasn't back to full health no matter how many times he roared that he was. He didn't need her ministrations. She wanted his, though she was sure he'd be too weak for the wild loving he'd shown her. She couldn't forget that wonderful night when he'd taught her how to be a woman, let her learn about his passion. She wanted more. Sometimes she was emboldened to ask how soon he would like her to join him on the nuptial bed. It was only a wispy wish. She couldn't bring herself to query him so. Besides, she didn't want him to recall their night of love. What if he remembered the blood of her virgin wall and how he'd shattered it? She didn't want those questions, so unless they spoke of his health she didn't initiate conversation with him. She was on the horns of a dilemma, wanting him, yet not wanting him to discover the secret of Rhys's birth. What a quandary!

Since his slow recovery she'd watched him. She was quite sure he didn't remember their wedding night. She was torn between confessing and being forever silent. Now and then she caught his gaze upon her. More than once it'd seemed he would speak of something. He didn't.

Not in her wildest dreams had she ever pictured such wild and wonderful doings between a man and woman. When she'd pictured herself with Tarquin it'd all been a sweetness of stolen kisses, squeezed hands, perhaps the daring of a hand at her waist. Never had she envisioned such a tempest as she'd had with Hugh MacKay, skin to skin, mouth to mouth, body to body. It had been beautiful. Her dreams since had been chaotic and hotter than she could've imagined. So many times she'd woken up, dampness between her thighs, a need, a want pulsating through her. It had taken all her resolve not to go to him, tell him of their wedding night and their loving. He knew of his sickness. He'd thanked her many times for her succoring. He had no knowledge of their coupling and she didn't enlighten him.

It seemed it wasn't to be. Not since her wedding night had she been with MacKay. Since their return to the main holding of MacKay, overlooking the North Sea, they'd not shared a bed. The castle was imposing, twice as large as the one where their vows were exchanged, with countless large sleeping chambers. She'd struggled to hide her disappointment that he'd not attempted to secure his marital right. Yet she also knew that for a lusty man like MacKay the weakness in his body wouldn't allow him the strength he needed for conjugal visits. Did all women have such wondrous couplings? She suspected not. She'd put her frustration aside. He needed to recuperate, to come back to full health. Then he would approach her. Each day he was better, stronger, though sometimes she noted the white visage that spelled fatigue. She wouldn't make explanations of their nuptial night unless he asked the question. Even then she'd hide from him her virginity in order to protect Rhys and his legacy. She sighed, knowing she was fortunate he didn't know, but sad that he didn't recall that wondrous night.

"Why are you staring at the castle, maman?"

"I . . . I like the look of it. Do you?"

He nodded. "I want to stay here. Eamon says I will because now I'm a MacKay." His missing tooth gapped when he grinned. Then he frowned. "I think my steed has a stone."

"I'll check for—"

"No!" Rhys held up his hand. "Eamon says I must take care of my own steed."

His "steed," a robust Highland pony, its long hair almost touching the ground, was a sturdy beast, not much taller than Rhys with the stolid personality needed to cope with an exuberant five-year-old. She hadn't wanted him to ride anything. Hugh had convinced her it was safer to give Rhys his own mount to protect against another occurrence of trying to ride the much larger and more unpredictable destriers.

Morrigan watched him struggle for a few minutes, then she looked toward the castle again, thinking of Hugh, who'd gone to look upon other portions of his vast holding.

The castle was very large, but it had charm. It was similar in design to the first castle, and to most in Scotland, England, or Wales. The similarity ended there. Roomier, with more amenities, it was built more solidly. With huge well-drawing fireplaces, it was not nearly as drafty as her own home in Wales had been. Almost every wall was covered with rich tapestries that kept out the dampness and gloom. The wood trim was glossy and came from the huge trees in the south.

Morrigan had found her new home a pleasant surprise. The enormous staff was congenial, well trained and independent. It seemed all MacKays were like that. They could argue among themselves, and none thought himself less or more than the other because of chore duties.

The rooms were well designed, spacious. The kitchen didn't smoke into the great room. Even the upper rooms could be easily warmed. There was more than ample space to move about, for a boy to play and run. Clan MacKay had been kind to Rhys; each member who was in contact with him seemed to bend over backward for the adopted heir.

Morrigan had begun to enjoy her new home. If deep in her soul she longed for a repeat of the beauty of her wedding night, for the hot and wonderful joining that had made her a wife, she'd learned to be content with what she did have. There was heat in her husband's eyes when he looked at her . . . and a question. Did he recall? Was that why he'd not joined her in bed? He thought her to be a slut because she'd enjoyed their lovemaking so much! Most women thought child making a duty. Perhaps it was wrong to like it.

She'd always been sure she would marry Tarquin one day. She was quite sure their coupling would not have been as it was with MacKay. She wasn't sure how she knew, but she was positive.

She looked at the landscape. A safe haven for Rhys and herself. Nothing could make her feel more secure than that. Perhaps one day when she and Hugh had been wed for many moons . . .

She forced her mind to other things, quite sure her secret longings should stay buried.

Now that Hugh was gaining in strength she had to wonder what their future as man and wife would be. Would they make a child together? Her body heated and froze just imagining it. To have a child in his image would be great joy.

She looked around at the cool, sunny day. Soon the weather would turn cold. The wind would turn to ice and frost. For now it was almost balmy. She'd not been led to believe that such weather existed in the cold north.

Morrigan inhaled the freshness of the breeze, closing her eyes in delight. Hugh's had been a long, careful convalescence. His strong constitution had helped effect a relatively fast cure. He could've died. She knew that, as did other MacKays. After Hugh had demanded a full explanation from her and Diuran, her healing abilities had put her on call from other MacKays. They'd also offered their friendship and their respect. She'd been awed by their open affection.

For many days she'd advised and medicated MacKays as well as their laird. It had confined her indoors. She'd been glad to leave the castle today, only because she needed exercise, fresh air. So she'd gone riding with Rhys. Though she thought that MacKay needed care, he'd raised such a ruckus about being kept in any longer that no one could've stopped him from going to inspect another holding some leagues away. He'd glared down any who looked as though they might gainsay him.

"No, I won't rest anymore," he'd told her, his chin jutting out much like Rhys's when he was in a temper. "And if anyone tries to stop me, I'll go over the top of them."

Morrigan had wanted to laugh. Her husband was wild-eyed from being ill. He'd been a horrible patient, his bellowing heard throughout the castle; his threats to all and sundry who would dare try to medicate him were many, varied, and colorful.

"How gallant," she'd murmured. "Threatening to throw Dilla, Ardis, and me down the steps, no doubt." The women had stared bug-eyed at her when she smiled.

He'd rapped his fist on the bed table and glared. "I've done none such, and you know it."

"Do I? Then why is the clan wagering that none of us will last the day?"

He'd glared first at her, then at the others. "They aren't," he'd muttered.

"Really?"

"Really," he'd said in more chastened tone. "I'm going to check the eastern hectares. I won't be long." He'd hurried from the bedroom as though they'd try to stop him.

When Morrigan laughed, the two women had looked at her aghast, then their lips had quivered, too.

"He's well enough, milady," Dilla ventured.

Morrigan smiled. "I'll find Rhys and take him riding. I've neglected him."

"I shouldn't worry," Dilla observed dryly. "He has half the clan at his beck and call."

Knowing how demanding he could be, Morrigan had winced. Then she'd left the women to find him.

She had seen to Rhys whenever she could in the last turn of the moon, but it'd always been in the confines of the castle. She'd sensed he'd not felt bereft by her absences, but she needed to see for herself that he was fine.

She had to smile. He had not been as glad to see his mother as she'd been to see him.

"One would think you weren't overjoyed to have me with you," Morrigan had mentioned when they'd gone to the stable. She'd tried to look woebegone. If truth were told she was delighted that he'd taken to the clan so fully. He was happy with his new status, and every day he sought out many members of the clan. The twins, Avis and Conal, were usually on his heels. It pleased her. In Wales he'd not been so forthcoming. Of course, then her own worries that his identity could be discovered might've made him imitative of her worry. Now he seemed to have thrown off any cares or concerns he'd had. His concentration on all things MacKay gave her a measure of security. That he could make a pest of himself she had no doubt. There were no end of keepers showing the youngster how to go on and how he should handle himself as an inheritor to MacKay. Morrigan was quite sure his self-worth had swelled along with his circle of friends.

She smiled as she recalled how her long face and question about being glad to see her had affected him.

Rhys squirmed. "You are not a boy, maman."

"True."

"Then you don't have fun like us."

"I see."

He grinned. "So I can go with Eamon."

"No. You'll go with me." She'd almost laughed aloud at how his expression had gone sheepish.

Now, as he remounted, she eyed him. "Do you enjoy your lessons?"

"Some. I'd rather play with the twins," he told her as he turned his pony, then mounted with care, as though his steed were indeed a destrier.

"Oh?" She felt guilty that she'd had even less time for Conal and Avis, though Lilybet and Dilla had told her they slept across the corridor from Rhys, ate as he did, and had every care as well.

"I like them. They take lessons with me now. I like it better. They make learning Latin and Greek not so bad."

She smothered a smile. "I see. That sounds good."

"It would be better not to learn it at all." He grimaced. "Avis thinks it's stupid. Conal likes Latin and Greek." He pursed his lips. "Eamon shows them everything he shows me. And they have horses, now, and they can ride." He looked proud.

"And did you help to teach them about riding?" She was sure he had by his look. Now that MacKay was better they could be a family. Such thoughts made her dizzy with heat.

"I did."

"I'm glad." Morrigan nodded, feeling reassured that the two youngsters who'd been such outcasts were being cared for, even though she'd not had the time to tend them. Her husband had taken all her concentration. And it wasn't just healing that filled her mind. Her thoughts always flew back to their wedding night. If only Hugh remembered . . . then again, that could be a bad idea. Dilla, who'd helped so much, had exclaimed about the blood on the sheets thinking that the laird had emitted it from his system. Morrigan hadn't disabused her. What would she say if he ever quizzed her about that night? As his wife she was honor bound to be honest. As Rhys's guardian, she'd made a vow to keep his identity hidden.

There were so many facets to her husband. Would she ever know all of them? He intrigued her, not just for his natural leadership, his caring for his clan, but for his intelligence, his interests in all levels of life. None of her family had ever been scholars though none had been unlearned. She'd been tutored in all aspects of leadership and learning. Her uncles had thought it useless. Her father had persevered.

It delighted Morrigan that her husband was as learned in script and parchment as she. He had an intense knowledge of many topics from the classics to agrarian management, and the running of the long-haired Highland cattle called stoats.

Most of this she'd learned from Diuran, Toric, and Dilla. She'd become even more informed by studying the personal library that he kept in his suite of rooms. The study of the stars marched with new methods of planting, along with the battle planning of Pericles and Alexander. His interests crossed the line between eastern mysticism, Christianity, and the study of the ancient beliefs, primarily the credos of the Druids and Vikings. He had all the Greek poets in their native tongue, as well as the Latin scholars. Most of the tomes were well thumbed. Not often was such found outside a monastery. Pondering her unusual husband, she let her horse follow Rhys's pony.

When the going became arduous she called out to Rhys to stop, then she moved to his side, careful not to let her larger mount bump his. Not far beyond the land sloped down to the sea that boiled onto the rocky strand. Loud, wonderful, awesome they stared down at the cauldron.

"Let's hurry, maman."

"Wait! We must use every caution, Rhys. You must follow me closely, and carefully. 'Tis a most precipitous descent and we must be sure of our footing." Morrigan wasn't sure about the decline. Mayhap 'twould be better to keep him on the escarpment.

"I can get down there," he insisted when she continued to hesitate.

"Good. You must still let me study the way first."

"Eamon says down there beyond those rocks that stick into the sea be a place for swimming," Rhys told her, his voice raised to be heard over the crashing waves.

"There is a place for swimming," Morrigan corrected his usage, as she often did when she needed time to think. Should they go down to the strand? It was quite beautiful and very warm. They could walk barefoot at the water's edge. "And have you gone into the waters with Eamon?"

Rhys shook his head, looking glum. "He catches me out even when I told him I know how to swim."

Morrigan nodded, intending to thank Eamon when she saw him. She knew full well how set on an idea Rhys could be.

After looking at the two possible ways down to the strand, Morrigan decided against the descent. Though she was sure Rhys's pony would be surefooted, she wasn't that convinced that Rhys would be able to keep his seat in the steep places. When she was about to tell him they'd stay on top, he nudged his pony around her, cantering to the edge, then starting down the path. Stunned, she was frozen in place for precious seconds. If she hadn't been fearful she'd startle him or his pony, she would've admonished him, and called him back. Any distraction could unseat him, or unbalance the animal under him. She dare not do anything but follow him.

Gritting her teeth, she kicked her horse into following the boy.

The descent in some places was almost clifflike. Leaning back in her saddle to equalize the weight, she kept her eyes on Rhys, her heart in her mouth, her attention nailed to the boy and animal in front of her.

Her body was pearled with dampness when they finally reached the strand. The unseasonably warm weather in Scotland had seemed like a blessing until that moment. Now her clothes stuck to her, her face was on fire, and she was damned mad at the boy.

"Wait right there," she called to Rhys, trying to get her breath. She rode up next to him, breathing hard, from fear rather than exertion. "You . . . you are never to do that again."

"What?"

"You know what I'm speaking of, young man, so don't try to play dunce with me." She glared at him, until his face fell. "I would've led the way 'ere we should descend. You knew that."

Knowing full well he'd crossed over the line, he waited, chin thrust out, wariness in every line. "I din't do nothin'."

"Anything. And you did. You know you should've waited until I said it was all right to descend the cliff. It wasn't safe, and I wasn't about to risk it. You sensed that. Didn't you?"

He nodded. "I wanted to be on the beach," he muttered.

"Be that as it may, you were wrong." She dismounted, letting her innards get back to rhythm, watching him as he got off his steed, biting back a smile, though she still felt shaky. He was as unruly as some of the destriers in MacKay's stable. Enough said. They hadn't been together in too many days. She wasn't going to ruin their time by badgering, but later there would be another lecture in obeying. His discipline had been lacking. Among the MacKays he was more apt to get a chuckle than censure. Morrigan was going to set some new, firm rules. For now he was safe, and that was most important. "Promise me you'll not do such a thing again."

He nodded. "I won't, maman."

"Would you like to collect shells?" Morrigan pointed to the bits and pieces scattered on the strand.

He brightened. "Yes. First, I have to tie Caesar very carefully. That's what Eamon said."

Morrigan nodded, being as solemn as he was about the appointed task.

"Eamon says if you take care of your d's'ter, he takes care of you."

"Correct," Morrigan said, eyeing his pony that was half the size of her horse, not even close to the dimensions of the warhorses used by the MacKays.

Following his lead, she tied her steed, then began to seek the lovely creamy and silver shells strewn on the strand. Over and over they exclaimed over a rare find. The net bag that'd been attached to Morrigan's saddle began to bulge with beach treasures. Though they talked in sporadic sentences, they'd wander away from each other, then back together again. Morrigan was sure he was not far from her.

"What do you think of this one?" Her smile fled when she turned. "Rhys! Answer me." Dropping the shell, she hiked up her riding costume, catching the long skirt between her legs, hooking it into the gem-covered belt around her middle. She ran up the beach, and around an outcropping of rock. "Rhys!" she shouted. Then she saw him, breath sobbing out of her. He was bobbing in the sea. "Rhys!"

"Maman! Look!"

She had a blurry impression that something or some-one was in the water with him, but she didn't take her eyes off the boy, his short arms lifting in the swim stroke he'd been tutored in since babyhood.

"No!" Morrigan shouted as he continued into deeper water!

Stripping down from her heavy bliaut, underdress and headdress to her shift of lightest lawn, she kicked off her stockings and elkskin boots. Thanking the Celtic gods and goddesses for the Welsh good sense that grounded males and females in all manner of self-preservation, including swimming and the use of weapons, she moved to the edge of the strand. For long moments she eyed the shifting waves, the strong retreat of the water, angst building in her. The tide was strong; the rolling waves could pummel one down in deeper water. Once down, a person could become disoriented, kicking hard to the bottom instead of up to the air. More than one died in the sea from striking a rock on the bottom.

Then she was flinging herself into the chilly water that days of sun hadn't warmed that much. Her eyes stayed on the boy, who seemed to be getting farther away. The tall waves hid him much of the time, but Morrigan stroked hard, determined she wouldn't come out of the water unless Rhys was with her. She was

strong, used to cold water, unafraid and able. It would
serve her well. They'd come out of this, with God's help
and St. Dafydd.

Hugh MacKay was restless. Some unnamed need or
want chewed his innards. He wanted to get back to his
major holding, to Morrigan with the green gem eyes. It
annoyed and titillated him that his new wife could have
such a magnetic hold on him. They'd not been together
as man and wife because of the poisoning that'd sapped
his strength, but he wanted her as though she'd been a
part of him for years. And if his people didn't stop hovering over him like he was a sickening we'en, he'd
strangle the lot of them. He wasn't about to wait any
longer. He would claim Morrigan for his wife, and soon!

A full turn of the moon and more they'd been wed,
and he'd not touched her. His illness had driven him
mad with frustration. It'd taken too long to heal. Then
he'd chafed at the akin weakness. He'd wanted her, and
not had the ability to take her. Too many others had hovered over him, determined to bring him to full health.
He'd wished them all to perdition. All he wanted was
his wife.

But the dreams! They made him hard even to say the
word in his mind. Why would he dream of a strumpet so
like his wife, when he could have his wife? Why didn't
he have his wife? He ground his teeth, muttering epi-
thets. The visions had been so real, he'd wanted to ask
his men the name of the beauty. She'd looked like Mor-

rigan, but wasn't. Damn! How could such a powerful loving be imagination? Impossible! What other explanation could there be? Madness.

"What drives you, Aodh?"

"Hugh, cousin." Correcting Toric was a ploy. His cousin was more than aware of the necessity of the Anglo usage. They'd embarked on a new life. Though their grip on MacKay holdings was tenuous, to a man they were sworn to keep it. Nay! It was the need to keep his cousin from probing that he'd corrected him. Not even to his closest companion since childhood could he confess the colorful passion that danced in him.

They rode ahead of the men, as they often did, so they could converse. More often than not their discussions would be on the clan, a subject important to both of them. Now he needed to distract Toric from his question, which he didn't know how to answer, even if he wished to, and he didn't.

Toric sighed. "Hugh. Do you worry about those who would've taken your life?"

Though news of his sickness had gone through the clan, and there were many whispered suspicions, Hugh had not issued dicta on the occurrence. That something had happened on his wedding day, most knew. All the details were only given to certain ones, such as his cousin Toric. Not that he didn't trust all the MacKays. He did. There were some given to gossiping, to exchanging information with passing drummers and vendors. Hugh thought it best not to broadcast everything until he was sure who was friend or foe. He would've sworn on scripture that none of the MacKays had betrayed him. Until he had some knowledge of the perpetrators he thought it best to keep his counsel except with a chosen few.

Hugh had followed a long-held rule with his clan. Only to the unmarried stalwarts would such a threat as his assassination attempt be revealed. Under no circumstances must the married men be involved. There'd be no holding any of his people back if they suspected a threat to his life. He'd not have the clan threatened by the decimation war could bring. They'd had enough of that. If the clan was attacked all would be at the ready and called upon to act.

The clan could be in danger of extinction without the buttressing of family. Endangering family men was folly and counterproductive to the safety and longevity of MacKay. Years of war and fracas had sliced into the huge family, removing some of its greats. The clan needed time to recoup.

Since the moment the word went out that the chief had been taken to his sickbed, the guards had been doubled, certain changes made in the protection of his castle and other holdings. Additions to the holdings were put into place, buildings secured, walls remortared, weapons honed fine. Secret exits and entrances had been searched and either boarded up or guarded. Some had been reinforced with iron webbing that formed a gate.

Nothing was left to chance. Lookouts had been doubled and sent on wider perimeters.

"You wander again, Hugh."

"I will admit to you it sits in my thoughts about the attempt made on my life. What angers me is there seems to be little clue to the culprit. Though I have no doubt I shall find who did it, until then I will take every care to stay alive and protect what's mine."

"Could your wife have done the deed, then feared for her life?"

Toric had put words to some of his thinking. "Diuran swears that my lady put every effort into saving me, at great cost to herself." Hugh took a deep breath, looking over his shoulder at his men. "She knew that Diuran would've killed her had I expired."

"True, as would any MacKay."

Hugh smiled. "Each has had their feelings toward her undergo a change, so I'm told. Many know what she did to save me, and they've sworn unspoken fealty." His smile crooked. "I wonder if she feels this. I would say my wife's intuitive."

"Aye. Dilla swears she can see through the next sennight."

"Though I don't subscribe to such, I do find her reasoning to be uncanny. Methinks she'd be a formidable enemy, one not easily stopped. Yet I don't sense an antipathy toward me. I don't think it's there."

Toric sighed. "I agree. I wish I could factor our enemies. I will continue to search, but I don't think my hunt will take me toward your wife. Your Morrigan is a beautiful and intelligent woman. Our people speak of it amongst themselves. Even dour Gordon has become her champion. He tells me any clan would be hard put not to be proud of Lady MacKay."

"True." Hugh looked around at his men, noting that they, too, scanned the countryside where they rode, that more than one rode point. All around him were outriders. Vigilance had been his byword since he'd been a lad. Anger soured his innards for a moment as he pondered how close he'd been to Heaven or Hell. Had it not been for the wife he knew so little about, he'd have been abiding in one or the other. And if she'd imbibed she would've been there with him.

"When I first saw Morrigan I thought her a made-up lady like those that come from Alexandria and beyond," Toric mused. "Not in all my days had I seen such vivid coloration, such rarefied beauty. I was not the only one whose breath was taken by the sight of her. It was as though she outshone the sun that very day."

There was vinegar in Hugh's look. "I would bash men for less, cousin."

Toric laughed. "I know that."

Hugh relaxed. " 'Tis true there are more and more who become devoted to my lady." He hesitated.

"There's a question in thy voice," Toric said in Icelandic, a language usage common in the north. "What think thee?"

They'd dropped back to a trot. Hugh's restlessness took them up to a canter once more. "I tell you true,

Toric. Though I've been suspicious of everyone who was our guest that day, including the king, I must say I cannot include my wife among those."

"Chancy. We would've drawn and quartered her had there been the least suspicion of her, mayhap."

Hugh smiled. "After telling me, time and again, that you found my beautiful spouse regal and lovely?"

Toric shrugged. "I wouldn't shirk my duty."

Hugh was still laughing when he saw the outline of the battlements, his destrier picking its way to the cliff path high above the sea that fronted his favorite holding of the many belonging to Clan MacKay. Around the bend in the way they rode was the main road to the castle and he was anxious to be there. Mayhap he'd tell his spouse that they could become man and wife that very day. He smiled when he envisioned the look she'd give him. Haughty, a bit tremulous, unafraid.

"By God, what's this I see," Toric exclaimed, breaking Hugh's reverie.

His sweet ponderings died a sudden death when he saw two people in the sea. Reining in Orion, he stared, aware that the MacKays behind him were doing the same.

"Can you see who it is, Hugh?"

"Yes." He'd know that hair anywhere, wet or dry. More times than he could count, he'd opened his eyes when ailing and had felt the satin thickness on his face as his wife had bent over, ministering to him. Now it was streaming out behind her as she struggled to reach the boy in the high sea. It was damn cold in that water despite the balmy day. He also knew she wasn't bathing and that the boy was out there with her . . . beyond her, out of reach. Would she get the lad? Could he get to either one?

He nudged his steed into a reckless gallop along the cliff top, then down the face, even as the shouts of alarm went up from his men.

Thundering down the steep incline, he cursed his wife, God, the sea, and the horse beneath him for not flying to the strand. If any harm came to her . . . he'd damn well follow her into the next world and wrench her back. His need for her was suffocating him, catching him between fury and desperation.

Lathered up and shaking, his horse jumped down the last twenty feet to the rocks edging the water. Shaky and wobbly for a moment, it galvanized itself to speed at Hugh's hissed urgings. Orion responded, galloping along the strand unmindful of rocks, holes, silt, and the wet sand that sucked at its hooves.

Hugh was maddened with fear. The sea was capricious. He'd swum in it all his life and he knew what danger there was atop and beneath the surface. The pull of the tide in and out was not unknown to him. Getting in its demon grip could squeeze the life from a man, filling him with water and drowning him. "Hang on, Morrigan." He spat the message through his teeth.

Flinging himself off his horse, Hugh stripped the clothes from his body, throwing the raiment, his sword and knives to the ground. In breeks and nothing else he threw himself into the surf, pounding toward his wife. He knew, without issuing any commands, that there'd be a host of MacKays following him into the wild water.

Morrigan was tiring and that made her fearful. If she was fatigued, how could Rhys cope? He would be flagging. How could she know where he'd be if he went under when one of the waves hid him from her? Time after time she thrust herself upward, struggling to see, to keep him in sight. In one of her many forays upward to spot him, she'd seen the dog who looked more like a long-haired stoat than a canine and she knew why Rhys was in the water. He loved all animals, and was fearful of none. Her arms felt like lead as she pushed harder. She had to get him before he got beyond the natural protection of the rocks jutting into the seas. Beyond them who would know what capricious waters would pull and toss them. He could be crushed upon the rocks before she reached him. Waves splashed over her, filling her eyes and mouth. Desperation had her redoubling her efforts, hands outstretched, and seeking.

As strong as he was, as well trained in water ways by Welshmen as he was, Rhys was a child, a brave and sturdy child, but still that. That fear filled her.

Her grasping hand clutched something. She pulled. "Rhys!" she breathed.

"Maman," he gasped, coughing. "I . . . save . . . the dog."

She looked over his head. The shaggy beast looked back at her, looking marked up, but not tired. "Let go of the dog, Rhys. I must get you back."

"Bring the—"

Words were torn from his mouth as strong hands went past her and grabbed him.

Gulping air, Morrigan scrambled to get ahold of Rhys again.

"No! Let go, madame. I have him." Lifting the child, Hugh thrust him at Toric behind him. "Get him out of here."

"Dog!" Rhys demanded, swallowing water.

"Eamon has him. Toric has you. No more talking." Hugh looked at his wife. "And I have you."

"I . . . I can make it." Morrigan wasn't sure she could. Water filled her mouth; her arms were tired. Even as stripped down as she was, her undergarments had weighed her down and fatigued her.

"I know you're a battler, milady. Give over this time and let me take you," Hugh whispered to her.

She nodded, unable to form any more words.

The waves crashed over them time and time again, the strong pull of the water yanking them deeper.

Only Hugh's strong stroking kept them on course. How he managed to keep her above the water amazed Morrigan. She had to admit that without him she might not have been able to bring Rhys back to shore.

All at once she felt herself lifted from the water.

"Good Christ! You're bare." Hugh turned so his body shielded her from the others. Then he bellowed for a tartan.

"I'm not bare, fool. Do stop jerking me around in a circle. Would you have had me wear my heavy bliaut into the sea? If your plan was to have me drown, 'twould be the best way."

"Even choking on water you've too much to say, wife."

Though his mouth twisted into a smile there was little humor in the words. Nay! They sounded harsh. His eyes hadn't stopped their perusal of her.

She tried to bring his attention away from her body. "I'm sorry you're displeased."

Eamon came down the strand on the run, whispering to Hugh, then handing him the fifteen yards of fabric that made up one of the clan's plaids.

He grabbed a proffered tartan, spinning it around her, enveloping her from head to toe. "No, you're not sorry I'm displeased, wife. You never are. Hell! You fight me at every turn." His eyes narrowed when her face reddened. "How is it my words overset you?"

She'd been thinking of her wedding night and how he'd made love to her. She'd not fought him, then. Nay! She'd cooperated, helped, been brought to dizzying heights she hadn't imagined in all her days. He'd not recalled. She couldn't forget, nor could she tell him the truth. Somehow it'd become tangled in all the other deceptions that'd seemed to weave themselves into the fabric of their vows. Once when she'd been a child she'd been playing hide-and-seek with her brothers. They'd been down in the dungeon of her father's castle. She'd been running and had gone full tilt into a cobweb that had wrapped about her face and neck. She'd felt smothered, afraid, and disoriented. The same sensation took hold of her each time she tried to tell Hugh the truth about her and Rhys. Time had tied her in even tighter knots of dissembling.

"What is it, milady? Are you still in fright?"

"Yes." She told him the truth.

"Don't fear. I won't let you go." He lifted her in his arms. "If you wish to swim in the sea I'll go with you. Don't ever go alone again."

"Rhys—"

"I know about the boy. Eamon has assured me that he is fine and given me the bare bones of his deed. The lad has too much courage."

"He has," Morrigan averred, shivering not from the cold. "I feared I wouldn't be able to reach him," she muttered, biting her shaking lips.

"You did." Hugh hugged her close. "You're as intrepid a warrior as I've ever seen. How you fought to get to him!" His smile crooked. His hold tightened. "I could've lost you, wife. Who then would fight with me?" He grinned when he saw the sparkle of battle in her eyes. It'd been his hope to distract her. It would seem he succeeded.

"Who indeed?"

"Why, wife, one would think you would be angered if aught but you solaced me."

"Solaced? I thought you said I battled you."

"There's the paradox, sweet wife. You do both."

"How have you managed to survive?" she quizzed in honey tones.

"From what?" But he knew the answer before she phrased it.

"That conceit of yours that blossoms over the land."

"One wonders." He grinned down at her, liking her spunk, relieved that she could jest with him.

"Does one?" She pushed at him, but he didn't release his hold, nor the warming massage he'd been giving her arms. Then she heard a five-year-old laugh. What if she hadn't reached him? Never more to hear that bell-like sound. All at once she hugged Hugh. Everything he did made her love him more. Love? Mayhap she would have to accept the feeling growing in her for the MacKay. That very day he'd saved her and the child of her heart. If he kept going on in such a manner she'd be swamped with love for him. "Thank you for what you've done."

"He's mine now, too. What father wouldn't want his son rescued, as well as his wife?" Hugh asked her.

When she felt his mouth on her wet hair, a shudder went through her. Hugh had tightened his hold even more. Mayhap he thought her chilled. Instead she burned with a wanting of him so great, it shook her frame.

"You could catch the ague from a chill, Hugh MacKay. You're not that long up from a sickbed."

"Aye, and you cared for me well." He kissed her cheek.

She trembled. "And you were a bear of a patient."

He laughed. "You're not to worry, wife. From now on Rhys will have a guardian, night and day."

Morrigan opened her mouth to thank him when the boy's shout drew her attention.

"Maman! Look! He's saved."

Morrigan struggled to free herself.

"No. I'll take you to the boy." Hugh carried her high on his chest, seeming oblivious to the delighted smiles of his men.

"Have you no shame? Your men look upon us." She couldn't define the wonderful heat, the sense of well-being.

Hugh glanced at her, his eyes warm. "Of course they do. They watch over us."

"'Tis unseemly to have them see us this way."

"Nay, 'tisn't. You're my spouse. 'Tis my job to care for you." His clasp tightened. "Be at ease, woman, you're where you belong."

"Your . . . your good health, you've just come out of sickbed," she gasped.

"I'm fine."

Breath caught in her throat, words stuck there. Morrigan didn't continue the argument. She'd known him a matter of weeks. She was firm in the opinion that Hugh MacKay could be set in his ways on some things. This was one of those and he wouldn't change. If she were truthful she'd admit she wanted his hold. Lord help her! "What is that, Rhys?" She pushed against Hugh's shoulders. "Let me down. I want to see the creature."

Hugh allowed her feet to settle to the ground, but kept his arm about her. He laughed. "Not a dog, exactly, lad. 'Tis a long-haired mastiff brought by Vikings when they followed Eric the Red to the many worlds he discovered. Some say they are a sea wolf, for though they are very strong and determined, they are usually gentle." Hugh went down in front of the animal, who growled softly. As though he hadn't heard the warning, he put out his hand, letting the animal sniff. "They are better than any man in the water and are tireless in heavy seas. I do not think this creature would've sunk beneath the waves, though I see marks of abuse on him, and no doubt he's been weakened by them." He looked at Rhys, his voice as stern as his features. "Now do you see that you must use greater discretion in your deeds?" At the boy's nod he smiled, rubbing the still damp ebony coat of the huge canine.

When one of the MacKays brought stores from the leather bag on his horse and began to feed the ravenous animal, Rhys begged to help.

The warrior looked at Hugh, who nodded.

Morrigan watched her husband go into detail about

the large animal with the long black fur that had curled into waves and ringlets with wet. The wide muzzle that stayed close to Rhys held a pair of wide-set intelligent eyes. He outweighed the boy by more than seven stone, but showed no antipathy toward Rhys. The boy was enthralled and made no comment when he was stripped of his clothes and garbed in warm tartans.

"Rhys—"

"Rhys will go with Eamon and Toric to the castle. The dog will accompany him. I will take you, madame."

"Stay!" Morrigan said to Hugh. "I would speak with them," she said, indicating his men.

She didn't see the astounded glances shared by the MacKays. Their lady stood her ground against the mightiest MacKay! Their smiles were tinged with respect, liking, admiration.

Hugh noticed, wry mirth touching his innards. "Then do so, wife."

Morrigan made a curtsy, her gaze touching all the men. "To all of you I give my gratitude." She looked at her son, then at the men nearest him. "Thank you, Eamon, and you, Toric, and the rest of you for your brave kind deeds this day. I can never repay you, but I shall always be in your debt." Morrigan turned her back on her high-handed husband, feeling irked at the way he delegated the happenings around him. To be chief of the clan was one thing. To lord it over her wouldn't be tolerated. She was so busy castigating him in her mind, she didn't notice the warm glances from the clan members.

Hugh watched his men, a mix of ire and amusement on his face.

"Our pleasure, milady," Toric answered. "Rhys has shown his mettle as a MacKay. His next lesson will entail discretion as dictated by his laird." Toric looked at the boy, who nodded.

Toric grinned along with the others. "Rest assured I shall watch him, milady."

"My thanks."

Before she could say more, Hugh lifted her and carried her back to his destrier being held by a young MacKay warrior.

"I would've said more to Eamon, as well."

Hugh shrugged, tipping her closer to his chest. "He's well able to handle things. Besides, you've bewitched enough MacKays for one day."

Agape, Morrigan stared at him. "I did no such thing. I merely thanked them."

"Merely? I think not. They were magnetized by you, as iron can be to special slate."

She smiled. "Foolishness. You saw what wasn't there."

He stared at her. "And are you posturing, wife, that you don't notice how you've enthralled my men?"

"Silly," she breathed.

"Nay, and I'll tell you true, I don't need more reasons to be taken by you."

"What?"

"Nothing."

She frowned, then tried to smile at the young man and

glare at her husband at the same time. "You are Kenneth, are you not?"

The young MacKay reddened and swept a deep bow. "And eager to serve you, milady."

"Thank you."

"You needn't charm all my men, wife."

Morrigan sucked in an angry breath. "I wasn't—"

Before she could finish he swept her up in front of the cantle on his steed and climbed up behind her. She could do little more than wave to Rhys, who waved back, though he made it obvious he was much more interested in listening to what Eamon was telling him about the dog next to him. "He should be put into a hot tub."

"He will be there before you, wife," he whispered.

Not sure she'd heard right over the pounding of horse's hooves, she didn't respond, though her heart sounded against her chest like a blacksmith's hammer. "My horse—"

"Will be brought by the men."

"Thank you."

"Our son dotes on animals, I'm thinking."

Morrigan's breath caught in her throat at the "our," happy that he'd not continued on with a discussion of her in a tub of water, yet shaken by the intimacy of his inclusion into Rhys's life. "Yes, he does. We . . . we didn't have many on our holding." She sighed. "He was lonely, you see. We were so isolated. Our . . . our neighbors were not near."

A wealth of meaning was in her words. Hugh cursed.

"What angers you, sirrah?"

"I can imagine how hard it was for you, how some might've shunned you for the sin of having a child."

She took in a shaky breath, biting her lip against the need to confess. Once again only the pledge she'd made to Gwynneth about the protection of Rhys kept her silent. "My family was a buffer."

"That you kept and raised the boy makes me esteem you, wife. I know it must've been lonely because you were far from your family."

Morrigan nodded, more touched than she could say by his words. "My holding was by the sea. My brothers had lands closer to Cardiff on the other side of Wales." She leaned back to look up at him. "For Rhys there'd been nothing except the grazing animals and a few children. The farmers were kind, but they returned, at some distance, to their own places in the evening. Most of them had a hard, busy life, eking out what they could from the stony soil."

"I see. You, as a royal of Wales, Princess of Llywelyn, were protected by the Llywelyn name. Under that umbrella was Rhys's guardianship as well, but, since you were thought by some to be a fallen woman, few had sought your company."

"Yes," she breathed, stunned by his plain speaking.

"I never trust the sanctimonious."

She exhaled. "Neither do I. I had the monies from my father, the holding, and a few family retainers, but there were few distractions or play for a young child. We had no pets. Rhys had few playmates until the twins. Now he looks on them as kin."

"I'm glad he has the twins, and they have him."

"And the dog." Morrigan chuckled, her angst melting in the heat generated by her spouse.

"Not to mention all the many other MacKays of similar age."

Morrigan laughed. "And the older ones who dote on the three. You have good people, Hugh MacKay."

"Thank you," he answered, his voice husky. "You are a most fascinating woman, wife."

Hugh grew contemplative once more. "And were your neighbors standoffish?"

Morrigan nodded, not affronted by the question because she sensed no censure in her husband. " 'Twas the way of it." It was like lifting a rock from her soul to speak thus with him. "So different in Wales. Too many of the close neighbors, though cowed by the power and money of the Llywelyns, were aloof."

"I can imagine. Persons of good standing often let me know how disappointed they were in me and my clan when we were renegades. Some didn't need words. Their looks were enough." He kissed her hair, muttering endearments in Gaelic.

"I really didn't mind for myself, Hugh. And, fortunately, for most of that time Rhys was too young to notice. Shortly before leaving Wales, he'd begun asking questions about his friends. It puzzled him that he couldn't play at their homes, nor would they come to his. It wasn't easy to talk with him about it. Of course I wasn't totally unhappy with the arrangement . . ." Her voice faded, her face reddening when she realized what she'd said.

Hugh kissed her cheek. "The solitude had ensured Rhys's anonymity."

"Yes." His understanding shook her. So much had opened her eyes. It'd been glaringly obvious, since coming to Castle MacKay, that Rhys had been starved for the masculine interest and input he'd received from Hugh's men. That he worshiped Eamon and Toric was obvious. That he eagerly sought out the twins and was glad they were family was quite as clear.

"What are you thinking?" Hugh said softly.

"Of Rhys, and how happy he's been since coming to Castle MacKay."

Hugh tightened his hold. "Then I vow you must stay."

Morrigan smiled. "It seems we will."

"Aye. I'll not let you go."

Her head whirled at his words, at the warmth of his hold, how his clasp didn't loosen as they ascended to the first glen at the base of the hill leading to Castle MacKay.

Hugh spoke to all those they passed, and was patient with every query. It astounded Morrigan how thoughtful he was with old and young, how all seemed important to him.

"Her ladyship is fine, Geordie. She tried to save our son in the sea." Hugh's words carried to others passing by, and they turned to tell others.

"Och, aye, and does it surprise ya', laird? She had the stuff in her from the beginnin'. Did ya' no see she was a stalwart one? Och! The noo. Ya' couldna been lookin'."

Morrigan stared, not comprehending the rapid Gaelic or the glowering looks. "They're angry with me?"

"Nay! See how they touch the tartan that covers you. They're in awe, wife, though they would wish that they had taken the risk, not you."

She twisted around to look up at him. "True?"

He nodded.

"Nonsense. I wouldn't have let them take the chance for me."

He chuckled. "They sense that, too. 'Tis one of the reasons they revere you."

Her face was still angled upward. The surprise on her features was obvious. Then she reddened and looked away again.

"Believe it, wife. I tell you true."

"I—I'm touched," Morrigan said, her voice breaking.

In moments there was only the sound of Orion's hooves hitting the stony path as they climbed the incline to the castle.

"Look at me," he whispered into her hair.

"I . . . I cannot turn my head." She could but she didn't want to look into those power eyes. He made her feel weak, and then she'd start remembering their wedding night, and that could make her damp in the most alarming places.

His hand came up and cupped her chin, edging it

around so he was looking down at her. "That doesn't hurt, does it?"

"No," she said on a wheeze of air. Those wild and wonderful eyes. They were a warlock's gaze to be sure.

"Do you know how I felt when I saw you in the sea? Seeing those waves breaking over you and pulling you deeper and deeper, farther and farther."

"I can . . . swim," she faltered, not answering his questions.

Hugh's hands moved over her, his strong thighs guiding the steed. His voice had a hoarseness, a harshness. "I wasn't sure I could get to you in time. If you had gone down would I have been able to find you right away? That tore through my head. I damned near killed my horse getting down there."

"I'm sorry. 'Twas not my intention to hurt this wonderful—"

"That has nothing to do with what we're saying, Morrigan. Dammit! I could've lost you." His voice rose though he tried to control it. In his agitation he kicked the destrier. Orion took umbrage and leaped up the last few feet to a stretch of flat land close to the gate.

Morrigan was thrown back against Hugh, gasping.

His arms tightened, keeping her there. "I have you."

"I know. About the other . . . I'm . . . I'm sorry. I had to—"

"I know. I just don't want you or the boy endanger like that. I would have you take Diuran with you w ever you go. And Eamon has already volunteered t the boy's mentor. He's a good teacher, and there's not much he doesn't know about the clan and its holdings. Father Monteith will continue to instruct him in his lessons, but Eamon will be his guardian. I'd trust him with my life. How do you feel about that?"

She nodded. " 'Tis sensible."

He chuckled.

She felt his lips pressed to her temple. More than breathing she wanted to turn her face to his, lift it for his kiss in that openmouthed way that he had. He'd turned her to fire once before, and she wanted the flame again. She'd never desired anything more.

"Why did you stiffen? Do my people frighten you?"

Morrigan focused on the group that'd begun to gather around them in the bailey, to follow them. "Oh . . . no. They've been most kind to me." She shook herself out of her reverie, smiling at those, letting Hugh answer the many queries about what had happened, why Lady MacKay was coming back all but unclothed to the castle.

"Where is the lad, Hugh MacKay?" The question came from the center of the group.

"Have no fear. He's with Eamon and Toric."

Their relief almost brought tears to Morrigan's eyes. What people the MacKays were! And she and Rhys belonged amongst them.

He put his mouth to her hair once more. "See. I'm not the only one who fears for you."

"I'm honored by the caring."

"As well you should be, milady."

She looked up at him, hearing the warmth in his voice. The heat in his look there had her all but sliding off Orion's back.

SEVEN

Today's today. Tomorrow, we may be ourselves
gone down the drain of Eternity.

Euripides

It'd all changed. Morrigan could feel it in the air that
crackled between them. Even the voices of those who
waited upon their trenchers seemed to have differing in-
tonations. No one stayed long in their presence. She and
Hugh were among the throng who always crowded into
the great room. Was it not custom for the laird and his
lady to eat among those who chose to join them?

"What think thou?" Hugh quizzed her in the ancient
Celtic that'd been the language once common in Scotland, though now it had dribbled into Gaelic. Wales,
alone, kept to the purest of the ancient speech, and used
it as the common language.

Morrigan smiled, aware of the effort it took him to
speak the ancient tongue, and how he honored her by
doing so. She had difficulty focusing on his question.

His eyes, as they'd done since their nuptial night, held her in thrall. "Of your people, milord?"

"Of all of it."

She wanted to dissemble, to find anything but the truth to tell the stalwart leader of the MacKays. "I like your castle and your people," she began, faltering when his smile twisted in mock query.

"That pleases me." He smiled, his eyes lingering on her form. "What else, wife?"

"I . . . I sense there's a change between us." With her face fiery red she stared into his eyes, watching that strong mouth curve upward.

"Astute of you, wife." He leaned toward her, holding his tankard to her lips. "I would have you quench your thirst, if it pleases you."

"It does."

"And you please me."

His words spilled over her like hot molasses, clinging, touching, somehow bonding her to him more than she'd been. "I . . . that's good."

"Isn't it. Will you drink?"

She hesitated, then sipped the strong ale. "Thank you."

He smiled, setting down the tankard near hers and lifting his hand to her unbound hair, letting his one finger twist through a curl. "I'm glad you're not wearing your headdress. Even the veil is too much."

" 'Tis permissible indoors. Of course, I can don it—"

"I would choose that you never cover the ebony fire of your tresses, love."

"You would?"

He nodded. "You're quite lovely, wife, in all parts and altogether."

She inhaled a shuddering breath. "Thank you."

With a slicing look he sent the troubadours, the attendants, the food servers on the run. More than one giggled or guffawed as they left.

With a mix of mirth and trepidation, Morrigan's mouth trembled into a smile. "And what do you do if they disobey?"

He grinned. "They don't."

"Why?"

He tipped his head. "Because I'm answerable to them. As chief I must see to their welfare and that of their families. They trust that I'll do the job. I can't betray them. Though they comprehend the enormity of the work they respect that the well-being of the clan is to the best interests of all. So, because I'm their chief, they will honor my chores, and give me fealty. If I let them down . . ."

When his voice trailed, she tilted her head. "What happens?"

"They have the right to choose another. I can either honor their choice or make war."

"What would you do?"

He grinned. "I'll not face the choice. Keeping one jump ahead of just doing well will keep me in place."

"And you represent what's best for the clan?"

He nodded. "At this point, yes." He leaned toward her, kissing the corner of her mouth. "Not that I don't love our discourse, Morrigan, I do. If the gods are good we will have long turns of the sun to discuss every facet of living. I'm eager for it. At this moment, I will admit something else holds my attention."

She swallowed. "And that would be?" A shaking began in her innards, spreading up her legs to her chest and along her arms. She wanted to hold him, to tell him about their night of love, how beautiful it had been, how much she wanted it to happen again.

"I want to be with my wife this night."

The trembling increased at her thighs and between. " 'Tis your right, though 'tis not full moon even as yet."

"The sun won't betray me," he told her in lazy heat.

"Will it not?"

He shook his head. "Like the sol it is, it will drop behind the hills and let me have a long night."

"You are used to having your way, gaining your wants in most everything, including this," she told him, her voice unsteady.

"Only with your blessing. I'd not frighten you since we've not been together." He kissed her ear. "Though I know you're not unversed in the ways of coupling, I would that you want it, too, with me, as I want it with you."

She turned and looked into the eyes so close to her own. " 'Tis true, I've known this coupling—"

"I don't ask for details," Hugh interrupted, a flash of anger there.

She hid a smile. His words released her from her growing anxiety about telling him. It could be put off since he'd rather not hear. One explanation would course into another, then another, carrying them back to Rhys's birth. She wanted him to know the truth, even if she was leery of explaining to him. Would he resent her secrecy? Would it change the warmth growing between them? If only she could explain the pledge she'd made to Gwynneth, how important it was to protect Rhys.

When he touched her cheek, she smiled at him. She wouldn't bare her soul now, not taint this fragile moment of their relationship. A burgeoning relief filled her. Mayhap she would chance it on the morrow.

Neither would she question his irritation. It gave her a wispy sense of power she'd rather not dwell on at present. It was a joy to be released from revealing her deception. If truth were told he would, no doubt, disbelieve it anyway, so why stretch the thin thread of closeness. It would be too brittle not to shatter if she told him; it was stretched to breaking as it was. "Then I'll give none."

His smile twisted. "Good." He moved closer on the bench. " 'Tis too busy here."

"No one is about, sirrah." She turned her head and scanned the great room.

He leaned forward again, pushing aside her silken

tresses and putting his mouth at her nape. "I know, but I would seek our couch, wife. What say you?"

Her body flamed, as did her face. "I would not gainsay you." She looked up at him. "Nor would I find it displeasing."

He was speechless.

"No answer, milord?"

"I can't phrase one," he told her, his voice hoarse.

She reached up and touched his mouth. "And are you so poleaxed, Hugh MacKay, by what I said? To hear the women of this castle discourse on you, 'twould seem you have a coterie of females each night, and never the same one."

Hugh grimaced. "They don't say that."

Morrigan was beginning to enjoy herself. "Shall I tell you what they say of your private parts?" She thought them quite beautiful, but she couldn't reveal that. When he looked even more taken aback, she chuckled. "Very colorful descriptions." It delighted her she'd shocked the mighty chief of Clan MacKay, that he stared at her more than a little dumbfounded. "What say you?"

Hugh glared. "You make sport of me." His smile was feral as he leaped to his feet, then leaned down to scoop her from the bench. "You're a most shocking lady, Morrigan MacKay."

She clutched his shoulders, not sure what he planned. "I'm surprised you would think anything shocking."

He strode across the great room, laughing, his elkskin boots making little sound on the stone floor. He stepped up into the entry, eyeing Dilla. "My lady has need of a tub of the hottest—"

" 'Tis been done, laird, and has been waiting this age. Twice the hotness has been refreshed," Dilla admonished, one eyebrow elevated. "The boy has been bathed and put to rest." Dilla inclined her head. " 'Twill be a miracle if our lady doesn't catch the ague."

"No, no, really, I'm fine." Morrigan pushed at Hugh to no avail.

"I'll see to it that she stays healthy, Dilla," Hugh told his attendant.

Dilla sniffed and stalked down the hall to the kitchen.

"She's annoyed with us," Morrigan whispered.

"Nay. Not with you, with me. She's ready to skewer me," Hugh said with a chuckle.

Morrigan watched him as he climbed the stairs, seeming as unaffected by her weight as by Dilla's words. He was the chief, but he took rebuke as his men would. She might never understand the wild Scot with the strange outlook who happened to be her husband. Not that she hadn't heard of him in Wales. Ballads were sung about him. Poets regaled one and all about the exploits of the great MacKay. No one had ever underscored his sense of fairness, only his ruthlessness, his canniness, his ability to conquer. No scribe had ever told of his goodness, his strong sense of justice and total commitment to his clan. The MacKay she knew had many more parts than the scholars could ever guess.

"Planning to help Dilla, wife?"

She chuckled as he threw his shoulder at their door, banging it open. "Oh, you've found me out. A spear through your middle. Foolish me. I thought to surprise you."

He smiled.

"The many women didn't describe you well enough, I'm thinkin'."

"How's that?"

"They didn't tell me of your versatility in handling them."

Hugh kicked the door shut, then strode to the middle of the room, his eyes on her. He paused near the bed, his head thrown back, laughter spilling out of him. "Christ's blood! What all did they prattle about me?"

Morrigan bit back a smile. "Methinks I should say nothing, else I shock you again."

"Worried about me, are you?" He let her slide down his body.

She nodded. "I would spare your sensibilities, good chief."

"Has anyone ever said you have a cutting tongue?"

Morrigan pretended to ponder. "Not more than a legion, I'm thinking."

Roaring with mirth, he looked down at her, a delighted look on his face. "Just when I think I know you, you show me more wondrous faces, Morrigan." He frowned.

"What bothers you?" Her words were out of breath because he'd begun removing her raiment.

"There're times when I'm almost sure I've known you." His brow furrowed. "Unlike the witches of Orkney and the priests of Rome, I don't believe in another life, except perhaps Valhalla, yet I have the surety I've seen you in my dreams even before I saw you on our nuptial day." His scowl deepened. "I've seen you since . . . during my illness. Fever can do that."

Morrigan caught her breath. He thought it'd been a dream he'd had, not the truth of the greatest lovemaking in the world, the most unforgettable moments of her life. She longed to ask him if he'd been swirled into the whirlpool of love as she had. If only she'd known that this day would come, that she could come to love and trust Hugh MacKay, she would've talked to him before the poison had taken him. She was more than sure she loved him now. Should she trust that love and tell him of Rhys's heritage? Nay, not yet. Soon, when they would sit together and talk. She'd not pondered a time when there'd be trust between them. It was a fool's game to conjecture. She'd been too afraid before their wedding of any Scot, especially the chief, to have ever confided anything to him. If only . . .

"What do you ponder that wrinkles your brow, wife?"

"Sometimes we feel a connection to another on first meeting." Such dissembling! Tell him. Words rose in her throat, then fell back again when he cupped her chin in his hand. "What?" she faltered.

"I want to look at you and be close to you."

"You may."

"I want you to want our joining as much as I."

Her skin trembled with the need to tell him how much she wanted him, how the night with him had changed her life, given her a belief that they could deal very well as man and wife. What would he say if she told him she longed to have his child? She lifted her hand to his face. "Shall not our feelings manifest themselves as . . . we . . . ?"

"Love each other?"

She nodded.

He smiled, then stepped back, letting her undergarments slide to the floor, pooling at her feet. He stared. "You're too lovely, wife." He looked toward the steaming water in the copper tub. "I would gainsay this, but 'tis for your good, and you must have your tub."

Disappointment rattled through her. " 'Tis a most alarming tub. How does one drain such a large one . . . that could hold two?"

His head swung back to her, his smile widening. "I hope I read your meaning, sweet one. I would want to hold you in the hot water until we grow hotter than the fire behind the tub."

She shook with the boiling in his gaze, her body reaching out for him, though she hadn't moved. "Doth sound most dangerous and intriguing," she said in Celtic. They were making love with words! She was wet for him already. Just the thought of the many times they'd loved that night, of all the ways he'd pleasured her and taught her to pleasure him. She felt weak and so very eager.

He leaned toward her, his mouth touching her nose. "You've no need to wish for it, wife. I promise 'twill happen. But, if you wish, I would seek a boon first."

Startled, she gazed up at him, feeling dizzy. He held her so tight in his gaze it was like another intimate embrace. "That would be?"

"I would have you call me Hugh."

A chuckle of relief escaped her. "I would grant that, sir . . . Hugh."

He laughed and caught her under the arms, bringing her close.

He carried her over to the tub, still holding her when he leaned down to test it. Then he lowered her, and stripped off his own raiment. Water sloshed over the side when he settled behind her. He began to lave her with the soft bits of fleece he took from the nearby washstand.

Feeling daring she took a section and turned, washing him with the fragrant soap, smelling of attar of roses, urging him to turn his back. He leaned against her, looking up at her.

"I don't usually wash with that soap." He scowled at what she held.

She laughed. "Don't growl, mil . . . Hugh. 'Twill fade before the morrow."

"Do not speak of the morrow. I want the night." He

leaned back, staring at her as she leaned over him. "I have a great heat for you, milady."

"You do?"

He nodded. At her wide-eyed look, he shook his head. "Don't fear this, Morrigan. 'Twill be right between us."

"I don't fear." She couldn't look away, feeling a sweet entrapment in his gaze. When his mouth moved upward, hers descended. It seemed to take forever; it was too slow for her. Reaching down, she caught his lips with her own, clinging.

The water swirled around them, the laving forgotten in the everlasting enjoyment of touching each other, of sliding limbs in and around the other. The slickness of their bodies was a heady inducement to more of the same.

Hugh groaned, feeling his body explode with want, the sensations wilder and hotter than the steaming water surrounding them. He caught her to him. "I want to go slowly."

Out of breath, she leaned against him. "Nothing with us has been slow."

"What do you mean, wife?"

Though his voice was husky with emotion she caught the puzzlement and stiffened. She was tempted once again to explain, but she was quite sure this wasn't the time. "I—"

"Never mind." Hugh muttered something else, then locked his mouth to hers.

Rising like Poseidon from the sea, he clasped her to him, spinning around, frowning.

"The laving cloths are there," Morrigan said, pointing to the stack not far from the bathing stool.

Hugh stepped out of the tub, grabbing a bunch and casting them over her as he carried her to the fire. "I'll not let you chill."

"I'm warm."

"I'm hot," he said.

She tried not to laugh. In truth it caught in her throat. When she looked up, he was grinning.

When he let her slide down his body, she reached for the drying clothes.

"No, let me, wife. I would relish the chore."

She didn't answer. Taking a cloth of her own, she began to minister to him in the same way.

Eyes met and locked as though there was no other in the world but the two of them.

"I would have you and give you joy," Hugh whispered.

"I would have you and give you joy," Morrigan said in Welsh, knowing it would take him longer to factor her words.

He smiled. "And do you know that's been accomplished?"

"What?" Not that she cared. Words dribbled from her lips. Little had meaning except his wonderful eyes.

"We've come together with words, good wife."

She nodded.

As though their bodies were starved for each other they pressed closer even as they dried.

As though another force propelled them they moved toward the bed.

Hugh lifted her into it and followed, his body tenting hers. "I won't hurt you," he whispered, his head between her breasts.

"I know," she murmured, her smile slipping when he lifted his head, studying her.

"You say strange things, Morrigan."

"Perhaps because strange things occur when we are together." When his mouth opened in query she moved her body against his, feeling breathless at the immediate fire in his eyes. "I like this," she murmured, quite sure she'd never been so unfettered. Her life since her father died had been uncertain, sometimes frightening. Now she felt more unafraid, more secure than she ever had. He would think it was because she was a woman who'd known a man, that she had experience in wonderful lovemaking. One day she had to tell him that the joy she'd found learning about body touching had come from him.

"So do I." He kissed the cleft between her breasts, letting his mouth slide back and forth between the soft, creamy globes.

When he took her nipple into his mouth and sucked, she called out, her body rising against his.

Cupping her buttocks, he held her while he ministered to both breasts, his mouth wet and warm, his body hardening.

Feeling dizzy, unhinged from any other person but Hugh, she could only hang on with hands, mouth, and eyes as he built the beautiful mountain they'd climbed once before, though he had no knowledge of it.

"Don't fear me, beloved."

"I don't fear you, MacKay," she muttered back, inching closer though they were already touching shoulder to toe.

He lifted his head, eyes ablaze. "I want your love, Morrigan."

She threw caution to the winds in the building fire. Limbs tingled with a want only he could assuage. "I want yours," she told him in short breaths, wondering at her audacity but not willing to call back the covenant.

Hugh stared at her. "What if I'd refused the king's request to wed you, my beauty?"

"You would've had a hole in your life, as I would've had in mine." Passion had given her power. The restraint she'd put on herself since Rhys's birth seemed cut loose, severed from the anchor that had kept her tongue in check. She smiled when he shouted with laughter. When he shook his head, she posed the question. "Such is not the way of it? This loving? To talk to each other as we are, to laugh?"

He shook his head. "None I've known." He smoothed the line in her forehead. "I've had other women, wife, as you've had men, but no one has titillated me so, no one has made me so hot, or made me want to know more about them. What say you? Think us to be a match?"

She nodded, tracing his mouth with her finger. "Having come from a country of upheaval, I'm not fool enough to think that all could go smoothly in any alliance, milord."

"Hugh," he murmured, brushing his mouth over hers.

She repeated his name. When her voice came out hoarse and squeaky she glared at his mirth, though she wanted to laugh. " 'Tis your fault I sound like a mouse among the rushes."

"Nay! You have a sweetness to your words." He grinned. "Not too many rodents have that."

She tapped his lips with her fingers. "You're not amusing, sirrah."

"Hugh," he whispered again, taking her mouth in a strong kiss that went on and on, fire licking through him. From the moment of seeing her, he'd wanted to make love to her. From somewhere deep inside him came his vision, his dream, of the two of them.

"Hugh?"

He ground his teeth. " 'Tis nothing, sweet one. You just take my breath away."

Morrigan hesitated. When she would've pulled back from him, he groaned and hugged her close.

"Don't leave me, wife."

"I don't wish to, but—"

"Then don't."

Her body began to undulate, her hips grinding against his aroused body. His hand began to massage her back, her belly, her legs and arms. She rubbed against him, letting her body slide up and down his, feeling a dizzying potency that rode her like a wild thing.

"Stop," Hugh said through his teeth.

Morrigan opened her eyes. "I displease you, milord?" He'd loved her actions on the night of their first joining. Had she done something wrong?

"Hugh," he muttered. "No, wife, you please me too much. I cannot love you in a slow seductive way when you move so. 'Twould go too fast." He swept his large hand over her hair. "All about you excites me, wife."

"I'm pleased."

His eyes narrowed, flaming over her. "And you shall be even more pleasured, my sweet one."

He laved her breasts with his tongue, moving down her middle. His tongue then moved in her navel as though he'd already begun the magic cadence that'd driven her mad on their spousal night.

When he moved lower, she remembered the wild beauty of the first time and she began to tremble.

He lifted his head. "Don't fear me, beloved, I would make you hot."

She reached down, pulling his head down to her again. "I would have it, too."

Then his tongue entered her and she would've screamed if she could've found the breath. Instead only a gasp escaped her as he began the wonderful dance that sent sheaves of fire through her body.

Moans mixed with endearments as each urged the

other to higher peaks of joy. Morrigan heard cries, not knowing if they were hers or Hugh's.

Her body began to shake as though with ague. She felt the same taut trembling in him. Clinging to him, she grew hotter as she whispered love words to him. Higher and higher he took her until she thought she couldn't stand any more.

In a burst of delight, colors flashing around them they rose together, clinging, joining, never wanting to part, hammered together by the very love that seemed to tear them apart in passion.

They held each other in the quaking aftermath, trying to gulp air, their bodies slick with love dew, their limbs flaccid.

When Morrigan felt his stillness she thought at first he was asleep, but when she looked up at him there was such an arrested air about him, it flashed through her he'd been disappointed. "What? Hugh?"

He embraced her, kissing her hair. "Look not so worried, wife. 'Tisn't you, my love, that makes me ponder. Our first time was all that Heaven could want." He squinted down at her.

"What?"

"I had the strange sensation that we'd loved before, that we'd joined our bodies at another time." He grimaced. " 'Twould sound unreasonable to you."

"No. It . . . it sounds most intriguing."

"Does it, wife?" With a crooked smile he leaned down and kissed her long and hard. When he lifted his head, his smile broadened. "You are as out of breath as I."

"I am."

"And my dreams of you do not distress?"

"No. I'm happy you dream of me." She buried her face in his chest, not wanting to face him. "And . . . and how did that make you feel?"

"Strange."

"No doubt."

He lifted her chin. "None has ever touched me as you did, my love. I tell you true."

Tears filled her throat. She couldn't speak.

" 'Tis not a time for sadness, my beauty."

"No. 'Tis joy I feel."

"As I do."

Curled in his arms, she let sleep overtake her. Loving this man, feeling so safe, she swore to God and all the gods and goddesses that she would protect her beloved Hugh.

Daybreak came with a kiss.

"Good morning, my love."

Morrigan smiled, lifting her hands to his face. When she went to move, her mouth dropped. "I . . . I fear we are connected."

Hugh grinned. "I know we are. I find joy in it."

"Then we must be content." Even as she said it, she could feel his hardening body within her.

He smiled. "You have a power, wife."

"Nay! 'Twould seem you do."

He laughed, his mouth running over her. "I could eat you at my trencher, wife, in very small bites."

Meaning trickled through her like fire. "Then there'd be no more of me."

"Ah! But that's why I content myself with nibbling only."

How could such mundane words have such heat? She was flushed with wanting once more. She pressed her breasts against him.

"Nay, wife, I canna' allow it. 'Tis too torturous for me."

"You like it not?" She was being coquettish. Foolishly so, since she was more than sure that he liked it very much. So certain was she that she twisted her body against his, so that he turned within her. It elicited a long, whispered curse from those lips so close to her own.

"No! Not yet." He held her tight.

"Yes," she whispered back, feeling the sensations erupt in her, gripping him hard, wanting the wild cascade that could shake her to her soul.

"Christ!" Hugh muttered, scooping her even closer, plunging into her as she rose to meet every thrust of his with her own.

In blinding light they came together, spinning out of the chamber, beyond any constellation, holding each other in the wonderful world only they could create.

"I will never let you go, wife," he mumbled into her hair.

Morrigan lifted her head with an effort, he held her so closely. "What if I say the same?"

"Say it."

The slumbrous look to his eyes had her trembling. "I will never let you go."

He laughed, catching her lips, his tongue tangling with hers. "Good," he told her when they were both breathless. "I will gladly give you the chains to bind me."

She laughed with him, then sobered. She reached up and traced his cheek with one finger.

"Why so solemn, wife? Did you not find joy in our coupling?"

"You know I did." She inclined her head, swallowing. "I have something to discuss with you."

" 'Twould seem it has great import to you."

"It does. It's about our marriage day. You see—" The sudden banging on the heavy wooden door to their chamber interrupted her.

"Maman? Don't, Eamon. It's all right. I can go in. Maman! Open the door. Someone has shut it too tight."

Hugh laughed when Morrigan stared at the chamber door, aghast. "I shall tell Eamon to let him in."

Morrigan yelped, skittering across the bed and off it, grasping at a coverlet when her husband stared at her. "Tell him to go away," she said through her teeth. "Stop looking at me."

"I can't. You're too beautiful, wife. I want you again."

Stunned, Morrigan glared at him. "Stop this, you'll kill yourself."

He grinned. "I'll chance it, milady."

"Not now."

"Maman!" Rhys bellowed. "Stop pulling me, Eamon. I can go in."

Morrigan had to clear her throat three times before she could speak. "I'm coming, Rhys. I . . . I was napping."

Hugh guffawed, earning a wifely scowl. "Eamon," he shouted. "Take him to the great room."

"I'm trying, Hugh. By God I am."

"I can go in, Eamon." Rhys was still shouting that as his voice faded. Eamon must have persevered.

In short order the chief of the clan and his bride met with the vociferous Rhys. Hugh looked content, lazy. His spouse looked distraught, shooting warning glances at him every few seconds. Those of the clan in attendance, and as usual there was a goodly number, looked at one another, struggling not to smirk.

Rhys came running toward them, flinging himself at Morrigan, then looking up at her, his brow wrinkled. "I told Eamon it was all right if I went into your room. It is, isn't it, maman?"

"Well—"

"Most of the time it is," Hugh interjected. "Some of the time it isn't."

"Oh." He seemed to struggle with the ramifications of that. As he was opening his mouth for another sally, Hugh continued.

"And of course those times you're not admitted you will go out on your horse with Eamon."

Rhys straightened in his mother's hold, a slow smile dawning. "O' co'se." He inhaled, then beamed at Morrigan. "I like him."

Used to his blunt pronouncements, Morrigan had to admit that Rhys still rocked her at times. Now was one of those. "I'm glad."

Rhys nodded. "Just as well, since we must keep him."

Morrigan bit her lip, not looking at Hugh and ignoring the smothered mirth sailing around the great room. "There is that."

Rhys nodded, grinning. "Now, I'll play kickball."

"What did you want, Rhys? You haven't told me."

He looked pained. "You told me I was to tell you when I left the castle. I told Eamon that, but he said it was all right not to tell you. I told him you'd wallop the two of us." He nodded sharply at the titters he heard, then grinned. "I like it here."

"I'm glad," Hugh said, his tone solemn.

"I thought so," Rhys said, equally solemn.

The coughed chuckles, barely masked giggles rose again, making the boy smile at those around them. "I'll play kickball now."

"You must be careful," Morrigan admonished.

"I'll keep my eye fixed to him, milady," Eamon reassured her.

Rhys nodded and ran from the room, Eamon at his heels.

The others in the great room seemed to disappear just as fast.

"I think you should've said that to Eamon," Hugh whispered. "My warrior looked harried."

"What is that?"

"You should've warned him to be careful. The boy will wear him out."

Morrigan shook her head. "Rhys is a handful."

"He's a lad. I wouldn't want our son to be any other way."

Morrigan looked up, smiling, catching his mouth with hers when he leaned down and kissed her. "Hugh . . ."

"I know you want to talk with me," he said against her mouth. "This is more pleasurable."

Someone coughed at the top of the steps leading down into the great room.

Morrigan would've pulled back if Hugh had let her.

Holding her close, he looked up, frowning. "Dilla?"

"Milord, I've been told there's a cavalcade coming. Would you have me prepare for guests?"

"Guests? We just had wedding guests crawling all over us. I thought I was to be alone with my bride," he grumbled.

Morrigan tried to ignore Dilla's smile but knew she'd reddened.

When MacKay looked around at her, noting her color, he frowned. Then his look lightened. "Rest easy, beloved. Dilla's had an armful of children, and Andra still chases after her."

Morrigan frowned.

Dilla laughed. "I'll see to all, milord."

"Don't make them too comfortable. I'll not want them around for long."

"Hugh!"

He whirled as though the sound of his name on her lips shocked him. "Should you call me by name at any time, I'll be there, beloved." He reached down and scooped her into his arms, carrying her out of the great room and up the stone stairs.

"Will you?" She circled his neck with her arms, holding him.

"I will. 'Tis my covenant to you."

She pressed hard against him when he entered their chamber and kicked the door shut. In moments he had her out of her clothes, kissing her, squeezing her bare skin with questing fingers.

"Hugh, we can't . . ." She wanted him so much she wished the arrivals to perdition.

"I know. I hate it." He kissed her again.

Morrigan forgot what she was going to say. "I . . . I should ready myself to greet our guests." She was repeating herself! Why did words seem so meaningless when all she wanted was Hugh's loving? She yanked at his tunic until it was removed.

He pulled back from her. "Do."

She inclined her head. "When you leave."

He shook his head.

Morrigan looked down at herself. "You must. I'm unclothed."

"I know. I unclothed you. How could I forget?" He moved back from her, his gaze going up and down her form.

She felt deliciously hot, but not shamed or embarrassed. His body was so beautiful and she loved looking at him.

Sighing, she backed to the bed and sat down. "We must be sensible. We cannot have what we had before when others expect our presence."

He approached, leaning over her, bracing his hands on the bed to both sides of her. " 'Twas wondrous what we had. I would have it again and again."

She gasped when he lifted her up once more, holding her aloft in front of him. "Sirrah . . ." At his shake of the head, she started once more. "Hugh—"

"Ah. Better." He touched his mouth to hers, his tongue intruding. They clung as though they couldn't let go.

Morrigan sighed into his mouth when he pulled back.

"I don't want it to end, either, beloved." He kissed her again. "Soon we'll be alone." He released her, grimacing. "I can't look at you without wanting you, wife." He scowled toward the door. "See to the fools who interrupt us. I would talk to Toric."

Eyes widening, Morrigan stared after him. "But . . . but you must greet—"

"I'll be there, wife," he called back.

"You're not fully clothed," she whispered, not sure why the thought of Dilla or any other seeing him that way would anger her.

After his departure a vacuum ensued when nothing seemed alive or moving.

Then, like clockwork, the castle was put in motion again. Morrigan donned a robe, sighing at the joy in her life with the wonderful MacKay.

In moments hot water was being trekked across to the caldarium. Morrigan had heard of the special rooms for hot baths that had come with the Romans when Hadrian's wall had been built. She knew that there were a few Welsh who had them. She'd never seen one until coming to Castle MacKay.

" 'Tis ready, milady," Mavis said, peeking at her from the aperture leading to the caldarium. "If you would prefer I will lave you—"

"I will do it, Mavis. Thank you."

The attendant beamed. "The boy is with Eamon, milady. The guests have been given tidbits at the trencher board. Garments have been taken to the laird. I will put bricks on your bliaut, milady. All is in readiness, as you would wish."

"I thank you." Morrigan couldn't help but like the friendly MacKays. Nor could she fault the seeming ease with which they organized everything. None seemed to hurry or fret, but a great deal was accomplished in short order, and done well.

She hurried through her laving, wondering if the rules

of etiquette used in Wales were the same as those of Scotland. She would need to have instruction so that she wouldn't offend by omission of act or commission of error.

She washed as she pondered this, astonished at her body's tenderness. A vision of Hugh rose in her mind, their coupling a colorful memory.

Hurrying as best she could, she dressed with Mavis's help in a very plain cloth of Cathay gown with an embroidered bliaut over it. The rich sea green made her hair glow with a thousand red lights through the ebony. Though she wore little jewelry, her spousal ring, surrounded as it was with diamonds, was opulent enough. Her head cover was a filmy veil with a circlet of gold holding it in place.

The attendant returned to put the chamber in order.

"You are most lovely, milady," Mavis remarked, her tone shy. "All MacKays are most proud of your beauty and acumen."

Unaccustomed to compliments from her rough-hewn family, Morrigan felt emotion rise in her throat. "I thank you for your kind words." She reached out and squeezed Mavis's hand, then turned toward the door. She missed the look of wonder on the attendant's face.

She descended the stairs almost at a run, wondering who it could be, wishing she'd asked Mavis.

Dilla was at the bottom. " 'Tis Lady MacKenzie and Lord Kieran who await you. They seem extremely overset. I've given them refreshments."

Morrigan touched Dilla's arm. "Thank you. Lord MacKay is with them?"

Dilla bit her lip. "Not yet. 'Tis the mare, you see. She's about to foal, and her time is never easy."

Morrigan wanted to laugh, but didn't. Being Welsh she realized how important the equines were, and how some were more dear than others.

Dilla moved aside and Morrigan moved to the top of the step leading down to the great room. Lady MacKenzie was there, threading her hands together. Kieran had crooked his arm on the high mantel, resting his forehead there.

Morrigan paused. Mother and son did, indeed, look overset. "Good day to you."

Lady MacKenzie was on her feet, about to rush toward her, arms wide, when she stopped, eyes dilated as she looked at Morrigan. "Surely 'tis a new fashion in mourning."

"I . . . I beg your pardon." Morrigan looked at a very surprised Kieran, whose gaze seemed locked to her raiment. "I don't understand."

"Do not try to be brave, milady," Kieran said, his strong voice solemn. "We heard from the runners, and came as soon as we could."

Lady MacKenzie opened her arms, her smile sad. "We've come to solace you, my dear."

"You have?" Morrigan tried to think who could have expired in her family.

"Yes. We've heard all the details from the runners."

"Runners? What runners? For what?"

Lady Maud MacKenzie studied her, then eyed her son. "This has been too much for you, has it not, poor dear?"

"Madame, I—"

Hugh burst into the room, smiling at her.

Lady MacKenzie gave a sharp cry and swayed.

Morrigan rushed forward. She and Kieran reached the woman at the same time, catching her as she swooned.

"Christ!" MacKay smacked the gong to the side of the wide entrance to the great room. "I've not had that effect on females."

Morrigan looked over her shoulder, frowning. He shrugged.

Dilla came running, eyeing her laird.

"Get something for her ladyship. She's fainted."

Dilla nodded once and was off at the run.

Hugh then moved past his wife and Kieran, lifting Maud into one of the heavy fireside chairs so much favored by Egyptian builders.

Morrigan dabbed her hanky in cool wine and wiped Maud's forehead. "I think it was you that worried her, Hugh."

"Why?"

Kieran glanced away from his mother for a moment. "Runners came from the king telling us you were killed."

"What? How could that be? No one knew I was ill but the clan. And none thought me dying."

Kieran shrugged. "I could wish that such a message had never been sent. It devastated my mother."

"I'm so sorry," Morrigan said, looking up, feeling confused. "I don't know how that happened, or how such a rumor spread to the king's runners. If I had known such a thing was happening, I would've stopped such gossip." Her glance slipped to Hugh and back again. "You see I was closeted with him all through the first night. In the days following his affliction he needed constant care. I never even thought to send messages." Contrite, Morrigan looked back at the quivering Lady MacKenzie, whose eyes had fluttered open. "Lie still, dear lady. Soon you'll be put to rights."

Kieran nodded. "I understand. No doubt 'twas one of the handmaidens who sent word."

Morrigan inhaled, her voice shaking. "'Twas a terrible time. Sometimes I didn't think I would save him."

"I beg pardon. 'Tis not like me to swoon. I couldn't credit my joy at seeing Hugh . . ." Tears welled in Maud's eyes.

"Shhh. All is well," Morrigan comforted.

Hugh watched her, then his gaze went to Maud. "Morrigan is right. Be at ease." Questions left his mind when he noted the haunted, pain-filled look on her face. Maud had been through plenty. Her husband had expired early, his treasures scattered among various lenders. There would've been even less than the castle they had and the small holding if Ermuth hadn't expired in his bed from overeating. None of the MacKenzies had ever been too stable. Ermuth had taken it another step and wagered on anything that moved until he'd depleted his inheritance beyond repair. Now she'd received another blow. She'd thought him dead. Then he appeared in front of her. "Don't fret yourself, Maud. All will be well."

"Thank you, Hugh. Your wife is a most caring female."

"She is, indeed." His heart swelled in his chest as he looked at Morrigan. "To be sure she is an excellent purveyor of medicaments. My life would've been forfeit had she not been so knowledgeable. You are in good care, Maud. All the MacKays trust Morrigan."

Morrigan's smile was fleeting. "Some do." She looked down at Lady MacKenzie, gratified to see color in her face, the glazed look gone from her expression. "I will order a special tea for you, milady, if you please."

"Thank you. A restorative would be kind."

Morrigan nodded and turned when she saw Dilla hovering in the doorway. She made her request and the other woman answered.

"I will get what you need, milady."

"Thank you." She turned back and saw Kieran smiling. "What?"

"You trust your new family, I see."

Hugh said nothing, his arms crossed in front of him.

Morrigan's gaze skated off him and back to Kieran. "They are MacKays, and therefore to be trusted." She felt Hugh's warm glance. When Kieran laughed she smiled.

"You've indoctrinated her, Hugh," he said, grinning, his relief at his mother's smile obvious.

"Nay! She saw the light herself."

Maud chuckled, trying to sit upright.

"I think you should stay still, Mother," Kieran warned.

"I shall. Ah, here's your woman with the mixtures."

Morrigan smiled. "Thank you, Dilla." She took the small cloth bags from her, going to the fireplace. She spooned small measures into the kettle that steamed between Dilla and herself.

Pouring some into a cup, she carried it over to Lady MacKenzie, holding it while the other woman sipped. When Maud sat back, Dilla came forward and pushed a stool in front of Lady MacKenzie's chair. Then she placed the steaming kettle, some cloths, and a plate of tiny scones on a small stool.

Lady MacKenzie smiled, lifting her cup again and sipping. "This is a delicious brew, Morrigan. You must tell me how 'tis fashioned."

" 'Tis a mix of teas, milady, from far-off lands, plus a good share of sassafras to keep the body balanced."

Maud nodded. "I know the worth of such mixes."

When Dilla turned to go, Morrigan followed her. She felt Hugh's stare though she didn't look at him. "Dilla, did someone send messages about the laird's illness?"

Dilla frowned. "I'm not sure. I know there was consternation among the people. Even if nothing was sent abroad, the word went out, far and wide, to be sure. Some thought he was lost to us." Her glance went past

Morrigan to her laird. "Woe to us if we lose him. So many covet the treasures of Morgan." She looked back at Morrigan. "You saved him for us. The debt can never be repaid, milady."

"Thank you." She touched Dilla's arm. "I could wish that no such message had been sent to Kieran's parent. She was most distraught."

"That she was."

Morrigan wanted to ask Dilla more, but in deference to her guests she couldn't linger.

Dilla smiled. "We love him, as you do, milady." She turned and hurried back to her kitchen.

Morrigan was frozen to the floor, knowing full well her mouth had dropped, her heart had stopped. Did all the MacKays know? No! How could it be? She was Welsh. She hid her feelings well. She sighed. Of course it was foolish to love a wild Scot. Too late—

"What ails, my love?" Hugh said, coming up behind her, his mouth in her hair.

"Ah, nothing. I was listening to Dilla."

He leaned down and caught her lower lip between his teeth, his body hiding her from the MacKenzies. "I would have you give me the same engrossing attention, love."

EIGHT

It has been related that dogs drink at the river
Nile running along, that they may not be seized
by the crocodiles.

Phaedrus

Edward Baliol was cross. No! He was damn well furious, though he struggled to hide it. Years of warfare when he hadn't known foe from friend had taught him to school his features, give no thoughts away. Right now it took every facet of his being to keep him from screaming the castle down, calling out his army to smite those who would gainsay him.

He'd waited a sennight for his most prestigious and powerful lord, a man reputed to have larger coffers than his own. Not that he would ever know for sure. The MacKays were a canny bunch who kept many secrets concerning their clan among themselves. It'd been a thorn under more than one skin, including the king's, that not a hint of MacKay private business was bruited about. Not natural! Were there no tale-wagging MacKays?

One close-kept knowledge that annoyed him more than any other was the hiding place of the huge treasure that many had sought, none had found. Edward had no doubt that Hugh MacKay was in control of that hoard just as he was in charge of his clan. None of his operatives who scoured the countryside when he'd been at war with MacKay had ever turned up a clue. There was no way of secreting a spy in the clan. MacKays knew family and kin from generations back. Fifth cousins were as known to them as brothers were.

Despite his ire, Edward admired the MacKays. They, too, had learned their lesson at the hard taskmaster of war and defeat. At another time he might have commiserated with their leader on the similar vagaries of running a country and a clan. Not now. Edward was in no mood to excuse or discuss anything except the topic that had roiled his spirit for days. He'd ordered Hugh MacKay to present himself at once. In fact, he'd wanted him in front of him the very day the message was delivered, though it might have killed a horse to do it. That had been Edward's plan. MacKay had had other ideas, it would seem.

Hugh entered the great room of the king's castle and knew the monarch was in bad tid.

"You tarried for a good reason, I'll be bound," Edward said, his mouth hard.

Hugh nodded. "And you are annoyed, good royal, unless I read you in error."

"You don't. My temper simmers."

"I was with my wife, first as her patient, then as her husband."

Edward's brows drooped lower. "I'd heard you nearly crossed over to the other side, Hugh. What think you? Did Heaven or Hell await you?"

"Hell, of course. I have Heaven with my wife."

Edward sat back, a reluctant smile on his face. "You rogue. Only you would end up with a beauty, one who has already produced a son, and will no doubt deliver another in time. Not for you the fry-faced harridans who dog much of the aristocracy."

Hugh grinned. "Forsooth, I agree that there must be an angel at my beck and call. How else could I have managed to find an earthbound one!"

"You've become like the sonnet makers, I'll be bound."

Hugh laughed. "If it would please her, I would try it, though I think I'd make poor work of it."

"I would that I could command you as strongly." When Hugh opened his mouth to retort, Edward waved him to silence. "I know, I know, you couldn't be in sickbed and here at the same time." His smile twisted. "Though some of your foes would gainsay me. They believe you're in league with the King of Darkness, himself. Ergo, you could be two places at once."

"They'd be wrong. My wife's good ministrations and beauty kept me housebound."

"I would still like a touch of your wife's power."

"So would I. She has well and truly caught me and she has won my people to her side."

Edward chuckled. "Will I have to fight all of Wales next?"

Alerted, Hugh settled back in his chair. "You're contemplating war?"

"My English cousin, the other Edward Rex, has been making unpleasant sounds. His voracious hunger for lands and treasure has given him a wandering eye."

"I thought his ravenings were directed toward France."

"So they are, but I sense he would make all of this land his"—Edward swept his hand around his great room—"before crossing La Manche to tackle our Gallic cousins."

Hugh frowned. "He'll set the world afire, and there'll be no quenching it. I'll not see one MacKay sacrificed for his greed."

Edward smiled. "I have your covenant you'll not fight with him, at his side and with his banner."

"You have." Hugh paused. "You should know I have no taste for war, now. MacKay holdings are where they belong. My people are knitting their lives back together. I'll not see all the striving and good works raveled for Edward of England or for what doesn't belong to him."

Edward sighed. "That righteous remark has not stopped many."

"No, but I tell you this. No MacKay is grist for Edward's mill. I'll let him know that. Too many of mine have perished. Too much of what was ours was taken back at too great a cost. There'll be no MacKays on English Edward's sacrificial altar."

Edward Baliol sat back. "They could come at us without warning."

"No, they couldn't," Hugh averred, stretching his long legs in front of him. "MacKay ground is covered and watched." He cocked a brow. "So is all land that abuts it, including royal holdings."

"I see." Edward chuckled. "You're a rogue."

"You repeat yourself."

"I do." Edward frowned. "You tell me you're protected."

"I am."

"Yet someone, or more than one, breached your defenses on the night of your espousal, Hugh."

Hugh glowered. It stung to know he'd let his guard down to some degree, even when he'd thought to have covered every hole a foe might find. More than one MacKay had come to him decrying the deed that almost finished him. His people would go to battle in an instant if they discovered who his assailant had been. Hugh would never let them. He would handle the dog himself.

It'd become borne upon him in the long days of convalescence, when he'd had time to ponder the deed, that the enemy could've been within the confines of the MacKay holding, even as his bride had been. Had the small army of Welshmen who'd accompanied Morrigan to his lowland holding been hiding the would-be assassin? Had the perpetrator been among other guests? Reason told him it was probable. A gut voice protested his wife would have had no part in the attempt on his life. He'd pulled apart more than one scenario, studying it, then another. His research was enough to absolve his wife of any blame. She'd put herself at great risk, medicating him, letting Diuran know what she was doing. His wife had courage— The royal's throat-clearing drew his attention. "I was thinking of Morrigan," Hugh explained.

Edward smiled, shaking his head. "What a boon I've given you."

"You have."

Edward hesitated. "You don't think her culpable? Able to be part of the assassination attempt?"

Hugh drew in air, taking his time. "She risked much to save me when she might've made myriad excuses about my death. My people are not that easily duped. They've had years of survival training when our entire clan was threatened. They suspect most persons unless they are blood kin. Still, they trust her. I trust her."

Edward nodded. "You don't know the culprit, do you, or have an inkling of his identity?"

Hugh shook his head. "I will, no matter how long it takes." He eyed the king. "An unforeseen happenstance saved me, and my wife. I won't let either of us suffer such a brush with death in the future."

Edward cocked a brow in query. " 'Twould seem you think a miracle occurred."

"Not far wrong. If I believed in such, I would label this one as miracle."

"Explain."

"Had she taken some of the same brew, at the time I did, we'd have both gone down into deep malady. No one would've heard our groans through the heavy door. Even if they had they could've been too late to save us, or not had the knowledge to counteract the poisons."

Edward inclined his head. "There's truth in what you say."

Hugh nodded.

Edward rubbed his chin. "Even so most wouldn't have intruded at the sound, figuring that the bride and groom had begun their pleasures anon," Edward said in sour humor.

Hugh grimaced, his head jerking up and down in rough assent. "And none would've attended us until it was too late."

Edward steepled his hands and looked at Hugh. "And the word went out you were dead."

Hugh nodded. "Not just my godmother heard this. Throughout the Highlands—"

"And England—"

"—the messengers went far and wide. Someone planned my end with great care, and the announcement to all and sundry." He frowned.

"What?"

"I'm still not convinced who the target was."

Edward frowned. " 'Twas you."

"Or 'twas Morrigan . . . and mayhap the boy."

"Why? The boy would not taste your spirits."

"What if some was given to him as medicine after we were taken care of?"

" 'Tis farfetched, Hugh. What has the lad? Naught but the name of Llywelyn. True it has the power of persuasion in Wales, its personages listened to in all considerations of how Wales does business. It ends there, for there's little else for him to inherit, except through his mother. Her monies and holding will be his. That would not compare to the Llywelyn brothers' holdings."

Hugh shrugged. "Not so. He's my heir . . . in part."

Edward frowned. "There is that, but what of your wife?"

"What of my wife?" The vision of Morrigan rose before him, in his bed, spread beneath his gaze, her warm creamy skin her only cover.

"She has little of value, though she is regent of Trevelyan . . ." Edward's eyes narrowed. "You think this endangered her? On your spousal day? She requested the regency."

"I know. To my knowledge there is no one who would contest her right to be such, nor think her claim without merit." He glowered. "I will admit the thought preys upon me."

Edward sighed. "I cannot see the danger there. In estates that lie fallow for generations, in much of Wales, it is regnant populus, not regnant rex, that assumes power." Edward's smile twisted when Hugh's harsh laugh cut through his words.

"'Tis true. Many are as independent as my wife."

Edward grimaced. "Those wild and woolly Celts rule themselves in that iron countryside."

Hugh shrugged. "What they do in that godforsaken land matters little to me unless they mount a force against MacKays."

"And your king, surely," Edward offered, his tones dry.

"Surely." Hugh's voice was touched with the same irony.

Edward's lips tightened. "I would need to know, at once, if they mounted a campaign. Any hesitation in countering could cost much." He showed his teeth. "English Edward would foster such a move to bring me to heel."

"Your people who move among the Celts would tell you of such."

Edward's lemon smile acknowledged the hit. There wasn't much Hugh MacKay didn't know about the goings on throughout the land. "Why doesn't it surprise me that you would know about the network of spies I've had to spread through the countries and holdings abutting the royal ones? Mayhap your wife would tell us about the underground of Wales."

"Mayhap my wife could have loyalty to her own. She's not been in Scotland that long that she should eschew all her past life and loved ones," Hugh pointed out, his tone even.

Edward nodded. "And you wouldn't push her to do?"

"No."

Edward's mouth twisted in a smile. "I would not dice with your spouse. She fears nothing and chances all."

Hugh nodded, a shiver of trepidation washing over him as he recalled her in the sea trying to reach Rhys. "Too plucky by half."

"What means this?"

Hugh related the tale of her daring.

"I would think on this." Edward scowled. "Perhaps 'twasn't an accident that the Viking water dog was there. Such a thing could entice any lad—"

"I've pondered such a happening."

Edward ground his teeth. "In one fell swoop the boy and the woman could be gone, pulled to Poseidon's castle by the tides. The blame could've been aimed my way . . ." Edward faltered at the rage on Hugh's face. "I would not have you think I'm not mindful of what a loss it would've been to you."

"Greater than you know." Hugh had no illusions about Edward's order of importance. His survival as king surmounted any obstacle, preceded any other venture in priority. Hugh's first thoughts were still the MacKay clan. These had expanded to include one glowing-eyed wife, twins, and one mischievous son. He'd never thought about commitment except to clan. Since the advent of Morrigan and her son his attitudes on much had changed, including fatherhood and being a husband.

"If there is chicanery among the Welsh, if there's a plan abroad to sacrifice the woman so that they could undermine my throne—"

"If any come at Morrigan, from any direction, there will be war, and I'll lead it," Hugh vowed. "There'll be no holding back. None will survive the assaults Mac-Kays will make on those who've threatened my lady. That's my covenant."

Edward studied his greatest warrior. Even he, who trusted MacKay, quivered under the threat. "Please believe I do understand."

Hugh eyed his monarch through a red haze of fury, his mind turmoiled at the thought of his wife and his three children in peril. "I'll not tarry long with you. We'll make our plan and then I return to MacKay."

Edward nodded.

"Milady, I think I see horsemen yonder, though I know not the insignia," Diuran remarked, his voice low.

Morrigan stretched in her stirrups. "I think 'twould be Welsh, though I'm not sure. Unless the sun fools me, I see the green and black of my family's guidon . . . and perhaps one other." She smiled when she saw MacKays come out of the woods surrounding the cortege. "We are ready for all who come at us, are we not, Diuran?"

He chuckled, settling his arms over his steed's neck. "That we are."

She laughed and cantered around him, checking to see that Rhys and Eamon were at her back.

Eamon allowed Rhys to follow his mother, then pulled up next to Diuran. "And did you hear how she referred to MacKays as Us?"

Diuran nodded, grinning at his cousin. "She is a wonder, our lady is. No wonder the laird cherishes her as he does."

Eamon nodded, his eyes on Rhys. "And he is going to be a great MacKay, as will be Conal."

"To be sure."

"I believe little Avis will grow to be a most comely lady." Eamon reddened when Diuran laughed.

The two galloped to catch up to their charges, their eyes checking on the outriding MacKays, who nodded back at them. All would be well. Their lady and the lad would be protected.

Morrigan was taken aback when she saw her cousin Cumhal. First she was elated, but when she studied his somber visage she was alarmed. She urged her steed forward, pulling up short in front of her relative. "What goes?" she said in Welsh.

"Goll has been taken. We're to ransom him." His face twisted when he faced the Scots who now surrounded him. He turned in his saddle until he looked at each group of grim men. "Do they think to cause me fear?" he asked, his Celtic words filled with disdain.

"They seek to protect the wife of their laird and his adopted son." She took a deep breath. "And we have given our name to two others, you should know."

Cumhal blinked, ignoring the last part. "Then 'tis true the boy is heir to MacKay?"

Morrigan nodded. "To some of the estate. He's an adopted MacKay, as are the other two."

"But he is still a Llywelyn, and I hope you've so informed him," Cumhal growled.

Morrigan's chin lifted. "All the years until this one you've shown little interest in the boy. Now you wish to claim him as Llywelyn?"

Cumhal swallowed. "I may have been remiss in my duties—"

"May? There's no question you were neglectful."

Cumhal winced, eyeing the MacKays. "Not so loud, cousin."

Morrigan sighed. "They are my guardians. Rest assured they won't berate you."

Cumhal nodded, licking his lips. "I'm glad the boy has been accepted, Morrigan."

"I hope so. You can see the sense of the course MacKay has taken with the boy, and the other two, I'm sure." At her cousin's reluctant nod, she was sure he didn't see, but like most of her iron-necked relatives he'd not admit to it. "There is little of the Llywelyn estates for him to inherit, except for monies and isolated holding, ergo, if he inherits a portion of MacKay wealth his future is secured. True?"

" 'Twould seem so."

Though his scowl didn't clear Morrigan could tell by the arrested gaze that her cousin did see the merit of Rhys being a MacKay. Being a tightfisted Llywelyn, Cumhal would not want any others to delve into the family coffers lest some touch his portion. If the boy was given enough by MacKay there'd be no need for him to search out more among the Llywelyns.

Morrigan was satisfied she'd get no more protests on the subject of Rhys being a Llywelyn. She patted his arm. "Come, cousin, let us go back to the castle. You shall be refreshed as will your coterie, then we'll talk strategy." Morrigan waited.

Finally Cumhal nodded. He was the most taciturn of her many cousins. He could be truculent and bull-headed, and he could set folk's backs up without trying hard.

The other side of him was his honesty. Morrigan had never known him to take unfair advantage of anyone. He and Morrigan had become close when he'd come to her father's holding to be trained as a lad.

Unlike some of the lesser-connected Llywelyns who came from the far country, he didn't subscribe to the narrow uses of women as playthings and birthing ob-jects. Neither he nor Goll had ever looked upon her fa-ther as a buffoon, not to be reckoned with, because she'd been educated and trained to such a high degree. There'd been some among the Llywelyns who'd dared to voice such. Her brothers had shouted them down, and threatened them with dire consequences if they ever dared gainsay their father, head of the family Llywelyn.

Yet there'd been controversy when the pact with England and Scotland had been put forth.

Goll and Cumhal had been voted down in the family's decision to offer her to MacKay. They'd both been vehemently against it, arguing that there were other methods to be tried before offering up their cousin as a sacrifice. They'd apologized to her and to her brothers once the final decision had been made. Morrigan had thanked her cousins for their support. Others in the family had offered her condolences that she would be married to a Scot. More than one had whispered that she, a fallen woman, was lucky to snag anyone. She should marry the Scot to solidify their positions. The sacrifice was worth it.

Morrigan had longed to point out a few things to the unctuous Felim, older brother to Goll and Cumhal and designated head of the eastern portion of the family. He was in charge of all when her brother Califb or Drcq were away, or her cousin Boyne from Hibernia was not in residence. Felim, to her knowledge, had never made a sacrifice of any kind for anyone or anything connected to Llywelyn. She'd often wondered how sour he would be if she ever pointed out how happy she'd been at Castle MacKay.

That Felim felt he could send a demand of any kind through Cumhal was obvious. Since he'd not bothered to be part of the Welsh contingent who attended her nuptials she knew her worth to him. Now, because something had happened, she was needed to perform a service, anything that wouldn't involve effort from him, or monies. No doubt it had to do with gold. Unless she missed her guess, Felim would know she was regent to Trevelyan. He and some of the other Llywelyns had tried to lay claim to the large and well-endowed estate because of their connection to Gwynneth. They'd been stymied by Edward Baliol's declaration on her espousal day. If he intended to ask her for Trevelyan gratuities, he'd be disappointed. Morrigan had no intention of letting any of the sticky-fingered Llywelyns slice, dice, and cube the estate belonging to Rhys.

They arrived back at Castle MacKay. Refreshments were seen to by Dilla. In short order, Morrigan was alone with her cousin in the great room.

"Does Felim have a plan?" She asked this, full knowing that Cumhal's older brother rarely had anything in order much less a layout of anything. He was more inclined toward chaos.

Cumhal's mouth twisted in mirth. "Strategy is not my brother's strength."

"I agree. I was hoping he'd changed. Since he hasn't and you are here as his emissary, may I assume that he would like a . . . contribution of some sort from me or the MacKays?"

Cumhal exhaled. "Not from the MacKays, but he does wish something from you, cousin."

"Go on."

Temper began to simmer in Morrigan as Cumhal went through the long list of reasons why she must sign her regency over to Felim. "And he will administer the estate, and pay back any monies that need to be borrowed from it for the ransom."

Cumhal had been striding up and down the great room, his reluctance obvious.

"And you think this is wise, Cumhal?"

He hesitated. "I could never believe that it is just to divide the portion belonging to another's estate." He grimaced. "But there is no living Trevelyan to suffer." His features hardened. "My twin brother is at risk. We must do all we can to free him from the yoke that holds him by the throat."

"And who holds this yoke?"

"I know not."

"How is that? Surely those who hold Goll must have sent some sort of missive, if only to inform you they held your brother."

"That's true, they did do that, but there was nothing about the identity of those who held him."

"Strange that Felim didn't inquire about such. I know he hates to part with a pence of his own."

"That's true." Cumhal looked thoughtful. "I've been remiss. I should've asked questions of Felim. If truth be told, I was too worried to think straight. When Felim commissioned me to contact you, I was glad to do something positive."

"I understand your worry, cousin. I would that we

know more. Where is he being held? How much gold is required to free him?"

Cumhal shook his head. "I should know all this. I don't. I'm not sure that Felim does."

"And is Goll well?"

Cumhal looked startled. "How would we know that? I suspect they might've tortured him. 'Tis expected. We'd not be informed of that."

Morrigan bit back a retort. So reckless. "Cousin, there must be enemies of Llywelyns known to you and Felim. Why wasn't a well-armed contingent sent to each holding?"

Cumhal flinched as though she'd struck him. "I've acted hastily and without thought."

Morrigan nodded. "So you have. If Goll is waiting for you to rescue him, he must be resigned to death."

Cumhal reddened, his mouth a hard slash. "We had no monies."

Morrigan tutted. "Don't try to fool me, cousin. Felim should've sold his cattle. Those destriers of his are worth much." She also knew that Cumhal had little monies of his own. When Felim had assumed control of the eastern branch of the family he'd bequeathed his brothers little. Goll had a small fortune inherited from a godmother. Cumhal had very little.

Cumhal stopped, his mouth drooping. " 'Tis true. The penny-griping fool. He could've done such."

Morrigan turned away with the pretense of pouring more tea. She didn't want her cousin to see her growing ire. She had the surety that not one MacKay would've acted so thoughtlessly. Maybe she'd become more of a MacKay than she'd figured. How Hugh would laugh at Cumhal's clumsiness.

She gestured to Cumhal to refill his goblet with ale. She sipped her tea and watched him. "Tell me this tale again, cousin. Start at the beginning, if you please."

It didn't take long for Cumhal to reiterate his tale, restating everything he'd just told her and expanding it.

"... so we cannot sign any compacts with those around us until Goll is ransomed back to us. That puts our bartering in limbo, and as you know, much of our revenues come from the marketplace. But how can we move on anything profitable when we don't know our foe? You can see how uncomfortable that would be if we were to sign a trade tract with the rascals who hold my brother—"

"My advice is to send some unknowns through the countryside. Word will have gotten out despite all efforts to be secretive. Someone will know who's holding Goll. Then you can make your move to free him."

"That is wise, but there is still the matter of monies. If Felim can't sell his cattle fast enough—"

"They will have to wait, then, won't they?"

"You are now regent of Trevelyan, Morrigan. You have the authority to release gold to us." Cumhal glowered. "You must admit 'twould be simpler to work through you than wait for Felim."

"Is that how you see it? And how do you think 'tis

simple for me to steal what isn't mine? For that's what this would be. I cannot in conscience release gold to you that belongs to the family Trevelyan. 'Tis not honorable."

Cumhal began pacing the great room again, then swung around to face her, his frown deepening. "Of course the House of Llywelyn, on its word, will sign a note of payment—"

"Hush your whisht," Morrigan said, her patience at an end. At her cousin's puzzled look at the use of unfamiliar Gaelic, the not quite hidden smirks of the MacKays who stood guard at the entrance, she took deep breaths trying to force down her ire.

"What is this you speak?" Cumhal quizzed. "I don't speak Gaelic. You know that."

"I said I needed quiet to think," Morrigan said, not looking when some of the MacKays, who understood Celtic and the Gaelic she'd used, chuckled. She hadn't been able to bring herself to tell her stolid cousin to shut up in the Celtic he'd understand.

Cumhal looked around him, his brow furrowed. Then he stared at Morrigan. "You always cared for my brother as though he were your own."

"I did, and I still do. I will do what I can to free him."

She didn't remind Cumhal that Goll had upbraided her more than once about her adultery and the subsequent birth of Rhys. Since he'd apologized at the birth of the boy, and they'd been on fairly good terms since, it was not something that needed chewing and spitting out again. "My feelings for my family are not in contention here. My honor is. I will not plunder an estate that doesn't belong to me, Cumhal. 'Tis thievery."

Cumhal spread his hands. "Then what can we do?"

"'Twould be better if Hugh were here. He would have an answer."

Cumhal looked astounded. "Then have you come to love this Scot, Morrigan? These vows were forced on you."

Morrigan took a deep breath, not wishing to go into the detailed explanation Cumhal would demand, once she began any at all. "I've had a change of heart."

Cumhal gaped at her. "Can it be you chose the Scot?"

"No, of course not. I'd never met or seen the man."

"You're Welsh and sworn to our good."

"I know that." She was glad they spoke in rapid Welsh. Even those Scots who had a smattering of the language would find it hard to follow. She didn't wish to air her feelings in front of the many attendants who moved in and out of the great room. "My feelings toward MacKay are my own, and they are between my spouse and me, and no one else."

"Where is this paragon?"

She inclined her heard, her eyes narrowing. "Don't malign him, Cumhal. I won't allow it. You are in his castle, and you are being treated as a guest because you're related to me." She lifted her chin. "If you dare to continue in such a vein—"

"I didn't think to fire your temper, cousin."

"—I would think nothing of having one of the burly Scots throw you bodily from this holding and bar you from it, henceforth. Be warned, I mean what I say."

Cumhal stared at her, blood chugging into his face. "I beg pardon. It was wrong."

"It was."

"Where is your husband?"

"He is destined to be in the king's grace for another sennight." She hesitated. "I don't like to think they speak of war. I fear they do."

"Ah, English Edward is growling. We have heard."

Morrigan sighed. " 'Tis true. So . . . I must make a decision on this."

"What will it be?"

"I will go with you to Cardiff to speak with Felim. We will devise a plan that will free your brother and my cousin, and I will not have to resort to chicanery."

Cumhal inhaled, his broad chest expanding as he nodded. "You are no cat's paw, as they deemed you would be."

Morrigan bristled. "And who made such a judgment?" She wished with all her heart Hugh was beside her. He would help her with this dilemma. Remembering his strong warm body made her own heat.

Cumhal lifted a shoulder, a smile on his face. "You know how men will talk."

"Fools, all!"

Cumhal's smile widened. "Your Llywelyn character has surfaced, cousin. You're a fighter."

"I am." And no one will undercut Hugh MacKay, or
gainsay him in her presence. The pledge that spurted
from her being in sudden and fiery commitment all but
rocked her.

"Cousin? Why do you dream?"

"I wish my husband were here. He would understand
my decision."

Cumhal nodded. "It went against my grain, if truth be
told, to consider plundering Trevelyan. Ruric was my
friend. Our cousin, though closer to you, was dear to me."

"And more dear to me than anyone can ever know,"
Morrigan whispered, her words not carrying to her
cousin.

"I liked it not that Felim is being wooed by those who
wish for the power and monies of Trevelyan."

Morrigan frowned. "Who might they be?"

Cumhal shook his head. "I know not, as I have said.
As always Felim is secretive with his many plans. More
than once I've wished he would discuss his plots and
stratagems. He thinks his mind can devise such. 'Tis not
been my experience that he has the wit to do so."

Morrigan's mouth lifted. "Even as a child, his games
were always full of twists and turns, had no beginning
and a rattle-tail end."

"Goll could keep him steady. And we need a good,
strong leader now. The two Edwards think to control us.
I think they mean to devise a way to thread us through
their schemes. If 'twere my chore, I'd not let them."

Morrigan wondered, not for the first time, why he was

never chosen as a leader for the eastern branch of the family. Stolid he might be, but he could factor and he had never put the family in peril. Some of Felim's schemes could do that.

"More often than not you outwitted Felim and Goll in the games we played as children, Cumhal."

Startled, he blinked at her.

She laughed. "Did you not know you had abilities?"

"Aye, I knew. I didn't think anyone else did."

Morrigan chuckled. "Come, we'll sup and ready ourselves. Try not to worry, cousin. We'll manage and the name of Llywelyn will keep its honor."

"And you will accompany me?"

Morrigan sighed, thinking of Hugh. "We'll leave before light on the morrow."

The laird of Castle MacKay was in a rage. No one could approach him without getting the rough side of his tongue. He stomped about like a maddened destrier. Curses streamed between his lips.

Toric tried to placate him. "Fret not, Hugh—"

Hugh glared. "I come home after days and nights at court, bent double with ennui, riddled with expectations that Clan MacKay could be a target of English Edward, and you think I should be calm. I was expecting to see my wife, and she's not here."

"I know, but—"

"But nothing! I want to know where she is," Hugh spat, his mind painting too many horror scenes. Fright was making him ferocious. Either she was coerced or she went of her own free will. The latter seemed more likely, since there hadn't been a battle, and MacKays would have fought to a man to protect her. Neither would she have gone and not left a note with some sort of veiled warning if there was trouble. Instead the missive was short and not informative. His wife was canny. He respected her abilities. Right now he wanted her in front of him, explaining all. Then he would carry her to their bed where she belonged.

Why in Christ's name had she left? "There'll be war, lest I find her." He smacked the scroll she'd written her cryptic note on, the crackly papyrus all but ripping. As though he realized it could be destroyed, he looked away from Toric smoothing the surface over and over again. She'd touched it, scribed upon it. It was his link to her.

"Find me something, Toric, anything that will direct me. Our runners so far have taken us to the Firth of Forth. There the news falters." He ground his teeth. "If they've taken to boats, and I think they have, they're not manned by any of the clans close to me." He shook his head. "I should know more." He banged the trencher board again. "Find me anything that will set me on my path."

"I will, Hugh. I promise."

Toric hated to leave him. Never had he seen his stalwart leader so torn, so ripped with frustration and trepidation. When Dilla had confided to him that Hugh loved his wife greatly, he'd smiled, thinking it romantic prattle. In the last two days since their arrival back at Castle MacKay, he'd changed his mind. Hugh was mad for her.

He left the great room at a run. Rounding the rear tower, he saw Dilla by the large baking ovens and approached. "Our laird's soul is fair ripped. He grieves for her." Surprise, awe, and questioning were in his tone.

"He loves her better than life. One day he'll see that for himself." Dilla tried to smile. "The boy is moping as well." She looked around her. "Since she left many of them"—she gestured to the twins playing with Rhys and others—"have smiled little. Our Lady Morrigan was a sunshine on the dreariest of days."

"What can we do? Where in Wales would she be? Why didn't she tell us the exact location?" Toric knew that Dilla didn't eavesdrop. He also knew that others told her things, and that she was a favorite of Lady Morrigan's.

Dilla took a deep breath. "I do not seek to know all of milady's affairs. I do know she is honorable, that she would not betray our laird." When she saw relief flash across his features, she was irked. "Do you say that you suspect such?"

"No. I believe in our lady, too." He exhaled. "I'd feel better if I knew where she was."

Dilla looked thoughtful. "Mayhap we can find a trail."

"What are you thinking, woman?"

"Your cousin Fergus, brother to Diuran. He's close-mouthed, and he might know a little. He and Diuran are like two peas in a pod. Where one is, the other would follow. If Diuran spoke to anyone it would be he. Mayhap a word was said. I'd be surprised if he knew much, but—"

"Where do I find him?"

"In the crofter's hut, last I knew. He—"

Toric was gone on the run, the rest of Dilla's words spilled into the wind.

The journey had been arduous. First they had the overland trip through some friendly clans. Since the MacKay tartan was well known, 'twas necessary to stop and greet spokespersons who hailed them.

When they came to the outer islands they took small, shallow-bottomed ships across the heavy waters.

More than once Morrigan thought they'd be swamped. No one else seemed worried.

"They're expert seamen," Cumhal assured her.

Morrigan tried to smile. She wasn't as worried about being overturned in the cold sea as she was concerned about Hugh's attitude when he found her gone. She had no doubt he would be in a temper. She longed to see him, whether he was angered or no. She hadn't gone into detail in her missive because she was quite sure he would come tearing after her. There was no need for that because she wouldn't be gone long. Besides, he wasn't that long up from a sickbed and she didn't want him pounding over the countryside seeking her. She'd be home before he missed her.

Sighing, she tried to put him out of her mind. Instead she studied the isles they passed. Living there on many of them were the pirates who preyed on shipping and the heavy purses carried by merchants. Only the Vikings were safe from the marauders, since they were always heavily armed and were expert sailors.

"I think we took too few warriors with us," Cumhal pondered as they made a stop for provisions.

"Surely not. We travel in Scottish waters. My tartan and men are respected. When we are on Welsh soil, the name Llywelyn will guard us."

"I trust you're right, cousin." He kept watch as they loaded their belongings and the gifts necessary to face Felim in Cardiff.

Morrigan, too, studied the waterways and terrain. "We should have enough men to protect us. Diuran is one of the most able of the MacKays. He commands six strong men and true." She frowned, seeing Hugh in her mind once more. "Besides, I'd not put any more Mac-Kays at risk."

Cumhal smiled. "You are smitten with the clan as well as its laird."

She laughed, masking her morose feelings. It wasn't Cumhal's fault she missed Hugh so much, that she saw his face in front of her, awake or sleeping. She loved the man and longed for his loving. If she hadn't had so much faith in Dilla and the other women she'd have fretted about Rhys and the twins, as well. No matter what occurred in Cardiff, Hugh and the children were safe.

"You're happy, cousin," Cumhal said. "That pleases me. I shall do all in my power to find a plan that will placate Felim and release Goll, so that you might return to your family with all speed."

"Thank you, Cumhal. We will concentrate on Goll and where he could be kept. Once he's found, you can handle the rescue and I'll return to Scotland."

Cumhal nodded. "I've been thinking on that. If 'twere me trying to hide someone, I'd take my prisoner to Druida."

Shocked, Morrigan eyed her cousin. "You can't mean that. 'Tis an awful place, and has been abandoned by all." She shuddered as she envisioned the holding atop a rock cropping overlooking the sea. It had been abandoned by Llywelyns years ago and had been allowed to go to rack and ruin. She had only been there once, taken there by her father, when an old relative had abided in the castle. She had hated it then. It would be worse now.

"But no one can venture close without detection. That would be most important."

Morrigan thought of the holding that was adjacent to Trevelyan lands. They'd played there as children. Ruric had shown her and Gwynneth a hidden entrance.

"What think you?"

She hesitated. "I feel we must put every effort forth to a scheme that would free Goll." For some reason she didn't want to discuss the hidden entrance to Druida with Cumhal. Actually she didn't want to think of the holding at all.

"I will do as much and have pondered the problem." He smiled at her. "I thank you for your caring."

"We are Llywelyns." She touched his hand, then he put his over hers. She smiled widely. "Not since childhood have we been so close, I'm thinking, Cumhal."

"Aye. 'Tis a good feeling."

For days and nights they made their slow way through the islands, the crafts seeming flimsy on the tossing sea. Sleeping on the small crafts was well nigh impossible. Most nights Morrigan curled in her tartan near the bow.

When Cumhal approached and sat down beside her, he studied her. "I know you think of your family most of the time, but other things bother you as well, Morrigan."

"They do."

"Are you worried about Felim?"

Morrigan bit her lip, a little surprised that her cousin had sensed her concern. "I am. I know how he can be influenced, and how stubborn he is after adopting a plan."

Cumhal nodded. "Goll was forever after him. In fact, I think he was the only one of us who could sway Felim."

The words hung between them like iron weights. Morrigan inclined her head. "Is that why you think he's being held captive?"

"The theme is not without merit."

Morrigan didn't respond. When her cousin left her she went over and over their words. She couldn't find a solution, nor come up with the name of the miscreants who held her cousin. Tired, wrung out, missing Hugh and the children, she settled down on her pallet, her body aching. In moments she was asleep.

The sun was slow to rise the next day, the misty morning making the light opaque.

"Land Ho!"

The cry had all rushing to the rail. The foggy atmosphere was all but impenetrable. They sailed on, using oars only, watchful of outcroppings that could pierce the hulls.

The mist lifted a bit, and the outline was clearer. Land! And it should be Wales. It seemed to take forever to maneuver closer. Then they entered a small bay, the wind dying almost at once, the heavy seas slackening.

"This is not Bridgewater Bay, is it?" Morrigan frowned.

Cumhal shook his head, striding to the steering dais, and querying the captain. When he returned to her side, he was still scowling. " 'Tis said they cannot land farther south. There's been a storm and trees have fallen into the bay, causing great hazard. He's been instructed to stop here. I told him he should have informed us of that, and we could've gone overland and been more comfortable." He glared at the steersman. "When did he get his information? And why wasn't it brought to me at once?"

Morrigan bit her lip. "You raise good questions, cousin."

"I like it not." Diuran had moved up beside them. "I'll question the fool."

Morrigan watched her guardian flailing his arms as he quizzed the stoical steersman. "Diuran frets."

"He reveres you, cousin. As do his men."

Morrigan smiled and nodded. "They're my clan."

"Have you become Scot, then?"

Morrigan exhaled. "In some ways I'll always be Welsh, as you are. In other ways I've changed." Not even to her cousin could she discuss the wonders of her marriage bed, the tenderness of her lover and husband.

Cumhal looked at the sky. "Dismal. 'Twill not be a comfortable ride after our docking. Then again, it shouldn't be more than five leagues along the sea to the Cardiff road."

Diuran strode to their side. "The gomeril answered none of the queries to my liking. I like it not. Where are we to obtain horses?" He glared at Cumhal. "Milady has to have a worthy steed."

Cumhal nodded, surprising Morrigan by not taking umbrage. "I'll talk to the head boatsman." He was gone some time. When he returned he was frowning, glancing at Diuran. "I like it less than you. The fool says there won't be horses, then he assures me there will be."

Diuran bristled, gazing at the boatsman, then back at his men. MacKays began to rattle their swords, tightening their leather jerkins, fastening their tartans at the shoulder and waist.

Cumhal's eyes narrowed, then he saw to his own weapons.

Morrigan watched, then touched Diuran's arm. "I'm sure there's no need to worry." If only Hugh were here. He would get information and defuse tempers. She couldn't wait to put this journey behind her and get back north to Castle MacKay.

Diuran eyed her, his face somber. "We will be ready for anything, milady. You are Lady MacKay, precious to us, a foe to some."

She nodded. "Then I, too, will be on guard."

Diuran grinned when he saw her draw a short sword from her bag. She slung the wide belt around her waist, jamming the blade into the worked leather scabbard that carried the intaglio of Llywelyn.

Diuran touched the weapon. " 'Tis a true one, I can see. 'Twill be a fine day when I fashion you a new scabbard with the MacKay intaglio on its surface."

Morrigan smiled at the MacKays, who were chuckling, then went to the rail to watch as they bumped against a small landing.

"Don't think she can't use that sword she wields. It might look small to some, but I've seen her move it faster than the eye can follow." Cumhal grinned. "She tipped my brother Goll on his back at one of our tourneys when we were children. I often wonder if he ever forgave her."

Diuran grinned. "She's a true MacKay. She's made us proud."

Mouth agape, Cumhal stared at Diuran for a moment, then remarked, "She's considered a first-rate swordswoman in Wales where women are often combatants." His smile was fading, worry etching his brow.

Diuran nodded. "I've read of your Boudicca, though I'll see to it that milady comes to no such end."

"Have no fear. We have many intrepid women in Wales. They can stand their ground," Cumhal averred. " 'Tis pride it gives a man when his spouse is so able."

Diuran pursed his lips. "Do not think we don't admire the same. Have you never heard of Princess Iona?"

Cumhal nodded. "The Icelandic who became a Scot. Yes. There are many legends about her warrior ways."

"All true."

Cumhal smiled at Diuran, who returned it, an unspoken pact between them from that moment.

Cumhal pointed. "Look at her, ready to lead the way." He shook his head. "She was ever wrongheaded."

Diuran smiled. "She is our lady."

"There is reverence in the words. I see I must look upon my cousin with new eyes," Cumhal remarked.

In not too long a time they disembarked, taking their possessions with them.

"There're the horses." Cumhal pointed.

Diuran and his warriors watched as the steeds were brought to them, some of his men as alert as he, their eyes scanning the surrounding woody areas. The rest studied the horses, frowning.

"Not the best mounts, would you say?" Diuran said from the side of his mouth to Cumhal.

"No. I'd not like them if our journey was a long one."

When all was loaded, Cumhal helped Morrigan into her saddle, though she needed no aid.

In short order they were on one of the narrow stony paths that curve along the coast of Wales. One side was a sheer drop to the sea, the other was a thick growth of woody plants and greens, many stunted and bent by the strong ocean winds.

Morrigan tried to keep her mind on the tasks ahead, but she couldn't blot out the image of Hugh, and what he would say when she returned. He'd bluster and stride up and down the great room. Her heart beat fast at how she'd soothe his ire, placate his pique. He would tell her she should've waited for him. Sighing, she wished he was with her at the moment.

He'd taught her about love. She'd thought she knew quite a bit because of her experience on the farm with animal husbandry. She'd discovered she knew absolutely nothing about what was between a man and woman.

The tall, handsome, dangerous leader of the wild MacKays had taught her about giving, about gentle nurturing, and hot passion. Could she ever have conjured up such a wonderful amalgam?

"Milady?"

"Yes." She almost had to shake herself from her sweet thoughts. Hugh was so big in her life, in every corner. Through the haze of pondering she heard the urgency. "Something gives you angst, Diuran?"

"It does."

Morrigan looked around her. "You sense danger."

"I do." He turned in his saddle, making a hand gesture. The warriors broke into a canter around her. "You must be ready on our signal to ride hard, milady, to find the sea and—"

Before he could say more there was a bloodcurdling war cry. Men erupted from the glen to one side of them, seeming to come out of the cliffs as well.

"Ride, milady," Diuran called to her even as three men engaged him with swords almost before he could draw his own.

"No!" Morrigan shouted, pulling her short sword and kicking her lackluster steed into a charge. Before any of them knew she was there, she was laying about her, swinging her short sword at the nearest attacker. His yowl of anger and pain told her she struck right. When he turned, she slammed the flat of her sword against the backside of his steed. It shot forward, unseating the rider.

"Get back, milady," Diuran shouted.

She was about to obey when she saw two men creeping toward his back. For a moment she thought she recognized one of them. A cousin? No! It couldn't be. They'd not attack her entourage.

She pulled hard on the reins, turning the sluggish
steed around, and charging at the two who were intent
on taking Diuran from the back. She dug her heels into
the horse, cannoning forward, passing Diuran by inches,
gripping her reins with one hand, her short sword with
the other. A battle cry tore from her throat. More than
one MacKay gaped, before redoubling efforts to take
down the assassins who would dare assault their valiant
lady.

Morrigan plowed into the two back stabbers, the wide
chest of the horse taking the two men down before they
could collect themselves to escape. Momentum carried
her past the area of battle. When she succeeded in turning the large overexcited beast she saw that Diuran was
no longer in sight. Neither was Cumhal. She raced back
to the fray, waving her sword like a guidon.

"Stop! I am a princess of Wales. Cease this attack at
once," she commanded, not sure her voice or her authority would work.

Silence descended like a tattered cloak. Cries, moans,
groans of the wounded were the only sounds for several
breaths of time.

"You . . . don't command us, but you will come with
us."

Morrigan inhaled, looking around her. They had five
times the men. "I will see to my people first."

"No need. We'll finish off those who are not already
dead."

Heartsick, Morrigan's mind raced. "Wait! Since I was

their captive I claim the right to end their misspent lives." Off to one side she saw Cumhal stagger to his feet holding his head, blood oozing from his fingers. "I would have a dagger, if you please. The rest of you stand back." She turned and stared at Cumhal.

"Hold! I, too, am the captive of the Scots. I would do my share of finishing the rabble."

Morrigan stared at him, hoping she read the right message in his eyes. " 'Tis your right." God help him if he killed any MacKays. She'd burn his eyes out with a poker.

She took a dagger from the nearest man, noting its rusted edges. They were rabble who took little care of their weapons. They'd slay no MacKays if she could help it. Waving them back in imperious fashion, she strode to where Diuran was lying.

His eyes were closed.

She leaned over him, raising the dagger. "Spread your arm from your body, please," she said through her teeth. She saw a flicker behind his slitted gaze. "Go to the witch on the river. It leads from this place less than a league. Go south. Her cottage is there. Give her the word Taranus. Tell me you comprehend." The eyes blinked. "Dog of a Scot! You die," she screeched, bringing the blade down in his armpit, praying she didn't touch skin.

She rose to her feet. "Now, the next one."

Cumhal staggered close to her. "My turn."

"Tell them Taranus."

"Of course," he muttered, then raised his voice. "I'll strike down the dog," Cumhal swore.

Morrigan noted one of the intruders right behind her. "'Tis almost done, and needed doing."

Suspicion crossed his face. "You were a long time with the first one."

"Indeed I had to be. I called upon the Prince of Darkness to come take his soul."

Blanching, the man stepped back, as did his cohorts who'd been listening.

"And did you lose many?" Morrigan tried not to gag at the gore, at so many lying wounded.

"We'll finish our own."

Horrified, she watched the man dispatch his wounded comrades. No Welshman should treat his own like this! Who were these men? Mercenaries that prowled the countryside looking for any kind of killing work? Predators who sought out the weak to rob and slay? Not a word passed her lips though she quivered with outrage. One day she'd see them hang for this day's work.

"Mount up." The leader glanced back at his men.

Morrigan eyed the wounded Cumhal, blood streaming down his face, reeling from weakness and fatigue. "My cousin must be seen to at once. He, alone, freed me from the dreaded Scots." She saw the pernicious look the leader gave Cumhal and knew that he would've subjected Cumhal to the same treatment he would've afforded the Scots had she not been there.

Cumhal shook his head. "I'll be along on my own. I

have my own medicaments." He looked at the leader. "Of course you know you're on Welsh soil, that eyes follow your every move. If any even speak wrongly to the Princess of Wales, you'll be boiled alive in the black pools that come from the earth." Cumhal looked thoughtful. "Perhaps you've not seen it done." He pointed through the glen. "Yon pools are magical. A burning faggot put to them causes a blue flame to rise." He gestured with both arms, though the effort caused him to groan. "The man chosen is then tossed into the center. His howls can be heard for miles. 'Tis great entertainment."

Cumhal's ghoulish smile had some shivering, the leader blustering he was paid to deliver her intact. Morrigan would've smiled if she hadn't been so heartsick and worried about the MacKays on the ground.

The leader grasped her reins. "Come along." He glowered at Cumhal. "You'll have to catch up on your own. We mean to collect our pay before the sun hides."

Morrigan had barely time to wave to her cousin before they were off at a gallop.

Cumhal watched them disappear, then he went to Diuran. "Can you hear me?"

"I surely can. I hope 'tis not us you plan to fry."

Cumhal grinned. "Come, I'll give you what medicines I have, then we'll be on our way to find Diodura—"

Diuran clasped his arm. "No, we look for Taranus as Morrigan said to me."

Cumhal smiled, nodding. "He is the god to the ancients. There are some who practice the old ways like Diodura. She is a great healer. Witches are honored among us, not harmed as they are in other places." He turned around and looked at the others. "I'll try to help them."

Diuran struggled to a sitting position. "Dermot went down, I saw that."

In moments they buried Leamon and Deil, fashioned a tumbrel of sorts with sticks and vines, for Dermot. Only then did they begin their trek to the river.

NINE

Absence makes the heart grow fonder.
                                    Propertius

Castle MacKay was in turmoil. The lady was missing.
The laird was in high dudgeon. Parties had been going
out for days, trying to find her trail.

She, six MacKays, Diuran, and one called Cumhal, a
relative to Lady MacKay, seemed to have vanished in
the sea. None had seen them disembark at Cardiff, if
that was their destination. Messengers had brought the
word she'd been summoned to a family meeting there.
Yet none had seen her arrive, nor had any seen her
since.

"I want her found, no matter what it takes." Hugh
slammed his fist down on the trencher board, his bitterness palpable. Not since childhood had he felt so betrayed.

"You don't know that the scrolls are accurate," Dilla
began, earning her laird's wrathful gaze. "I do not care
if you proscribe me, I'll not believe she betrayed you."

Dilla's husband gaped at her, then went to her side. "I ask you to punish me for my wife's thoughtless words, milord. I'll not let her be—"

"Stop!" Hugh shouted, making man and wife jump. "I'm not angry with Dilla." He glared at her spouse. "Since when is it against the law for any MacKay to express an opinion?"

He grimaced. " 'Tis not."

"Then stop defending Dilla until she needs it and—"

"Where is maman?" Rhys shouted, tearing into the room and plummeting into Hugh. "I want her now. She needs me. Avis and Conal will cry if she doesn't come. She's to help us with our lessons." Despite his strong words, the lad's chin shook and his eyes were suspiciously wet. The twins stood in the doorway, faces and limbs quivering.

Hugh scooped him up, holding him close. For the five days Morrigan had been gone, and the three he'd been home, he'd hardly been separated from the trio. Hugh slept in Rhys and Conal's room on a cot. Lilybet had stayed with Avis. If either boy woke he could touch them. Lilybet often spoke of Avis's restlessness. Most nights Hugh didn't sleep, his mind boiling with anger and fear. Before the sun rose he was usually up, sending runners, waiting for the return of others. Morrigan! Her name rang in his head, in his chest, all through him—

"Where is maman?" Rhys leaned back in Hugh's arms. "She needs me. You must know that."

"I know. I'll find her and bring her back home. You

must believe in that. You're a MacKay. You must have faith in your laird." Hugh heard Dilla's smothered sob. From the corner of his eyes, he saw her husband pull her close. His insides were shredded with worry. No word in all that time. Five days and he didn't know where she was. His wife and her coterie seemed to have vanished. Runners had been all over Scotland, Wales, and England. Nothing.

Hugh inhaled. "We'll mount a new campaign." He eyed Toric, who'd hovered nearby since they'd found Morrigan gone. "I'll lead it. You'll stay with the boy, guarding him along with—"

The flurry and shouting at the gate alerted him and started him running. As Hugh passed Dilla and Andra, he shifted the boy to her. Andra lifted the twins.

Rhys began to wail the minute he was out of Hugh's reach. Tears ran down the twins' cheeks.

"Shh, we'en, 'twill be fine," Dilla crooned. "Will not our laird see to it?"

Rhys shook with his sobbing, though he nodded. "Maman needs me."

"She does indeed. What mother would not want to be with you, Avis and Conal. And she will be soon." Dilla swallowed her own sorrow, wise enough to know Rhys was saying he needed his mother, however many times he repeated that she needed him. She hugged him close. If truth were told, the three had become as dear to her as her own. "I'll take you to the kitchen, and we'll have sweets and a game. What say you, dear ones?"

They tried to smile but their eyes strayed to the great doors that'd been flung open by the laird, where the hustle and bustle of the bailey sounded loud and clear.

Hugh bared his teeth when he saw the litters bearing his men, MacKay horsemen surrounding them. He fixed his gaze on Diuran, who was held in front of Alex MacKay, his cousin. He was wounded; so were the others. Bringing up the rear of the ragtag entourage was a hag on a long-haired pony.

Hugh strode to the horse carrying Diuran, lifting the mighty warrior down as though he were a child.

"Hold, fool. Would you undo my work? Is his litter made for him? Where are my medicaments? Hurry, you foolish gawps. Do as I bid."

MacKays stared openmouthed at the raspy attack on their leader by the frail but fierce witch. Then as though burned by her words they ran in all directions to do her bidding.

"I'll carry him to his litter," Hugh said, his tone quiet but firm.

"Lord," Diuran whispered, his pain obvious. "She was alive five days ago. It's . . . taken . . . this . . ."

"No more talking," the hag interrupted. She stared up at Hugh. "She's not dead. I've seen it in my visions."

Hugh felt as though a great weight had lifted from his chest, though he only nodded. Why he believed the crone he wasn't sure. That she knew Morrigan seemed possible. That she might know where his wife was itched at him. He longed for Morrigan with a terrible ache. Underlying the longing had been a dread that their happiness was illusory, a fantasy that couldn't last. How could something so beautiful be forever? It was simpler to reflect that she meant to betray him, that her body and words lied to him when they'd been entwined in love. Why would a lie be more comfortable than the truth? She'd betrayed him only by not waiting for him, by not including him in her plans.

His heart filled with fury toward those who'd had the temerity to attack MacKays, especially his wife. There would come a reckoning. He'd see to it if it took his last breath. Those who'd come at MacKay would feel his steel. No one and nothing would come between him and his wife. Neither would any invade his clan without retaliation. It ate at him that all the long years of being exiled from his holdings had not been payment enough to ensure peace.

More than breathing he wanted serene days for his people, a long, warm life with Morrigan. If Fate was playing the malice game with him, if his beautiful wife was to be denied him, then he'd dedicate his life to his clan, to the elimination of those who would assault it. He would fight to the death to protect it.

At the witch's insistence he hurried Diuran to her care.

His dark thoughts prodded him to the healing room. Trying as he did to comfort Diuran, he couldn't drive the angst from his head. Where was Morrigan? Did anyone know?

When the MacKay women pushed him aside in the healing room, not questioning the witch's authority, Hugh backed to the wall. He had no intention of leaving. He never took his eyes from Diuran and the others.

Dilla came into the room. "The boy's with Mavis and other guardians, milord. Eamon is with them." She waited for his nod, then went to look at Dermot and Clovis. One of the women moved from the side of the sick, talking in quiet tones to Dilla, gesturing to the witch. Coming back to his side, Dilla waited.

"Well?" Hugh's voice was harsh.

"Two have died as you know, milord."

"Aye. Leamon and Deil." His face stretched tight over his bones, a muscle jumping at the side of his jaw.

"The others will live because of the ministrations of the witch, called Diodura. She's Welsh, and loyal to the family of Trevelyan."

Hugh's head swiveled toward her. "You mean Llywelyn."

She shook her head. "Leana said the name twice because it twisted her tongue. Trevelyan."

Hugh pondered that. 'Twas no secret that his wife was regent of Trevelyan. That that would be known by a witch, who was no doubt isolated from most of society, Welsh and Scot, made him wonder. Such persons had to stay by themselves because the many who believed in them were counterbalanced by the erratic disbelievers

who were known to stone, burn, or even skin them alive.
No, the woman would have little touch with society, unless in truth she saw everything in visions. Though
Hugh hung on her words that Morrigan was alive, he
didn't countenance much that came from soothsayers
and the like. He would quiz her as soon as he could. Did
she know where Morrigan was?

"I will have words with Diuran when he's able and
can speak with me," Hugh rasped, his fury barely contained. He glanced at Dilla. "And nothing to the boy."

"Aye, milord," Dilla said, sympathy in every line.
"She's safe. I know it."

His lips cracked upward. "Thank you, Dilla." He left
the healing room, his long strides ringing down the
stone corridor.

"Our lord hurts," Leana said, behind her.

"He's fair torn apart," Dilla said on a breath.

Cardiff looked the same to her, though Morrigan hadn't
been there much since childhood. Noisy with the clatter
of wagons, the shouts of vendors, the scurrying of sedan
chairs and their pullers, it had an alien feel. She felt
choked by the sounds. She longed for Castle MacKay,
the people . . . Hugh. She couldn't get him out of her
mind. Would he forget her? They'd shared so much that
she could never put aside. She'd had but one man, and
she loved him. How many had he loved? Still loved?
Was she even on the list? Countless questions assaulted
her even as she studied the world around her.

Whatever had to be done for Goll must be done speedily. It annoyed her that the fools escorting her hadn't listened to her directions. It'd taken three days to get there instead of one. Though she'd come to no harm in the company of the riffraff, she'd chafed at the waste of time. She had to get back to Hugh. She could almost feel him pulling her into his arms, planting small kisses along her cheek as he was wont to do. Sweet Mary! She missed him.

Stop! Stop thinking of Hugh. Torture! Think of Rhys and the twins. She did, but even then, Hugh was there. Always. Around her, inside her, filling her. Baffling. She'd not imagined a man could take over her life in such a way. Most of her existence had been dedicated to the crusade of saving Rhys and his inheritance. She'd been quite sure nothing could intrude on that. It would remain the prime mover in her life. Now there was Hugh, and she couldn't envision a future without him or Rhys and the twins. The children had become a force in her life. Her passion and emotion for Hugh had increased her love for the three children. Her life with them was all she needed, all she could ever want.

"Yonder, lady. There's the castle," the leader called Raulf informed her.

"I see," she answered as though she hadn't known. She'd told him she was a princess of Wales. Why hadn't he assumed she'd been to the castle? She was perplexed by the men who'd escorted her to Cardiff. Who'd hired such rowdies that would attack her coterie of MacKays?

Why were they set upon at all? How did they know they were coming? Cumhal had said nothing about sending a messenger. Had they been watching for them? Why wasn't an advance guard of Llywelyns sent instead of the no-name hooligans? All the questions needed answering. Felim would respond to the perfidy or she'd leave Cardiff that day and return to Castle MacKay, on her own if need be. Five days of journeying! Why had it been necessary to come such a circuitous way? She'd have answers or she'd skewer Felim with his own weapon. She scanned the men around her. Their bunch seemed smaller, and there wasn't a familiar one to be seen. What was the connection between these rowdies and her arrival in Wales? Obviously she alone would face those who held Goll captive. She'd not turn to Felim when she interceded for her cousin's release. Felim would be overbearing. He'd bluster and set up the backs of the absconders. No, she'd have to go alone. If only she had Cumhal interceding—

They approached the castle on a curving road.

In a flurry of trumpets and full-dress destriers, the welcoming committee disgorged from the castle in a feckless display that wouldn't have passed muster in Castle MacKay.

Felim trotted through the middle to pull his large steed up in front of her. "So, you're well, cousin?"

"If I'd not been set upon by marauders, I might've been better," she shot back. "As a princess of Wales I demand an explanation, cousin."

"What?" Felim growled, his many-layered features quivering with ire. "You were to be escorted to me, not set upon—"

"Oh?" she interrupted. "Then why am I escorted by marauders?"

Felim shifted in his saddle, setting his horse to sidling. "You were to be safe, brought to me by safe escort."

"My *escort* from Castle MacKay was set upon and dispatched."

Felim grimaced. "I had wished to avoid that, but the Scots were ever warlike." He whirled his steed, cantering back the way he'd come.

Morrigan stared after him. "Wait! 'Twas not Scots—"

"We'll speak of this anon," he called back over his shoulder.

Morrigan seethed. What went on in that convoluted head? He was no scholar; he didn't have the wit for intrigue. Like the puppeteers of Venice there was someone manipulating Felim's strings. Who would it be? What was the plan? Wasn't she here to help Goll? Damn her cousin! He'd answer all her questions.

He'd taken the news of the attack too well. It was unlike her mercurial relative not to spit fire over the smallest affront. He'd not been fazed by the news. This had been an assault on his family. Was she not the highest-ranking Llywelyn outside of Califb? Had her ham-handed cousin planned the action against the Scots? It seemed well nigh impossible. He'd never been known for his intricate thinking. Blunt words, clumsy actions were more his style. Did someone else devise the attack? Who held Felim in such thrall?

Felim turned in his saddle. "Come along. There's a chill in the air, cousin. There'll be warm ale by the fire."

Morrigan kicked her horse into the canter that carried her through the barbican to the bailey. When some of the people called out to her, she paused.

"How goes it, good Drulla, Ham?"

The attendants skated their eyes around her, then fixed on her again.

"Things have changed, highness," Ham said through his teeth. "Our farms have suffered."

As though they felt the approach of some of the horsemen, they bowed and backed away.

"Thank you for your greetings, good people of Wales," Morrigan said to the gathering, her slight nod at Ham and Drulla signaling her understanding.

"Blessings to you, good princess," came from a chorus of voices.

Even as she watched, Ham and Drulla faded back from the horsemen into the throng. They were fearful! What was going on in Cardiff? Much of the land farmed around Cardiff had been deeded to her by her father, so she could have the independence all Welsh women wish. It wasn't a large holding by most standards, but it produced, and allowed a good living for her tenants. She looked long and hard into the faces about her, anger building. If Felim had transgressed on her holding, if

he'd shown high-handedness to her serfs, she'd have his
eyes. First she'd have an accounting. If it didn't balance
she'd empty his coffers to do the job.

Wheeling her horse, she all but rammed the horsemen
behind her. "Remove yourself from my path, you en-
croaching fool," Morrigan demanded in her most imperious voice. "You crowd the people of Cardiff who
belong here, who pay their respects to a royal. Methinks
you don't have a place here. They do." Her voice carried
as she intended. For a moment there were smiles.

Startled, the men who'd convoyed her to Cardiff
stared at her, uncertainty in every line.

"Have you lost your hearing, dolts? Move!" She
glowered at the man and his companions, then galloped
through their midst, not looking back.

She was helped to dismount by another unknown,
then attendants bracketed her as she marched into the
castle, then to the great room that was jammed with people, most of whom seemed to be arguing with Felim. As
always her relative was relying on roaring over reason.

"Cousin."

Startled, Morrigan looked to the left. "Cumhal, how
did you—?"

"Shh. I'm here. Say no more. I'm here," he said,
struggling to speak from the side of his mouth.

"Where have you been?"

"Seeking Goll's hiding place and trying to discover
who is enemy and who is friend."

"And have you?"

"No. I tell you this, cousin, I fear we are in a den of knaves. I've had this feeling since we were set upon."

"I've had the same misgivings in this Llywelyn holding," Morrigan whispered back. She looked around her, finding many eyes riveted to them. If Cumhal was attempting to be unobtrusive it wasn't working. "I'm glad to see you," she said, smiling. "I'm sure the Scottish riffraff have been dispatched."

He watched her for a moment before nodding. "Back to their hell, I should think," he muttered, beginning to scan the room. "A nightmare, is it not? If Felim could learn but the rudiments of leadership we might have had a chance."

"Had? What does this mean?"

"I've heard talk of mounting a campaign. You and I know that Felim is not up to planning such."

Cumhal's bitterness wasn't lost on her. "That is not all he can't comprehend. He doesn't mention Goll, nor did he allow me to broach the subject. He's either run mad or he does not care. Which?"

"Both, mayhap," Cumhal said through his teeth.

"Wasn't it incumbent on you to take over if he has proved so incompetent?"

Cumhal shrugged. "Yes, if I had a standing army I might."

"He is so well protected then?"

"I wouldn't call it protection. More like congenial imprisonment, though my brother sees it not." Cumhal looked around him. "We cannot speak of this. There're ears everywhere." He inhaled. "Tell me of Tarquin. He shows bitterness over your marriage?"

"I shouldn't think so. 'Twas not his wish to tie himself to a woman who had a lad without . . ." She hesitated.

"Without nuptial words. I know of this. Why should it matter to him when it doesn't to us? I would've been at your Scottish vows had I been able to return from our island properties in time."

"Thank you." She lowered her eyes and her voice.

"You're welcome." Cumhal bit his lip. " 'Tis passing strange about Tarquin since rumor has it he feels bereft since your marriage. I cannot say I understand this."

"Nor do I. Tell me of this congenial imprisonment that you intimated."

"I can't. 'Twould not be wise for us to speak of it here. Another time and another place, I would say. The walls listen here."

"Indeed, 'twould seem so." She smiled, nodded, bowed. "Why have you not contacted my brothers?"

"I've done that. They've talked to Felim and gotten nowhere. His stubbornness is only surpassed by his stupidity when it comes to trusting the wrong people."

"And they are?"

Cumhal reddened. "I know not who directs him. That's what flummoxes me." He ground his teeth. "I would not lie to you, Morrigan." He swallowed. "I didn't think this when I summoned you, but . . . now . . ."

"What?"

"I think I've called you to hell. I like it not. There are

so many here I know not. Why are mercenaries crowding this great room?"

Morrigan took a deep breath when she saw Felim scan the room, then scowl at her. "Come, 'twould seem we're wanted."

"Be careful, cousin. More and more I feel 'tis a den of vipers we face. And I know not who they are, or when they'll come upon us." Cumhal shook his head. " 'Twould seem I've been tricked as well as you."

Morrigan stiffened. "And did you not even suspect this before you arrived at Castle MacKay?"

He flushed. "I have had a feeling something wasn't right for some time. I couldn't trace my fears to anything. More than once I called myself a fool for feeling such. I've tried to rid myself of thinking there could be a betrayal of family." He inhaled and exhaled, ignoring his brother's gesticulating. "Not until we were set upon did I come to the admittance that there is dread treason within our house." His glance slid to Felim.

Morrigan gasped. "Surely not. He has always been loyal. Besides, he isn't . . . hasn't—"

"The think box for intrigue? I agree. I can't factor who's behind this and how I can combat it."

"Cumhal!" Felim roared.

Cumhal's eyes closed for a moment. "He is ever discreet and unobtrusive."

Laughter bubbled through her ire. "Some things don't change." Her smile died. " 'Twould be easy to fasten blame on Felim. I don't think 'tis to our best interest to underestimate him. Neither do I think we can be complacent about others, inside or outside the family, who could be proctoring a conspiracy."

"You were ever acute in your reasoning, cousin."

"Thank you." *And if Hugh were here we would have answers instead of conjectures.*

"The two of you, come," Felim roared.

"We'd better hurry before he blows the stones off the battlements," Cumhal muttered.

Morrigan chuckled. Underneath the surface mirth a worm of worry ate at her. It was so ridiculous to think of someone trying to undermine Llywelyn, one of the power families of Wales. Yet the certainty it was happening crawled through her innards. *Hugh! I need you!*

Cumhal's mouth twisted upward as he led her through the squabbling throngs, the laughing, shouting hangers-on that crowded Felim's court. Not only didn't Cumhal's older brother mind the din, he encouraged it. Mandolin players who should've soothed, played too loud. Some were discordant enough to make one cringe. Vendors moved among guests shouting their wares. It was like a marketplace instead of a great room.

" 'Tis chaos. My brother is a better sheepherder."

"Aye, I'd not question him on his abilities in animal husbandry." She smiled and greeted many on the circuitous route to the fireplace where Felim was ensconced. She noted the many strangers who stared at her openly. There was no obeisance to her rank. Not that she cared, but tradition had always held that reverence would be shown her title, if not her person. She detected a thinly hidden insolence. "Cumhal, I think I sense what you've been feeling. There's peril here, enmity. Contact my brother Drcq. Tell him to find Califb wherever he is. Make sure he knows there's perfidy within our ranks. The name and House of Llywelyn is in jeopardy and we are assaulted by fools."

He nodded. "I will. First we'll have to see to my squalling brother."

"She's where she should be. The rest is up to you."

"I know. Do you think 'tis wise to trust our fellow dice players in this big game?"

"No. For now they're useful. Once the preliminaries are in place we can eliminate the extraneous—"

"Some of them wouldn't look upon themselves as such."

The one shrugged. "To fashion such an operation, to put it to work, takes time and people. Once this begins the elimination of those who could cause trouble for us in the future makes sense."

"Aye, it does. It's the delicacy 'twill take to make them disappear that eats at me. I'll not call down trouble on me and mine. Remember that."

"The rewards are great, as you know. You cannot wish a share of the treasure without paying the price. The choice is yours." He watched the other writhe with his greed, quite sure he'd finish him with his own good sharp dirk if the answer would be the wrong one.

"I never said I wouldn't take part."

He relaxed his hold on the blade. "Be patient. All will be as it should be."

"Let us not return to the others. Our presence is needed elsewhere."

"As you say."

The two smiled at each other, as though their minds were clear, one to the other. Their mistrust wouldn't be verbalized. Each had the other's destruction in mind. That could wait. The primary plan would go forward.

TEN

Submit to the present evil, lest a greater one
befall you.

Phaedrus

Hugh leaned over Diuran, trying to swallow his terror. It
had been riding him for days that he wouldn't get to
Morrigan in time, that her survival was in jeopardy.

Again and again riders had galloped into Castle
MacKay with the same news. She'd been seen landing
in Wales, even spotted on the outskirts of Cardiff. More
than one guaranteed that she would be at Cardiff Castle.
It made sense. No matter how he tried he'd been unable
to get information out of the castle in Wales. He dare not
make an open attack on Morrigan's family. Anything
that smacked of war would bring down the short-tempered
Welsh upon his neck. By the time the smoke cleared his
wife could be well and truly hidden, or worse. He didn't
want that.

Nothing mattered but talking to her, getting to the
bottom of the mysterious trip. All must be resolved be-

tween them. If she thought to leave him, he would convince her she was wrong, that her place was with him and Clan MacKay.

It soured him sorely to imagine her trying to escape from him. He would've sworn she felt as strongly toward him as he did her. His skin felt raw when he pondered rejection, even as his heart and mind told him that such thinking was wrong. Still, he would tell her how she'd erred in not leaving him a clear message, how she'd made a mistake in causing him such concern.

What if she died, was dead already?

His life would be forfeit if he didn't find her alive and well. No matter how long he strode the earth, he'd be dead to feeling. All the fire she'd given him would be snuffed out, and there'd be little to relish except his efforts for the clan, the twins Conal and Avis, and their son, Rhys. That would take all his waking hours. Sleep would elude him until the final sleep. He needed the wife he'd begun to love on first sighting. He knew that now. His heart twisted with the need to get to her, to bring her home to Castle MacKay.

Anger that she could have abandoned him mixed with the fear, the amalgam building to a helpless rage.

"Is Diuran dead, then, like maman?"

Hugh lifted his face from his hands, staring down at the boy next to him. He scooped him up into his arms. "Your maman is not dead. I love her, too, and wouldn't let her die."

Rhys couldn't answer. He buried his face in Hugh's neck, sighs shuddering through him.

Despite all his importunings, and distractions, their son Rhys became more listless each day. No matter how many times he told him he'd bring his mother back to him, the boy was losing faith. He didn't eat as he should. And though the twins longed for their mother, they worried about Rhys, as well. They hovered over him, more loving than any brother and sister could be. Still the boy grieved.

"Milord, forgive me. I know you fret," Diuran said from his cot, his voice weak. He tried to smile at Rhys. "I'm . . . alive . . . so is your maman."

Dilla moved next to Hugh and took Rhys. "You see? Diuran is MacKay. He wouldn't lie to you."

Rhys blinked, then nodded, twining his arms about her neck. "She must come home soon. She needs me."

"Of course she does."

Hugh watched Dilla leave the chamber, then he leaned down and touched Diuran's arm, noting that the fever had gone from it. "You worry that we fret. Nay, my friend, you brought Diodura to us. Had she not treated you, you and my men would've died." He ground his teeth as he recalled his conversation with the crone when the men who'd accompanied Morrigan had sickened even more on their return to Castle MacKay.

"I thought as much, good sir," Diodura had told him in halting Gaelic.

"What is it?" he'd said to her in Celtic, earning her gap-toothed smile. "That they've used poison on their weapons, I doubt not. Why did it take so long—?"

"Not long, good sir," Diodura had interrupted. "'Twas planned that if any lived, they might make it back to your side, to die after telling of the ambuscade. There're herbs and plants that would do this. There're mushrooms in our caves that can bring a euphoria that will induce instant obedience in the taker. Killings have been done by such, and wreaked havoc on families as a result." She shrugged. "'Tis a Roman strategy, I'll be bound. 'Twas brought down to us from the days of Boudicca." She cackled when his gaze narrowed on her. "I was educated by the great House of Trevelyan, as a healer and scholar. Long ago I was banished when the great Ruric the First was killed." She frowned. "His son and grandson were destined to be in my care, but their lives were taken betimes."

"That's how you know my spouse, by her connection to Trevelyan?"

She shrugged again. "That and other ways."

Her cryptic responses had set his teeth on edge. He knew it was more the delays caused by the sickening of his men, the worry about his wife, that fueled his ire. If he hadn't been so distracted he would've quizzed her. Since he owed a debt of gratitude to her, he restrained. His men would've died had it not been for the hag. There was a debt. He'd honor it.

Nothing preceded his need to get to Morrigan. Instinct told him she was in peril even if she was in the heartland of her family. His fears had mounted with each turning of the glass. Nothing would be allowed to get in the way of finding her. But he couldn't go crashing into Wales, even with a standing army, unless he was certain of her location. He had no wish to embroil his clan in a needless war. Nor did he want those who held his wife prisoner to be warned ahead. There were myriad ways she could be hidden from him. Death was one, but he couldn't dwell on that. It would've driven him mad.

Only if there was no other way would he commit his full complement of warriors. If it took that to get his wife back, he wouldn't shirk from it. He had to get to her!

Now, as he stared down at his almost helpless lieutenant, fury filled him. Time was passing. He knew so little. "Can you tell me aught of where she could be?"

Diuran shook his head. "They . . . set upon us, milord. Planned, I would swear . . . though they were rabble. They were to . . . slay us." Diuran closed his eyes as Diodura dabbed at the cold sweat on his face. "Milady . . . said . . . she . . . would do it." Diuran's smile wobbled. "Called . . . us . . . foul names."

If Hugh hadn't been so furious he might've smiled with him. "So?"

Diuran turned his head looking at the others lying in the healing room. "They . . . will . . . live"—he looked back at Hugh—"because of milady."

"How?" It rasped from his throat.

"She pretended to finish us with . . . dirks." His eyes closed. "She didn't . . . know about . . . the poison."

"No, she'd not countenance it," Diodura said, wiping Diuran's forehead again. "There would've been no way she would've left you had she suspected."

Hugh could hardly get air. It hurt his chest to try. When he spoke, his voice was raw. "You'll not return to Wales, woman. Some could discover how you've helped Clan MacKay. You're one of us now. A new place will be prepared for you in the castle. You'll never fetch your own firewood again."

The words bonding her to a safe haven startled Diodura. Her self-assurance seemed to melt on the spot.

"Nay, good lord. 'Twould not be to your best interests to sponsor me," she said, swallowing. "I hate the truth of it, to be sure—"

"Then think no more of it. From this day hence, healer, you will run this room and save our people."

Swaying with emotion, she clasped bony hands in front of her. " 'Tis not good of you to shatter a crone's feelings toward men. You undermine me." She bowed her head. "I thank thee."

"No!" He lifted her up. "I thank you for my men and to your god Taranus I give thanks as well."

She smiled. "You will do well, great chief." She gasped, her eyes widening, her body growing rigid, swaying, her teeth gritted, her hands turning clawlike.

Dilla moved to the laird's side. "She has a vision,

lord. Stay your hand," she told him when Hugh moved to support Diodura.

For long moments none moved in the healing chamber.

Even the ailing men stilled, eyeing the crone. Those nursing them paused. No one commented, well aware it was dangerous and blasphemous to interrupt a sojourn of the spirit into the phantasmic world.

Diodura seemed to travel back to them, though it was more a floating sensation than trodding. Her body shuddered, and she stared at each one in turn, then her gaze fixed on Hugh. "You must hurry, good lord. I see pain for her. My good child needs you." One tear trembled down her cheek. "Great peril awaits you. You must not lose faith. I cannot find her exact locus, but I would look for Cumhal and Felim."

"Yes, yes," Diuran groaned. "I'd forgotten. He ministered to us. He said he would go to Cardiff to help our lady." He stared at the laird. "I'd not trusted Welshmen. This one has honor. He medicated us until we were strong enough to depart."

Hugh breathed more easily. Morrigan had an ally. "Rest, good friends. I leave you in her care." Hugh nodded toward Diodura. "I go to Cardiff. The castle?"

She shook her head. "My vision told me naught of that, but 'twould be my first choice." She grimaced. "You must hurry. There was a blackness I couldn't see through, but I felt the agony."

Diuran groaned. "You must save our lady, Hugh."

"I will," Hugh said through his teeth. "You mind Diodura."

Diuran shook his head. "If she purges me again, I shall put my sword through her."

Hugh smiled for the first time in many days, though his heart thudded with trepidation. "Be stronger than she before you threaten her." He left the room on the run, calling for his horse.

Over and over Morrigan tried to bring up Goll's disappearance. From the first moment of greeting that had been her focus. Felim had put her off every time, fraying her temper and nerves. Had there ever been a more rock-headed person?

Morrigan found it a terrible strain. Felim was little help, always going back to the same theme: his course was the best course for the Llywelyn family. She tried every trick and wedge she knew to budge him from his course, to make him confide in her. If only Califb and Drcq were with her. They'd not tolerate Felim's ill judgment. Why had not the runners located them? It made her uneasy. Where was Cumhal? It'd been two days since they'd spoken.

"Felim, listen to me. I—"

"I have heard you, Morrigan. But you are a woman and do not understand the intricacies of policies."

"I comprehend more than you think."

Felim waved his hand at her, called for ale.

Morrigan exhaled an angry breath. If only she could

break down his barriers they might be able to come upon a course that would free Goll, and allow her to get back to Castle MacKay. She wanted to sprint out the door that very moment, find a horse, and ride north as fast as she could. She missed Hugh with all her being. She wanted and needed his good sense, his strong hand in managing her cousin.

" 'Tis a matter for a conference of the family. I'm thinking," Morrigan broached the subject again. "Those who formed the plan to accost me and my entourage must be found and punished."

Felim frowned. "They only harmed Scots. What is that to me?"

Morrigan kept her temper in check, though she itched to poke her cousin in his long quivering nose. "What of Cumhal? Is he not your brother?"

Felim pondered that. "He's more than equal to the task of caring for himself, Morrigan. Remember what a bully he was when he was a lad. Think no more on this."

Actually she recalled Felim as being troublesome, instigating mischief, then laying it on Cumhal when it didn't work out. She held her tongue, not wanting to get into an uproar if she pointed that out to her mercurial relative. They'd been arguing since her tattered arrival, and she'd gotten nowhere. "If you persist in doing nothing, then I, as a royal of Wales, will institute my own search for the predators who dared to set upon me." When Felim stared at her, blinking, alarm beginning to crease his features, she stared back.

"Listen well to me, Felim. I call for vengeance against those who attacked my coterie and my allies. Those Scots were friends to me, sworn to protect me. They were attacked with no provocation. The perpetrators will be found and punishment will be exacted. That's my covenant."

Felim waved his hand in the air. "Do not get discomposed over this. 'Tis of little importance."

"To me it's paramount." If Hugh were here, he'd override Felim's stubbornness. She closed her eyes for a moment, seeing her husband in her mind's eye. She wanted him here, putting Felim in his place, finding the ones who ambushed her Scots. Then she wanted him to take her in his arms, put her up before him on Orion and take her back to Scotland. "There could be war over this, Felim. Think on that."

A strange look shadowed his face, then it was gone.

Alarmed, Morrigan stared at her cousin. "Felim, who is advising you?"

Bellowing like a stung bull, he roared to his feet, stomping up and down the great room, scattering attendants like leaves in the wind. In moments the great room was empty, few wishing to risk the ire of their lord. "You dare accuse me of being led? I am the leader. None tell me how to go on, or how to manage my people." He swung his arm to encompass the messy room with its stained rushes, fireplaces that belched more smoke than heat, tattered tapestries. "Look at my castle and tell me it could be better managed."

"I will, and it could be by anyone," she shot back, anger spilling from her at last. "The lowest beggar in the land could've managed this better than you."

Dumbfounded, Felim stared at her, breathing in and out as though he'd run up a hillock. "I'll excuse your unseemly behavior, your nasty words, this time, for I know how women run to ill humors. My Mathilde is the same. That's why she rarely shows her face at this castle." His unctuous smile went over Morrigan. "She knows her place."

"Does she? Or does she avoid your presence because of ennui?"

Felim wrinkled his nose, his chin quivering. "No, no, that can't be it. She knows my importance."

Rage made Morrigan's mouth sour. She swallowed the wrath because she didn't want to send her cousin into one of his long harangues about his position in life, and everyone else's. "Perhaps we're off the point."

"You might be. I never am," Felim told her.

At any other time she might've laughed at his pomposity. Now it worried her. She knew something was in the wind, otherwise her cousin wouldn't have had that arrested look on his face. If he'd been flummoxed by another, coaxed into an unwise move, she'd better know it. All of Wales could burst into flames while her cousin was ranting how important he was. He'd not see one tongue of fire even if it licked about his boots. Fool that he was. Risking his pique, she decided to toss a verbal lance.

"I like it not if you've given over your powers to any other than Llywelyns."

Felim sputtered, reddened, blustered, enforcing the feeling that she'd struck the mark. "You speak with the tongue of a witch, Morrigan. All know my honor, my loyalty to the family." He glowered. "My leadership is never in question."

Of course it is, fool, she said to herself. You just never see anyone's point of view but your own. Countless Llywelyns and others know of your inability to lead, your predilection for confiding in the wrong people. Her mind boiled over with argument. It took every bit of strength she had to hold back. "Perhaps we should speak of other things . . . and come back to this." She'd never get too much out of him with a frontal attack. Her head ached with the need to have done with Welsh intrigue. Find Goll, get him freed, then get back to Scotland. Why had she bothered to come on this fruitless quest?

Slightly mollified, he nodded. "I think we needn't come back to it. I'm satisfied all is well."

"What of Goll?"

Felim blinked again, his face reddening. Then he looked away from her. "He's . . . fine. Don't worry."

Alarms went off in her head. A sense of danger seemed to dance around the room. It hit her with such force, she gazed around her. "What does that mean?"

"Nothing."

"We have to find him. Isn't what why I'm here?"

"There's another reason."

Suspicion sharpened in her. "Am I wrong in thinking that there's nothing wrong with Goll? That I was brought here under a pretext?"

"Certainly not."

His bluster made her shake her head. "You never lied well, though you tried." She slapped her hand on the trencher board. "Tell me the truth."

Felim stepped back, looking affronted. "I have."

"No, I fear not. Listen to me. I'd rather be back in Scotland. It angers me that my time was wasted in coming here."

"You're wrong," Felim blustered.

She shook her head. "No. I've struck the mark when I say your evasions are foolish and they waste my time." She took a deep breath. "I'll have no more of it. If I find you've conspired against me and mine, I will gather my brothers and get you out of power."

"You can't," Felim wheezed.

"You know I can."

"What more did you want to say, Morrigan?" His smile wobbled on being congenial, though he couldn't hide his grim and fearful acceptance of what she'd said.

"The invasion of Trevelyan holdings. As regent, I cannot think it honorable."

"Then give over the guardianship to me." Felim smiled. "That's the best thing to do."

"Since that was Edward Baliol's choice, not yours, and since he chose me, I think you should take that up with him," she riposted, knowing full well her cousin wouldn't seek out the King of Scotland. He'd never been to the "country of barbarians" as he called it, nor would he. No doubt he feared the monarch as many other Welsh did.

"Then make out an order to free up the gold to release our brother, Goll. You will be killing him, lest you do."

Morrigan had the distinct impression her cousin was repeating some directive. "No, I think you are killing him if you don't mount a campaign to look for him and punish the miscreants who dared such an affront to our family."

His startled anger let her know he hadn't expected nor wanted a reprimand. "Think you I've not done all I should?" His surly tone rang around the room.

"If all has been done as should be, we should know where Goll is by now. Mayhap he would be back with us." She held her breath, well aware of Felim's unpredictability. If only she'd waited for Hugh, brought him with her, he would've handled Felim, the fool.

"That is true," he muttered, his brow wrinkled in deep thought. "Things would work better if I had more control. Some say 'twould be better if I were the only leader of Llywelyns."

Who had drummed such a thing into Felim's thinking? Once more it would seem he repeated a well-worn theme. Who had filled his head with such? She closed her eyes for a moment, then opened them, forcing a smile. "Is not my brother Califb leader of the Llywelyns?"

Felim glowered at her. "He's always away on one

quest or another. He's a spiritless whelp who shouldn't be ministering the estates."

" 'Tis his right as chief." Morrigan had to agree that her sweet-natured brother didn't monitor his family holdings as he should. He was far more comfortable in the Land of the Pharaohs studying the ancient languages, digging around for artifacts that others considered useless. "If truth be told I needn't wait for Califb. Since Drcq is his lieutenant, and named to act in his absence, he can act. If you've displeased him, or betrayed the good offices bestowed upon you, he can and will bring down troubles on your house, cousin."

Felim swallowed. "I'm a loyal Llywelyn." He lifted his chin. "It is Califb who is in question. Did not one of the family confessors accuse him of being in league with the dead Pharaohs?"

Morrigan laughed. "That didn't displease Califb. He told anyone who would listen about it. He was delighted." In many ways her brother was impossible, Morrigan had to admit that. When it came to the good of his people he was openhanded and most generous. There were no slaves among the Llywelyns, and even those in the lowliest jobs drew pay and could be independent. Califb was loved by the people. Yet he tended to handle things, then be gone for long periods. Morrigan had the feeling her brother was sorely neglecting his tasks.

Felim threw out his chest, most of which had sunk to his middle. "I'm the man for the job. I consult good people and know what's good for the family."

"Then if you are as informed as you say"—she felt his hard stare—"and I'm sure you are, you must know 'twould be dishonoring our family if we invaded another estate's coffers. The Llywelyn name is too proud to—"

"You needn't tell me about family pride. I carry the banner of Llywelyn high and none can gainsay me on that." Felim discoursed for a few moments on his many virtues.

Even if his liabilities were pointed out to him, Felim would be the last person to accept he had them. Morrigan closed her eyes and prayed for patience.

The more needful Morrigan became to return to Castle MacKay, the more impatient she'd become with her stubborn cousin. "Nothing will be done with the Trevelyan trust. I decree it."

"You can't do that," Felim protested, looking fearful.

"I can and have. Now to the problem of Goll."

"I'm . . . I'm handling it."

"You're not. I've said over and over, Felim, that we have to have a plan, that we need to send out runners who will locate Goll so we might free him."

"You repeat yourself," Felim adjured.

"Because you don't listen," she riposted, her voice rising in spite of her determination to keep a cool head.

Felim floundered. "And have you a plan?"

Morrigan took deep breaths. "I thought we might put our heads together on this," she said, spacing her words, struggling to keep her ire in check.

"We can do that."

Counting backward didn't salve her temper. "First we must study what could occur if we take certain steps."

"What would that be?"

Reining in the retort that rose to her lips, she swallowed. "If we pay the blackmail, as requested, how will we know Goll is all right? What guarantee do we have that Goll is well at this moment? Have you inquired about his health at the present from those who importune you for ill-gotten gains?"

Felim glanced at her, scowling. "That might be dangerous."

It hadn't occurred to him, Morrigan translated. Why had they handed the keys of the eastern limb of the family over to Felim instead of Cumhal? True, Felim was older than the twins, Cumhal and Goll. Felim didn't even resemble his brothers that much.

Cumhal and Goll were taller, more muscular. Both the twins had the head to handle the many branches of business the family had. Cumhal, at least, was more caring about Llywelyns. Goll might've been more casual, but he wouldn't have allowed the family manse to decay in such a way.

Felim was worse than she recalled. He seemed to decide through his conceit, rather than using facts and figures to come to a conclusion. What was good for him should be good for the family seemed to be his credo. Feeding into that ego was the best way to control him. She was almost sure someone had.

"Where is he being held?"

Felim wrinkled up his nose. "Not sure. Maybe in Ireland."

"We should know that, and his condition before we entrust persons or money into a foe's encampment."

Felim got to his feet, striding up and down in the shabby great room. Once, in her father's day, it'd been a grand castle, all accoutrements of the best. The armor had glistened with care, there'd been no tapestries in shreds. It would seem Felim either had little gold for housekeeping, or it was being put to poor use.

Morrigan looked around for the maîtresse d'hôtel. As usual she wasn't there. No doubt steeping herself in some of the homemade ale in the cookery.

Stepping down from the dais, she went to the fire and swung the steaming kettle toward her. She tipped the boiling water into the pot she held, swirled it around, and tipped the water at the edge of the fire to a runoff through the bricks. Then she measured leaves into the pot and poured more boiling water over the whole.

"Perhaps you'd best make me some. My head aches," Felim complained.

Not from thinking, she was certain. The words ground in her mind the same way she ground more leaves with the mortar and pestle before adding them to the brew, along with more water. Arguing with Felim had had poor results over the last days. No matter how skewed his viewpoint, he'd only dug in his heels and found a number of foolish reasons to stick to his way of doing things.

She brought the kettle and mugs to the trencher and poured for both of them. "We have so much more able help in Scotland," she observed, hoping to find a chink in her cousin's armor.

"You're richer up there. The reivers are more agile." Felim laughed at his joke.

"Mayhap they are. I know I don't have to wait on myself because my help are in the kitchen downing the church wine."

"Are they?" Felim looked more surprised than displeased. "Oh well, the priest doesn't come until Sunday."

Morrigan closed her eyes and counted backward again, hoping it would calm her. It didn't. "That was a jest, cousin."

"What?"

"Never mind."

He frowned at her. "Do you know, Morrigan, I think you've become addled from living in the north. The mad Scots have made you one of them."

Frustrated, she was about to throw back a stinging retort when there was a flurry at the door.

Felim looked up from his sassafras tea. He blinked. "Well, by the gods, look who it is, cousin. Your favorite, I'll be bound."

Morrigan put down her cup and rose to her feet, eyeing her longtime friend. It seemed another age when she pondered being his wife. Relief that it hadn't happened almost made her smile. What would Hugh have to say if he knew that she preferred him to all others in Wales or Scotland? She missed him sorely, quite sure he would've made short work of Felim's evasions. She had to get home to her husband and to Rhys. She moved toward him, her hands held out in greeting.

"Tarquin! How good of you to come. I've been visiting Felim as you can see."

Tarquin approached, bending over her hands, his mouth lingering there.

Felim grinned. "Easy to see where your interest lies, eh, Tarquin?"

Morrigan looked over her shoulder at her cousin. "Since I'm now Lady MacKay, that shouldn't be a concern."

"That can be changed." Felim chuckled.

Morrigan frowned. "What does that mean?"

"He means that your marriage is at this moment being absolved so that we might wed, beloved." Tarquin bent to kiss her cheek.

Felim chuckled. "See, our ruse brought you, Morrigan, now you can be happy."

Reeling, Morrigan grabbed at the kernel of disbelief that was mushrooming into horror. "Then Goll is not incarcerated?"

Felim nodded. "He is, but he'll be freed when you marry Tarquin. Then the regent of Trevelyan will pass to him and the gold will be given to Wales, as it should be."

"This can't be," she whispered. "No marriage can be dissolved. Only the pope can do that, and only under special circumstances. Generally the wife goes into the convent, or the man to the priesthood—"

"Not this time. 'Tis arranged. Your marriage to Tarquin will take place on the morrow, right here."

Morrigan stared at her cousin, shaking her head. "It can't be done. MacKay didn't give his sanction to this. 'Tis infamous."

"No, 'tis right, beloved. You've wanted to be my wife, and I've wanted it as well. You're overset, but nothing shall stop our union."

"You can't."

"Shh, you're overset. I will get you something."

"No! I have tea."

"Good. I'll bring it to you."

Felim went to Morrigan, bending down to her. "You'll see. All will be well."

She shook her head. "Conspiracy! Can't you see it? You and Tarquin have been fooled. This will bring war—"

"Here you are, Morrigan. Drink this. 'Twill help."

She gulped the tea, feeling as though she was a hare in a snare. Swallowing the entire cup, she looked up at the two men. "You must see that this is the wrong way. . . . Oh!" Dizziness assailed her. "I . . . I should sit down."

Tarquin took her arm, leading her to the dais and the bench. He kept a hold on her, looking at Felim over her head. " 'Tis a tisane to quiet her. She is honor bound to MacKay, so she thinks. When she wakens all will be over and she'll be wed to me."

Felim studied his cousin. "I think this is the right thing." He frowned. "In some ways I think we should wait until she wakens."

"No! It goes as planned."

Felim glowered. "Don't give me commands. This is my castle." He looked down at Morrigan. "Strange. One would think she was fond of the Scot."

"Nonsense."

Felim glowered. "Don't gainsay me! I say she acted as though she loved him." He leaned over Morrigan. "Are you sure she's all right? Her breathing seems shallow."

"She's fine."

The door opened beside the fireplace so quietly, neither heard it, though one had been waiting for it.

The intruder moved up behind Felim with a truncheon, sapping him hard.

"Come, we'll take her out this way."

ELEVEN

**Always to be bravest and to be preeminent
above others.**

Homer

Hugh didn't even pause when he was accosted at the
gates of Cardiff. Sweeping through, his men at his back,
he heard the shouts and sighs of the populace.

"Invasion! Scots!"

He let Toric do the explaining. His eyes were on the
castle. Morrigan was there! She had to be.

Galloping through the barbican, then to the bailey, he
didn't pull up until his steed, sides heaving, slid to a stop
in front of the ironbound wooden door to the castle. He
slid off Orion, patting his neck, and gesturing to one of
his warriors to take the warhorse.

Men poured out of the door when the two parts of
the castle door were pushed outward, swords at the
ready.

Hugh glowered at the guardians who dared draw near.
"Stand back, or feel my wrath. Put up your weapons or

be slain. I've come for my spouse, Lady MacKay, and none shall get in my way."

The warriors hesitated, looking at one another.

"You can't find her here. There's nonesuch." The one who spoke stepped back at the sudden flaring of fury in Laird MacKay's face. When those large hands balled into threats, the warrior could've bitten his tongue.

"What mean you?" Hugh's query came on one angry breath.

"She . . . she was here. Not now. No one . . . has seen her. Some say . . . she was spirited away by demons. The same who smote our lord into constant sleep."

Hugh glared, digesting the halting, fragmented explanation. "Foolishness!"

"Nay, lord. 'Tis truth."

Hugh took a deep breath. Men scattered from the front of him as he drew his sword. "I would see for myself." He knew without checking that MacKays would be at his back, that their weapons would be showing.

The men in front of him melted back like softened wax, allowing a path into the castle.

Hugh narrowed his eyes against the gloom and saw one figure in the great room, next to the fire. "You! You brought my wife to this miserable hole. For that your life is forfeit. First, tell me where she is."

Cumhal moved away from the fire, his hands at his side, his sword in the scabbard. "I would if I could. I've searched these two turns of the day for her, and find no trace." He grimaced at the angry mutters coming from the MacKays. "I've been gone since the day after she arrived. When I reached the castle after leaving your men with Diodura, I rode here as fast as I could. Following Morrigan's instructions to find her brothers, I left again, almost at once. I should've been back sooner. I know she would've waited for my response had she been able." Cumhal paused. "Finally one of my runners found Drcq. Califb is in the Land of the Pharaohs. My cousin will be riding full speed this way."

Growling, Hugh moved forward, dropping his sword. "I'll not wait for any other. I want my wife now, bastard. Speak now or I'll tear the answer from your throat."

Cumhal put up his hands to defend himself, but didn't try to draw a weapon. "And I tell you I don't know."

Hugh would've flung himself upon Morrigan's cousin, but Toric was there, holding him back.

"Stop! Hugh, listen." Toric had both arms around his straining relative. Though he put every effort into it, Hugh was bearing him toward Cumhal. "Listen! I've questioned the staff, so have the men. She was here. Now she can't be found. Runners have gone out all over the land. They can't find her." Toric eyed Cumhal in baleful study. " 'Twould seem her cousin is telling the truth."

Hugh stopped, almost toppling Toric to the floor. He looked only at Cumhal. "When did you last see her?"

"When I arrived the first time. We tried to talk to my brother. He was impossible. That's when she sent me to search out her brothers. I did. Your men—"

"They told me," Hugh interrupted, his tone harsh.

Cumhal nodded. "I'm glad they made it back to your holding." He paused. "Morrigan and I couldn't convince Felim to our way of thinking. We tried to get Felim to contact those who'd kidnapped my other brother, Goll—"

"So? Get on with it." Hugh strode up and down the great room.

Cumhal's glance slid to Toric, who grimaced and shrugged.

"Hugh MacKay knows you tried to help his men. 'Tis his worry for Morrigan that makes him rash," Toric whispered.

Cumhal nodded. "I, too, fear for her. This is Castle Llywelyn. This should be the safest place on earth for her." He watched Laird MacKay examine the lancets, then the fireplace, his hands pressing and thumping.

"Except for Castle MacKay," Toric muttered.

Cumhal glared at him, then looked back at MacKay. "What does he do?"

"He looks for—"

Hugh's growl of triumph sliced through the words.

"What is it, Hugh?"

"This is a way unknown to you?" Hugh turned his head, though he continued to press on the bricks nearest the tapestries.

"What?" Cumhal expostulated. "I don't understand . . ." Stunned, he watched the wall next to the fireplace swing open. "I . . . I never knew of this." He shook his head.

Hugh put his head inside, then went to the fire, pulling out a burning faggot, holding it high so that it shone into what appeared to be a narrow tunnel. "It seems someone has restored an old escape route."

Cumhal rushed to his side. He went down on his hands and knees and started to crawl inside.

Hugh's hand stopped him. "Where do you go?"

"To the end," Cumhal told him, his mouth grim. " 'Twould seem there have been plans at Castle Llywelyn that are unknown to me." He leaned into the tunnel again, and brought out a small piece of fabric, frayed as though it'd been torn. "I'm not sure, but this could be a scrap from Morrigan's raiment."

Hugh snatched it from him, staring down at it. Then he looked up at Toric. "I want runners, going to every section of this holding. Get more men if you must. Send messages to the border. The Ferguson, Johnston, and Douglas clans will have spotters there. I want every hillock in Wales combed until I find her."

Toric nodded, speeding from the room.

Cumhal stared at Hugh. "I cannot ask your forgiveness for leading your wife here. I truly thought it was to help my brother. Felim couldn't have known anything about this—"

"I want to speak to him now," Hugh snapped.

Cumhal shook his head. "My brother is upstairs, waiting to die. He's not been sensate since the day I found my cousin gone. He doesn't open his eyes, nor does he speak. His breathing is shallow. Only a little water has he had in three days because the women force it down his throat." Cumhal swallowed. "I'm afraid the blow he suffered has rendered him at death's door. I'm sure 'twas then that Morrigan was taken."

Hugh cursed, looking around the room. When he spied the decanter, he went to it.

"I can bring you nourishment if you like," Cumhal offered.

Hugh shook his head, sniffing. "This has an elusive fragrance. Would it be the same poison that downed my men?"

Cumhal frowned. "There was no poison. They were wounded. I was there. I saw the rabble that attacked us." His mouth soured. " 'Twould seem they ached to slay me as well. 'Twas Morrigan who saved my hide, for they didn't want to kill me in front of her." At Hugh's speculative look he curled up his fists. "I give you my word I sensed infamy at the time, but didn't see it directed at your men or Morrigan. I thought I was the target."

"Why?"

"Among those who attacked us . . . I thought at first one belonged to a member of my family who holds me in antipathy." He lifted his hands. "I'm sure now I was mistaken."

"Why?"

"Because I didn't see him, or his likeness, again while

we fought or after that. Nor did I see him when I came to Cardiff and I looked." He hesitated. "How did you save the men if they were so afflicted?"

"You sent them to Diodura."

"I did." Cumhal nodded. "She would've recognized the symptoms."

"She did. I'm in your debt for that. Had she not succored them they would've died soon after reaching Castle MacKay." He glared. "She told me that the tincture was refined to cause the delayed death. She told us if they had begun to lose the use of their limbs they would've been beyond saving."

"What devil's brew was this?"

"She called it tincture of hellebore that'd been on the swords of the opponents."

"Hellebore? How would the rabble I saw know about such concoctions? Only the wisest of witches can brew poisons to react as they wish. Surely . . ."

The noise at the entrance pulled Hugh's gaze. "Speak!" he demanded of Seamus, one of his men.

"An old one who makes basket from the reeds on the edge of the sea"—Seamus sputtered each word, out of breath—"approached me, saying he saw men from the castle come out as though from the wall, carrying something to the river."

"Whence?"

"He knew not the exact time or place, Hugh. It might've been a day or more past. More importantly he

did say there was an old castle on the river, abandoned
by the Llywelyns many—."

"Druida Castle!" Cumhal yelled. "I know it."

"Horses!" Hugh bellowed. Then he turned to Cumhal.
"You'd better remain here. Your brother may need
you—"

"And you think I might take my sword to you when
you attack my relatives. Is that it?"

Hugh shrugged. "I've no time to argue."

"Neither have I. I'll set attendants on Felim." His
smile was grim. "I didn't think to question if my brother
had been given a potion and this is what makes him
sleep. I'd thought it was the lump on his head that held
him in thrall. I'll talk to the attendant who minds him,
then I'm coming with you. Morrigan was set upon.
She's your wife, but my cousin. Llywelyns don't take to
backstabbing."

Hugh inhaled. "'Twould seem there's a question
about some."

Cumhal reddened but said nothing. He left the chamber on the run but was back in moments. He listened as
the Laird MacKay rallied his men, then he followed him
as he entered the narrow tunnel behind the fireplace.

Morrigan knew she ailed. If she could keep her scattered
wits in place she might be able to factor why, and how
to neutralize. She had skills! Use them. Her foggy
thoughts couldn't seem to bring energy into play. When
she lifted her head the world spun. Hugh! Come to me.

In a sudden misty memory she recalled their love-making. At once there was a quickening of her blood. How her chest hurt with desire.

She could feel his hands going over her, his mouth following the hands, carrying her into ecstasy. Her arms reached up to enfold him, to bring him closer. She closed her eyes, feeling his kiss—

"What think you? Can we take her down and have her sign the papers?"

"She must."

The chamber door shut.

Morrigan didn't open her eyes. Her wits, though not sharp, told her she was safer pretending to be sleeping and listening than trying to convince Tarquin and Goll to release her. Tarquin had talked of bedding her! Exchanging vows with her! He was mad. She'd not allow him to touch her. Only Hugh could. As cloudy as her mind was, she would've known had Tarquin or any other man touched her. If any tried, she'd do all she could to kill them.

Why? Why had they set upon her? What did she have they could want? Trevelyan? Edward Baliol wouldn't allow it. Nor would she allow anyone to touch Rhys's legacy.

"Once she signs the holding over to you, we'll be done with her," Goll said.

Tarquin shook his head. "I think not. I would have the vows spoken between us and keep her as wife." He frowned. "Even Felim said I was to be wed to her two days past. I will not wait on this." He glared. "Had you not decided to eliminate Felim he would've put his arguments for my marriage before Morrigan. She would've been easier to handle."

" 'Tis nonsense, man. Felim believed she was to be married to you at his castle. I fed him such to lever him to our side. How could you have spoken vows with her? She's been insensate since we took her, in and out, not able to speak most times. We'll put her signature on the papers and have done with it."

"I would have her as wife. I would know what draws the Scot to her."

" 'Twould be foolish to keep her, she would know too much and might talk to the wrong person."

"I want her." He shrugged. "Maybe not for long. Who knows? She might bore me. I will try her. Besides, she will be the winning roll of the ivories if the Scot declares war upon us."

"Then make sure she's neutralized."

"Where do I keep her until I can inform MacKay that she's no longer his wife? He'll come at us hard and fast. His reputation is bruited about all over Scotland and Wales. When he makes war, he wins."

"Not this time. The plan calls for him to die as well."

Morrigan was dizzy. She couldn't have heard right. 'Twould bring about all-out war across Anglia, Wales, and Scotia to threaten the Earl of MacKay. He was her husband. She was Lady MacKay, no other. Hugh! Come to me. Why were Tarquin and her cousin conspiring?

They had a good share of land to command. Why would they need hers or the Trevelyan holding? They couldn't have either. They didn't need more. She'd have to speak to Califb and to Hugh. Did they say they would kill him? Never! She'd not let them.

"Trevelyan Castle is a most delightful place," Tarquin mused. "I'll not find it uncomfortable to reside there—"

"Not for long," Goll interrupted. "I want that holding. It rightfully belongs to us."

Tarquin's eyes narrowed. " 'Tis my wife who holds it."

"Seek not to go over your station, Tarquin. You might marry a Llywelyn. You'll never be one."

Morrigan paid little attention to Tarquin's cursing. She was more concerned with Goll's treason. She struggled to argue him down on that point. Nothing came out but a moan.

"Ah, she comes out of it. Let's get her downstairs to the chapel."

Tarquin drew back. "We must get the women to change her clothes. If the priest sees her in disarray there'll be questions."

Goll cursed. "All right. Hurry them. The quicker we get this done, the better I'll feel."

"Aye." Tarquin went to the door to hail attendants.

Goll looked down at her. "Well, cousin, finally you'll be of some use to me. With Felim and Cumhal out of the way, next will be your brothers. Wales will be mine. I've worked long and hard for it." His gaze seemed to leave her. "Too hard to share it with anyone." His laughter had an evil sound. "With the help of my friends even the wealth of MacKay is open to me now."

Morrigan fought against the fuzziness. Who was there to stop Goll if not her? She had to ask him questions. She had to tell him about Rhys. No! She couldn't do that. Hugh! Hugh! I need you. Who had put Goll up to this? Had he always been perfidious? She'd thought him nasty at times, not treacherous. His thought processes were not that impressive. Could he have conspired with English Edward?

It was as though she'd entered another world as the clothes were stripped from her body. Neither Goll nor Tarquin left the chamber when this was happening. Neither did they turn their faces away when she was disrobed. Morrigan would've been horrified if her muddled mind hadn't been more ensnared by the danger these two could bring to Rhys and Hugh.

"She has a lovely form, to be sure," Goll murmured, his eyes sliding to Tarquin. He smiled at the avidity on the other's features. "No doubt you'll want more than a taste of her before she's sent to her heavenly reward." Goll chuckled.

"No doubt. I may want her for more than a taste, but I'll control her so that she does not interfere with you." Tarquin looked at him. "Does it not bother you to ponder sentencing your childhood playmate to death?"

"Not a whit. And do your scruples decry her demise if she does not please you in bed?"

"No, but I fear 'twill not suit me to send her heaven-ward until she does cause me ennui. My lust overrides my need for Trevelyan. I would keep her alive for a time. At least until I'm sated." His gaze fastened to Morrigan once more. He didn't see Goll's speculative gaze on him, the tightening of those lips that looked more feminine than masculine.

Goll touched his arm. "Mayhap we might both use her . . . together. What say you?"

Tarquin frowned. "I've not done that. I would taste her first. If she is adequate you might be included," Tarquin said, his manner lofty, his gaze going back to Morrigan almost at once.

"How things stay the same," Goll whispered. "When I was a lad, you, Felim and Cumhal were ever deciding what was right for me. How strange you would think it hadn't changed."

"What?" Tarquin looked back at him as the last bit of clothing was shoved onto Morrigan.

"Nothing," Goll murmured. Then he glanced at Morrigan and scowled at the attendant. "Her hair, fool, brush it or something and get that headdress on her. Wait! Leave the necklace. She needs it not." He put his hand out for the exquisite piece.

"Morrigan's father gave those to her mother." Tarquin glared. "Those gems belong to me as her spouse." He grabbed Goll's wrist, twisting it. "You surprise me. For a narrow man you have much strength in your arms."

"Yes. Hunting is helpful." Though his mouth smiled, and he handed the necklace to Tarquin, his eyes were cold. He looked around at the attendant who'd dragged a coarse iron comb through Morrigan's hair, snapping her head up and down in ruthless determination to be done. "Get her on her feet. We'll drag her between us."

"Be discreet," Tarquin warned. "We can't let the priest think she is anything but shy."

Goll nodded.

Down the stairs they went, all but dragging Morrigan until they reached the bottom.

Hugh sat forward on his saddle, staring at the dank, dark-looking pile of stones. "We can't make a mistake on this," he said through his teeth. "I don't have a good feeling."

Cumhal stared at him, wondering if those who defied this man ever lived very long. " 'Tisn't easy to enter this enclave without being seen. It's been well placed on that spit of land that juts past the river to the sea. Water on two sides, open space on the third."

Hugh eyed him. "Would it seem strange if the ancient who built this had the same idea of entry as the one who built Cardiff Castle?"

Toric grinned at his laird, his smile touching Cumhal. "I ask to check this out, Hugh."

Hugh shook his head. "No time. We go forward, one at a time, lookouts as usual." He sucked in air. "We assume 'tis the same, and we hurry."

Toric's smile faded at the hoarse urgency in his laird's voice. He turned, gave the hand signals, and they went forward at a gallop, following Hugh without question.

Cumhal was right behind Toric, his horse almost touching the hindquarters of the one in front of him.

Hugh went through the heavy copse of trees fronting the river, then let his steed drop down into the water, letting it swim to the side of the battlements. He didn't even look up to see if there was a spotter. His bowmen would take care of that. In speedy inspection he checked the walls, guessing at the placement of the great room.

He almost shouted for joy when he saw the clumps of brush, heavier, thicker in one spot. He went to it as fast as he could, then was off Orion before the horse had halted. The steed was taken from him at once by a MacKay.

Hugh gave no orders, assuming, and rightly, that his MacKays would disperse into battle strategy.

Pushing, shoving, testing, barely reining in his urgency, Hugh worked without pausing over the crumbly stonework. Then there was a godawful squeak and squawk of raw stonework abrading mortar. It sounded clarion clear and strong even through the roar of the wind howling off the sea.

Hugh held his breath, expecting an outcry, but he didn't stop trying to make the opening wider. Before he could request it, Toric put a flint and flambeaux into his hand. Stretching into the opening, he lit the torch, noting it was covered with mold and webs.

Plunging into it, he led his men in the circuitous tunnel that led upward in shallow and steep rises. Small piles of rock impeded them, crumbling about them as they moved. Hugh didn't halt his forward thrusts.

When he heard voices he paused, his men stilling as soon as he did.

Words came in shadowy echoes through the walls.

"I fear your new bride has wedding-day nerves, Sir Tarquin." The speaker paused. "I wish I felt more sure about the papyrus stating the annulment."

"You can be sure it's authentic. Priests from your monastery sanctioned it, as did the bishop. You saw the signatures."

"I did. Annulment is such a rare thing. I did not know it could go forth so quickly. Of course the MacKay is a powerful man and his wishes would be catered to by the Church."

"Just so," Tarquin murmured.

"I did not know that the MacKay preferred men to women and would put her aside because of it."

"Yes, 'tis passing strange. Her cousin and I thought it important that we speed this nuptial to spare her lacerated nerves. She suffered much being married to MacKay."

"Yes, she must have. I was glad to see her retire to bed. 'Tis sad for a woman when she's not wanted."

"Yes," Tarquin answered. "How kind of you to allow her to retreat to her bedchamber, Monseigneur. I'm sure when I take her to wife her nerves will settle. Mayhap we may have a child this year."

"Ah, that would be good for her."

"I think so. Do have more wine. We are quite proud of this vintage."

"Ah, thank you. Llywelyns and Trevelyans have vineyards across the sea, do they not? How kind of them to let you use them."

"Yes," Tarquin replied, eyeing the impatient Goll. "Perhaps you will allow me to show you our vineyards one day."

"How kind. I have a love affair with Provence. Our monastery is there, you see."

Goll moved away from the wall, but Tarquin waved him back.

It'd taken all Hugh's strength not to push through the wall and slay the three who occupied the room. Morrigan wasn't there! She was his first order of importance. The fool thought he would touch her, take her to wife. For thinking such he'd die.

The scurrying of rats and other vermin that seemed to fill the tunnel halted him not one whit. The torch had flickered more than once, but kept on burning. Wind whistled down the tunnel from the many openings caused by decay and neglect.

Then he stopped. He was at the top of the tunnel. Taking a deep breath, muttering a prayer to all the gods of yore, and to the Savior, he pushed hard with his shoulder. Nothing!

"Try one of the bricks on either side of you, about head high. I recall this in one of my uncle's holdings, though I'd never expected it in Felim's castle."

Hugh recognized the voice as Cumhal's. Though he still had his suspicions of Morrigan's relative, he obeyed.

Again there was a very raucous, tooth-grinding squeaking, and a narrow door pushed open.

Hugh drew his dirk, having no room to pull his sword, and pushed into the room. Rolling to his feet, he whirled, gauging the peril. No one—

"Hugh . . ."

The moan spun him toward the bed. She'd called him! When he was closer he saw that she'd made a sound, called to him, but her eyes were closed. She was so very weak. "Morrigan! Look at me."

She turned her head with great effort. She had to struggle to open her eyes. "Hugh! Am . . . I . . . dreaming . . . again?"

"No, love. I'm here."

She tried to lift her hand. It fell back. "I . . . die."

Hugh's heart nearly burst in his chest. She'd been poisoned as his men had been? Could he get her to Diodura in time?

He turned to his men. "We don't fight this day. We must get your lady to safety."

Cumhal glanced at Morrigan, then at Hugh's face. "I like it not. She won't—"

"She will," Hugh said through his teeth. "We must pass her down the tunnel. Get the horses. We ride for the sea."

Cumhal hesitated, then went back into the tunnel.

Hugh looked around the room, noting the chalice near the bed. No doubt it carried the poison.

"God help me. She must be saved," he muttered, then dove into the tunnel cuddling Morrigan. He didn't want any to touch her, but for speed, he had to pass her downward to his men. One MacKay remained to make sure the door was safely shut behind them.

TWELVE

Give me where to stand, and I will move
the earth.

Archimedes

Hugh hovered over her, each night sleeping with her held tight in his arms. Each day he rarely left her room, except to wash and clothe himself.

Only once did he show himself down in the great room and only long enough to give instructions to Toric. Then he'd leave at once and go back to his wife.

Cumhal had returned with them to Castle MacKay. He strode up and down the room, glancing at Hugh's chief lieutenant. "What plans do you make, Toric?"

Toric looked at Cumhal. "You expect too much if you wish our trust. Our lady could have died in that rubble called Castle Druida. There were none to help her. Now you quiz me on what we'll do."

Cumhal flushed. "I can't expect you to trust me, but I will stay here, and follow you into battle if I must. What was done to Morrigan was done to me. If Califb was at home where he should be, he would be summoning armies to right this wrong."

"But he isn't, is he?" Toric shot back. "Our lady has two brothers, Drcq and Califb. Neither protected her from the vermin. Had she died we would have burned all of Wales, Cumhal. Believe that."

Cumhal nodded, not trying to hide his bitterness. "I would've helped you, Toric MacKay."

Toric nodded, though his visage didn't lighten.

In the upper chamber, Hugh hovered as Dilla and Diodura changed her clothing again as they'd been doing on and off since he'd brought her home three turns of the sun past. They'd risked heavy seas, and nearly killed their horses to get her back. Now they would wait.

He leaned over the bed.

Diodura glared at him. "Move back, gomeril. You're in the way."

Dilla shook her head. "The witch presumes," she muttered.

Norah, another MacKay, gasped. "None has ever called Hugh MacKay fool, in any language, including Gaelic."

Dilla glared. " 'Tis of no import."

Norah winced, nodded, then went to gather the soiled linen.

Hugh took it in stride. "She doesn't change."

"She's been poisoned, fool. What do you expect? Had not she the courage of Trevelyan and Llywelyn she would've died the first day."

Hugh had stopped wondering at the witch's persistent mentionings of the family Trevelyan. As far as he knew his Morrigan wasn't even related to the family and was regent because the holding marched with her own. "I want her well."

Dilla bit her lip. "I would comfort our laird in his anguish, but there are no words that could assuage."

Andra, who stood with her, put his arm about her. "He's lost a stone of weight with worry, ye' ken." He kissed his trembling wife.

As though she felt him calling to her, Morrigan whispered his name.

Diodura cackled. "The herbs are working on her."

Hugh dropped to his knees, pressing his face to the covering near his wife's face. He'd never cried in his life, not even when he'd once nearly been flogged to death by a captor as a young man. Now he could barely speak with the emotion that choked him. "I'm here, beloved."

Her eyes lifted as though they were weighted. She tried to smile. "I needed . . . you. Our babe—"

"The children are fine. And I'm here." He looked up at Diodura, who was rubbing her hands together, and to Dilla, who was holding her apron to her mouth, tears running from her eyes.

"Hold . . . me . . ." Her words were barely out of her mouth when Hugh scrambled into the bed and caught her close.

"You can never leave me again," he told her, his voice torn with the worry that had weighed him down.

"No."

Diodura backed away from the bed, turning to Dilla. " 'Twill not be easy to speak to them of the babe, though I think Lady Morrigan knew she carried."

Dilla shook her head. "Have you told him?"

Diodura shook her head. "Soon."

"God helped them before. He must now."

"He will." Diodura frowned. "But there are rough waters ahead."

"How can that be? Our lady is back safe to us. We are protected here in Castle MacKay."

Diodura released a long shuddering sigh. "I trust your sight is stronger than mine."

Dilla stared after the witch when she shuffled away, her brow furrowed. "Andra, we will go. I would pray for them."

Andra looked puzzled. "She is getting better."

"The witch says there's trouble ahead."

"Och, no. They will prosper and have other bairns."

"I will pray 'tis so." She glanced once into the bed-chamber heated by a roaring fire, then closed the door. She shivered, as though someone walked on her grave.

Hugh muttered love words into her ears, his hands caressing her, warming her. Though he was totally aroused by holding her, his happiness was greater to have her safe in his arms again. It rocked him that even if they were never intimate again, he would want her, need her, keep her. "When you are well, love, I shall take you to a small hut on the cliffside. You'll see the Orkneys and watch the wild water while I warm thee," he said, in the ancient Icelandic tongue of his mother.

When he leaned back to smile at her, her tears were there, though she was trying to fight them back. "Beloved! You're in pain!"

"No, no." She clutched him when he would've risen from their bed. "Don't leave me. I'm not in the kind of pain that demands Diodura or Dilla." She inhaled a deep, ragged breath. "I need you."

He moved beside her, gathering her close. "Tell me what hurts you so."

"I think I lost our child when I was at Castle Druida. Dilla has not said, nor Diodura, but I sense it is so. What was given me in Druida loosened our spawn from my womb, I'm sure. I will ask Diodura."

Her breathy words speared him. Agony, such as he'd never known, filled him. More than once he'd been wounded in battle. No laceration or contusion had pained as this did. His arms tightened. "Do you need attending now, beloved?"

She sighed. "I didn't want you to leave me, but perhaps I need cleansing." Since this was never done by any but women trained to be attendants, Morrigan thought nothing of it when he rose from the bed.

Hugh went to the fire, pulling the pot toward him and pouring the steaming water into another flatter pot. Then he collected clean swaddlings, and turned toward his wife again.

"You are hurt by my words, Hugh." She tugged the tartan up to her chin.

Seeing the movement, eyes narrowing on her, he comprehended her restraint. "Beloved, we have lost a child. We will grieve. But we have three other children who give us joy. Never ponder I could not think you the most perfect of wives, the most beloved of mothers." He edged back the tartan. "I see only a beautiful woman who shares my pain. Don't shut me out of that."

"No," Morrigan answered, a tear running down toward her ear.

Hugh leaned down and caught it with his tongue. "Fret not, Morrigan. We have our two wonderful sons, Rhys and Conal. They'll grow strong and tall, and bring us much joy. Our beautiful daughter Avis will be the warmth of our lives and make us proud."

"We could have more . . ." she began, then paused. "That angers you?"

"Not at you, beloved. We'll not speak of having other children. You are ailing. 'Tis not necessary to have another child. Three are more than enough."

"But . . ." Her words trailed when he lifted her sleeping raiment and loosened the soiled wrappings. She watched him as he washed her. "Your strokes are more than gentle, husband."

"I revere you, wife. To touch you is an honor."

"You warm me another way. Though I am fatigued, and my body sore and wrenched, my mind spent, my spirit wretched, my being responds to you as it had on first sighting you."

"Stop, wife, you're seducing me." He chuckled, though his hand tremored.

"Good. You've enthralled me, husband. It seems ages since our wedding, though it was mere turns of the moon. Yet, in my heart, it's as though I've always been with you, that we've traveled through many lives to be together."

Hugh had lifted his head, his hand poised over her. "Wife, you warm me."

"I . . . I have the feeling I've always known you."

Pleased, he grinned, taking the soiled wrappings to the fire and tossing them in there. He stared down at his hands, colored with her blood. Anger and sorrow shook him. "And so you have, beloved. Since you'll be living with me for eons forward, we shall discuss it fully." He looked over his shoulder. "For now, I shall get into bed, and we'll nap together." He used hot water and soap to lave himself.

"What if I should want more?"

"Though weakened from your ordeal, you cannot resist teasing me. For shame."

"I'm most happy to be home."

Hugh glowered at her. "You'll not tempt me, woman. Behave yourself." He slid in next to her, catching her close.

Morrigan put her hand on his chest. "Mayhap I already have tempted you. I feel the thunder. Here." She poked him.

"Do you?" He let his mouth rove her face and hair. "To be truthful, you're a sore trial to me."

She laughed and wound her arms around his neck, stifling a wince at the pull from her middle and lower body.

Hugh kissed her over and over, trying to blot the anguish and fury from his mind. They had come at his Morrigan! For that they would pay dearly.

Tarquin stared at Goll, his face mottled, ire and trepidation chasing across his features. He would like to be gone from Druida, but Goll wouldn't hear of it. Since Morrigan's disappearance he'd been like a madman. "How could it happen?"

"Quiet! Do you think I'm not trying to figure it out?" Goll looked around the shabby great room draped in cobwebs, dirt everywhere. Then he strode to the front door, pushing it open, the grating sound of it abrading the ears as it cast off slivers of wood to the stone floor.

"What bothers you?" Tarquin inquired, his tone pitched too high. "We should leave this place. By this time messengers will be on their way to Califb—"

"He's in Egypt."

"Well, Drcq and your brother Cumhal are not. If word goes out to your cousin Boyne of Hibernia, there could be a bloodbath. Morrigan is a favorite of his. Boyne is not patient. In fact he is ferocious."

Goll studied him. "You think I don't know my cousin. I do. As for Califb and Drcq, I discount them. Neither cares for any woman, including their sister. One dreams of the Land of the Dead, the other only of war and glory." Goll's mouth twisted. "I'll give both of them plenty of it when I take over Trevelyan."

Tarquin's face seemed to swell. "I was to take over Trevelyan. She is my wife according to our writ." He frowned. "What does it matter? She's escaped."

"Yes. And I wonder about that, since she had a strong enough potion to kill her."

"What? I was to taste her first."

"Forget that," Goll said, his face creased in thought. He thumped the brick closest to the window, grimacing as mortar powdered around him. "What bedchamber did she reside in here?"

"At the top of the stairs. I don't know which one. It was the least dirty, and spacious enough." Tarquin shrugged. "What did it matter? She wasn't going to remain there long if she hadn't pleased me. I wouldn't have needed to keep her long. Replacing her with another wouldn't have been difficult. To gain the wealth of Trevelyan she would've made me a widower quite soon, I'll be bound." He looked thoughtful. "Unless of course she pleased me, as I've said. Then she would've lasted longer."

"True," Goll said, hiding his disgust with his coconspirator.

"What do we do now?"

"We find another way to get Trevelyan. My other . . . friends have varying solutions to tangled problems. I'll consult them this day."

"What of the others in this scheme? Why haven't you discussed them with me?"

"You didn't ask, and the less prattle about something like this, the better."

"I don't like to be kept in the dark."

Goll swallowed the sharp retort. No need to alienate the fool. He turned and left the room at a run, ignoring the screeches behind him as he mounted the stairs, two at a time. He threw open the door of the first chamber, going right to the fireplace. Nothing! Even as he heard Tarquin ascend, mouthing complaints, his hand found the indentation.

When the narrow door swung open, he ground his teeth. He had the panel shut before Tarquin entered. One day he would seal the fate of his stupid collaborator.

Hugh had his maps on the trencher board. More precious than gems to a strategist, they were papyri given to him by his Viking neighbors in the Orkneys. He pored over them for days, when he wasn't up in the bedchamber with his bride. He'd let no one feed her, change her, dress her, since she'd begun recovering. He had the unholy sensation that if she was out of his sight for too long he could lose her. That was never going to happen.

He pressed the papyrus flat, looking it over, pondering his moves as he'd been doing since finding Morrigan. None who'd plotted against her would survive. Nothing would save those who'd attacked his wife. They'd terrorized her, and tried to kill her. For that they'd forfeit their lives.

"When think you?" Toric asked, leaning over the crackly parchment.

"Soon," Hugh said through his teeth. "I want to see Morrigan well first."

Toric smiled. "Methinks my lady does well. I heard her shout at you yesterday."

Hugh grinned. "She can make her feelings known."

Toric laughed. "The children thrive because she's returned."

"They have." So had he. He could eat and drink without it coming up in his throat as had happened when he hadn't been able to find Morrigan.

MacKay men and woman bustled about the great room, working at an assortment of tasks, some whistling and humming. Things had gone better with their lady back.

"Hugh."

Everything in the great room went silent. Chattering, ale mugs clanking, shuffling of feet, laughter, ceased.

There were gasps, the loudest coming from the laird when he turned and saw who stood there.

"Morrigan! You must not be out of bed," Hugh thundered, racing to her side and scooping her up in his arms. "You could catch a draft." He turned his back on the wide open door of the castle, a cold wind blustering through it. His words were hardly spoken when the door was slammed shut.

"I'm fine," she told him, her arms around his neck.

"You're skin and bones," Toric blurted, reddening when she smiled at him. "Forgive me, Morrigan."

"The weight will come back, too fast, I fear."

"You were never heavy," Hugh whispered to her, cuddling her high against his chest and starting for the stairs.

"Wait!"

At her imperious command, Hugh halted. "What, beloved? You must go back to your upper chambers at once."

"Why the maps? You are going to seek revenge against those who held me, aren't you?"

Hugh wanted to lie. He couldn't. He nodded.

"You mustn't," Morrigan cried. "I'll not have you among that den of trolls again. I don't want it. I won't have one MacKay hurt. I'll not have you wounded. Hear me well."

Stunned MacKays listened, mouths slack. No one ever told Hugh MacKay what he should do. English Edward tried. So had Edward Baliol. Neither had succeeded. Now a slip of a woman, who only came to his chin, who was Welsh no less, was telling him he couldn't wage war.

Mackays rattled their weapons, not sure what side they should take.

Hugh didn't hear. He was staring down at her fragile face, its stubborn set, the slight quivering in her chin. "Fret not, beloved. If you don't wish it, I shall not do it."

Some warriors said later that they couldn't believe their ears, that their knees went weak. Most smiled, poking one another. Their lady had become dear to them. That she could handle MacKay made her even more important.

"What say you, Hugh?" Toric queried, laughing, knowing he risked a slamming into the wall later.

Hugh looked at him. "My wife says no." He glared when MacKays began laughing. "I'll thrash the lot of you," he growled, reading their minds.

"You won't do that either. They're MacKays and I won't let you hurt them," Morrigan whispered.

It was heard. MacKays doubled over in mirth, the words sweeping through the great room and out to the bailey, as one MacKay threw open the door and shouted it as he was running out, slamming the huge oak behind him.

Hugh looked down at her, trying to frown. It didn't come. He was so damned happy to see her moving about, he couldn't push the smile away. "You'll be running the clan, I'm thinking."

"Sooner than you think," she shot back, making him roar with laughter. "I love to see you this way, warm, alive, happy. We have a joyous life, husband. We cannot risk it with a war upon miscreants. They won't dare approach MacKay land, so we are well rid of them."

He sank down onto a bench, still holding her. "I like it not that you're a good stone lighter than you should be."

She shook her head. "Not really. Besides, you've lost as well, Hugh." She put her hand to his cheek. "Fret not. All will be well." She paused, swallowing. "We'll bear a child."

His hands clenched on her. "I'll not want you bearing unless you're well, beloved. I won't be put through that again. When you were unwell 'twas too great a cost."

"Calm yourself," she soothed. "I know a deep part of you won't be calmed because of your fears. Be at peace, Hugh. Don't think we won't have a child. We can. I feel it."

He stared down at her, as though he didn't comprehend. " 'Tis not the babe that hurts me, though the loss of such is an agony." He looked into her eyes. "Do you not know I couldn't lose you? That is my greatest fear, beloved." He marked her stunned expression. When she pressed her face to his chest, he embraced her. He felt her struggling with emotion, her breast heaving against his.

She leaned back, staring at him. "I didn't intend to love you."

He grinned. "I'm irresistible."

"Boor," she chided.

"I also love you." He knew she loved their verbal jousting as much as he did. He wanted to kiss her, to love her, but she had to regain her strength.

She glanced around the now-empty great room. "I do love it here."

Happiness rivered through him. "It's a most wondrous place because you are."

She touched his cheek. "You overwhelm me with your words, Hugh." She pulled his head down and whispered. "Take me to our chamber."

He recoiled. "I . . . can't," he said, his tone hoarse. "You need rest."

"I need you."

"Morrigan," he breathed. "Don't test me this way. I can't hurt you."

"You can only hurt me by rejecting me." She stroked his jaw.

"Diodura—"

Morrigan smiled. "She assured me I could resume my wifely duties."

"Duties?"

"Her words, not mine."

Hugh surged to his feet. "I can't gainsay a soothsayer, one who mended my men and told me you were alive."

When his voice shook at the last, Morrigan twined her arms around his neck. "I knew you'd come for me. I fought to live, knowing that."

Hugh kissed her, his mouth clinging to hers, his heart pounding against her. "My sweet, are you sure . . . ?"

"Very."

"Damn, I love it," Hugh said, sounding like a gleeful boy.

Morrigan laughed.

He strode to the stairs, mounting them, three at a time, as though she were the merest feather he carried.

She pressed her face into his neck.

"Fear not to hide your blush, love. Our peoples know I love you."

Myriad MacKays exited from chambers, then hustled back the way they came, giggling and chuckling behind their hands.

"I have no shame. I want my husband."

"Not as much as I want you."

When the door shut behind them in the chamber, she pushed at him to let her down, so that she stood in front of him. "I have something to say to you, husband."

"What?"

"Nothing matters at this moment in time, except you . . . and me."

"I agree."

She smiled. "I want your strength, the same intensity of purpose that discovered where I was and brought me to you. I have a hunger for you."

"As I have for you."

She moved closer, reaching up to slip her hands around his neck. She edged him closer to the thick tartan in front of the fire. She pulled him down so that they were kneeling, facing each other.

Hugh muttered a blasphemy as his hand curved up under her breast. His hardness touched her and she arched into him. He hissed invective, the desperation behind it making their touching erotic, so sensual. When she rubbed against him, purring her pleasure, his mouth closed over hers again.

He loosened her outer garments, only breaking contact when he had to slip it over her head.

Morrigan was just as busy, pulling open his woolen jerkin and trying to slide it down his arms. She looked at his chest, the dark, russet hair, arrowing down to his belt. She tugged at that.

Pushing her hands aside, he slid off the belt, pushing down so that his clothing left him naked just above his high chausses. He waited for her shock. It didn't come.

She looked her fill, then smiled up at him.

He lifted off the rest of her raiment, staring at her in the sheerest of cloth of Cathay undergarments. When he closed his eyes and took deep breaths, her chuckle was short of air as well.

"You tease me, wife."

"Yes." Her airy giggle had a quiver to it that enticed him.

"You are Helen and Circe in one, beloved."

"You don't like it?" she whispered.

"You know I do." He caressed her bare thighs.

"I had not thought to ever have this," she murmured on a sigh when he kissed her breasts.

"Neither did I," he muttered, rubbing his lips from breast to breast as they rocked together.

She moved back from him, lifting her silky garment

over her head, watching as his face reddened, his breath quickened.

"You are Circe."

"I want to be yours."

"No other."

With the last of her raiment discarded she melted down to the tartan, relaxed as a cat, a wanton pose, her hands free of her body, the fingers curled as though she'd reach to grasp him.

Hugh gulped air, rising to his feet, his gaze fastened to her, as he threw off his chausses, his sword clanking to the stone floor.

Flames outlined him, and she took his measure. "I want and need to fix in my mind how you look at this moment, Hugh."

He paused. "Do you?"

"Yes. You make my heart thump, Lord MacKay."

"I'm scarred from shoulder to foot, beloved."

"I would kiss each one. I care for your form, Hugh. I did not think that I could ever look upon a man this way." She smiled. "I must say I enjoy it."

He laughed. "Make sure it's only mine. You can see what you do to me, beloved."

"All of you is hard, I would say."

He chuckled, feeling blood pump through his limbs because her eyes were on him. He dropped down beside her, taking her breast into his mouth, sucking there, then tantalizing the fullness with his tongue. When her body quivered against him, he had to fight down the need to take her. He lifted his head, his thumb pressing over the rosy nub. "I can't stop watching you, beloved. You were made for me."

"As you were for me?"

He nodded, bending to take the other nipple into his strong flexing jaw, so that he both sucked and blew on the surface. Her gasping sounds pushed his hands over her in softest caresses, each touch setting him on fire.

Responding to the lightning in her body, she arched again, rubbing against him. "I feel your fire, Hugh MacKay. I've never wanted food or drink more. Mayhap you will drive me mad with wanting."

"Nay! I'll be the one, to be sure."

"Don't worry that I will break, husband. I won't."

He eyed her. "I want not to hurt you, yet I would love you in every way."

"Do."

He leaned up from her, drawing her knees up, easing her back when she would've risen. He smiled at the instinct to cover herself, though she'd just encouraged him to love her all ways. He wanted nothing more.

When he lowered his head, she reared up, calling his name.

"Shh. This is what we both want, beloved."

"Yes."

He opened his mouth, finding her woman's place, and placed his lips and tongue there. In slow and even cadence, his tongue took her over and over again.

Morrigan's protests broke to rusty groans of encouragement.

He felt her rise to the peak, then crash in sudden and full climax.

Taking in air as though she couldn't get enough, her body glistening, she looked up at him, shocked, eyes wide. "Hugh?"

"I'm with you, beloved."

Face glinting with the same fever as hers, his body slick with it, he placed his hands on both sides of her. He levered himself over her, entering her with slow, careful strokes.

He watched her, teeth gritted, he edged out, then in again, trying not to hurry, to hurt her. She was such a perfect fit for him, sweetly snug, warm, damp.

When she clutched him, taking more of him, grasping his buttocks, rolling herself tighter into him, he began a tightening motion of his own. Again and again he sank into her, sweat beading his face, air wheezing from his body.

He saw by her sudden gasp, her widening eyes, that she'd begun to share his thunderous questing. When she gasped his name, thrusting back with every thrust of his, he went mad with want.

She was giving to him, more and more. Hugh couldn't believe the wonder of his beautiful lady.

He slipped his hands beneath her hips, cushioning her, tilting her more toward him. Each deepening motion carried them farther into the wondrous land where only they could dwell. Not in all his life had there been such.

"Hugh!"

"Yes, beloved."

"More."

"My love!"

All his energy turned on this, his breath seemed to leave him, ragged, uneven.

Morrigan began the ascent again, pulling him with her.

When the stars burst around them, they sobbed their names, their love, their need.

Long moments they held each other, embracing, stroking, gentling their breathing.

" 'Tis a most wondrous happening. No wonder people marry."

Hugh laughed. "Not all go to heaven as we did, beloved."

She looked up at him. "Why not?"

The question arrested him. He mulled over her question, again taken at her perceptive powers, her level of learning, emphasized by her questions. "Because they cannot find what I have in you, beloved."

She smiled. "And I must have the same in you."

"I would agree."

Morrigan laughed. "Good things have happened to me."

Hugh tried not to let the tumult of emotions show. For him the words brought back how easily she was taken from him, how cavalierly they'd diced with her life. He'd not let her out of his sight again. He touched her neck, rubbing his hands over the silky surface.

"What think you?"

"The necklace that you wore is gone."

She nodded. For a moment sadness filled her, then she smiled. " 'Tis paltry compared to our being together."

He nodded. "But you loved it."

"Yes. 'Twas a gift from my father to my mother. It'd been in his family many years. Some said 'twas sacred to Llywelyns."

"I will regain it."

She touched his face, shaking her head. "No. I'd not want it if it cost one drop of MacKay blood. 'Tis a bauble, nothing more."

Hugh recalled the exquisite cut of the gems, their deep flashing hues, the richness of the gold that bound them. He smiled, but made a secret covenant.

"You ponder other things, Hugh?"

He wanted to evade, not bring up that time when she was in those bastards' clutches in Wales. Truth won out. "I cannot brush away that time when you were in jeopardy."

Her hand cupped his jaw. "I'd not play you false by saying I wasn't frightened. I was. Not seeing you and our children again would've been hell on earth for me." She nipped at his chin. "I also was quite sure you'd find me. And you did, and brought me home. I have my joy again, Hugh. 'Tis all I need." She shook her head. "I didn't think you'd come through the wall."

"You saw me." His hand whorled over her middle.

"I did, though I couldn't move or say much, nor was I sure you weren't a vision."

"I thought your eyes were closed."

She grimaced. "They were slits, I think. I could see you, but it was as though there were bars to my vision. I couldn't make anything work as it should."

"Beloved!" Torn as he'd never been or thought to be, he enfolded her to his chest, kissing her hair.

"I feel your heartbeat against my cheek," she murmured. "It warms me."

"And you heat me, beloved."

She looked up, her eyes alight. "Surely not again."

His face changed, his eyes narrowing. "Are you not well?"

Morrigan laughed, feeling more carefree than she'd ever been. "I am. I am. I just didn't think you could do . . . that so quickly again."

Hugh's eyes glinted over her. "You turn me to fire with your look. I thought you knew that."

"I'm beginning to, husband." She leaned up and kissed him, her mouth clinging to his.

"Good," he muttered, his mouth sliding down her neck to her chest. "You're so beautiful. I need you."

"As I need you."

For the next hour they spent many ways telling each other that, with embraces, touches, kisses. There was no need for mere words.

THIRTEEN

Chaos: A rough, unordered mass of things.
                                        Ovid Naso

Morrigan had been disappointed when she'd had her monthlies, though Diodura told her she would bear a child in good time.

As time went by, it seemed that every MacKay was dedicated to keeping her wrapped in swaddling. Annoyed and amused at the way they rushed to take all chores from her hands, she had to use ingenuity to free herself from the loving shackles. Hugh was the greatest offender. He acted as though she'd break in a thousand pieces if she took a walk.

Many times she took strolls with the twins, Rhys, and their huge water dog called Odin after the Viking god. The fresh air revived her, good food restored her. Her health was returning by leaps and bounds.

Strolling outside one day when the children should have been at lessons, she went to the stable and saw a tall, strapping MacKay leading a spirited filly around on a rope, crooning to the horse as though it were a baby. She went over to the enclosure formed by thick branches woven with hemp. Leaning her chin on the top rung, she studied the animal. Sleek, not large, but quick. Certainly not a destrier, but more for the kind of trick riding the warriors in Wales would do with sword and lance.

All at once the man saw her, his face reddening. His bow was ragged as the steed bumped him in play.

"You're Rufus, aren't you?"

"I am, milady. 'Tis glad am I that you're well," he said in Gaelic.

"I thank thee," she answered in the same way. "What do you call her?"

"She has no name until you give her one. She's to be yours when you're well, milady. Hugh has decreed it." He rolled his eyes. "Oh woe, 'twas to be a surprise."

Morrigan laughed, hiding the rush of ire toward her spouse. When was she supposed to be well? When she was sixty turns of the moon? She was more than fine at that very moment. "Good. Saddle her for me. I would ride this day."

Rufus's mouth dropped, his eyes skating the perimeter of the enclosure as though he'd call for help. "Milady—"

"I'll saddle her myself," Morrigan told him, her momentary regret for upsetting Rufus overridden by the need to get out and stretch her mind and body in the fresh air.

"I'll do it," Rufus said, reaching for the sidesaddle that

most women used. When Morrigan shook her head, pointing to the regulation saddle, Rufus reddened, shaking his
head. "Milady, you've . . . not . . . the . . . split skirt."

Not that he would've approved anyway, Morrigan
was sure. "As you say, I'm not wearing the right raiment. Use the sidesaddle." She nodded her head, acqui-
escing to his wishes. One day she'd remember to don
the split skirt fashioned for her in Wales, made of the
smoothest skin of the sheep, and soft as down feathers.

Rufus exhaled his relief.

Morrigan eyed the sun, then gave the horse handler
her widest smile. "Are Rhys and the twins at their studies, Rufus?" Knowing full well that all MacKays
seemed to know what every other one was doing, she
awaited his reply. Mayhap her three children would be
studying or about their chores. Mayhap not.

Rufus looked up at her. "Milord wants us not to tell
you aught that would alarm you, milady."

"Then Rhys, Conal, and Avis must be doing something terrible."

Shocked, Rufus shook his head, not quite hiding his
misery.

No doubt he'd been informed to tell her nothing.
Morrigan vowed to talk to her husband.

"Conal totted up his words and his special duties with
the Greek studies, milady. Rhys did his stable chores.
Avis joined with the cooks when she was through with
chores." He coughed. "All three have finished their
lessons for the day and were given a choice of games."

"And what did they choose?"

Rufus swallowed. "They're out at the jousting field with Eamon, milady."

Morrigan hid her chagrin. How like her children to be there. No doubt Rhys fooled his instructors into shortening the lessons so that he and his siblings could get to the practice field. Rhys and the twins had far too many people running hither and yon to please them.

"I won't be long, Rufus."

"I'll go with you, milady."

"No need," she told the hapless stable attendant. "I'll be going down to the practice field. I'll not be far."

"But . . . milady . . ."

"Fret not," she said over her shoulder. "You must mind the horses."

"Yes. And I have to wonder what side of my chest the laird will grab when he slams me to the ground." He sighed.

Morrigan loved the smooth gait of the filly, who was fresh and eager to run. Letting her have her head on the wide glen leading to the practice field beyond, she sensed the joy of the horse as she gathered herself and sped down the glen at a gallop.

Wide-eyed MacKays watched their lady fly over the field, jumping hedges and laughing out loud.

More than one dropped the tool they'd been using and hurried after her, concerned and curious.

"She's wild y'un, our lady is," Tolphus muttered, breathing hard as he ran along on his bandy legs.

"Och, aye, though she's braw, I'll be sayin'," said Beamis, panting, then glaring at the many who were joining them. "'Twould think 'twas a circus they'd be seein'."

"Och, aye."

Unaware of the cavalcade at her back, Morrigan raced on, elated, joyous.

Reining in the excited filly, who reared back, she stared down the shallow hill to the flat area called the jousting or practice field, not surprised to see the twins and Rhys with their wooden weapons learning to handle themselves against some of the MacKay warriors. It would seem a goodly number of MacKays had cut short their chores to entertain the threesome.

Laughing, she leaned on the pommel of the high saddle and watched the tableau of the eager children intent on their lessons.

Easing the filly down the slope, she was very quiet, but Rhys saw her nevertheless, and ran over to greet her.

"Maman!" Rhys shouted. "Come see me slay Eamon."

"Me, too," Conal shouted.

"I can, too," the quieter Avis said, more shy than the boys.

Morrigan approached, acknowledging the bows from the men in their leather aprons. She eyed Eamon. "Bloodthirsty lot, aren't they?"

He grinned. "They are indeed, milady. They would slay all of us."

"Leave us a few MacKays if you will," Morrigan told the children, who grinned back at her. It touched her heart at how healthy the twins were, how they could move swiftly with the leather breeks that'd been fashioned for them, fitting over the legs and up over their hips. Dilla had assured her that they were getting stronger each day, that perhaps one day soon they would not need braces for their limbs.

"Come and fight us, maman," Rhys insisted.

When Eamon would've interceded, Morrigan waved him back. "And who will I fight?"

"Not me," Rhys answered. "I could hurt you. You can fight Urdred." Rhys pointed to the largest of the warriors, whose face reddened.

"All right," Morrigan concurred, earning a horrified look from the MacKays and consternation from Urdred.

"Milady, I—"

"Mind your weapons, Urdred," Morrigan instructed, going to the armorer, overriding his reluctance and choosing a short sword. There were blades covered with leather and the wooden weapons with rounded edges. Morrigan chose a leather-bound sword, preferring its balance.

"Milady, I couldn't—"

"Of course you can," she told the large man who'd come to her side and bent down to speak.

He inhaled a sharp breath. "I'll be put to death if you

get bruised," he said, accepting his fate with a glum expression.

"No, you won't, my friend. I've been trained. And we're only jousting."

"Yes, milady," Urdred replied, dour acquiescence in every syllable. "Someone should tell me mither. She'll want time to fashion a proper send-off for me soul after the laird slays me."

Morrigan laughed.

Donning a leather apron that served as a shield, she approached one of the arenas designated for the training of hand-to-hand combat, the manus a manis, so favored by the Romans and Greeks. Though it wasn't as exciting as the wrestling, Morrigan would never choose that, nor would she be allowed to do so. It crossed her mind that it would be most entertaining if she taught Rhys and the twins a lesson in the Celtic body throwing favored by the Welsh.

Hugh rode back with Toric at his side, swinging around the outcropping of ground that all but masked the road leading to the road to the castle. He frowned up at the watchtower, hidden by brush and trees. The sentry had given him the merest salute before he'd turned back to something that seemed to be holding his attention.

"What is it, Hugh?"

"Conan seemed distracted." He pulled Orion up, listening and glancing around him.

Toric cocked his head. "I see naught, but I hear a cheering of sorts. Are there games this day?"

"But for those practicing on the jousting field, I know of no other."

Toric grinned. "Shall we see? Perhaps Urdred is thrashing one of the arrogant young whelps."

Hugh smiled, hiding his eagerness to get to Morrigan. He'd only been gone the morning. Still he felt a loss, a need to get back to her. There was an acid amusement to accepting the hold she had on him. The wonder was he didn't mind. Nay! He wanted it, desired her to take all of him, embrace him. Years of balancing his wants, his personal needs, behind the pressing business of reclaiming his rights, his title, his holdings, and keep all in place, had kept him aloof from deep feelings toward a woman. He'd come to prefer such a way.

With Morrigan it was different. She was his life. She'd brought him light and a wild serenity. He couldn't explain it. Neither could he live without it.

"Ho! So that's the reason for the cheering," Toric said, laughing. He'd ridden ahead of Hugh. Now he leaned back against his cantle, his one leg up and curved in front of him. "A rare sight indeed," he muttered, slanting a look at his chief as Hugh came up beside him.

"What tickles that macabre sense of humor now, cousin?" Hugh walked his horse up the rise and reined in next to Toric, his eyes scanning the practice field below him.

"See," Toric goaded.

"Christ almighty!" Hugh said through his teeth. He would've spurred forward, had not Toric stayed his hand.

"Don't distract them, Hugh. Those are practice weapons, but if handled poorly someone could get hurt."

Hugh stared down at the tableau in the glen, at the clusters of cheering and gibing MacKays. His wife was dueling with Urdred, one of his most able warriors! Damn her!

Morrigan was getting winded, but she also hadn't had so much fun in a long time. She'd longed for the strong physical workouts she'd had with her brothers when she'd lived in Wales. Califb hadn't been home as much as Drcq, Cumhal, or her Hibernian cousin Boyne, but she'd managed with them.

Though she panted, it cheered her to see that her ability to avoid hits from her adversary and to land some on him, had made Urdred settle down into the mode of fighting. He was as good as Califb, the best of her brothers, at manus a manis. Perhaps not as quick as she, but he was stronger, and knew how to use his weapon, both as sword and cudgel. More than once she'd had to leap to one side or risk a spank on the thighs. She knew he had no intention of hurting her, as she had no wish to mark him, but the strategy of the battle, the wit to know the adversary's move before he made it, spurred both of them. She'd always loved it and had begun at the age her brothers had because her father had insisted she be well conditioned in the mind as well as the body.

Round and round they went, dancing in and out of the other's reach, tapping, tipping, the crowd cheering and making wagers.

Morrigan noted a change in the sounds of the crowds, but she didn't turn her attention from Urdred.

Figuring it was time to end it, she gambled on her memory. She had to be exact when it came to putting the right force in the right spot. Only then would Urdred's own power catapult himself end over end to slam backward on the ground.

Tumbling the formidable Urdred would take exquisite timing, placement, and energy. She counted and angled herself around for the best place to enter his sphere of combat and do the routine. It would be faster than the eye could follow. One slipup could tumble her under the warrior, or worse the leather on either weapon could slip and she could risk injury that way.

Hugh had moved up to the gathering, afoot. Many had noticed him, though he'd spoken to no one nor taken his eyes off his wife.

"Papa!" Rhys's voice caroled through the cheers.

Hugh nodded to the three children who raced to him. He leaned over them, kissing each one on the top of the head. "Shh. We must watch maman and learn."

"You're talking through your teeth," Rhys said, in his matter-of-fact way. "Maman would tell you it will ruin them."

"Would she?" Hugh ignored the titters circling near him, moving around the children and getting himself into position to interfere. Enough of this! His wife instructing the entire clan in manus a manis? Under his ire was a burning pride in her agility, her almost careless handling of the weapon. She'd been taught well.

Just as he was about to call a halt, he saw her gather herself and move under Urdred's guard. Fury and fear nearly made him bite through his tongue. She was going to try to tumble Urdred, a most capable wrestler.

Morrigan counted to five, then swung her body inside, seeing by Urdred's widened gaze that he hadn't expected it, that his counteracting would come too late. She grabbed for his digits, twisting, turning, thrusting her body under his. She put every bit of power she had into the move, knowing full well she'd never tumbled anyone so large as Urdred.

With an unholy yowl Urdred spun, his toes pointing downward until they left the ground. His body spun high for an instant, then he crashed to the ground on his back with a huge whoosh of air, his own strength and momentum delivering the force.

The silence in the glen was total for several pulse beats. Then the roar began, growing like the thunder of the sea wind in a wild storm. MacKays jumped up and down, pummeling one another. Even the losers in the many wagers grinned, paid up, and shook their heads.

Rhys and the twins yelled and screamed, delighted with the event though they weren't quite sure what had happened. Had their mother bested Urdred, the grand warrior? It could not be. Yet it seemed so.

Hugh shook off Toric's restraining hand, not sharing his laughter.

"Hugh! Come back. She's won the day. She deserves the accolades."

Hugh ground to a stop, glaring at his cousin over his shoulder. "She's been very ill. Do you think this could be good for her?"

Toric laughed. "Ask Urdred, cousin."

"Hush your whisht," Hugh growled in Gaelic.

Toric laughed all the harder.

A dazed but grinning Urdred looked up at Lady MacKay, shaking his head, his eyes glinting with admiration. "You would teach me thus?"

Morrigan nodded. "I would."

Urdred's mirth burst forth. "Methinks I'd be invincible."

"No doubt." Morrigan laughed with him.

"Milady, you are . . ." His voice faded. He looked past her, his smile going sour.

Morrigan knew without looking who was coming. Little by little talk ceased, mutterings grew. Hilarity was smothered by excited whispers. She turned, her chin up. "I'll not let you blame Urdred, a most fine warrior," she told Hugh. "He's a most valiant MacKay, and I shall show him the way of tossing that we do in Wales."

"Brought to you by the Vikings," Hugh murmured.

"Mostly by the Celts if truth be told."

"Are you all right?"

Standing in front of her, chest heaving, was her beloved husband. Morrigan could see Hugh was caught in an amalgam of angst boiled in anger, frustration, and primarily fear. She also glimpsed his pride that had her own swelling. She knew he didn't know how to express his myriad emotions.

"Tell me, Morrigan."

She put her fists on her hips, pleased with herself, her head cocked up at him. "I'm just fine. Never better."

He reached out and lifted her into his arms, kissing her on the lips long and hard.

The cheers of the MacKays rose to a crescendo.

Morrigan tore her mouth from his, her feet still dangling above the ground. "Watch yourself . . . MacKay. I . . . I might . . . do the same . . . to you as I did to Urdred," she told him, out of breath.

Her words blew through the crowd like a storm. Laughter rose like the clouds.

"Or I to you," Hugh whispered for her ears alone.

She scowled at him, her face reddening, her own mirth rising to meet the crowd's. "Say you're not angry."

"I'm not. I was afraid," he admitted. "And I didn't like it. You draw my blood with your antics, wife."

"Have no fear," she whispered, her hand lifting to stroke his cheek.

"Maman! Do the same to Papa," Rhys shouted, his thunderous child's voice piercing the mirth.

He ran over to them, thrusting his arms up to Hugh, the twins at his heels.

Hugh had to put her down to scoop up the three, who giggled and waved to those around them. "It's time to go back to chores."

"No!" Rhys stuck out his lip. "I want maman to do that to you. Tip you over."

Hugh stared at his son. "You will be a great leader I'm thinking. By wiping out your father, 'twould seem."

The jest shot around the throng, the MacKays chuckling. What a wondrous thing it would be to watch their lord and lady tussling in the Welsh manner. Ballads would be sung for generations!

"No, I will not engage your mother in such. She has just come from a sickbed. I would not have her ailing afresh."

Morrigan was sure Rhys would argue, but he nodded along with the twins. When her gaze fell on the crestfallen Urdred, she sidled toward him, touching his arm. "Stay, my friend."

"Milady, I would not have hurt you . . . I wasn't thinking when I agreed . . . I cannot tell you how sorry I am."

"No! Don't think that. I'm very well. The laird cossets me too much," she said, being more blunt than usual. "I would not have you think anything but the best of our encounter. And I shall teach you the tumble that—"

"Do you include me in that?" Hugh interrupted.

Morrigan looked around him for the children.

"Eamon and Toric have taken them to the castle for a nuncheon." Hugh eyed the rigid Urdred. "You'll learn this tumble, as will the rest of us."

"I shall teach them," Morrigan interjected.

Hugh opened his mouth to retort, when Urdred touched his arm. "What?"

"I take full blame, laird. I should not have let our lady risk—"

"Hah!" Hugh snorted. "When you learn how to tame this wild Welsh woman, you must, indeed, inform your laird. For I don't know the secret."

Morrigan laughed with the other MacKays near them, patting Urdred's arm to reassure him.

The obvious adoration of the huge MacKay warrior had Hugh closing his eyes and stifling a groan.

Whipping Morrigan up into his arms again, he whirled around and strode to Orion.

"Hugh, I don't think the laird of MacKay is supposed to carry his wife about the place."

"Well, I'm sure as hell not letting anyone else do it."

Morrigan chuckled, feeling happy, content. If a little sadness touched her heart when she thought of their lost babe, she didn't dwell on it. She would pray to carry another MacKay and God and the goddesses of Boudicca would safeguard the we'en.

Hugh placed her on his saddle, one soft word quieting the destrier. Then he popped up behind her, encircling her with his tartan, arranging it around her back and legs.

She smiled. "I'm not cold."

"I'll not take a chance you'll catch a chill."

She cuddled close to him. "Then you must keep me warm." She saw the hot look in his eyes, and knew the look reflected her own.

"I intend to keep you safe, always," Hugh said into her hair.

"I know."

"Do you?"

"Yes. I've trusted you since the first day." She looked up at him, troubled that there were still things she must tell him about Rhys and herself. Her worry now was not so much about Rhys and the stewardship of Trevelyan, but that Hugh might put a force of MacKays to war to ensure Rhys's rights. She'd not have one MacKay embroiled in such. What a coil! Would all troubles be settled one day so that she could confide her innermost secret to the man she loved more than her life?

"Perhaps I should put you to bed now," Hugh murmured.

"That might be wise." The thundering of her heart almost blotted out his low chuckle. She would tell him her secrets later. Now she wanted to be loved.

FOURTEEN

The cause is hidden, but the result is well known.

Ovid

Morrigan watched him dress, loving that scarred body, and the feel of it under her. Even knowing that the scarring was old, she couldn't quite stem all her fear.

"If you keep looking at me that way, wife, I'll be back with you."

She laughed. "I would not hate that."

Hugh whipped around, strode to the bed, and lifted her up to him. "Do you know how beautiful you are, Morrigan MacKay?"

She loved being suspended in his arms. "If I am, you have made me so." She could feel his body hardening.

Hugh shook his head, eyeing her up and down. "No, my love, you've been beauteous since the womb. No one could change that." He grinned and brought her to him, rubbing his mouth over hers. "Perhaps I will take credit for the glint in your glance, the heat that I love."

She brought her hands up to clasp his hips. "Hugh, I would talk with you, if you please."

"It will always please me, love." He sank down next to her, taking her into his arms. "I find I'd prefer to talk a little later."

"Hugh!" Reluctant humor bubbled up in her as his mouth went to her breast. "We always do this."

"How wise we are," he said, his mouth stroking her skin.

"I—"

The pounding on the door jarred her upward, Hugh's low cursing an accompaniment.

"What?" Hugh growled.

"Messenger!" Toric called through the heavy door.

"Handle it."

"I did. It says that there is trouble, that a scroll comes from the king brought by your godmother."

"Devil take the lot of them," Hugh growled.

A muffled laugh was heard from Toric.

Disappointed, Morrigan moved away from him. "You must go."

"You wished to talk to me. You're more important."

"No. The clan must come first," she said, making a moue. "I like it not that you leave, but I'll not let you stay, good Hugh."

"Beloved, I command you not to seduce me with those wondrous eyes. Is it not enough that you have brought my clan under your spell?" He rose from their bed.

Morrigan looked her husband over from head to toe,

feeling possessive of that strong body, that great mind, his wondrous caring. "As long as I've captured you." She'd not thought to dare make such an open, flirtatious remark to him. Even now her temerity stunned her. Yet that sinewed body wooed her as words could never have done. She wanted him. She loved him. Now had been her time to speak of the deceptions and need to hide Rhys's background behind lies and restraint. When she'd wanted to keep him with her to confess all, it couldn't be done. Soon, there'd be time enough for explanations. Their love was so secure now, she no longer feared his rejection.

"You have succeeded," he whispered.

Wrung from her reverie by his honeyed tone, she cast back in her mind to recall what she'd said. The memory shook her. The words had spilled out on their own, not to be called back. She touched his cheek. "Then I've won much."

He crossed to her side and kissed her hard, then moved back to don his raiment.

Fully dressed, Hugh strode to the bed again. "Will you come down, beloved?"

Morrigan nodded.

His eyes went over her, a pulse beating in his throat. "Your words have unmanned me, Morrigan love. Do not come out of that bed until I leave the chamber or I'll not be able to depart."

Feeling lazy and joyous, she fell back on the coverlet, waiting for the handmaiden Hugh would send. She closed her eyes and let the past hour relive itself in her mind.

Hugh didn't like the funereal glances aimed his way when he entered the room. He noted the king's courier off to one side of the room, waiting his turn to speak. In deference to the priest and his mother, he would wait.

Hugh eyed his godmother, not speaking. Lady Maud MacKenzie was not only a relative, she'd been his mother's best friend. Though a distant relative of his mother's, she'd lived in his mother's household from babyhood. Younger than his mother, just a child when he'd been christened, she'd been treated as close family always. That she'd married a relation of the MacKays had been no surprise. Hugh had known her all his life, and as his godmother she was worthy of his care and respect. At that moment he wished her to perdition, wishing he could go back up the stairs to his wife, rather than welcome kin.

He sighed. "Greetings, Godmother, Kieran."

"Greetings, Hugh MacKay," mother and son said in chorus.

Hugh eyed them and waited. His godmother was given to histrionics at times. He could be patient. Maud and her son had been part of the MacKay household since he'd reclaimed the estate. Hugh couldn't deny them.

If the rumor was true, and none were quite sure about

it, Edward of England had been about to crown Kieran as keeper of the MacKay holding before Hugh had made his compact with that monarch and Edward Baliol. It would've been a righteous choice since Kieran was related by blood to the MacKays. If Hugh hadn't threatened to battle both kings and their armies, he might've lost his heritage.

If truth be told Kieran had a blood right to Clan MacKay. His father had been second cousin to Hugh's father. Owen MacKenzie had been a profligate who watered away his holding with fruitless enterprises. Though Maud had a substantial portion from the Sinclairs and Lindsays, Hugh's mother's people, Kieran had been left little by his father.

Hugh felt a strong kinship to the two because they'd always supported him. He swallowed his irritation and smiled.

"Good day to you, Godmother. And to you, Father MacKenzie." He smiled when Kieran looked pained.

"Call me by my name, cousin. We've never stood on ceremony with each other."

"True." Hugh sighed.

Both priest and godmother looked worried. If they knew how eager he was to see the back to them, they might really scowl. He didn't want to talk to them when he could be intimate with Morrigan. He laughed to himself when he thought of what his godmother would say if he voiced his thoughts. " 'Twould seem all is not well by the looks on your faces. What news?"

"Hugh, I fear there are rough roads ahead and I like it not." His godmother held up her hand. "I'll not interrupt the messenger, who should speak first." She gestured to the man who stood to one side, an urgency to his movements, though his manner was deferential.

"Fine." Hugh waved his hand at the king's courier, and went to the trencher board to pour some ale.

The courier coughed, then spread his papyrus, reading. "Milord, by writ of his Royal Highness, Edward Baliol, it has come to his attention that a scroll of annulment has crossed the desk of Edward of England. That your marriage to Morrigan of Llywelyn is nullified—"

"Good Christ Almighty! You daresay this to me in my own castle!" Hugh flung his goblet against the fireplace, denting it. "No more!"

The messenger coughed. " 'Tis not my wish to offend you, lord—"

"You have. And Edward Baliol has incurred my everlasting wrath if he thinks that some paltry scroll will end a marriage sanctioned by the Church and witnessed by hundreds."

"My lord, if you would hear me out—"

Hugh whirled, teeth bared. "Nay! You'll find yourself fortunate if I don't skewer you!"

"Hugh!" Morrigan stood at the entrance to the great room. "What mischief is this?"

He saw how startled she was by his ire. Her confusion

fueled his temper. "Leave!" Hugh commanded the messenger, who looked both frightened and determined.

"Hugh! Wait. His words can't hurt us." She went to him and touched his arm. "Can you not see he's been instructed to say all the message?"

"I'll not hear it!" He bellowed.

Morrigan looked first at him, then at Lady MacKenzie and Kieran, then at the messenger. She laid her hand on her husband's arm, then gazed at the courier again. "Begin at the beginning and finish the missive."

The messenger swallowed. "If it please milady."

"It doesn't please me," Hugh said through his teeth, his arm going around his wife as the messenger made a new start.

Morrigan reeled as the words filled the room. She clutched Hugh, who enfolded her in his arms. "How . . . how can this be? We would have to sign an annulment agreement and we haven't."

"I would say that someone has used our signatures freely."

"The annulment is counterfeit? How would Edward of England countenance it?"

Hugh exhaled. "He and I have never been friends. He would seize any weapon to come at me. He uses this."

The messenger coughed. "There's more."

Morrigan nodded. Hugh growled.

"The aforesaid statement was brought to me and has been issued to you. Since I was there when your nuptials took place, since I know there was no impediment to the vows, I will do all in my power to aid you if you choose to answer these charges. Signed Edward Baliol, Rex."

Silence spun about the room.

"All . . . all is not lost. Edward has seconded us, Hugh."

"It doesn't matter what any say. You're my wife."

Morrigan looked up at her husband. "What shall we do?"

"Nothing. I repeat, you're my wife, under God and Scotland. Nothing can gainsay that. I won't let it."

Kieran MacKenzie cleared his throat.

Hugh's baleful glance fell on him. "What?"

"My feeling is that this can be set to rights in short order. If my lady goes to Edinburgh, talks with the two Edwards, if she avers that her vows are correct, all is cared for in the proper manner, if she swears on her name and the good book—"

"She did her swearing when she took her vows. That any dare to gainsay that means war," Hugh shouted.

"No, we mustn't," Morrigan pleaded. "None must die over this."

"Listen, Hugh, I beg," Kieran added his voice. "Again I say if she goes to Edinburgh—"

"She goes nowhere." Hugh ground out the words. "She's been ill."

Maud groaned. "Then we are undone. Can't you see, godson, that Kieran is right?" Her gaze slid to Morrigan. "My poor child, what ails—"

"She's better," Hugh interrupted. "And I'll not see her in fever over this."

Morrigan touched Hugh's arm, then glanced at the messenger. "Then we must study alternatives." She licked her lips. "Perhaps all can be accomplished by doing nothing, by remaining in our castle."

"I feel you err in this, my dear," Maud whispered.

"No, she doesn't," Hugh averred. "If she stays here, as my wife, which she is, none can gainsay her. All MacKays will swear to her validity as Lady MacKay. All but a few of my clan witnessed her rites and vows."

Kieran bit his lip. "This is true. I, myself, was on the altar, but I fear Mother is right in this, cousin."

"I don't agree," Hugh said through his teeth, keeping Morrigan in the curve of his arm.

Kieran looked pained. "You can keep them away from Castle MacKay, but you can't stop the order of dissolution, Hugh. It's in the works. Copies have been scribed and sent to Rome as we speak. If the cardinal becomes capricious and starts to act on it, on his own, he has the authority. All my objections will have little effect." Kieran winced. " 'Tis better to face him on this. If I can I will convince him to travel to Rome, which he loves to do, have a private audience with the pope. It will add to his stature to do so."

"Pompous ass," Hugh muttered.

Morrigan bit back a smile. Not too much impressed her strong-hearted husband. "Kieran is right. Perhaps he could accompany the cardinal. He could add his arguments."

Kieran nodded. "By the end of the season all could be put to rights, Hugh. If we stall on this, if the cardinal feels an affront to his authority he might sign the dicta. Your vows will be considered invalid. Once done 'twould be a tangled weave to be sure, not so easily handled. Surely you can see the need for discretion, for moving correctly on this."

"They can bloody well keep their noses out of my business and my life," Hugh ordered. "Morrigan is my wife, and no other's. That will not change."

Morrigan slipped her arm around his waist. Though it was unseemly she had a need to reassure her beset husband. "I will always be your wife."

Kieran spread his hands, his beseeching glance touching Morrigan. "True." He inhaled. "But there are considerations."

"Nothing is important but my wife and the clan."

"Hugh, listen," Morrigan urged. " 'Tis not our plan to have anger thrust against our people."

"I'll listen." Hugh kissed her cheek. "Go on, Kieran."

"If 'twere just your life and holding to protect I would back you on this." Kieran paused.

"Well?" Hugh shot at him.

"I'm being blunt because I must be. I would like it not if any issue of yours was declared ineligible to be your heir because of bastardy."

Hugh's roar of rage brought MacKays on the run, weapons drawn.

Morrigan freed herself from Hugh's hold, leaving her husband and going to the side of the two leading Mac-Kays, a very tense Toric and Diuran. " 'Tis of little import, my friends. You may retire."

"Pardon me, milady, I would do so. But first I would know why your hand shakes," Diuran said through his teeth, his gaze shooting about the great room.

"I would as well," Toric mentioned, scanning the area.

"Toric!" Hugh shouted. "Would you say my marriage vows to milady were valid?"

Toric nodded. "I would. Why would I not when I was there to hear them freely exchanged?"

Hugh gave a hard laugh. "Point taken. I'll hear no more."

"Are there any so foolish as to gainsay this?" Diuran's words stopped all discussions and murmurings.

" 'Twould seem the two Edwards think so," Hugh answered.

Morrigan glared at her husband. "Hugh—"

"Then this MacKay declares war on the slime who would malign our lady," Diuran shouted.

"Oh, Lord," Morrigan muttered. "What next?"

"Did he just declare war on England and Scotland?" Lady MacKenzie quizzed in fading accents. "How can this be?" She sank back against her chair, waving her veil in front of her. "Our lives are forfeit."

Morrigan hurried to her side. "No, ma'am, 'tisn't so. There's no thought of war. I beg you not to overset yourself. Men can speak unwisely, but I can assure you my MacKays wouldn't dream of waging a war on such as this—"

"We would!" Toric and Diuran shouted in unison, the bellowings bringing even more MacKays to stuff the room to overflowing.

Morrigan turned around, glowering at Diuran and Toric. She stamped her foot. "Desist! I'll not hear any more of war from any of you. Hear me well. Not one MacKay shall have a bruise over this." She waved her hand. "Think you I'll have any of the clan piped to their grave? Never! Do you hear me?" She stamped the other foot. "I have decreed it. Do you understand? Do you hear me?"

"They'd hear you in Edinburgh," Toric muttered. Then he lost his grin when Morrigan turned her furious gaze on him. "Sorry," he mumbled.

Morrigan inhaled. "I should think so." A little more calm, she went to the clusters of MacKays mulling about the anteroom. "All is well, my friends. No need to fret. Go about your business." She smiled. They smiled back. No one moved.

"Have you been insulted, milady?" Urdred moved through the throng, his large body quivering with feeling.

Morrigan shook her head. "No. No, truly I have not."

"You have," Hugh pronounced behind her.

MacKays bristled, growling to one another, uttering dire threats.

"I challenge any and all who've done this," Urdred shouted.

Morrigan winced at the yell, her ears ringing. "Stop!"

No one paid attention. Instead they muttered among themselves, discussing battle plans.

She whirled around, scowling. "Hush your whisht, Hugh MacKay, at once. I'll not have our people embroiled in such nonsense."

MacKay mouths hung open at their lady's temerity in telling the laird to be quiet. Had anyone ever done that to Hugh MacKay? Certainly not since he'd been out of leading strings.

Hugh approached her, his eyes glittering with purpose, a vinegary mirth outlining his features. "Then let our people decide for themselves if there is need to move on this assault to your virtue."

"Aye!" thundered the gathering, intent and purpose on every visage.

Urdred waved his claymore in the air, as did others. "I'll draw and quarter the spalpeens who dared such a falsehood."

Morrigan raised her hands for quiet. Some listened, others continued to fret and argue.

"Hugh, have a care!" his godmother intoned, shaking her head. "Would you have your wife wrapped in shame with no alternative but to enter a convent?"

"Not bloody likely. Morrigan stays with me," Hugh stated, his hard smile touching the throng of protesters.

Then he fixed his gaze on his wife. "You're mine," he mouthed for her alone, though others saw it.

Morrigan smiled and nodded.

"Let us ponder together, pray on this," Kieran said, adding leverage to his mother's argument.

"No!" was the battle cry.

When the hubbub subsided, so that those who would speak could be heard, Kieran approached Hugh. "Let me try to talk to the cardinal before blood is spilled. You can meet me in, say, three days in Edinburgh. I will have softened up the prelate, God willing. You can sit down with him and voice your valid arguments. Then all of us will go to Edward Baliol. We'll enlist his help in facing English Edward. Let the two of them thrash out any disagreements they might have. You know they will see the validity of pacifying you in your cause. They've nothing to gain by siding with the Welsh who instituted this annulment. The cardinal, needing the good wishes of the two kings, will add his support, bringing the papacy to your side. All will be settled amicably."

Silence whorled around the great room in puffs of uncertainty, agitation, ponderings, and disbelief. Credibility was slow to come to the irate MacKays, yet reason argued that MacKenzie was speaking sensibly.

Hugh began to pace.

"Listen to him, Hugh," Morrigan urged. " 'Tis a good plan, one that could work. We need to take all steps to protect our own."

Hugh stopped suddenly and grabbed her so quickly,

she caught her breath. "I'll not let anyone take you from me." He didn't bother to lower his voice. The mutterings from the clan members answered him.

"I wouldn't be parted from you." She patted his cheek. "We will just take care of this problem, then relax." Her smile widened. "Or ready ourselves for the next mare's nest."

His heavy brow lightened and he leaned down to kiss her nose. "We'll do that." He brought her closer to his chest. "I like not to leave you."

"I like it less," she said into his shirt.

Smiling down at her, he kissed her cheek. "We will have our life. I'll be back in a few turns of the sun."

"That quickly?" She tried to smile, but her heart twisted at the thought of being parted from him. She saw the glint in his eyes that told her he understood.

"Faster, mayhap."

Hugh looked up at Kieran, nodding. "You go to the cardinal. I'll bide my time, then join you and we'll go to the king. I'll contact you in two turns of the sun hence."

Kieran blinked. "I must go at once, then." He grimaced at his mother.

"She can stay here," Morrigan offered.

Lady MacKenzie rose to her feet, her grace giving truth to how young she'd been to bear her only child. "How kind you are, Morrigan, but I will go with my son and add my voice to his. Another advocate won't hurt." Her smile crooked. "Who knows? We might clean up the matter even before Hugh joins us."

Morrigan's importunings were put off, and soon the MacKenzie entourage was leaving the gate. "Think them safe in their quest, Hugh?"

He nodded, keeping her within the circle of his arm. "MacKays will guide them through lands belonging to those friendly to MacKays." He smiled down at her. "Kieran is well known in the Highlands, and since his ministry takes him to Edinburgh several times in the turning of the moon, he will be passing many acquaintances."

"Good. I wouldn't want anything to happen to your family." She sighed. "You think we can placate the cardinal, so that the papacy won't be involved?"

"We will, or we'll live here alone with our clan. No one can take my wife or my title from me."

Morrigan burrowed into his chest, loving it when he wrapped his tartan around her. "I feel better already."

"Good, I wouldn't want you tired when I say goodbye to you."

"Hugh!" Morrigan looked around them, but no one was close to them. "You talk too freely, sirrah."

He lifted her into his arms. "I will tell you more, if you like, and I'll whisper it against your skin from your neck to your ankles, beautiful one."

"Hugh," Morrigan whispered, her body singing at his words.

They retired early, taking berries, oat cakes, and ale to their suite. They eschewed the food. Instead they embraced, far into the night, the whispered words of love which, in truth, was all the heat they needed or wanted.

The next day Morrigan spent all her time with Hugh and the children.

Arms entwined, Hugh and Morrigan watched their three at their riding lessons.

"Our Avis is becoming as intrepid as her mother," Hugh said, smiling.

"I'm that proud of her and the boys," Morrigan told him in Gaelic.

That evening they supped with the children, then they retired early, loving deeply, neither mentioning their separation the next day.

Just as the sun was making an appearance Hugh rose. Morrigan ate a small meal with him, then insisted on riding with him to the perimeter of Sutherland land, their nearest neighbor, her horse bumping his from time to time.

"You're not to worry, love," he told her, knowing that she was remembering the last time they were parted just as he was.

"Neither should you," she riposted. "None could rip apart a MacKay vow unless they had Ajax's ax."

Hugh chuckled, leaning over and scooping her from her saddle to settle her in front of him.

Toric chuckled, catching up her reins and twisting them around his wrist. "Will she not be a burden, cousin, if you troll her all the way to Edinburgh?"

"Are you saying I'm too many stone for him to carry, Toric?" Morrigan eyed the laughing MacKay. "Because if you are, I challenge you, here and now, to a jousting on your return."

"Done," Toric said, eyeing the MacKays who surrounded them, who were already making wagers.

"We'll see about that," Hugh murmured into her hair. "When I return you'll be too busy in my bed for that nonsense."

When Morrigan reddened and pushed at her husband, the MacKays laughed louder. Even though she was sure they hadn't heard, she knew they would surmise what Hugh had whispered.

They parted on a knoll. He kissed her repeatedly, then gave terse instructions to the men who surrounded her.

Morrigan watched him out of sight, her heart pleading for him to come back to her as soon as possible.

FIFTEEN

Fortune is not satisfied with inflicting
one calamity.

Publius Syrus

Hugh and his men usually went into any fracas with
heads high, grim humor slashing their mouths. Their
fateful acceptance of injury and death came from too
many years of warfare.

When Keith began to hum a MacKay battle ballad,
Toric dropped back, shaking his head.

"We've always done this," Keith assured the second
in command to the laird.

"So we have." Toric slanted his gaze forward. "Not
this day, I'm thinking. Hugh is deuced overset about this
business." Toric frowned. "I can't say I feel any better.
How in God's name will he live if the cardinal goes
against him. English Edward will have the reason he
needs to snap at our heels."

"Scotland's king must support his greatest lord,"

Keith averred, his teeth baring in a snarl. "None must try to blacken our lady's name."

"And that is what is tearing him apart. Lord MacKenzie hit the nail on the head when he mentioned bastardy. That it could sully the name of any child spawned between Morrigan and Hugh would be a burden too great for him. Before the birth, our lady could be jeopardized by the epithet of whore, as she was once before—"

Keith bleated his rage, his steed reacting to it and rearing. The other MacKays heard the same and began cursing.

Hugh looked back, pulling up his destrier. "What's amiss?" His eyes scanned the thick copse ahead. Better to be safe than sorry, though they were on the edge of Graham land. Donald Graham had been his ally through it all, so he wasn't too concerned.

"We speak of our lady," Toric answered, getting the rough side of Keith's tongue for owning up to it.

Hugh let his horse drop to a trot as the others came up on him. "Worry not. She'll be fine."

"Say what you will, Hugh, if any so much as thinks evil of her, I'll skewer him even if it's the king himself," Keith said, earning ayes from his clansmen.

"If I don't get to him first," Hugh interjected, earning some mirth from the men, though firm intent didn't die from their eyes.

Perhaps their discourse diverted some of their caution. To be sure, they were prepared as they entered the tunnel of trees, letting their eyes adjust to the difference in light.

"Aiyee," Carmody let loose a battle cry. "Above us."

Hugh turned in his saddle, catching the man who leaped atop him. He rolled off the destrier to the ground, bringing back his fist to smash it in the face beneath him. Before he could land another blow, another one was there, cudgel held high. He brought it down on Hugh's temple.

Too many turns of the sun. Too many long nights, alone in the big bed. The phrases ran around her head as she stared from the parapet as she'd been wont to do the past sennight.

"What is it, maman?"

Morrigan looked down at Conal, the frailest of her three children. He was more apt to get the rawness of the throat than the other two. He was also more in tune with what she felt. He amazed her.

"All is well, my son," she told him, smiling down at the lad, who'd grown inches since coming to live at the castle.

"You worry about Papa."

She nodded, too concerned and fatigued to dissemble. "Yes. I had hoped that—"

"He will be fine. He's a true MacKay," Conal interrupted, something he rarely did.

Morrigan leaned down and kissed his forehead. "You warm my heart, dearest."

Conal wrapped his arms around her hips. They hugged, not moving.

A flurry beyond the gates drew her eyes, and she straightened, her heart beginning a painful thudding.

Conal called to his sister and brother, and Rhys and Avis joined him at the ramparts.

"Who is it, maman?"

"I don't know, Rhys." She covered her brow with the side of her hand. " 'Tis an entourage, I think."

"Papa!" Rhys yelled, running to the narrow stairs that would take him down into the main area of the castle.

"Don't run, Rhys. I would wish you to watch over Avis." Morrigan knew that would stop him, and it did. The three were very caring of one another, and were almost inseparable.

He frowned. "I do." He waited for his sister.

Conal smiled up at her and followed.

Morrigan clasped her hands and sent up a prayer of thanks.

By the time she freshened herself, then hurried down to the great room, she was almost sure it wasn't Hugh who'd arrived. If it had been he, there would've been a greater clamor, more of a bustle for refreshments. Cheers would've risen to her suite.

Hiding her disappointment, she moved into the great room, a smile fixed to her face. When she saw the dour messenger and his coterie, alarm frissoned her spine. Putting her chin up, she approached. "I am Lady MacKay."

"This be for you, milady." The messenger handed her the metal cylinder, then stepped back. " 'Tis from Lord Kieran, Father MacKenzie."

Morrigan nodded, spreading the rolled parchment on the trencher board. She took deep breaths, the words dancing in front of her eyes.

Dear Cousin,

   To bring you this news tears at my heart, but I must persevere. I cannot find Hugh. He never came to Edinburgh. I've sent runners almost every day since three days had passed, when we were to meet. No one has sighted him, nor his men. It's as though Scotland has swallowed them. I fear they've been attacked by the rascals who prowl our land. I don't wish to alarm you, but I sense that something drastic has happened to Hugh. I've sent runners to Edward of England and Edward Baliol. No one has news of him.

                              Forgive this sorry missive.
                                   Kieran MacKenzie

Morrigan crumpled the letter in her fist. She thumped the table with that hand, over and over again.

"Milady?"

"Who went with Hugh, Diuran?"

"Why you know, milady. 'Twas Toric, Dylan, Keith, Carmody, and two attendants, Wull and Davy."

"Do you think them capable? Can they care for themselves?"

"Milady, you jest. They are prime MacKays, strong, able, and unafraid."

Dry-eyed, she turned to him, taking deep breaths. She shoved the letter at him. "Read it."

Diuran took the crumpled sheets, perusing them twice.

"What think you now?"

White-faced, Diuran stared at her. "They are either dead, or confined, milady."

"So I feel." She inclined her head. "I will not think them dead."

"Nor will I."

For long moments she stared into the fire, knowing full well that the power was hers, that if she took MacKays into the fray, some could die. Her heart squeezed with the agony of that. MacKays were her family. She loved them all. God and all the deities help her, she prayed. It was left to her to make this awesome choice.

"Milady?"

She shook herself from the reverie, facing him. "Awa'," she said in Gaelic. "Bratach Bhan Chlann Aoidh."

Diuran sucked in air, straightening to his full height. When Morrigan again raised her voice in the MacKay battle cry, "the White Banner of MacKay," he answered her in kind.

Morrigan lifted her chin, shaken. "Ready yourself, Diuran, and a full complement of warriors. Leave the castle guarded and manned. Andra and Dilla will have the last word. Guards will be everywhere. Extra guardians on our children. Bring all families on the perimeter in closer to the castle, or into the bailey itself. Leave nothing to chance, no weak links.

"Have the shepherds bring the sheep and stoats onto safe ground. Make sure they're armed. Let loose the battle dogs to keep company with the guards and shepherds. The battlements will be manned night and day. Food will be brought in and stored. Water sources will be guarded with available streams and rivers channeled to our use. Prepare the blacksmiths. Advise them that they will work from dawn to dusk. Keep the lamps low and hoard the oils. Linens balled and wrapped will be soaked in these. Ready the flambeaux and catapults. Enlighten the friendly clans of what we will do."

"What is that, milady?" Diuran's voice was faint.

Morrigan took a deep breath, baring her teeth. "War. Like Boudicca, Queen of Wales in olden time, I'll not let any strike at me and mine with impunity. Those who would try to abscond with one MacKay scone, from this day hence, shall pay the stiffest price. Those who would threaten any MacKay will answer to our steel. Once and for all they will see that we won't allow usurping without a fight. They who have dared attack our laird shall pay full measure for their perfidy."

"Whom do we battle, milady?"

"Any who dare to harm our laird, or who think to lay a hand upon him, or his people. England and Wales to start."

Diuran stared at her for long moments, then he slammed his fist across his chest like his Viking ancestors. "Aye, we will. From this day forward they'll feel our wrath and none shall gainsay us." He ran from the room.

Morrigan looked up at the crest above the fireplace, a right hand grasping a sword. "I'll find you, my Hugh, or die trying. I canna' give you up," she said, tears falling from her eyes, as she lapsed into Gaelic. When she heard the light cough, she turned to face Dilla, swiping at her eyes.

"Milady, you mustn't go. 'Tis not that long since you were abed with . . . with . . ."

"Yes, yes, I know. I thank you for your concern, good Dilla, but I must go. I will lead the MacKays," she said, her voice hard. "We will find our laird."

Dilla nodded, her eyes filling. "I shall guard the children with my life." She gulped. "My Andra will die before aught breach our defenses."

Morrigan nodded. "I know that. Thank you. I'll bring Hugh back, you know."

"You must. He's been the savior to Clan MacKay."

"And he will continue to be so."

Dilla bit her lip. "My Andra would go wi' you."

Morrigan shook her head. "I'll take Urdred, your

cousin, instead. I would like Andra's cool head here. He knows how to protect the castle. He will be in charge."

Dilla's mouth worked as she hurried closer to Morrigan. "He'll not fail you."

Too choked with emotion to answer, Morrigan embraced her, smothering her own sobs when she heard Dilla's.

Hugh knew he must be hurt, and in a dark place. He could see nothing, nor could he move a muscle. It took moments to factor he'd been spread-eagled and tied with thongs. He smelled the freshness of the leather. That meant it didn't bode well for him if he was bound for long. The ancient Phoenician trick was still very effective. The raw leather would dry and bind, and as it did it would cut and choke the flow of life's blood from the limbs. The agony would be long and drawn out as the body died by inches, withering and pulled from its sockets by the inexorable bindings. He'd seen men scream in anguish as their limbs were yanked loose from their bodies by the shrinking hide. A favorite ploy of English Edward. Had he been caught in the maw of that deviate? Who would protect the clan and Morrigan if he died? No! Damn their eyes! He wouldn't be taken that easily.

His head hurt when he tried to recall. What had happened?

"Hugh? I heard you move. Can you hear me?"

"Toric? The men? Are you all right?"

"We're all here, but we're not all right." Toric groaned. "They've broken my legs, I fear. There won't be much time for me."

Hugh cursed. "Listen to me, cousin. You don't die. You hear me?"

"Only the devil himself and us could hear you in this hell pit where they've flung us, Hugh. We're in the bowels of Satan's lair, I'll be bound."

"What does it matter? We've fought our way out of worse hells. I command you to fight."

Toric's chuckle was weak. "I'll do my best to live, cousin. God knows they hit us hard. They've killed Wull and Davy."

Hugh grimaced. "They were but boys. How could they have harmed anyone?"

"They couldn't, but 'twould not be as sporting with them."

Memory was returning. They'd been leagues from Edinburgh when they were set upon by rabble.

"They've begun games with you? Damn! Are we in Wales?"

"We are. They came at us from the trees if you recall."

"I'm not too clear on it, cousin. My head aches so I know a sap of some kind was used."

"Cudgels. We've been here three days when I've been aware."

"More than five turns of the sun," a weak voice added.

"Carmody? Are you well?" Hugh struggled against his bindings, but he couldn't move.

"They've blinded me, Hugh."

"Christ almighty."

"I'd rather they'd killed me."

"You'll not despair. You're a MacKay. You'll learn to fight with your ears and nose and sense of touch. Forget your eyes." Hugh was too gruff. Anger and frustration choked him. What barbarous cowards waged war in such a way? "Dylan?"

"I'm here, Hugh. I've not been touched. They're saving me for this day, I'm thinking."

"No! This time they'll take me."

"Nay, Hugh. You must lie low. We will find a way to get you out," Keith said. "They should be coming for me or Dylan next."

"Listen to me. Are you bound?"

"Yes," came the chorus of answers.

"Not I. They blinded me and tied my hands, not my feet. I've freed myself."

"Good, we'll rely on you, Carmody, to free us. When the time is right we'll strike. No more sport with Mac-Kays. Are you with me?" The ayes were low but firm.

"When they come for us, you'll pretend to be bound." Hugh winced when Carmody sawed at his bonds. "Whoever they take will fall down, making them drag the person. Whoever it is will groan and sag like wet sand. The focus will be on that. They'll be angered. That's when we take them." Hugh groaned when he fell to the ground. He rubbed his limbs over and over, trying to get life back into them. "Remember not to move until they're looking away. We can't make a sound because we won't know how many are outside the cell. Whatever happens, be quiet and calm." He ripped away the bandage wrapped around his head and eyes, feeling the sting.

"They didn't mean to succor you with the rag, Hugh. They would keep you sightless," Carmody told him, his hands going over his chief.

"Fear not, my friend. They'll pay, then we return to Castle MacKay."

"I wish for that."

"They masked us all," Keith said.

"All are free," Carmody mentioned, as he stumbled from one to the other. "Shh. I hear something."

"Did I not tell you all would be well with you, Carmody?" Toric told him, then groaned.

"Damn! Toric, how is your pain?"

"Bad, but there's a numbness to it. I can do what I must, Hugh."

"Good. When next they come, and if Carmody is correct, 'twill be soon, we attack, no matter how armed they are, how strong they think they are, we will best them. Will you fight with me, MacKays?"

"Aye!"

The resounding affirmative was muffled by a greater sound.

"What is that?" Toric tried to heave himself up, but he fell back, moaning.

"Shhh. It comes from beyond this holding. Someone approaches the castle," Carmody said. "Mayhap 'tis an assault."

"Aaagh!"

"What is it, Keith?"

" 'Tis the bindings they put on my arms. Carmody, can you help with these? There be spikes wrapped in the thongs. I thought I could stand them. 'Twill not be easy to cut."

"I'll bite them through, if I can't release them," Carmody vowed.

"They'll pay for this." Hugh's mind had begun to clear, at least enough for him to try and factor who his enemies were. Goll, Morrigan's cousin, would be one. That bog-bound slime Tarquin would be another. That he coveted Morrigan's holdings and monies was enough, that he would take her to wife was intolerable. This time he would die.

More shouts and yells signaled even more of a disturbance beyond the castle. That sound filtered down reassured the MacKays that they were not in a well-built holding. In a proper dungeon, no sound would penetrate.

"Is it an assault, then?"

" 'Twould help us if 'twere," Keith answered Toric.

When the MacKays heard running and raised voices they went still.

"You know what to do," Hugh muttered.

"Aye."

Heavy grating was pulled open, rusty hinges squawking a protest. A torch was thrust into the cell.

Before the light hit him, Hugh tried to bend away from it, make himself invisible.

"Where is the leader?"

"In there. Go. I'm at your back."

There was a flurry, a yelp, a scream. The torch fell and sputtered out in the rancid dampness of the stone floor.

"Hugh?"

"I'm here. What goes?"

"The two of them have gone to visit Satan, their master," Keith said.

"Good. Get over here, and help me with Toric. Find the torch and see if there's a flint by the door."

In short order the cell was lit, the keys of the keepers pocketed, their bodies slung upon the vermin-covered pallets.

Toric was strapped between Keith and Carmody.

Hugh stared at them. "You'll make your way out into the throng. Move freely, and don't slink. Find any old cart. Put Toric into it, and get away to Scotland."

"No! We'll not leave you."

"You will . . ." He paused when he heard more running. They doused the torch and waited.

Just outside the cell there were queries.

"Where be Timon and Bemis?"

"Killing the prisoners, I'll be bound. We'll have to tell them what's occurred. Naught can believe it. I could've sworn my eyes deceived me. Who would've thought she dared? Like Boudicca she comes. 'Tis a sight, is it not? How can we go against her?"

"If we don't they'll slay us and enjoy the sport."

"I like it not. She be a princess of our land."

Hugh stiffened, his movement causing a sound.

"What be that?"

"Bemis is strangling the prisoners. He's a man who likes his work, to be sure."

"Let's get the weapons and leave. I don't like dungeons."

"You work in one, fool."

Soon the carping faded. The clanging and banging of weapons accompanied the attendants back out of the dungeon.

"Hugh, I can't let you face them alone," Toric said in fading accents.

"Stop. You know I cannot let you hold me back."

"That's not why you send me away. I can't make it back anyway. Let me fight at your—"

Sounds of battle penetrated their cell.

"Let's get out of here first." Hugh struck at the flint and relit the torch.

Being undermanned and at a great disadvantage, they took what weapons they could and climbed the curving stairs, littered with refuse, out of the dungeon into a shouting melee of men who scrambled every which way with weapons. There was little order. That would be to MacKay advantage.

Dylan grabbed a Welsh jerkin, pulling it over his head and donning the woolly headdress. He grabbed the arm of a running man. "Who attacks us?" he said in halting Celtic.

"The damned Scots led by our own Princess Morrigan."

"Damn that woman," Hugh cursed, proud, fearful, angry all mixed in with a love that almost choked him. "Why didn't she stay home?"

"She couldn't," Toric managed. "It's not her nature." He tried to laugh. Instead he fainted.

A hand reached out and touched him. "Let me. I can care for him."

Hugh looked around, his eye widening. "Diodura?"

"No. Her sister. We are twins. I wasn't banned, though I've hated it here without her. My name is Latura. I have her skills, and I know thee, leader of the MacKays. My visions have told me you succor my sister." She glanced at Toric. "I can make him well. I will need aid to move him."

Carmody moved to her side, then looked at Hugh. "I will meet you at Castle MacKay, Hugh MacKay. Fear not that I will have Toric with me."

"They've blinded you, but you're unafraid," the crone mentioned. "Fear not. Your courage will not fail you. You will see with your heart and become a wise man among your own."

Hugh smiled at her. "I agree. Have a care with them."

Latura nodded. "Come, we must hurry," the hag whispered to Carmody. "Soon they'll take note of us." She eyed Hugh. "Go through there," she said, pointing to a chamber. "There's an opening to the bailey, seldom used." She eyed him again. "I didn't know how I was to free you. Diodura came to me in a vision and begged me to find you." Her mouth drooped in mirth. " 'Tis well you're as adept as they say. You freed yourself."

" 'Tis our way," Carmody answered for his laird.

"The gods have smiled on you, their leader," Latura told Hugh.

"Thank you. You will find sanctuary with the Mac-Kays as your sister has done, if you choose. Get back to Scotland with Toric, good friend." Hugh clapped Carmody on the shoulder, then they turned toward the chamber.

"Go with God, Hugh. Bring back our lady," Carmody whispered into the air.

"Fear not. He has the good wishes of the gods and goddesses. None will defeat him."

"Thank you," Carmody whispered, hefting Toric and letting the witch lead him.

SIXTEEN

A great love goes here with a little gift.
                                          Theocritus

Morrigan sat her destrier like a warrior, the split skirt she'd only worn on her holding in Wales serving her well. She'd endured the stares of the MacKays when first she'd left Castle MacKay, sure they were shocked. It'd astounded her when she caught their smiles of approval, their nods of appreciation. The leather garment had been tanned to a lightness that was far more comfortable than the heavy skirt she would've used for the sidesaddle. They'd been traveling all day, and when the moon was full, at night.

She'd used all the good shortcuts through Wales that were unknown to any not of Welsh background. They'd not be expected to come that way. Now that they were at Goll's holding, her being shuddered with the certainty Hugh was near. Every pulse beat told her so. She could almost feel him.

"What of Cumhal, milady?" Diuran said at her right.

"I don't know. He told me when we parted after the laird rescued me that he had family business. I've not heard from him in some turns of the moon."

"I would not hurt you, milady, but I tell you true I trust not any of the dogs who'd betray our laird, and since we don't know them all, I'm wary of most," Urdred said on her left.

"I trust none but our clan at this point, good friend," Morrigan said, praying that her guess was right, that Hugh would be imprisoned at Goll's holding. It saddened her to suspect Cumhal, but she'd trust no one until she had Hugh back in the Highlands where he belonged. If he wasn't here, if she was wrong— No! She wouldn't think of that. "Diuran, sound the trumpet."

He nodded and waved to the hornsman. "What challenge do we send, milady?"

The horn sounded. Once. Twice. Three times.

"You'll see," Morrigan murmured, watching the battlements. When she saw movement there, she gulped air. Though it was too far for her to be sure, she'd have wagered all the treasures in her holding that it was Goll standing up there.

She waved a hand to the hornsman, who brought her the trumpet to speak through.

She clasped the horn, then before any could guess at her intention, she clambered up upon the back of her steed, bracing her legs on the wide saddle. She prayed the horse would be the same steady steed she'd had in Wales. To her relief he was immobile. The test would be when she shouted through the horn. "Urdred, you will hold my reins."

"Aye, milady. Should you not come down from there?"

"He's right, Milady Morrigan. Hugh will have our eyes if aught happens to you." Rufus MacKay grimaced when her steed sidled.

"Shh," Morrigan admonished. Putting the horn to her mouth, she shouted. The horse sidled again, then was still.

"Ho, Goll, you feckless coward, stand down and meet your doom. I, Morrigan of Wales and Scotland, throw down the gauntlet. You are challenged to a joust with me alone, you son of bog slime!"

"Milady!" Diuran begged, the MacKays muttering at his back. "Seek not a personal challenge. Let us do that."

"I beg you let it be me, milady," Urdred importuned.

Morrigan ignored him and the pleading Diuran. "Goll! You hear me, craven dog that you are. Hide not within. Come out and fight me. I challenge you in the name of Llywelyn and MacKay. I will serve your head to the wild dogs and they will vomit you out of their mouths."

Such dire threats were only thrown at sworn enemies. The insults were so rife as to call forth a blood feud.

Curses were thrown from the battlements along with the cheers of MacKays, the warnings from Goll's warriors.

"Face your destiny, you lowly cur, you slime that only bogs produce, you filthy traitor to Wales and all honorable Welsh! Entrails of a swine you are, feces of a mad dog," Morrigan shouted until she was hoarse.

Silence shook over the cold glen surrounding the castle. As the wind whistled from the sea, rattling the leafless limbs of trees, her invectives seemed to echo in every ear.

"Milady, I will be your champion," Urdred demanded.

"Or I," Diuran pleaded.

Morrigan shook her head, keeping her eyes on the battlements. The faces disappeared.

Long moments passed. Little was heard but the wind.

Then the godawful squeak and squawk of the drawbridge being lowered brought all to attention. The drumbeat and clarion challenge of the horn sounded through the air, battling the sea noises.

Hugh lunged forward, caught about the middle by Keith.

"Not now, laird. 'Twould endanger all if you were to appear. The sight of you would be the impetus for a battle. Ere we reached our lady she could be pierced by yon weapons." He pointed to Morrigan. "She is most vulnerable and exposed where she is. We must be most discreet, Hugh. Let her have her way for now."

Hugh shook off his large warrior. "She's challenged him," he said through his teeth. "If he accepts he could charge and kill her."

Keith shook his head. "A ploy to draw him out, to be sure."

"Pray you're right."

"I do, laird. Trust her. Our lady is just testing the waters. She would not joust with her cousin. 'Tis a trick to pull him out of the castle into the open, so she might quiz him to your whereabouts."

"Is it? Don't be too sure. She's daft with courage, damn her eyes," Hugh muttered, then subsided, watching the people around him. "Prepare yourselves."

They nodded, solemn intent in every gaze.

Dermot lifted a piece of metal from the ground. The sun was watery but mayhap he could catch a beam.

Hugh saw and nodded.

"Be of good heart, Earl of MacKay. Your lady is surrounded by her people. Not one among them would not give his life for her, Hugh," Keith said. "Wait for the propitious time, then we'll take the day, and rescue our lady."

"I'll not see her threatened." Hugh bit off the words, his voice hoarse.

MacKays murmured agreement.

All had their eyes on the Princess of Wales, who stood atop her steed, her chin up, short sword in her hand. Welsh hearts were proud even if she was going up against her own. MacKays quivered with anxiety, though their visages said they, too, thought her gallant and intrepid.

Through the opening from the bailey rode the Welsh contingent, their battle flags upon spears.

Goll had his leather shield and hat upon his head, his own sword drawn. "Cousin, you'll die this day," he shouted to Morrigan.

"One of us will," Morrigan answered. Then she slid down to a seated position. "You came at my husband like the traitorous dog you are, Goll. For that you've forfeited your honor. As the ranking royal in our family I pronounce you proscribed, that you are unfit to keep the name Llywelyn. Henceforth, you are Goll, the Nobody, and proscribed in all things Llywelyn, and throughout Wales."

Her curses rang in the wind, going to every ear. No one had thought to hear such. Mouths drooped in shock. Eyes widened in surprise. Most had never heard such sanctions against any of the leading families. That the princess should oust a relative meant there was nowhere for him to go, that he was lost to blood ties.

"Damn you to hell, Morrigan," Goll shouted back.

"Arm yourself to face this MacKay, cur dog," Morrigan yelled.

MacKays watched her, appalled, as she readied herself. "You will all stay back unless I'm beset from others. I order this. Understood?"

Urdred shook his head, then nodded when she made him swear.

"I like it not," Diuran told her.

"We're here to get our laird. We will," she told them, swallowing the quaver in her voice.

MacKays made a tunnel of themselves, arms at the ready, every other one facing an opposite way, the hillocks, trees, and outcroppings manned by MacKay warriors.

"I go forth. Bratach Bhan Chlann Aoidh!" she shrieked. MacKay pipes sounded into the wind, preparing her way on the huge arena where men on opposite sides looked like bugs to the other.

White-faced MacKays watched every move as their lady moved out into the flat land facing the holding, her steed sidling in nervous reaction to the pipes. Though the destrier looked too large for her, her queenly stature gave lie to any weakness some might utter.

"Come out, cur," Morrigan shouted. "Meet me on your day of doom."

Hugh was busy, though he watched every move she made. He went among his men, head down, proud that though MacKays recognized him, they kept their silence.

Morrigan's slow progression to the center of the ground that would be used for their jousting caught the eye of the hordes of Welsh who pounded into the area from the surrounding holdings. Word had gone out that Princess Morrigan had issued a challenge to her cousin. Death to the loser.

Timed to the second when most would be watching

the tableau unfolding, Hugh went to the men brought by Morrigan, seeing them, letting them see him. He gave them terse instructions. Few were needed.

"There will be more than one assault on her person," Hugh told them. "Watch for this."

"Hugh, look. They seek to come at her from the side," Keith said, strapping on a weapon supplied by another MacKay.

"Handle it." Hugh's eyes swept the area, catching the movement off to the other side. "Urdred—"

"I see. 'Tis our job."

Hugh didn't even check to see if it would be done as it should. There was no need to instruct MacKays. Their instincts had been forged in battle; their mettle tested against formidable foes. They knew how to face down the enemy, prevent takeover. Had they not done so since babyhood?

"Milord," another from the group surrounding him got his attention. "We must do something now. Our lady—"

Hugh waved his hand. "I would we could. I sense my spouse has a stratagem in mind. Though I see it not, I cannot interfere as yet." Cold sweat dribbled over his body as he poised himself to move. Because there were so many MacKays he could slide among them, doubled over, all but hidden from those from the opposite side. His heart squeezed within him as he pondered the fate of his wife if he was unable to reach her. Timing was going to be everything. If he missed a beat, his wife could die.

Morrigan waited until her cousin was a distance away, but facing her. They were in jousting position. "Before I skewer you I would have the people of Wales know of your perfidy."

"You stall, cousin," Goll shouted, standing in his stirrups. "I come at you, armed or not, prepared or not. Brace yourself."

"Wait! Are you so fearful of hearing your transgressions voiced aloud? Ask the people of Wales. Let them decide."

"I'll not let you stall—"

"Yes! Tell all. Tell all," called the people.

Goll seemed transfixed that they could question him, that they had the temerity to do so. "Quiet!"

"Is it your plan to muzzle all who think freely, cousin? I think not." Morrigan raised her voice, her scathing tones not lost on the populace.

"Nay! Nay!" the burgeoning assembly caroled. "Speak out, Princess! We have the right to hear."

"Quiet, fools!"

In his ire Goll didn't see Morrigan's smile at first. Then he caught it, realization coming in fulminating fury. "You'll die!" he shouted, spurring his destrier, paying no heed to the shouts of "Foul!" that followed him.

"No, fool, you'll hang for being the treasonous scum you are. Wales has no place for such as you." Morrigan would have preferred a longer contretemps with Goll, a more prolonged insult match, a greater time to prick at his ego. In such a way she could turn the gathering populace against him. No person of sense would go against the people. In such a Punic combat there'd be no winner, if the people decided to take a hand. As she watched her cousin's horse circle, readying itself to gallop down the glen toward her, she knew her time for bluffing was over. The people were restless, questioning. Would they rise up against Goll? There was no time to question that. She had to prepare herself to meet his sword.

Hugh paused in his preparations, listening to her, his anger not abating at his wife for endangering herself. His admiration for her courage and ingenuity grew in spite of his ire.

"I, too, fear for my cousin," Cumhal said, appearing at Hugh's elbow.

"Then why the hell didn't you stop your twin?" Hugh said through his teeth. "You come and go like a wraith. Why were you not there to aid her?"

"I was sent on a wild-goose chase, Hugh MacKay. I've come back this hour. My people are telling me many things about my brother."

"I'll listen later." And if he lied he'd skewer the bastard before he could get near Morrigan.

At the sudden silence, Hugh straightened. Goll was going to charge Morrigan! No more time. Damn the woman! He'd convince her once and for all that she was not Boudicca, but his spouse, and he wanted her safe.

Once more he glanced at the two who held the assemblage in thrall, their steeds exhaling steam and pawing the ground. The pewter-hued sky with its ponderous clouds drooping over them seemed a fitting canopy for the combatants.

Then he heard Goll's furious squawk. As though on hidden signal, the silence broke into growing roars as the crowd reacted. Morrigan and her cousin were racing toward each other, weapons pointed out front, battle cries issuing from their throats.

Hugh cursed, then grabbed at the nearest destrier. The rider quickly dismounted, giving his armor to his laird. Hugh flung himself into the saddle, eschewing armor, holding a sword with one hand, reins with the other. Could he catch her? Digging his heels into the destrier's sides, he sped after his wife, MacKays parting like the Red Sea in front of him.

The cacophony of yelling, huzzahs, boos, and wagers became a hoarse mix, raging to crescendo. Warriors dropped weapons to watch. All cheered a favorite.

Hugh heard nothing but the pounding of the blood in his brain, urging him to go faster.

Welsh watched Scot and vice versa, in wary study. At least they did when they could tear their eyes from the glen as Morrigan, Princess of Wales, Lady MacKay charged at her cousin, Goll of Llywelyn, respected

baron of one of the oldest families in the country. Unheard of! That a Llywelyn would battle another? Mayhap in barbaric England or Scotland old families would
do such. Not in Wales, and certainly not the Llywelyns.

Some shook their head, disbelieving. Others were
awed, staring, mouth agape. None could leave the fray.
One day children would listen to the sonnets about the
time when the Llywelyns made war on each other.

Neither adversary gave quarter, nor held back. They
galloped at each other, full tilt, sword at the ready, grim
visaged, both determined to end it their way.

Tarquin of Cardiff had all but decided how to handle
matters until he saw MacKay. His self-importance had
taken a beating since dealing with Sir Goll of Llywelyn.
Though they'd been acquainted since childhood, Tarquin realized he'd never really known the complex Goll.
Things had gone poorly of late. Nay, it'd begun to go
down when the lords of Wales had decided that Morrigan should marry the Scot. All his plans for wealth and
status had flown. When Goll had suggested a solution to
Tarquin's myriad financial problems, it'd seemed an answer from Heaven. But not lately. Too much had gone
awry.

Neither English Edward nor Edward Baliol had come
out strongly for the decree of annulment. Neither had
they gainsaid it, but it'd gone on too long. Morrigan had
disappeared before they could make her sign the script
and before she could pronounce her vows to him. And

there were the suspicions that grew with each passing
day.

For weeks he'd been sure that Goll was undermining
him in some way. He didn't know how. Hell, he didn't
know all of Goll's allies. What if they were the enemies
of Tarquin? He was very sure he had to protect himself.

As he watched Morrigan and Goll, the distance shortening, he had the surety his problems would soon be
solved. They'd both be killed. He would inherit
Trevelyan because he would insist that a marriage had
taken place, and was legal. He, then, would set his men
on Cumhal, and take over the Llywelyn holdings to the
west. Nothing could suit him more. Was not his family
almost as old as Llywelyn? If his father had had the
monies and holdings belonging to Trevelyan and Llywelyn, he would have been a baron.

When he saw MacKay come out from a group of his
men, racing after his wife, he almost fainted. Turning to
the mounted men around him, he shouted, "Get him!
Him! The Scot." He pointed to MacKay. "He's a traitor."

When the men hesitated he swung at them with the
flat of his sword. "Go! Go! I will lead you," Tarquin
screeched at them. Then he lashed his own steed forward. "We must kill him!"

Only three followed.

Hugh wasn't blind to the dangers surrounding him, the
numbers of Welsh who would count it a triumph to slay

him. Still he'd waved off his men as he saw Morrigan
rush to engage her cousin. "I'm sending that fool who
dares to attack my wife to his grave," he muttered.
Though he hadn't ordered his men to follow, he knew
they'd be at his back.

"I heard you and I'm with you," Cumhal said, ap-
pearing at Hugh's side, his horse as lathered as Hugh's.
"You needn't trust me. You can't order me away. And if
Morrigan doesn't finish Goll, he's mine."

Hugh didn't bother to respond. He'd have the fool
called Goll beheaded in a trice. His relative could deal
with the corpse any way he chose. Another time he'd
deal with the elusive Cumhal, who never seemed to be
there when Morrigan needed him.

Hugh put all out of his mind but Morrigan, even as he
felt her cousin pounding toward the jousters with him.

Headlong down the jousting field, more than a half a
league in length, he and Cumhal rode head to head.

"Attackers!" Hugh waved his sword in signal.
Cumhal seemed to comprehend and veered toward Tarquin and his men.

Hugh cursed when they managed to cut him off from
getting to Morrigan. He recognized the Welshman. He
had to go through him and his men to get to Morrigan.
So be it.

Full tilt, Hugh went right at Tarquin, who screeched
orders, excoriating the laggards to charge the Scots.

Even as his few men tried to stand their ground, Tarquin gave way, galloping back the way he'd come.

Hugh ignored the others racing through them as they scrambled to get out of his way.

Welsh loyalties were being ripped apart, torn in two directions as the family Llywelyn polarized itself.

"He'll die for the temerity of wanting her," Hugh hissed, leaning over his horse's neck, urging it to more speed.

Cumhal managed to hear him over the din, and smiled. "He desired gold more." Even putting everything he had into it, it wasn't easy to keep up with Hugh MacKay.

"He'll live until I skewer your twin, and get my wife from harm's way." Hugh lay over the destrier's neck, urging the animal in the reckless run to overtake her in time.

Scots faced their adversaries, challenges issuing from every throat. Chafing at the bit, they awaited the laird's directive, though more than one shivered with dread. It was not a good sign that their lady was in the forefront of battle.

SEVENTEEN

And now I have finished a work that neither the
wrath of love, nor fire, nor the sword, nor
devouring age shall be able to destroy.

Ovid

Morrigan was so stunned when Hugh shot past her, she
couldn't react. Her sword dribbled downward, her destrier slowed, her focus left her cousin to be burned into
the man who'd elbowed her out of the firing line. "Wait!"
Her admonition came out a husky mutter.

"You! Son of Satan, this day you'll join your master
in the nether kingdom," Hugh bellowed.

More than a few crossed themselves. No one should
call upon the demon world. Gazes narrowed on Goll.
Was he consorting with a succubus? He'd never bothered with neighboring girls. Had he married a demon's
daughter? Macabre tales flew from mouth to mouth, the
deep-seated fear of the devil's kingdom giving their
imagination free rein.

As though Goll sensed the growing antipathy of Welsh and Scot, he reined in his steed. "My cousin has need of a barbarous Scot to do battle with me?"

"She's my wife," Hugh bellowed, pulling up as well.

"Nay! She's but a whore!"

The roars that came from the throats of the Scots bent the trees, shook the heavens. Many more shouted protests came from the Welsh.

Had not a grim-visaged Urdred contained them; if Diuran, his features contorted in rage, not stayed them, all MacKays would have flung themselves at the Welsh, stormed the castle, and turned the holding to ashes.

Tarquin pulled up his steed, bitter that those Welsh at his back had paid him little heed. He could've had it all. Goll and Cumhal killed along with MacKay. Then he would've taught the Llywelyn tart about obeisance.

He'd always known that Morrigan commanded great loyalty. That she should still have such power, that it should come from all sides, boiled his innards. It stirred his vitriol that those who should be under his command looked to her who'd married a Scot. He'd make her pay for her sins.

He studied MacKay. He'd made the world stand still. Welsh and Scot eyed him. The contretemps between Goll and MacKay took center stage. It was like a tale from Homer. Ire had Tarquin grinding his teeth, though he couldn't take his eyes from the tableau in the glen.

Reason told him that whoever won, he could be in danger. Something must change that.

Hugh MacKay was fighting to control his black humors. Temper was eating at him. Tarquin blessed the fact that Goll was his target, even as he vowed to have Morrigan's cousin killed if he survived the day.

Studying the MacKays, he noted their fury. It would be put to good advantage. Tarquin would triumph. Then he'd make sure that Morrigan kept to the vows she'd made with him. He knew the annulment and vow taking could be questioned, but there'd be no one to do that. As soon as he had control of her estates, Morrigan and her brat would die. For today, once the balance of power was his, he'd keep her locked away until she was no longer useful. There were other women, more interesting than the haughty Llewelyn shrew. He'd have his place in the aristocracy at last, commanding armies, fraternizing with kings. Mayhap one day he'd be King of Wales, as was his due.

He pulled his mind back from delicious ponderings and settled on what needed doing at that moment to further his cause.

He'd hated the Llewelyns for years. They thought they were born to be fawned upon, catered to by all and sundry. He had fought for every bit of space and stature he'd gained. The marriage to Morrigan would've been a coup if the earls hadn't decided to bestow her on MacKay. Who'd think the Scot would be so incensed over losing an adulteress, or that he'd fight the decree of annulment? The barbarians were hard to understand.

Goll threw another challenge at MacKay.

Tarquin read the signs and spurred his steed down the aisle of Welsh archers who screened him from the combatants and the Scots. His victory was at hand. He could almost taste it.

Morrigan had moved up to the side of Cumhal. "If you've come in good faith, you're welcome. If you've come to support the slime who faces my Hugh, I challenge you now."

Cumhal's smile was sour. "I've come to reclaim the good name of Llywelyn."

"Don't insult me. The Llywelyn name has not been sullied by such as your brother. He has disgraced himself, not my blood. He has not the wit or grace to be any other than he is, a by-blow of Satan."

Cumhal studied her, his smile slow in coming. "We've all underestimated you, haven't we, Morrigan?"

Morrigan's chin lifted, her glance sliding to the two shouting combatants. "Not Hugh MacKay. He knows my worth as I know his. If your words are true, good Cumhal, you'll take your place as head of your branch of the family. If you play false I'll hunt you down and kill you."

"Even if all is not right at the moment, I'm sure your life will come about, Morrigan. I respect you, and never would deceive you. You can believe in that."

"Thank you, cousin. I'll not give any covenant except to Hugh until this day is finished. If he falls"—grief choked her for a moment—"I will take up his banner, and I shall war against my family and all others who've dared to take up arms against MacKay."

"Fair enough, cousin." Cumhal's glance held admiration. Then his gaze turned to the two facing off each other, as was custom. Men could come onto the field of battle, call names, list their grievances, shout threats until such time as both were ready to charge. "I would tell your spouse 'tis my fight not his."

"Have a care. Do not attempt to break my husband's concentration."

"I seek to do battle only with the dog who had betrayed me and mine. If our older brother Felim, who was three kinds of a fool to trust Goll, ever speaks or knows any of us again, 'twill be a miracle. Felim didn't have the wit to see he'd been duped. He thought he was doing the right thing, cousin."

"I will admit that Felim is rash and foolhardy, but neither do I see him as traitor."

"He was stupid to trust Goll. It cost him his senses. I know full well 'twas Goll who struck his mind askew. For that I will demand payment."

" 'Tis just."

"Wish me well, cousin."

"I do," Morrigan whispered to his back, aware that he was no match for his brother in swordplay, manus a manis, or any other war game. Goll was a past master.

She'd been sure she might get hurt battling him. She'd also been positive she could win. Hugh didn't know her cousin's tricks. Cumhal didn't have the devious mind to accept that his brother was as tricky as he was. She had no intention of taking her eyes from Goll Llywelyn.

A flash of light struck her eye. She knew, before she turned to trace its path, that it'd been the watery sun hitting steel. Armor or weapon? Since none had moved among the onlookers in the glen, she scanned the castle battlements and saw the flash again. Fixing her eyes on the spot, she made out a metal visor. That could've caught the sun. Why was a warrior up there when the battle would take place on the field? An archer! An excellent one if he expected to hit a target from there. Even the lower lancets would be too long a distance. The light hit again as though the archer had a bejeweled visor. What was his target? Why was he readying himself? Had he a long bow that could be pulled with enough force to kill a man at such a distance? It would take an outstanding bowman. Drawing an imaginary line down to the ground, she gasped. His objective was Hugh!

"Ambuscade! Ambuscade!" Morrigan screamed, kicking her horse to a gallop down the glen toward Hugh.

Hugh turned. When he did, Goll charged. So did Tarquin.

So did Cumhal. He leaned over his steed, whipping it to furious speed, as though he would reach the battlers. "Brother, I'll end this infamy this day. You treacherous dog," Cumhal muttered. "You would attack another when the foe's focus is elsewhere. If I die this day, I, Cumhal of Llywelyn, will stop you, Goll."

Hugh was aware of the danger, as both Tarquin and Goll charged him. What worried him was his wife, riding recklessly behind him, yelling something he couldn't make out. He felt some relief when he glanced back and saw Cumhal and Urdred racing after her.

He studied the two men coming at him from opposite sides. Dilemma! How to take them? He was sure he could; he was also pretty certain he'd take a wound or two in the doing. He stiffened when he heard the pounding hooves at his back.

"I'm for Goll," Cumhal shouted, going past Hugh at a gallop. "Tarquin is yours. Watch him, he's fast and tricky."

"So is your brother, if what is said be true," Hugh called after him. Then he looked away and watched the other come at him.

Readying himself, he checked his sword. He heard the whistle of the missile cutting the air. Years of survival training had him taking defensive measures, without thinking. He flung himself to one side of his steed. "Aaagh!" Hugh yowled as the arrow tore through the fleshy part of his left arm, the force rocking him back, staggering him. He heard Morrigan's scream.

"Stay back, wife," he shouted, putting down his sword and breaking the arrow. The stump would remain where it was until he finished the man who'd dared to try to take his wife. An unforgivable crime. "I want this one." He slid to the ground when Tarquin was almost on him. He lifted his sword and smacked the flat of it over the nose of Tarquin's destrier, making the angry steed rear.

Thrown off balance, Tarquin couldn't bring his sword into play. Trying to turn the steed did no good. He lost his seat and his advantage. Scrambling to his feet, he swiped a hand over a mouth frothing with ire.

"I'll kill you this day, Scot."

"So you say," Hugh answered him, shaking his head to clear it. Had the shaft point been poisoned? He would only have moments then before his vision blurred. When the Welshman took his stance, Hugh read the movements of the well trained. It would be challenging. He had a taste for it.

Morrigan pulled at Urdred, who held her firm. "I would go to him. You mustn't hold me back."

"I cannot let you distract him, milady. That is why I detain you. I wouldn't keep you from your laird."

Morrigan patted his arm. "Good Urdred, you are thinking for both of us." She winced when she saw Tarquin strike at her husband. "Cur. I would dispatch him myself."

Urdred leaned closer. "Fear not. Our laird is more the man than any Welshman living, wounded and unarmed."

Morrigan chuckled, though her worried gaze stayed on her husband.

As though he realized what he said, Urdred stammered an apology. "Milady . . . I didn't mean . . ."

"Nonsense. I understood. Do you think I don't know that MacKays are valuable, that they are my people? Shame on you for not knowing that, good Urdred."

Morrigan didn't see his protective smile, his soft look for her alone.

"I did know this, milady, and—"

Diuran poked him on the back, then leaned over him. "Did you hear our lady?"

"Just now . . . ?"

"No. When she screamed 'ambuscade' and looked up. I saw no one, but when this is settled"—he jerked his head toward the combatants—"I will tell the laird and we will besiege the holding."

"Good. I'll be at your side."

Diuran sucked in air. "Evenly matched, more's the same," he said in Gaelic.

"Aye. 'Twould not be so had not some dog shot our laird."

"I agree," Morrigan said, standing in front of the two. "I'll find the accursed vermin, I swear as Princess of Wales."

When the two men looked at each other over her head, neither smiled.

"We will do all to aid you in finding the dog, milady," Diuran whispered.

"I know that," Morrigan stated, not taking her gaze from her husband.

Back and forth they went. Hugh had not underestimated Tarquin's strength or his talent with the sword. He knew he was tiring, that his strength had been sapped by the arrow. He had to end the duel, and he intended to be the winner. Morrigan! Every time he thought of her in the clutches of his opponent, his thrusts strengthened.

She'd yelled just before he'd been hit. She'd been watching and then raced to his aid. Was there ever a more intrepid woman? No wonder she revered Boudicca. She was her modern soul mate.

Hugh was brought back to the combat when he felt a slice up his side. He countered, then moved inside and struck his forearm against the other's shoulder.

Tarquin stumbled back, steadying himself. Gritting his teeth, he rushed the Scot. "Why haven't you weakened? The broken shaft still protrudes from your upper arm. Damn you!" he gasped.

Cumhal was still atop his horse though Goll had nearly toppled him twice. His twin was in far better shape. Since he'd spent much of his life working with weapons, testing himself, it was no wonder. Cumhal decided to bait his twin, figuring he needed an advantage. Goll's conceit could be it. " 'Tis amazing that such as yourself who looks like a girl could be so able with weapons. I compliment you on your skill, little lady."

Teeth bared, Goll urged his horse into another assault position. "You insult me, brother, as you've always done. Killing you will free me from your presence for all time."

"Nay!" Cumhal turned his steed and readied himself for the assault. "You've sought Lucifer as your partner, lo these many years. This day you can make him your lover, scab of the family." It was a gamble. Cumhal took it because it gave him the only hope he had of putting his twin off stride. Goll's greater skill with sword and ax, and excellent horsemanship, needed leavening.

"You'll die this day," Goll screeched.

Cumhal didn't move, even when the destrier under him quivered and pawed at the ground to answer the charge. Though Goll was a fair distance from him, he'd turned his steed once more and headed back the way he'd come. Cumhal needed an advantage. Goll was a master at the full jousting charge. He'd practiced his skills from childhood, never seeming to get enough of the battle games. He would finish him unless Cumhal found an edge. Goll was using a sword. He needed another weapon.

Glancing about him, he noted the lance carried by the lead soldier displaying the guidon. In one imperious gesture, Cumhal called the man to his side. "I want it."

" 'Tis Lord Tarquin's guidon," the man said, faltering.

"And I am Llywelyn. Don't gainsay me." Cumhal faced the man even as his peripheral vision told him his brother was gaining on him.

He looked up at the sky. His mother was in Heaven. Would she forgive him for killing his twin? She'd have to, for if he didn't Goll would most likely skewer him. If Goll came to power, Wales wouldn't be enough for him. He'd put the world to fire.

"Stand off, man, or you can be a victim," Cumhal said through his teeth, grasping the spear and swinging it hard to bring it to bear. The man looked down the field, then scampered back to his fellows.

Cumhal looked back at his twin. It startled him to see how close his twin was, how intent he was on killing. Not this day if he, Cumhal of Llywelyn, could help it.

Cumhal had to admit to a quaking of the soul when he heard his brother laugh. In truth he was in league with Satan. Remembering what his twin had put Morrigan through, Cumhal felt his arm gain strength when he aimed the spear. Letting the animal under him sidle, Cumhal waited, shoving down the urge to spur his own mount forward, to enter the fray at a gallop as Goll would want him to do. No, there'd be a chink in Goll's armor and he'd find it. Goll was faster, more agile, accurate, and better trained. Cumhal would rely on his factoring powers, his cool head to conquer Goll.

He gritted his teeth, hearing the cheers and jeers of the crowd. They'd be sure this would be an easy win for Goll.

Goll seemed as certain. "Prepare yourself to meet your Maker, Cumhal. You gutless dog, I'm glad to do the deed."

Not all could hear his shouts, but those that did crossed themselves.

Cumhal stayed still.

"Die!" Goll screamed.

At the very last moment, Cumhal moved forward a pace, put up the spear and kneed his steed into Goll's. His startled horse sidled hard as Cumhal figured. Momentum carried horse and rider into clumsy contact, surprising Goll and his horse that were coming full tilt.

Force met force with the screeching of horses and men melding with the clash and clatter of steel.

Cumhal saw the point of Goll's sword sliding toward him. At the very last second he swung his elbow, sliding the spear along the saddle, ducking the other way at the same time.

His horse screeched as Goll's sword sliced him.

The spear sped on its path along Goll's leg into his middle and out his back. The roars of the crowd rose to a crescendo.

Cumhal was almost unseated by the force. Goll was skewered.

"You've killed me, spawn of Satan," Goll screamed, blood spurting from his mouth. He was still fumbling for his dirk when death took him.

"Go to join your evil counterparts," Cumhal whispered. When a Welshman approached, Cumhal glared. "Throw him in the bog. Set it afire. Let him not be shriven."

The Welshman nodded, white-faced.

Brother has just consigned brother to Hell, came the murmurs. What an unholy day for Wales!

Cumhal leaned over his steed, taking deep breaths, his eyes moving to the two who still battled down the glen. He turned toward them, letting his horse pick its way. He patted his neck. "You've done fine this day. I'll see you succored." He hailed another countryman, giving the orders to care for his steed. He slid to the ground, his knees shaking, his hand going to his face.

When another horse was brought to him, he mounted in silence, head down, kneeing the horse toward the combatants.

Hugh's ears rang with the clatter of swords and shields each time he and Tarquin made contact. It would have to end soon. He was wearying and he couldn't risk that the slime lived. His men would protect Morrigan but Tarquin would try to prevail. He'd overheard the guards talk of how he'd said nuptials with Morrigan. If he, Hugh, were dead, the dog would try to make his vows to her stick. He would importune—

Hugh took another hit, though it was a flat blow, not a slice; he castigated himself for losing his concentration. Bearing down, his arm feeling as though it weighed ten stone, he eyed his opponent and decided to gamble.

Dropping his sword point, he fumbled for his dirk.

The Welsh roared, seeing victory for Tarquin, who

threw himself at the Scot, sword aimed at MacKay's chest.

Scots sighed, recognizing the ploy, frozen in place at the peril MacKay had put himself into to bring a quick end to the fray.

Hugh, still turned, saw the point of the sword coming at him. In sudden reflex, he brought up his own, slashing hard at the other weapon, deflecting it. In the same motion he came inside the other's guard, bringing up the dirk and jamming it into the chest of Tarquin of Cardiff.

Tarquin struggled to say something. All he could manage was a gurgle. Then he fell forward on his face.

EIGHTEEN

Think to yourself that every day is your last; the
hour to which you do not look forward will
come as a welcome surprise.

Horace

Swaying, Hugh tried to look back at Morrigan, who
raced to him, arms outstretched, calling his name.
"Beloved," he whispered, smiling, then he slipped to the
ground.

Urdred and Diuran lifted him.

Morrigan grasped him, screaming. "Latura!"

The hag shambled from the sidelines.

A burly Scot swept her up into his arms, while the
Welsh watched, mouths agape. He sprinted across the
field and deposited her beside Morrigan.

"Help my husband," Morrigan pleaded.

"Tut, tut, child of Trevelyan. Have faith."

Hugh opened his eyes. "She's not Trevelyan," he
muttered. "She's MacKay." He passed out, wringing a
cry from Morrigan.

"We must get him home to Scotland," Morrigan commanded.

Latura shook her head. "Not as he is. We must assume that the arrow could be tainted. Nay, nay, fret not. I will give him herbs to counteract poisons. In a few days if he's well, we'll send him home. For now"—she looked up at the castle—"he must stay here. Are there enough Scots to take the holding?"

The ayes bellowed over the glen.

Morrigan shook her head, a tear trickling down her cheek. "Let me speak to the people here. I want no more killing. 'Tis time for peace." Turning away from the MacKays, she walked toward the contingent of Welsh, stopping in front of them. "My people, this day I would've fought against Wales to protect my husband from my cousin. And I would do it again. I do not consider myself a traitor to my people. In all honor I ask a boon." She let her eyes roam along the rows of Welsh. "That you let me take my husband within the holding so that he may be tended."

"I, too, wish it," Cumhal said at her side.

The silence stretched across the glen, a raven cawing overhead.

As one the men moved back, forming a tunnel. As one they swept their hand over their chest. "Go forth, Princess, in peace," one said.

"Thank . . . thank you," Morrigan managed from a throat choked with emotion. "I am so proud to be

Welsh," she told them. The leather head coverings were swept off as many bowed to her.

Whirling, Morrigan glanced at Urdred, who'd been busy fashioning slings to carry Hugh in between two of the destriers. Although the large animals seemed to balk at such a demeaning task, they were brought to heel by the Scots.

Soon the entourage was entering the castle. Latura's shouted instructions were being heeded by attendants who appeared from everywhere to obey the barked commands.

Morrigan saw nothing but her husband. As soon as he was settled in the upper chamber, she set about aiding Latura in her ministrations. "He must live."

"He will, milady, for many years to come." Latura chuckled at Morrigan's blinding smile.

All through the rest of the day and into the night Morrigan and Latura labored, finally finishing with Hugh, bedding him down, then moving on to others, Welsh and Scot, who might need tending. Since there were far fewer to treat than there would've been had there been a full-scale battle, they were soon done and could take to their pallets.

Morrigan was asleep as her head touched the tartan that covered her husband.

In the morning her husband's groans awakened her and she was quick to check his bandaging. His fever was light, his skin warm but not burning. There was moisture to it, but not the sweating that comes from infection.

"I like it that you touch me, wife, but I could wish we were in our own chamber," Hugh said, a faint smile on his lips.

"Do not brag about your prowess in bed, now, good husband. It won't stand you in good stead. You've been wounded, but you are on the mend."

"I know. 'Twas only a paltry thing."

" 'Twasn't! You could've died if Latura wasn't here to succor—"

The door burst open as she spoke. Instinctively Morrigan threw herself across Hugh. He struggled to get her free of him and get the dirk that was next to his pillow.

Morrigan relaxed, sighing. "Latura, you gave me such a fright. Why have you come . . ." The words died on her lips at the witch's pasty cast. "What's wrong?"

"I know not. I woke from the vision, mystified." She leaned back against the chamber door. "There're guards throughout the castle?"

"MacKays are always on the watch. No one need instruct them." She ignored her husband's chuckle.

"Then we must check the grounds," the witch instructed. "I know not what it was, but I'm disturbed by it."

Morrigan nodded. "Can you not place the peril so we might take action?"

"Shh, love. Diuran and Urdred are in charge. Naught can happen," Hugh hastened to assure her, though his voice was weak.

"Why are Toric and Carmody not with Keith and the others?" Morrigan smiled at Hugh, the smile freezing when he looked away from her. "Tell me."

"Carmody was blinded. Both Toric's legs were broken."

"Dear God in Heaven!" When she gasped, placing her hand over her mouth, Latura approached the bed.

"Grieve not, good lady of Trevelyan. The men are on their way to Scotland, and have safe conduct. I, myself, succored them."

Teary, Morrigan nodded her head. "Thank you, good friend." Through her agitation Morrigan noticed how preoccupied Latura was, how she kept looking at the door. "You mustn't worry. No MacKay would let trouble come to their laird. In a day or two he'll be well, and we'll be on our way back to Scotland."

Latura was wild-eyed. "I see danger, Morrigan of Trevelyan. I cannot place it, so the jeopardy for all is great."

"Why does she call you Trevelyan?" Hugh moved his head on the pallet. "Let me up. I want to talk to my men."

"No! I'll bring them to you." Morrigan shook her finger at him, ignoring his question. She would answer at another time. "Don't you dare move, Hugh MacKay."

Latura cackled, though she didn't cease her study of the room.

"She's a harpy is she not, Latura?"

"You love her. She loves you. Aught else means little."

Hugh smiled, his gaze going back to Morrigan. "Too brave by half, my little beauty."

"So are you," Latura riposted, then she went around a MacKay coming through the door and left the chamber.

Morrigan stared after her, then gestured to the nearest MacKay.

Diuran appeared at once, his face creased with concern. "Milady?"

"All is well. The laird wishes to speak to the men. Since all can't fit in this room, bring representatives, and he shall state his case."

"I will," Diuran stated, slamming his hand across his chest. "I will follow any and all dicta you give me, also, milady, including battling at your side." He turned and ran down the stone steps leading to the entry, calling out to Urdred to guard the chamber.

Men seemed to erupt from the walls, surrounding her.

Morrigan smiled at the MacKays. "You are a credit to your clan."

"Nay, milady," Urdred informed her solemnly. "You are."

Shaken, she glanced at each one in turn. "Thank you." She hesitated. "I should tell you that the witch, Latura, fears that all betrayal isn't at an end. Even she doesn't know whence it comes, or from whom. If 'twere anyone else, I might not give it credence. With her I do. I would ask you to be vigilant." She gazed at them. " 'Tis not my wish to think of my people, the

Welsh, as disloyal to me, but some might feel I've betrayed—"

The nays interrupted her.

"Thank you, but I think we should ponder all avenues in which an assassin might appear. I beg you to question the smallest thing that seems strange to you."

Diuran went by with his group of MacKays, eyeing them in open curiosity.

"I will talk to you later," Urdred told him, his features tight.

When Diuran disappeared into the chamber, and the door was closed, Urdred looked around him at the other MacKays. Without further words they drew their weapons and waited.

"We will keep to our posts, milady, and—"

A commotion had him spinning about, weapon high and ready. Another pushed Morrigan to the middle of the group, so that she was surrounded by MacKays.

"Let me up, you fools. I would see my cousin."

"And I would look upon my godchild."

Morrigan exhaled. "Rest easy, friends. 'Tis Father MacKenzie and Lady MacKenzie."

The men around her melted back, though they still hovered close.

Maud MacKenzie came forward, hands outstretched. "However did you manage such a brilliant move, my dear? We are all in your debt that you saved our Hugh. We've come to see him."

Morrigan smiled. "You are in truth an archimage,

dear lady. How else could you've come this far and this rapidly?"

Lady Maud waved a hand before embracing Morrigan. "Nay, I think not. Would that I could speak their hocus-pocus, though. 'Twould be a fine talent, I'm thinking. As for Kieran and myself, we've not come a great distance. A friend's holding is just beyond this one and across the border."

"Dunsinane? Has he come around to Hugh's way of thinking, then?"

"He has. But let us not talk of mundane matters when I would see Hugh for myself."

"Of course. This way. How are you, Father?"

"Kieran, please, Morrigan. We are family."

Morrigan smiled and opened the door. "There he is. Hugh, you have company."

Hugh opened his eyes, studying the newcomers, bidding them welcome.

"Hugh!" Lady Maud sailed across the room, bending to embrace her godchild, kissing him many times on the mouth.

"Maud, Maud, I'm not dying." Hugh smiled.

Morrigan saw his tiredness, but she was loath to send Hugh's family away. When she saw Kieran with his unguents, she went to him. "Surely he doesn't need the last rites. He's getting better."

Kieran smiled. "I know. I would give him the blessing for the ill, to speed his recovery, if you wouldn't mind."

Morrigan shook her head. "He needs all the blessings he can get."

"Wife, how can you speak so?" Hugh's gibe had mirth, though his voice was raspy and not as strong as it should be.

She laughed. " 'Tis my duty to keep you holy."

Everyone laughed, especially the MacKays who'd lingered in the room after the new arrivals.

Morrigan noticed how Maud was frowning as she looked about her. She moved close to her. "Something upsets you, milady?"

"Methinks there are too many persons in this room, taking up the good air needed by the laird," Maud chided, scowling at the MacKays' jocularity. "Tsk, tsk, this is a sickroom. You must go, good sirs," she said as she chased the attendants from the room.

"There, that's better. We can move about more freely, and you"—Maud pointed to Hugh—"can get your rest."

"And I can get on with this," Kieran said, smiling.

Content to stay out of the way, Morrigan backed toward the tapestry-covered walls. Now that Hugh was safe, she felt a lassitude, a numbing relief that her husband would recover, that they would return to Scotland. She wanted a peaceful life with Hugh and the children. The thought warmed her. Morrigan watched and listened to the banter between Kieran and her husband.

Idly she studied Maud, who'd moved back to the bedside, her eyes pinned to Hugh. Pale sunlight streaked through the window, making her rich headdress glitter.

As though all of life went into limbo, Morrigan went still, alarms going off in her being. A sense of peril seemed to crawl up her spine. She watched Kieran prepare his unguents and oils for a blessing of the sick, saw his mother hover over the bed to aid him. A revelation flowered at the same time. She recalled the battlements, the sun hitting what she'd thought had been armor. She looked at the gem-encrusted headdress.

"Wait!" Morrigan shouted, her hand going to the short sword at her side. "I've changed my mind. You will not put any of your oils upon his lips or anywhere on his person." She felt rather than saw Hugh stiffen, for she kept her eyes on the MacKenzies. She drew her sword. "Back away from the bed, Kieran MacKenzie, hands high if you please, and away from my husband."

"Hugh!" Maud raised her voice. "Your wife has run mad!"

"Has she?" In slow slides up the pillows, Hugh poised, then reached for the weapon on the side table.

"Don't!" Kieran hissed, throwing down the oils and grasping his own sword.

"So? What's this?" Hugh watched his cousin, in lazy scrutiny, settling his hands back on the coverlet. "What say you, wife? A viper among us?"

"More than one, I'm thinking," Morrigan answered in Gaelic. " 'Twas your virulent gaze I felt on the day of our nuptials, was it not?"

" 'Twas, you insolent Welsh slut."

"You poisoned the wine on our nuptial day, I would swear. And then you saw to it that Hugh was ambushed and captured. You concocted that story that the king knew of Hugh's death. Evil!" Fury filled her when Maud's mouth twisted.

"Curse you for not joining Hugh in the drink of death," Maud said through her teeth. "I watched you fawn over those crippled spawn of Satan, and knew you must die. You bring such filth to the clan. You and Hugh cannot have this clan. It belongs to Kieran."

"Don't malign ours. They are our children. And this clan is Hugh's."

"No!" Maud screamed.

"Hugh, I'm sure they didn't just arrive." She hauled in a deep breath, swallowing. "They've been here all the time." That was conjecture, but Kieran's glare assured her she was right. Did Maud bare her teeth just then? How was it she'd missed the agate hardness of those eyes? Morrigan shook with fury. "Guests of Goll's were you? You needn't deny it. Have you been in league with him these many moons? Did you not conspire to take from my husband, from me?"

Maud glared. "The MacKay treasures belong to me."

Morrigan was taken aback, though she masked her thoughts. "You're not a MacKay."

"Hugh was to marry me. It was decreed—"

"A lie," Hugh said in a calm voice.

"No! I gave years to your mother. I was not much older than you. When I went to your father and mother

and suggested that I should become your wife in time,
they smiled. Then, soon after they arranged my wedding
with MacKenzie, your cousin. It was wrong. When I had
my own son, I . . . we devised a plan to wrest what was
rightfully mine from our enemy." Maud gritted her teeth
when Hugh laughed. Then she glowered at Morrigan.
"How could you know about us? We made no mis-
takes."

"The truth of it is I might not have. 'Twas Latura had
a vision of an evil presence. Then you appeared. Perhaps had I not been so warned, nothing would've come
of my wonderings." She stared at Maud, anger rivering
through her. "There was another incident. I saw the sun
hitting your headdress as you stood upon the battlements yesterday. As you leaned over my husband just
now, the sun shone upon you again. Your penchant for
jewels has brought you down, milady."

Maud ground her teeth. "You Welsh spoiler! 'Twas
not you who was to wed the laird. I was. I had talked to
many of the earls. They'd promised to press my suit before Edward. Before 'twas done, the compact was
signed."

Stunned, Morrigan stared. Then her glance went to
her husband, who hadn't taken his eyes from Kieran.
"Hugh, do you hear?"

"I hear. Not an interdict from the pope himself
would've made me do it."

"Liar! You loved me," Maud said through her teeth,
sidling to the chamber door and throwing the bar across

it. "You think you can spurn me, Hugh MacKay, as your parents did? My son shall inherit your title and your holdings. All MacKays shall be under our heels."

"Why such venom, milady? Have you not been fed and clothed by them, lo these many years.? My mother took pity on you. My father bestowed upon you your only legacy. How foolish we were to hug vermin to our tartans."

"How dare you!" Maud drew a short sword.

"Was it not my clan that tutored you, even in using a weapon? Ungrateful tart," Hugh taunted.

"Never speak to my mother in such a way," Kieran bleated, swinging his sword at Hugh, even as MacKay took the bolster behind him and tossed it in his cousin's face.

Maud screamed and made a rush at Hugh.

Morrigan was there with her own sword. "Don't, madam. 'Twould not take much for me to kill you. You have threatened my husband, our clan—"

"Your clan? Hah! You're not a Scot. I am." The two women faced each other.

"You lied about the king's runners that day when you came to commiserate with me, did you not?"

"I was enraged that the two of you weren't beneath the ground," Maud spat. "You were meant to die with him."

"Instead we live." Morrigan couldn't look toward Hugh, though she feared for him. He was too weak to fight his cousin, even if MacKenzie was a poor swords-man.

Hugh clambered out of bed, his reaching hand grasp-ing his ceremonial claymore, that had been brought from Scotland under Morrigan's banner. Too clumsy for the chamber, better suited for the jousting field, it was all he had.

Kieran chuckled as he whipped the Venetian rapier in front of him. "Look to yourself, cousin."

"Kill him, Kieran!"

When Hugh staggered back, he hit the small table at the side of the bed, overturning it, and spilling Kieran's unguents to the floor. Shards of the container littered the area under Hugh's bare feet.

Thudding began on the chamber door. Shouts pene-trated the thick wood. "Hugh! Milady!"

"To me!" Morrigan yelled.

As she did, Maud charged her with her sword out-stretched.

Morrigan danced away, beginning a battle that would take too much time. Hugh needed her. "Think not to en-list the aid of any MacKay, Maud MacKenzie. They will see through your wicked ploys."

"My son will become the laird. The treasures of MacKay will be ours. Hugh had his opportunity. Now he must die."

"He never wanted you. Few would," Morrigan taunted, needing a leverage to help her finish off Maud. "Too many coincidences, milady. I vow only the crazed would give you homage if aught happened to our laird. Methinks you've taken on too much this time."

"Kill him, Kieran, and help me," Maud ordered.

"Your son, spawn of the devil that he is, will need all his strength to fight Hugh, and he'll not be victorious," Morrigan hurled at Maud, stepping away from a hard thrust. "Did you think to come at my husband with impunity? Have you forgotten MacKays outside this door who'd hunt you to your home in Hell if you come at Hugh? Already you've forfeited your life." Morrigan was fast losing breath. She'd underestimated Maud's skill. It took every effort to battle her and keep talking to undermine her. "Listen to the MacKays, Maud. Even now they call to us and threaten to break down the barrier."

Hugh stumbled and fell. He just made it to his feet, swaying there, swiping at his sweating face.

Kieran smiled. "Fear not, Mother. You'll die, Morrigan."

"Never!" Hugh cursed.

Kieran ground his teeth and charged, aiming his sword at Hugh. "And MacKays will hear that she attacked you, Hugh. I'll say I couldn't save you, but I killed her." The rapier swished through the air at Hugh's chest.

The heavy claymore came up from the floor, two hands on the powerful blade, slicing up and through the middle of Kieran MacKenzie.

"Traitor," Hugh rasped.

"No!" Maud screamed, then rushed to her son, falling forward on her short sword, impaling herself over his body.

The door crashed open, armed MacKays pouring through the opening, battle cries issuing from their mouths.

Morrigan threw herself at her husband. "Take me home, Hugh MacKay, take me home."

"At once, beloved. Not another sennight do we reside away from Castle MacKay." He looked at his men. "Diuran, get rid of the garbage. They're not to be shriven."

Diuran glanced down at the two bodies. " 'Twill be done."

EPILOGUE

Now is the time for drinking, now the time to
beat the earth with unfettered foot.

Horace

Scotland was warming again. All was serene, beautiful.
Even the wild Pentland Sea seemed more calm. Laughter could be heard in the distance as children romped.

Eamon and Urdred were playing a game with Avis,
Conal, and Rhys, and the laughter was loud and long.

"Life is sweet, is it not?" Morrigan asked her husband, as she suckled her babe to her breast. "The air is
so fresh. I had to be out in it today. What think you of
our Riordan, husband?"

Hugh was lying back on the ground studying her, one
of his favorite things to do. "I think he's a feckless lump
with no gratitude."

"What?" The mother in Morrigan rebelled at such
words and she glared. "How can you? He's the most
perfect of babes. He sleeps well. Dilla says there never
was a better we'en."

"He took his time at birthing. I'll not forget that."

"Dilla says 'twas not unusual."

"What does she know?" Hugh reared up on his elbow, to make sure the tartan was around his wife. "Did she have to pace the chamber while you suffered? No! I've never seen such agony in any battlefield as was in that birthing bed."

"Not so." Morrigan tried not to laugh as she recalled how it'd taken Diuran and Urdred to force him from the room when the birthing was done, and she needed cleansing. How horrified the women had been when the laird had insisted he would do the job.

"And don't mention those MacKays that thought it amusing that I was ordered from my own chamber. I've still not factored how I'll repay them. Never did I think Dilla would turn against me. I've pondered the torture chamber for the lot."

"You'll do nothing," Morrigan said, her face serene. "Or perhaps you'll punish them as you did Carmody and Toric. Putting them in charge of all that is MacKay, in land and monies, was a good plan. And a good job they've done."

Hugh frowned. "They have. Would that I could've taken their assault on myself."

Morrigan finished nursing and cuddling the baby and then returned him to the woven birthing sock that kept him so warm and safe. "You have, time and again, husband. They've told me so. Now, you dignify their courage by making them lieutenants over all your warriors. You've given Diodura and Latura happiness and security. All love you for what you are, just as I do." She touched her husband with tenderness.

Hugh eyed her. "When I look at you I don't know how I could've forgotten we loved that first time." He shook his head. "You told me of our nuptial night when we came home from Wales, and, in truth, I saw it all again, Morrigan."

She slid down next to him, gazing at the sky, then at him. "I know. It pained me to keep the secret of Trevelyan from you." She stroked his cheek. " 'Twas even worse to hold back about our loving." She smiled. "You recalled it all in what you thought was a dream, my love."

He rolled over so that his body tented hers. "And was I gentle with you your first time, sweetling? That has bothered me since you told me."

He did not mention that she'd dissembled and kept a very important secret from him. Not once had Rhys's true birthright, and her reason for needing to be regent of Trevelyan, concerned him. Rather he worried whether he'd been gentle with her when they'd loved the first time. This was not the first time he'd asked since she'd confessed all. She rubbed the Llywelyn medallion that Cumhal had reclaimed from Goll.

"My dearest Hugh, you are all of goodness to me, and you were then."

"Then I vow to keep and protect Trevelyan for our son Rhys. We will tell him, together, about his legacy, when he's older. There is enough of MacKay holdings and monies to provide for Conal, Riordan, and Avis." He smiled. Then it faded. "You are sure I was gentle with you, love?"

"You were and always will be all of beauty, all of passion and love. Our first loving was as grand and glorious as the others have been since. You caught me in your web on first meeting, and I wouldn't leave you if I could."

Hugh kissed her, his mouth warm. "Nay, I'm in your sweet web, wife. And I love the tangle. Swear you'll never leave me."

"Not in this world or the next."

They embraced, kissing over and over and murmuring love words as the laughter of their children echoed around them.

Fall in Love
with Acclaimed Author
Helen Mittermeyer

★ ★ ★

900-c